Easy Target

By Kay Thomas

EASY TARGET
PERSONAL TARGET
HARD TARGET

Easy Target

KAY THOMAS

ELITE OPS—BOOK THREE

AVONIMPULSE
An Imprint of HarperCollins Publishers

Excerpt from *Hard Target* copyright © 2013 by Kay Thomas.
Excerpt from *Personal Target* copyright © 2014 by Kay Thomas.
Excerpt from *Heart's Desire* copyright © 2015 by Tina Klinesmith.
Excerpt from *Desire Me Now* copyright © 2015 by Tiffany Clare.
Excerpt from *The Wedding Gift* copyright © 2015 by Lisa Connelly.
Excerpt from *When Love Happens* copyright © 2015 by Darcy Burke.

EPub Edition JUNE 2015 ISBN: 9780062290892
Print Edition ISBN: 9780062290908

10 9 8 7 6 5 4 3 2 1

For my big sister, Libby—
who taught me that reading is fun,
laughter heals, and champagne
is not just for special occasions!

Easy Target

Chapter 1

December
Africa

As THE TRUCK rolled to a grinding halt, Sassy Smith braced herself at the back door. This would be her one chance, and she wasn't going to blow it. They'd only been moving for a few minutes, so it wasn't a "rest" stop, at least she hoped not. She'd seen that horror unfold more than once since she was kidnapped off the streets in Niamey two days ago.

She wasn't absolutely clear on the time of day. She was guessing early morning, but it could have been midafternoon. Her internal clock was pretty screwed up. They were close to a town, if the warehouse they'd just been in was any indication.

If they unlocked the back, the doors had to swing out like a big gate, and that momentarily blocked the guards' vision. She'd have a three- to five-second head start to run once they opened. Given the terrain, that might be all she needed. Sassy was small, but she was lightning fast.

She slipped off her wedge heels as she stood by the doors and knotted the kimar scarf around her waist. It had long ago slipped from her head, but she didn't dare leave the truck without it. She had no idea where they were, and a woman with her head uncovered in some areas of this country might as well be wearing a neon sign and shouting into a bullhorn.

The women around her were already tuning up, moaning and wailing. Sassy took a deep breath and reached for that inner calm she could always find when everything around her was going to hell. Being raised by a crazy alcoholic had made that a necessity. Her brother, Trey, claimed that she had ice water in her veins.

Sassy shook her head. She couldn't think about Trey right now, or the Mexican prison where he was incarcerated for a murder he hadn't committed. She would shut down completely and be incapable of doing what had to be done here. She needed to focus. What had seemed not so bad initially had turned ugly and frightening in the past forty-eight hours. If she dwelled on her circumstances for very long, she'd lose her nerve.

Four women on the truck had been sexually assaulted on the journey across the Hoggar Mountains since Sassy had joined them, and that was just the tip of the iceberg. Sassy'd sat beside one and held her as she'd wept afterward. She had the terrible feeling she might be next if the way these new guards were treating her was any indication.

She dragged her thoughts away from that stomach-turning possibility and instead narrowed her concentration to the back door of the truck. This was just like when she'd been a runner back in high school. You waited for the signal gun to fire, and you never looked back until you crossed the finish line.

She wasn't weeping like the others in the truck; she was gearing up to blast out of here. If she was lucky, only one guard would be opening the door, and he wouldn't be expecting Sassy. She held a shoe in each hand, ready to brandish them like small clubs if necessary. She heard the padlock rattle in the lock and slipped into "the zone" as if she was in the starting block on the high school track years ago.

The door swung open, revealing a sliver of light, and Sassy immediately dropped through the gap to the ground, rolling under the truck and scootching out the other side, away from the traffic, before she'd fully taken in her surroundings.

The women were wailing; no one would "tattle" on her. She hesitated a moment, hiding herself beside the two large back wheels. They were on a busy road with a long stream of cars coming from both directions, but beyond that, she couldn't tell anything about her location. There was nothing but a long wall directly behind her. Why were they stopping here and opening the back door? They were in the middle of a town. A very busy town.

Was that a bridge?

She stared a moment. That was the Sidi M'Cid.

She'd been here once before on another story. This was Constantine. The market was just across the road.

Why would her captors stop here, in the middle of all these people? Why open the truck beside the Casbah? These men were not the sharpest tools in the shed. *Thank God.*

She studied the guard's feet by the back door and glanced at the wheel on the traffic side of the truck. The tire was as flat as her chest had been when she was eleven years old and praying for boobs every night.

The guard would be climbing in the back of the vehicle soon to grab the spare, but he still hadn't realized anyone had flown the coop. She crawled underneath the undercarriage to the traffic side of the truck and checked to make sure no one else was exiting the cab on this side. Seeing no one, she waited for a break in the line of cars coming from the opposite direction. Then she stood, tucked the shoes under each arm, and sprinted across the street. The gravel over the top of the warm asphalt dug into her feet, but she ignored the pain. The guard behind her yelled, but he was too late. Sassy slipped into the crowds and never looked back, disappearing into the Casbah and the anonymity of market day.

She was free.

She hurried through the labyrinth of stalls strung with the vendors' wares—scarves, food, embroidered baby clothes, electronics, linens, housewares, even chickens. Anything and everything one could imagine was found here. The shoppers were out in force as well.

Was this Christmas Eve? She'd lost track of the days while on the truck. But there was no time to dwell on that. She slipped the kimar up over her head and wrapped it twice, securing it as best she could without a pin or mirror. She shoved her shoes back onto her bruised feet and slowed to a more sedate pace, since a white woman running through the market would draw entirely too much attention.

She paused by a vendor selling beautifully woven rugs and glanced behind her. No one appeared to be following. But she couldn't be sure if the man from the truck was just good at tracking or had given up and decided it wasn't worth the trouble.

Either way she had to keep moving. She gazed to the Sidi M'Cid, its towers rising majestically in the air over the one-lane bridge. That would be her quickest way out of the area.

She looked closer. No, that wouldn't work. The bridge was cordoned off with police and official vehicles swarming it from both ends. She was stuck here for the time being, unless she wanted to venture farther into Constantine or try the urban gondola system.

Despite the sign ahead for one of the gondola stations, she wasn't ready to do that yet. Sassy wasn't scared of much—in fact, she'd do just about anything on a dare— but her fear of heights would keep her out of that egg-shaped car crossing the Rhumel Gorge unless someone held a gun to her head.

For just a moment she wondered if she'd made a mistake leaving the truck. She could possibly have found out where Elizabeth Yarborough was if she'd stayed with the women. Or if Trey's girlfriend had even been here in Africa, as Sassy strongly suspected. But the last time they'd stopped, the man in charge had looked at her with entirely too much interest and undiluted lust. He'd groped her thoroughly as he'd shoved her into the truck in the warehouse.

She'd known it had only been a matter of time until they'd pull her from the back at one of the "rest stops." As a reporter, she'd been on her own in too many dangerous areas of the world not to recognize the signs. And she wasn't dumb enough to think she could fight them off or talk her way out of it. She wanted to help her brother, but she wouldn't put herself in the position of being raped to do it. She'd be no help to Trey if she was a broken wreck or worse.

She refused to think about what this meant for Elizabeth. Her brother's girlfriend might very well have died on the Sahara crossing, if her journey had been anything like that of the women in the truck with Sassy. Even if that were true—and Sassy's heart ached to think it could be—Sassy had to find the evidence, anything to prove that Elizabeth hadn't died at the hands of her brother at a resort in Mexico, as the authorities claimed.

A wave of dizziness flowed over her. Lord, she was hungry. She estimated the last time she'd eaten a real meal. It had been almost forty-two hours ago. Plus she'd had precious little water on the grueling trek across the desert. She needed food now.

What was she going to do? She looked around her. She had no money, no phone, no passport, no way of proving she was an American citizen. She questioned whether or not going to the local police would help or hurt.

She hadn't had great luck with the authorities here in Africa since she'd arrived to investigate the human trafficking problem and the possible relationship to Elizabeth's disappearance. As a freelance reporter, she'd assumed she'd be ignored to some extent. The corruption was rampant in the government, but she was now certain that she'd stepped on someone's toes with her investigative reporting. If she went to the police station, would the authorities help her, or turn her back over to the men she'd just escaped?

December 24
Early evening

BRYAN FISHER SPIED the sparkling lights of Constantine on the horizon. It was a beautiful night, but he didn't give a damn about the scenery right now. He'd driven like a bat out of hell from the port city of Skikda once he'd learned that Sassy was in trouble.

All along the way, he'd been telling himself that she had to be okay. There was no way she was hurt. Sassy Smith always landed on her feet. But the other part of him knew that the men who'd taken her were vicious. He'd seen their handiwork, and there was no telling what could happen if they had her.

The kicker was he'd passed the truck and the women this morning on his way to the coast, catching up with his partner, Nick Donovan, and Nick's girlfriend, Jennifer Grayson. They were now on their way home after the harrowing week of attempted murder and kidnapping they'd had together in Africa. He still didn't know who was behind their troubles, but the Vegas and the Riveras were prime candidates in Bryan's eyes.

He hadn't known that Sassy had been on the truck he'd passed—or, rather, that she was supposed to have been on the truck. She hadn't been in the group of women he'd seen taken into custody by the Algerian military at the roadblock that had stopped him on his way through Constantine. He hadn't even discovered she was in trouble until he'd met with Nick and Jennifer in a café in Skikda earlier today. He still couldn't believe she'd been kidnapped.

Sassy was supposed to be in Niamey, writing her free-lance article on Mexican cartels and sex trafficking in Africa. She'd never intended to be part of the story itself. He ignored the cold sweat that had taken up permanent residence at the base of his spine ever since Jennifer had told him about Sassy being on the truck with the traffickers' load of women.

On his wild ride back from the coast, he'd almost chewed through an entire pack of Dentyne gum as he'd tried to contact Marissa Hudson, his boss and the co-owner of AEGIS, Armored Extraction Guards and Investigative Security. He'd had to settle for leaving her a voice mail. Risa had connections everywhere, and he needed her contacts at the embassy to find out what had happened this afternoon to that truckload of women after they'd been taken into custody.

But things were going to hell at the AEGIS office

right now with a warrant out for the arrest of Gavin Bartholomew, Marissa's partner. The charges were bogus, but Bryan feared they were enough to dry up Risa's resources in most embassies on the African continent.

Bryan was just approaching the Sidi M'Cid Bridge when an incoming text message dinged on his phone.

Call me, NOW!

He pulled off the road just before the bridge and hit speed dial. Risa answered on the first ring. "Glad you caught me. We're getting on a plane. I've got about thirty seconds before I have to turn my phone off. Here's the scoop."

He scrambled for a pen and paper, grateful she was cutting to the chase.

"I talked to my one embassy contact in Algiers who was still speaking to me. The truck had a flat near the Casbah in Constantine, by the bridge. Driver swears it was the only time the truck door was open before the roadblock. If Sassy Smith got away, it was there."

"Are they sure the driver is telling the truth?" Bryan couldn't shake the thought that Sassy was in a ditch somewhere after being used and discarded by the animals running this trafficking ring.

Risa cleared her throat, but her voice still had that hoarse tone that reminded him so much of Sassy's, even though their accents were different. "The same story was confirmed with a couple of the women on the truck, but no one actually saw Sassy get off the transport. That doesn't mean it didn't happen. Most of these girls were so out of it from dehydration and hunger, they didn't notice much of anything until they were being rescued."

Bryan squeezed his eyes closed and imagined what kind of shape Sassy might be in at this point. If she'd gotten away at the Casbah, where could she have gone?

Risa's voice interrupted his unhappy train of thought. "I'm sorry. I've got to go. Leave me another message, but on this new number." She recited the number that had come up on his caller ID. "It's a burner. The AEGIS numbers are most likely all being tapped at this point."

He didn't even have time to say *Thanks* or *Who is we?* He knew she was with Gavin. Bryan didn't believe the man was collaborating with the cartels, and Marissa was loyal to a fault. She wouldn't leave her partner twisting in the wind on some bullshit charges.

Gavin's wife had just died after a long, agonizing battle with cancer. Another example of how loving someone and losing them could eviscerate you. Bryan wasn't going to think about what kind of hell Gavin was dealing with.

If Risa could help the man by doing what she did, then more power to both of them. Whatever else was going on between them was none of his business. Hell, he was only a contract employee, not even a permanent hire for AEGIS. Nothing in Bryan's life was long-term anymore.

He hung up and looked ahead. The Casbah was just across the Sidi M'Cid Bridge. He studied the landscape a moment. He'd never been inside the market, although he'd seen pictures. Located in the oldest part of the city, it didn't look particularly welcoming at this time of night, with its dark, winding streets and narrow alleyways. But it would be the perfect place to hide if Sassy had escaped her captors here.

This would be like looking for a needle in a haystack. He comforted himself with the thought that he'd at least located the most probable haystack. He crossed the bridge and created his own parking space on a side street before diving into the maze of the Casbah.

Despite the objections of many Muslim religious leaders in the area, there were signs of the Christian holiday all around the market. Some things had been "adapted" to the area. On one side of the entrance, Santa's sleigh was parked with goats in the harness instead of reindeer. And on the other side—somewhat miraculously—there was a nativity scene complete with angels, wise men, and the baby Jesus. Given the religious climate, this was all most unusual.

Most vendors closed up shop when the sun went down, although there still were a few around the entrance to the marketplace itself. Fear for Sassy and what could be happening to her right now had him speeding up the incline farther into the labyrinth of streets. The deeper inside he travelled, the more lonely and desolate everything appeared, with only the occasional shop open for business.

Sassy, where are you?

If she was out here alone, she could be in just as much trouble as she had been on that truck. Bryan rushed ahead into the darkness, hoping for his own Christmas miracle.

Chapter 2

SASSY STOOD ON a corner deep in the Casbah, about to cross the street. She no longer worried about the men from the truck finding her. She'd been here for hours now. The traffickers were long gone.

Earlier she'd drunk from one of the older public fountains, using her hands to slurp water from the spigot. A vendor had taken pity on her and offered her a plate of the traditional flatbread and lamb sausage, so even her hunger was assuaged for the moment.

Her most pressing problem was being a woman alone on the street after dark. Here in Constantine, that seemed to signal that she was looking for male companionship, if the gaggle of young men following her was any indication. They were talking to her, some in French, a few in English, but their comments had grown increasingly bold and coarse.

They were in a darker area. Earlier there had been

shopkeepers and people about. Now the streets were all but deserted. Sassy felt the first real frisson of fear.

Suddenly the five young men surged forward to surround her.

"Back the fuck away from me!" she shouted in English.

She knew at least one of them spoke the language because of the lewd suggestions he'd been whispering for the past five blocks.

"That's not exactly the kind of fucking we had in mind," the English speaker said, and with that the men pressed in, edging her back into the alleyway they'd just passed.

Oh God, this is really happening. Her anxiety switched into overdrive, and a clammy sweat broke out on her forehead and back.

She took a deep gulp of air and struggled to steady her racing heart. She had to think. Concentrate on what Trey had taught her as a kid.

She stopped walking backward and braced herself, with her feet shoulder-width apart. There were five of them, and they most likely would overpower her. But she could hurt a couple of them before they got her on the ground. She rounded her fingers into the shape of claws so her nails would act as talons. They might take her down, but they'd carry marks.

The man who'd spoken in English signaled to the others. One guy came at her and grabbed her left arm, another came from the right. A third, smaller man grabbed her around the waist from behind and pulled himself close to her, his front to her back. She could feel his erection jutting at her rear end. Bile rose in the back of her throat, and she swallowed hard before flinging her head back to pop him in the Adam's apple with her skull. He let go of her immediately, cursing in French as he fell to the ground.

The first two men pulled her farther into the alley, backing her into a brick wall. One of them slapped her. She opened her mouth to scream and saw a knife in the fourth man's hand. He held it up as he approached, and no more words were necessary.

If she screamed, he'd cut her. *Oh Jesus.* After all this, was she really going to be raped in an Algerian back alley?

The fourth man came closer with the knife. He seemed confident that she was cowed and would no longer fight. She considered her options. Stop fighting and be raped and killed, or fight tooth and nail and be killed. There was no real choice. In that moment, she decided there was no way she could stop fighting.

She went limp, giving the impression that she was relaxing, then she kicked out with her feet, catching the fourth man in the upper thigh. She screamed in rage rather than fear. She'd been aiming for his balls, but the hit had the desired effect. He doubled over, most likely more surprised than hurt. That left the final man. The one who'd spoken so crudely earlier. He picked up his friend's knife and moved extremely fast. Before she knew what had happened, the blade was pressed to her throat.

A warm trickle of blood oozed down her neck as he pressed the steel against her skin with one hand and fumbled at his pants with the other. His body odor was foul. "I don't care if you're alive or dead when I do this." His laugh was more of a cackle, and she shuddered in revulsion.

The two men on either side of her tightened their grips on her arms. Tears prickled at the corner of her eyelids. This was happening. There wasn't any way out. If she screamed, he'd just stick that blade straight in and rape her as she bled out.

He yanked at her blouse, pulled up her skirt, and leaned into her, kissing the other side of her neck. There was no reasoning with him, and no cavalry was riding in to save her. She couldn't stand it. She took a breath to scream, and he pressed the knife a little harder.

"No," she whispered.

Now a rivulet of blood streamed down her neck. She could smell the alcohol on his breath. She was going to be sick.

His hands were sweaty on her hips, then her thighs, as he tore her panties. He pressed his lower body against her. She tensed for the horror to come, and closed her eyes to block out the inevitable.

Without warning, the man's weight was lifted up and away from her. Her skirt was hiked to her waist in front, but the back fell into place around her calves. Her shirt was torn open.

She opened her eyes to see the man she'd fantasized about in her teenage years—more than she'd like to admit—tossing the attacker against the wall. Bryan Fisher was throwing the guy into the bricks. The attacker's head hit the masonry with a sickening thud.

The two men who'd been holding her dropped her arms and started toward Bryan. But when they saw the gun in his hand, they ran like scalded dogs. The other two were already on the ground. Bryan had put them out of commission before he'd ever pulled the first one off of her.

Where had Bryan come from? Not that she wasn't beyond glad to see him, but how had he found her? And what was he going to do now?

BRYAN SPARED ONLY a glance for the three men on the ground before holstering his Glock. They weren't going anywhere. One had a broken neck, the other a cracked skull, and the third would be unconscious for several hours.

He felt the adrenaline spike as he looked at Sassy. Her blouse was torn, and the flowing skirt she was wearing when he last saw her in Niamey was dirty and hiked up to the point where he could see her ripped panties and tell that she preferred bikini waxes over Brazilians. The bra she wore looked like something featured in the X-rated dreams he'd had about her over the past six months, even with a torn strap.

She was shaking like crazy, and her eyes were huge as she stood in the shadowed alleyway. He was shaking himself. So grateful he'd found her before any more damage had been done to her, he didn't know what to say.

As it turned out, he didn't have to say anything, because she immediately began peppering him with questions as she threw herself into his arms. "Ohmigod!

You're here. How did you find me? What is going on? Are they dead?"

The questions came with the rapid-fire pace of a machine gun. Even when scared out of her mind, Sassy could pull it together, and she never stopped thinking. As a kid, she could cope with disaster better than anyone he knew, and as an adult, she hadn't relinquished the title.

A smile tugged at the corner of his mouth, and his body tightened with the inevitable response to that adrenaline dump and the lightning-fast switch from killing a man to embracing an abundant armful of warm woman. He knew the hug was an anomaly and decided he better enjoy it while it lasted.

He took a moment to hold her to his chest. "It's complicated. I don't know, and two of them are dead, yes."

Sassy still clung to him, even as she stilled in his arms and tried to step back. He held on to her a moment longer until her hands changed from grasping him around the neck in honest relief to an abrupt slide across his chest with a red-tipped fingernail. He let her go, but he didn't want to. The comfort of finding Sassy safe washed over him, along with the realization that no matter how hard he'd tried, he hadn't been able to stop thinking of her since they'd reconnected last summer after Trey's arrest.

They were both trying to prove her brother's innocence, but they couldn't seem to work together without fighting. Bryan knew that for his part it had more to do with wanting what he couldn't have, particularly if he wasn't sticking around. He wasn't the sticking type, not anymore.

Sassy didn't help matters by baiting him with outrageous sexual innuendos he had no intention of following up on but that struck entirely too close to home.

She looked up at Bryan; the usual taunting light in her eyes was nowhere to be seen. That obviously had something to do with what had just happened to her. With a jolt he realized that the sensual banter she typically subjected him to was most likely an act. He wasn't sure why she did it, but he sure as hell wasn't going to stand here and try to figure it out. Not with two dead men at their feet.

"We've got to get out of here." He moved away from her and took his button-down shirt off to slip it onto her shoulders, like he would dress a child.

He could tell she was still in shock by the way she allowed him to do that without argument. He also straightened her skirt, ignoring her torn underwear and pulling the edges of his shirt together around her waist to button it in two places across her chest.

"We're leaving now." He took her hand and exited the alley, picking up her kimar from the dirty ground along the way and draping it around her shoulders. They'd get it on her head in a moment.

He walked her down the street, anxious to put as much distance between them and the alleyway as possible. He wanted to get her out of the Casbah and into a western hotel immediately. It would be a trick leaving the country since she didn't have a passport with her, but he'd figure that out later.

She'd become very quiet, and he glanced down at

her as they hurried through the marketplace. Her neck was bleeding onto his shirt, and her mouth was swollen where one of those animals had hit her. He swallowed the rage that surged up at the sight. Getting her out of here was the priority.

Three blocks over, he stopped to drape and wrap the head covering around her hair as best he could. He took an extra minute to press part of the kimar against her neck to stop the bleeding. As he tucked errant strands of her hair inside the scarf, she seemed to waken out of her temporary stupor and take notice.

"Where are we going?" she asked.

"Not sure yet. Give me a minute," he muttered. For tonight a hotel was decidedly best. Particularly as he had no idea what the roads between the coast and Constantine looked like now in terms of roadblocks. Nick and Jennifer were most likely long gone from Skikda anyway.

"We're going to hole up till I can figure out how to get you out of the country, with or without papers. Those men who got away can identify both of us if they're so inclined."

"Okay."

If he didn't know it already, he would have been clued into something being wrong when she agreed so fast.

"Are you alright?" He dug out his pack of gum and handed her the last piece. "Did they hurt you?" His own voice was calmer now that they were farther away from the alley and he didn't see the knife at her throat every time he took a breath.

She shook her head and unwrapped the cinnamon-scented stick. "I will be. You just get me to a hotel room with a shower, and I'll be fine."

He squeezed her hand and kept moving. "You got it."

"How did you find me?" she asked.

"Jennifer Grayson told me you were on the truck with those other women. I backtracked from there with a little help from my boss's contacts."

The streets were darker than they had been when Bryan arrived. Everything was closed now. He kept hold of her hand as they walked.

"Thank God, Jennifer's alright. How did she get away?"

"Nick got her." Bryan reached for Sassy's waist when she would have tripped over a loose stone. "They're on their way out of the country as we speak."

"Good." She nodded but didn't ask any more questions.

He kept his hands on her, still so relieved he'd found her that he wasn't ready to let her go yet. Ten minutes later they were at the entrance to the Casbah, crossing the street to his car. They'd passed a half dozen people in total. No one seemed to pay much attention to them, although at six foot five Bryan himself was fairly noticeable. Unfortunately, they'd remember him if authorities started asking questions later.

He helped her into the car and slid behind the wheel. They were closest to the Hotel Novotel Constantine. It took less than five minutes to reach Place des Martyres. From there Bryan pulled into the hotel's private parking garage as if they already had a reservation. Fifteen minutes later, they were checked into the last available room.

Bryan explained that the airline had lost his wife's luggage, and the management provided a small bag of toiletries for Sassy. The room wasn't large by western standards, but it was clean and private, with a shower, tub, and a fluffy robe—but only one bed.

He'd think about that one bed later.

Chapter 3

December 24
Late evening

THE HOTEL RESTAURANT was open for room service for two more hours. While Sassy cleaned up, Bryan ordered food and looked through his own luggage for something she could wear. The best he had was a collared shirt that would probably come to her knees.

The shops downstairs in the hotel were closed, but the night manager had assured Bryan that they would be open first thing in the morning and Sassy could find some clothes there that would do.

For now he needed to figure out how to get her out of town. He could smuggle her out. Just like the women on that truck, but he'd rather do this legally. It would make for fewer problems later, particularly with all the issues surrounding the investigation of AEGIS and Gavin.

Anything that would make this easier in the long run and enable him to get back over here to Africa with ease was preferable. He heard the shower switch on and flashed on an image of Sassy under the water's spray. He immediately fought to turn his wayward imagination off. Those thoughts would only lead to madness.

Marissa could get them out of here fast, or he hoped to God she could. He called her and was surprised when she picked up on the third ring.

"It's me, Hollywood. Can you talk?"

"Yes, did you find the girl?"

"I did. We're in the Hotel Novotel Constantine, but she's got no passport." *And barely any clothes.* But he kept that information to himself. "Can you get us out of here?"

"Probably, but it'll take a few hours. I'll have to go through back channels to do it. All my embassy contacts are burned for now."

"Can Leland help?" asked Bryan.

"If his confidential informant is available, yes. If not, you're stuck with me."

"I'll call him," said Bryan. The quicker he got Sassy out of here, the better.

"Touch base with me in a few hours. What time is it there now?"

"Almost midnight."

"I probably won't have anything for you till the morning— Wait, it's Christmas. It'll be tomorrow night. I'm sorry I can't work any faster than that."

Bryan didn't curse out loud, but in his head he was screaming profanities. That one bed was going to put him right over the edge. He swallowed hard before answering.

"'S okay, we can hole up here. That's not a problem." Yeah, he could lie with the best of them. "I'll talk to you then."

He ended the call and tried Leland to see if his contact could get them out of the country any faster, but there was no answer. As he hung up, Bryan heard the shower turn off and again tried not to imagine Sassy standing less than ten feet away—wet, warm, naked.

Jesus. He stood up and walked to the hall door. He was going to go crazy in the next twenty-four hours here with her. And he felt like a complete ass for even thinking that way right now considering what she'd just been through.

He had to figure out how to get them out of here while keeping his hands off her. That had been a problem ever since she'd hit puberty. More than anything else, Sassy was why he'd left town two weeks after he'd graduated from high school and joined the Marines.

Bryan's grandmother couldn't afford to send him to college, so he'd let the government educate him. That had turned out to be a very good plan. He'd seen the world and gotten quite the education.

And he'd put thoughts of Sassy behind him, or he thought he had, until he'd seen her again last summer. Since then, staying away from her had continued to be the wisest course of action. Whenever they met, he always made sure it was in a public place, or, if they were alone, he made sure it wasn't for long.

He assured himself that after Sassy's ordeal earlier tonight, their instant-combustion chemistry and keeping his hands off her wouldn't be an issue. She'd try to flatten his ass if he got too close, even by accident. He certainly hoped so. Otherwise, the next twenty-four hours would be his downfall.

SASSY TURNED OFF the shower and stood in the steamy enclosure for a moment. She'd considered soaking in the tub, but the steam made her feel cleaner. She hadn't felt this way since high school. The shaking had stopped on the outside, but inside she was still unstable and jumpy. If she focused for too long on how close she'd come to being raped or worse . . .

Those jitters weren't going away.

How had Bryan found her? God, did she even care? She was just grateful.

When he'd held her in that alley, she'd wanted him to never let her go. But she'd had to step away or risk him seeing how much he affected her. It was embarrassing how long she'd had a crush on him, but he was oblivious, thanks in part to her acting skills.

Sassy had learned a long time ago that her size and stature would work against her unless she used it to her advantage. Men would always think of her as someone they could use and take advantage of unless she turned the tables on them. So she automatically used an over-the-top sexual bravado and disdain to keep them at arm's length. And it worked surprisingly well, with everyone except Bryan.

Most men didn't know how to deal with it when she came on strong then used insults and sexual scorn about their not being able to handle her. It helped keep her would-be predators off balance. They didn't mess with her once she used what she liked to think of as the "Jessica Rabbit" persona. She wasn't really bad; she just acted that way.

Men she'd known over the years would laugh like mad if they knew her brazen innuendos and scoffing were all an act. "Sexy Sassy" was really "Scared Silly Sassy" just playing a part to keep the wolves at bay. But with Bryan, she didn't know what she was doing. Turning on her usual ego-crushing dialogue after flirting with him was next to impossible because Bryan knocked Sassy herself off balance.

Not because he'd ever come on to her, but because she had been attracted to him for as long as she could remember. What was real and what was pretend was a jumbled mess, and her "bad girl" act was even more pronounced whenever he was around. She flirted like mad but couldn't seem to flip the switch to the withering sarcasm that she used to keep other men at a distance.

Part of her would love to see Bryan's face if she just walked into the bedroom and whipped off her bathrobe, but that wasn't happening. God, if he really knew the extent of her play-acting, he'd either laugh his butt off, or run for the hills.

Still, her experience—or lack thereof—wasn't going to be an issue tonight, even if there was only one bed. Right now, she just wanted out of Africa, and on a plane headed home. Surely that would keep her emotions on an even keel.

She squeezed a small dollop of complimentary hotel toothpaste on her finger. The minty smell mixed with the lemon verbena scent of the soaps, lotion, and hair products she'd used earlier in the shower. She brushed her teeth and took a moment to study her face. She didn't usually go without makeup. The purple shadows under her eyes were so dark they were practically bruises.

Lovely. She looked like death warmed over. She gave the mirror a final glance and decided she'd stalled long enough. Tightening the belt on her robe, she opened the bathroom door.

BRYAN SAT AT a desk across the room from the bed. He was still struggling with how he was going to survive the next twenty-four hours with Sassy in a hotel room when he heard the bathroom door open. The citrusy smell of the hotel toiletries wafted into the room ahead of her. The scent of warm, clean woman wrapped around his head and his balls and squeezed. *Jesus.* He was a sick son of a bitch for even thinking of her this way, and he was never going to survive this.

She was wearing an oversized hotel robe, or rather it was wearing her. The thick terry cloth fell to her ankles, and the sleeves hung below her fingertips. Her wet hair was slicked back, with a couple of blonde curls springing loose around her temples. There was a Band-Aid on her neck.

She should have looked like she was twelve, but her blue eyes were distinctly older. Wiser. And despite the exhaustion shadowing her face, she looked like every wet dream he'd ever had since that summer he'd understood he had to get out of Springwater or do the unthinkable.

He needed to say something to establish some distance here, but the lump in his throat made that impossible.

She drifted into the room and plopped down on the bed in front of him. "So have you ordered us anything to eat?"

"Didn't know what you'd like," he mumbled. "I ordered a little of everything."

She opened the spiral-bound menu on the bedside table and perused the mostly Algerian and French dishes. "Ohh, yum. Did you get oysters on the half shell with champagne?"

She looked up at him with that sly, flirty glint and a lilt in her voice, but something about this wasn't ringing true. He wondered again if that off-the-charts sexuality she oozed was real or some kind of performance. Instead of wanting to nail her to the wall, he found he wanted to cradle her in his arms.

"Stop it. Just stop it. I can't do this with you." His throat felt as if he'd been gargling gravel.

Her smile dimmed a bit. "You're not 'doing' anything," retorted Sassy, but there was a definite shudder in her voice, too.

He stood and started toward her. "That's just it. I can't . . . Shit." And there it was, the reaction he always had to Sassy. Cussing and lust combined.

Now that he knew what he was looking at, he recognized her sex-kitten act for what it was—an act. As much a self-defense mechanism as the left hook he'd taught her with Trey years ago.

"Was there some sort of injury you sustained?" Her tone was low and sultry, but he heard another distinct tremor as well.

She was deliberately misunderstanding; he knew she was. But he didn't know why. The woman had almost been raped tonight. Why was she doing this?

His confusion combined with her exasperating words stung just enough to make his tone change. "No, I wasn't injured in Afghanistan. But I'm not going to screw my best friend's little sister, either. It wouldn't be right."

He sank down to the mattress beside her, so irritated at her that he was no longer worried about touching her. He'd never thought he'd be quite so crass about it. But this conversation was long overdue.

She stared back at him a moment, the defiance in her face the first real emotion he'd witnessed since her meltdown in the alleyway. "Well, maybe it wouldn't have been right when I was fourteen. But what's wrong with me now?"

He glowered at her a moment more before what she was saying registered. She looked almost as surprised at her words as he did.

"God, woman, absolutely nothing. I just—"

"Then why did you leave home like that? It was so quick you hardly said goodbye. You abandoned Trey, your Gran, and me so fast, it made our heads spin." Tears welled in her eyes as she stuttered over the words, and he was lost.

He knew it even as his palms itched to hold her. He'd left them because he was eighteen and on the verge of doing something that would have destroyed his relationship with the three people he cared about most in the world. He'd been so mixed up about his feelings for

Sassy; he couldn't stay. Leaving had been the right thing to do—the only thing to do—but he'd never considered how it had made Sassy feel.

"Nothing's wrong with you. I just didn't realize till now that you'd really grown up."

Inwardly he groaned as Sassy leaned back to look down her nose at him. *How ridiculous did that excuse sound?*

"What I meant to say was that, um . . . I didn't understand that you . . ." He clamped his mouth closed because while he was babbling like an idiot, he was at least smart enough to see that he was also digging a hole with a backhoe.

She narrowed her eyes at him, and he stared back. Everything that had happened earlier tonight faded as he did the thing he'd wanted to do for the past six months. He reached for her, pulling her into his arms and cradling her to his chest.

She melted against him without hesitation, and the feel of her body against his was better than he'd imagined. Her soft curves, in all the right places, registered with his brain and everything below his belt as she tucked her head into his shoulder.

He shouldn't be doing this. He knew it. She'd been traumatized earlier.

She sighed against him and tilted her head up. He looked into her midnight-blue eyes and saw a vulnerability there that had been shadowed before with all the sexual bravado she'd been throwing his way since last summer.

Still, he hesitated.

She looped her hands behind his neck and pushed his head down toward her. She smelled . . . different than he remembered. Her scent, which normally had him so mixed up, had been washed away with the shower. She kissed him, carefully moving her mouth against his, and he froze.

He was kissing Trey's sister. She moved her hand down his back and pressed closer against him. Her breasts were soft against the firm wall of his chest.

Her tongue was in his mouth and he stopped thinking—about everything, about Trey, about why they shouldn't be doing this, about where they were. His hands were in her robe and he moved them up her sides along her ribcage. She moaned into his mouth as her palms slid to his waistband. The robe slipped from her shoulders, catching at her elbows.

He looked down. Her breasts were the perfect size, with nipples a dusty rose that had pebbled with the cool temperature of the air conditioning. Her waist and hips were covered with the white terry cloth, but he caught a glimpse of blonde curls between her legs. His cock throbbed against the back of his zipper.

He gently tugged the robe from her arms and she slid one of her hands under his shirt, brushing one of her fingertips across his stomach along the way to his belt buckle. He kissed the side of her neck, then pulled back to slip his T-shirt off.

The gray cotton tee fluttered to the floor. The feel of her satiny bare skin pressing into his chest had him almost coming right there, but he took a deep breath, swallowed hard, and put his hands on her waist. His fingers rested on either side of her hips, and he moved his thumbs down across her belly lower and lower, finally lifting her up so that she could swing her leg over his lap to straddle him.

Her robe puddled over his hands, leaving her completely exposed. When he touched the top of her pubic bone with his fingertips, she startled, and her eyes focused on his for the first time since she'd kissed him. But the expression there was completely different from what he'd been expecting.

Instead of being in the throes of passion, she looked . . . scared? He pulled back and was about to ask her what was going on when there was a brisk knock at the door.

"Room service."

Chapter 4

SASSY JUMPED AWAY from him like she'd been burned, pulling the robe with her across the bed. Bryan could do nothing but stare as she practically cowered at the headboard. Guilt and confusion simultaneously swamped him.

What the hell? There was no way he'd misread this, was there? She'd been all over him. She'd kissed him. It hadn't been *that* long since he'd been in bed with a woman.

Sassy had obviously changed her mind about having sex with him, and that was fine. But she hadn't said a word. He felt like shit.

If that knock on the door hadn't come just now, would she have gone through with it anyway? On top of everything that had happened to her tonight, that horrified him.

"Are you okay?" he asked softly.

She nodded, refusing to make eye contact. "I'm fine."

Bryan knew enough about women to know that "fine"

was code for something else here. Unfortunately, he had no idea how to access the codebook.

The knock sounded again. He made no move to answer.

"Are you sure?" He stared at her, but she never looked up from the bedspread. There was no way he was going to just leave this alone. "Did I hurt you?" he asked.

Bryan was a big guy, and he didn't think he'd leaned into her or crowded her in any way. He certainly hadn't crowded her the way he'd been planning to before he'd seen the expression on her face.

She looked up at him then. "God, no. I just . . ." She took a ragged breath. "I'm just not as up for this as I thought. It's been a . . . difficult night," she mumbled. Her earlier bravado had completely disappeared.

Jesus. That was putting it mildly. "Sassy, I . . ."

"Don't worry," she muttered. "It's not like you did more than grab my ass."

Bryan tried not to be insulted.

He'd done a bit more than that. They'd been about to have sex. And there was no un-ringing that bell. Was this some weird delayed shock reaction? The knock sounded once more, insistent this time.

"Coming," he called out. Then almost snorted at his choice of words. *Not hardly,* he thought. He rolled off the bed, buttoned his jeans, and answered the door.

SASSY TIED HER robe tightly around her waist and struggled to regain equilibrium as the room service waiter rolled a cart laden with silver-topped domes into the room. What had she been about to do? God, she'd been undressed and in Bryan's lap. If the waiter hadn't arrived when he had, she'd be having sex right now.

Not that having sex with Bryan was a bad thing. It would probably be a very good thing. But he would know.

And she wasn't ready for that, particularly tonight. The explanations involved and dredging up the past were more than she could take after the day she'd had. Right now, she just needed to get a grip on her emotions.

The waiter pulled the serving domes from the plates with a flourish. Bryan hadn't been joking, he really had ordered a little of everything from the menu. Pastries, a fluffy omelet, cut fruit, a dish she didn't recognize but that looked heavenly and smelled divine. Who would eat all of this?

Bryan turned away from her as he took the check from the waiter. The skin on his bare back was smooth, with a deep tan and well-defined musculature. Her throat went dry. Even the man's back was beautiful.

His waist tapered and his tan line stopped just above the top of his jeans. She tried not to stare at his butt, focusing instead on the strip of light-colored skin just below his waist as he bent over the desktop to sign the tab. He must weigh at least 230, but from what she could see, he was all muscle. She assumed it wouldn't be a problem for a man his size to eat everything on the table the way he'd been about to gobble her up earlier.

Bryan locked up behind the waiter and leaned against the door to stare at Sassy in silence. The heat of his gaze had her feeling more than a little intimidated. But something stirred deep inside her as well. Why couldn't she just slip back into her usual saucy persona, complete with scathing barbs? If she didn't, how was she ever going to survive here without throwing herself at him again?

The scent of the food wafted around them, and she broke the silence. "Even with you helping, I'm not sure I can begin to make a dent in all that food."

Her stomach growled, and a smile kicked up at the edge of Bryan's solemn lips. "Well, we can certainly try," he said.

Thank God. They weren't going to discuss what had just happened. She stood beside the bed as her emotions over the room service interruption swirled inside her like a child's spinning top. How did she really feel? Confused, embarrassed, disappointed?

Relief *should* be the overwhelming emotion of the hour, because Bryan didn't know her carefully crafted personality was a lie. Hopefully, he never would.

She nodded toward the mattress. "This other thing earlier. That was a mistake."

"Ya think?" His eyebrow lifted as he spoke.

She couldn't tell if he was hurt or being sarcastic. Instead of answering, she gave a nonchalant shrug and ignored him as she sat down to eat.

He stayed by the door. "Look, Sassy. I just want to get you out of here and back home. But we're stuck until I hear back from Marissa Hudson, my boss. Until then, I need you cooperative."

His tone and choice of words had her lashing out

before thinking it through. "So you thought you'd screw me into compliance?" That wasn't what she'd meant, but she was so off-kilter, she'd slipped right into her autopilot defensive mode.

Bryan looked at her as if she'd slapped him. "Hell no. I just . . . Jesus, that's not how it was at all and certainly not what I meant. I'm so sorry if it felt that way . . . I . . ."

His words made her feel steadier. Throwing him off base helped in return, even if it was playing extremely dirty and bitchy. This kind of balancing act she was used to.

He was still staring at her as his stricken expression hardened into something completely unreadable. "I assure you, it won't happen again."

Even as her heart sank, Sassy smiled and tried to tell herself that her tactic hadn't backfired. But deep down, she knew it had. If she was honest with herself, what she really wanted was him holding her and telling her everything would be okay. But if he'd just said that it wouldn't happen again, he'd all but taken a vow.

She'd heard those words before, when he was eighteen years old and she was fourteen. They'd been on the back porch of his house playing a handheld video game. She could still hear the trailer's air conditioner wheezing and smell the honeysuckle combined with the stink of the compost pile from Bryan's grandmother's garden around the corner of the cement patio.

Bryan's Gran called Sassy Sarah Ann, but she'd been Sassy to the rest of the town for as long as she could remember. Her brother Trey hadn't been able to say Sarah

Ann when she was born. Only two years old at the time, he'd called her Sassy instead. The moniker had stuck.

For once her brother hadn't been around. Normally he and Bryan would have been torturing the tagalong little sister with some ridiculous dare that was either death defying or humiliating, like climbing the twenty-five-foot tree in the cotton field across the highway or singing her dinner order at the top of her lungs in McDonald's on a Friday night. Initially, these "challenges" had been Trey's way of keeping Sassy in her place, since she was always hanging out with them. But over the years Bryan had adopted it, too.

She'd been hanging out with Bryan by herself that day and taking turns playing on the Game Boy that they'd had forever. For once she wasn't being dared to do anything. In fact, Bryan had been listening attentively as she'd been talking about a boy in her class who she had a slight crush on.

"Bobby says he doesn't like me because I don't have 'experience' like Tracy Rave or Julie Milver," said Sassy, inching closer into Bryan's chest to see what he was doing on the game.

"Tracy Rave is a slut. You don't want to have a reputation for that kind of experience." Bryan pushed back with his shoulder and hip a bit to keep Sassy from taking up too much space even as he scooted over on the sofa cushion to let her see the screen.

In her innocence Sassy really hadn't known precisely what Bryan meant by "experience."

"You mean she's a good kisser?" she asked.

"No, I mean she gives good—" He swallowed and shook his head. "That's right, she's a good kisser. Among other things." He sank lower into the sofa. "Geez, hasn't your mom ever talked to you about this?"

She rolled her eyes at him. Unless Sassy could fit herself into the bottom of Bess Smith's bourbon bottle, there was very little chance she and her mother would ever be having a heart-to-heart conversation. Bess rarely said much of anything to Sassy beyond "Where are my smokes?" and "Is there any more Jim Beam in the cabinet?"

Bryan's Gran was more of a mom to Sassy than Bess ever was. For the first time Sassy didn't mind so much, since she liked seeing Bryan uncomfortable and blushing as he tried to talk to her about what Tracy Rave's "experience" meant.

"Why don't you show me?" she asked.

"What?" He startled beside her as he turned on the cushion to study her face. "Are you nuts?"

"No, I just want to know what it's like to kiss a boy. And since you say Bobby's a turd, I think my first time should be with someone who's not."

Bryan almost looked relieved. "You want to know what it's like to kiss . . . I thought . . . never mind what I thought."

"Would it be that horrible to kiss me? C'mon," she said, tossing her head impatiently. "I dare ya."

She loved being the one to say it this time. He leaned back for a moment and stared at her through gray eyes that were usually a bit sleepy and sometimes a little sad. But there was nothing sleepy or sad in them right now.

There was an expression there she'd never seen before and couldn't identify.

"You sure about this, Sassy?"

"Absolutely," she grinned, completely unaware of what she was asking for.

Everything slowed to what felt like a standstill on that old ratty couch when he set the game down and put his arm around her. The air conditioner kicked off. It was unusually quiet. She held her breath without realizing, and the next thing she knew Bryan was kissing her.

His lips were warm and soft against hers and his breath smelled like the Dentyne he liked so much. She leaned into him and sighed as he brushed his tongue against the seam of her lips, and she figured out fast that she was supposed to open her mouth instead of just grinding her lips against his.

He pulled her closer and swept his tongue into her mouth. She felt funny with a flutter deep in her tummy and leaned even further into him. His tongue tangled with hers for just a moment longer, then she moaned into his mouth and he jumped back as if she'd bitten him.

One month after that kiss on the sofa, Bryan had graduated from high school and joined the Marines. Sassy hadn't seen him again for almost twelve years, not even for his grandmother's funeral, until Trey had been arrested in Mexico. Two days later Bryan had shown up out of the blue looking like a live action hero from the movies, and offering to help Trey any way he could.

Sassy had recognized him immediately standing on her mother's doorstep, but it had still been a shock. And while Bryan might have changed dramatically since she'd known him in high school, the expression on his face the first time he'd kissed her was exactly the same as he'd worn just moments earlier: positively stricken.

"LET'S EAT," BRYAN said as he stalked toward the room service cart. "It's going to be a while before we hear back from Marissa." He was so mad at himself, his tone sounded much harsher than he intended. Sassy brought out the absolute worst in him, every time.

He never cursed around women, yet with Sassy he felt as if he was in a constant state of having hit his thumb with a hammer. What was it about this girl . . . this woman?

She sure as hell wasn't "a girl" any longer. Sometimes it felt like he could just look at her and raise his body temperature. That's why he'd left home so abruptly. Nothing good would have come of his staying in Springwater the summer he graduated. He wasn't going to seduce his best friend's baby sister then, and he wasn't going to do it now, either.

Trey Smith had enough trouble. Six months ago in Mexico, he'd been found early one morning passed out and covered in blood in a boat he'd rented the afternoon before with Elizabeth Yarborough to take a sunset cruise.

No body had been found, but witnesses claimed to have heard Trey and Elizabeth arguing in the hotel restaurant before they'd left for the marina. Trey had no memory of what had happened beyond renting the boat and leaving the dock. He admitted to having had a heated discussion in the restaurant beforehand, because he'd been worried for Elizabeth's safety in the village where the Peace Corps had had her stationed.

Cartel violence had increased dramatically in that same area, and he'd wanted her to come back home to the U.S. early or request to be moved, but she'd refused. The next morning everything had gone to hell. Elizabeth was missing, presumed dead, and Trey had been arrested.

Sassy was convinced Elizabeth was alive. But while Bryan didn't think Trey had murdered the woman, he wasn't so sure she was still alive.

He snuck another glance at Sassy, perched on the edge of the bed in that ridiculously oversized robe, and felt his heart rate bump up. *Jesus.* It was going to be a long night.

He flipped on the television to a BBC news channel. The Christmas Eve mass from the Vatican was being broadcast. Bryan wasn't Catholic or particularly religious, but his Gran had gone to church, and he'd attended with her often. Until now he'd only thought about today's being Christmas Eve in terms of how it would affect their getting out of Africa. The mass seemed an appropriate background for dinner.

Peace on earth.

He stared at the screen. Peace was such a foreign concept. He wasn't opposed, but with everything happening right now, it felt extraordinarily out of reach. He listened to the chanting and tried to focus on the liturgy. Anything to keep his mind off Sassy and that one bed.

Chapter 5

December 25
Late afternoon

BRYAN HAD GOOD memories that involved Christmas. But this had been a bizarre holiday, filled with waiting, impatience, and awkwardness. Being shut up in a hotel room for most of the day with a half-dressed Sassy had been surreal.

Despite the manager's assurances of last night, the hotel shop had been closed all morning, along with every other shop immediately around the hotel. Bryan didn't want to go back to the Casbah, so he'd decided to wait a few hours before trying again. He and Sassy had passed the time catching up on what their lives had been like since Springwater, even playing Texas Hold'em for a while until she suggested they switch to strip poker. God, the woman really would say anything about sex. This very grown-up Sassy was not at all like the girl he'd known back home.

After a late room service lunch, he left the hotel a second time in search of clothes for her. A few blocks away, he hit what felt like a Vegas jackpot when he found a combination boutique and grocery store that was open. The clothing might not be Sassy's style, but he managed to pick out what he assumed were the right sizes.

It was half past six when he got back to the room. Vibrating with tension, Sassy met him at the door. "I checked my voice mails while you were out. Trey's attorney called. They're moving up the timetable for the trial. It all takes place right after New Year's on January third. That's just over a week from now."

This was very bad news. Unlike the U.S. courts, in Mexico defendants were considered guilty till proven innocent. And the judges were extremely engaged in the investigation of the crimes involved.

Sassy paced the room with nervous energy. "Trey's judge is expected to rule on the case immediately after the trial. We're running out of time."

Bryan took a deep breath. He'd thought they would have at least another couple of months before the judge's ruling. This added a whole new layer of urgency to finding answers for Trey. Bryan needed to be home, or at least on the North American continent, to help his friend.

While he seriously doubted Elizabeth was alive, he knew voicing that thought here would be a mistake. Besides doing nothing to help Trey's precarious situation, it would only ratchet up Sassy's anxiety. He wasn't sure how to help her right now. He wanted to hold her, but after the fiasco of last night, touching her seemed a recipe for disaster. Instead, he handed her the bag of clothes he'd just bought.

She looked at the simple offering inside the plastic sack and gave him a wry grin. Beyond that she said nothing, which surprised him. He expected some sarcastic comment about his selections, but she slipped into the bathroom to change without a word.

He was staring at the door and puzzling over her reaction when his cell phone rang. It was Marissa. The meeting was set to take place in a hotel across town where Sassy's passport and cash would be delivered for their trip home. Risa had also arranged for a flight out of Mohamed Boudiaf International there in Constantine. How she had done it on Christmas Day, Bryan had no idea. But he didn't ask. All he knew was that they were checking out tonight.

Thank you, Baby Jesus.

He explained the plan to Sassy though the bathroom door and began pulling his own belongings together and packing to leave. He shook his head, still surprised they'd made it through the past twenty-four hours without fighting or sleeping together. Aside from feeling grumpy, grouchy, and horny, he was beyond grateful that temptation and Sassy would soon be out of his hair.

When she reemerged moments later, she put her other, impossibly dirty clothes alongside his in a plastic bag. Nestling her belongings into the duffel bag beside his Dopp kit, she packed with him as if they'd been together for years. For some reason the idea of packing a bag together felt as intimate as kissing her, and he had no idea why. He stared at the white plastic bag a moment before zipping the duffel, then straightened and caught her staring at him.

"We're just like an old married couple, aren't we?" she muttered, echoing his thoughts so completely that he wondered if he'd spoken aloud a moment.

"As if," he snorted. "Let's get out of here, Harriet."

She winked and grinned for a moment. He had the urge to lean in and kiss the dimple at the edge of her smile, or better yet, push her to the mattress and finish what they'd started yesterday. But he managed to get a grip on himself. That was not in the cards, and he was moments away from making it out of this hotel room with most of his sanity intact where Sassy was concerned.

"Let's go. We have just enough time to get across town and meet Marissa's contact."

"But I don't want to go back home. I think we can find Elizabeth here."

He stopped with his hand on the doorknob.

"Are you crazy? After all you've been through in the past four days? Where would you start looking? You don't even know for certain that Elizabeth was ever in Africa."

"But Juan said she was put on a boat in Venezuela. Wouldn't that—"

"Juan Santos, your contact?"

She gasped. "How did you know that?"

"I don't think you should depend on what old Juan told you. He has, or I should say, he *had* a somewhat dubious reputation."

"Had?"

"Juan's dead. He tried to kill Nick Donovan yesterday morning on the Sidi M'Cid Bridge."

Sassy put a hand over her mouth.

"Nick told me before I came to get you. It seems Juan was notorious for lying when the truth would do. That caught up to him yesterday."

"But why would he have lied to me?"

"I don't know, Sassy. I think the more important question is, why would he have told you the truth? According to what Nick learned yesterday, Juan lied about pretty much everything, even when he didn't have to."

She stared at the floor a moment longer before shaking her head. "I came here to Africa looking for Elizabeth because of what Juan told me. I can't believe—" She stopped herself. "I don't want to believe it was all a lie." She moved to the door but didn't make eye contact. "God, we're running out of time," she repeated. "Trey's running out of time."

He nodded. What had she traded to get the trafficking routes for the women he had seen on the side of the road in Constantine? He thought of the kiss they'd shared last night and wasn't sure he wanted to know. He also didn't want them to walk out of this room at odds with each other.

He couldn't argue with Sassy and keep her safe at the same time. He had no idea if Rivera's men were still looking for her or not. With Ernesto Vega dead, things were most likely in utter chaos, but he wouldn't take chances with her safety.

Regardless of what was happening with Trey's case, getting Sassy home to the U.S. was the wisest course of action for now. Convincing her of that would be the problem. He decided to wait until he knew how they were getting out of Africa before pushing the subject of going back home any further.

"Why are we meeting so late?" she asked on the way to the elevator.

He grabbed hold of the new subject with gusto, happy not to be bickering. "It must be because of the holiday. Marissa warned it would take a while to get everything together. I'm not sure who we're meeting across town. She just told me where to wait, and said that they'd find us."

He turned in their hotel room key, and they caught a cab. The streets were bustling, much more so tonight than the evening before. The cab dropped them in the driveway of the Hotel Hocine, and they walked inside to meet their contact.

Bryan did a double take when he saw Gavin and Marissa seated in the lobby drinking coffee. He grabbed Sassy's elbow and pulled her with him to the white leather sofa.

Gavin stood. "Merry Christmas."

"What are you two doing here?" The hair rose on the back of Bryan's neck. There was a warrant out for this man's arrest in the U.S., yet Gavin was in Africa instead of trying to clear that up?

What the fuck?

He shouldn't be that surprised. Gavin had a way of turning up in the most unexpected places. The first time they'd met was in an army hospital in Afghanistan. It had been crazy unexpected and a godsend at the same time.

But with AEGIS under investigation, could Bryan really be one hundred percent sure of Gavin? Loyalty was incredibly important to him. But Bryan was experienced enough *not* to take it all on face value, even though his and Sassy's options were so very limited right now.

Still, if Gavin was dirty, Bryan was the pope. He'd worked with Gavin too long and seen the man in too many situations to accept anything else. His gut check was not buying that Gavin could be corrupt. Bryan squeezed Sassy's hand and hoped like hell he wasn't being naïve.

"Don't worry about me, Hollywood. Only in the U.S. do they want my head on a pike."

"So far," added Marissa with a grim smile.

Gavin raised a shoulder in a shrug and pointedly ignored the comment. "Risa figured we were the logical ones to deliver the travel documents. Nick is already on his way home, and Leland is still on crutches." He studied Sassy with undisguised curiosity.

"Whatever the reason, I'm glad to see you," said Bryan. But even as he reached out to shake Gavin's hand, Nick's words in Skikda came to mind. *We can believe whatever we want. It's what we can prove that will matter.*

Bryan was still holding Sassy's fingers in his other hand and dropped them when he realized he was squeezing a little too hard. "This is Sassy Smith, Trey Smith's sister." As he introduced Gavin and Marissa, Bryan fought the urge to put his hand on Sassy's back.

What was it about his always wanting to touch her?

One of Gavin's eyebrows shot up. "Elizabeth Yarborough's Trey Smith?" he asked.

Bryan nodded and forced himself to meet Gavin's stare. While he *had* told Gavin that Trey was a friend when AEGIS had been hired to look for Elizabeth, he had never told his boss about the connection between himself and Sassy and exactly how AEGIS had come to be hired.

After Elizabeth's disappearance and Trey's arrest, Bryan had gone to see Sassy at her mother's house, explained what he did with AEGIS, and offered to help. In turn, Sassy had introduced Bryan to Elizabeth's parents and encouraged them to hire AEGIS to help find their daughter. The Yarborough family vehemently believed in Trey's innocence, which had made for some heartrending news coverage. Even so, Bryan suspected Gavin had never told anyone else at AEGIS about his connection to Trey Smith.

That suspicion was confirmed when Marissa put her hand out to greet Sassy. "I must say that it's a surprise to meet you. I had no idea until now that anyone in AEGIS had a *personal* connection to Elizabeth Yarborough before her parents came to us." The look Risa shot Bryan would have melted glass if he hadn't already been so fried by everything else happening.

SASSY GLANCED SIDEWAYS at Bryan as she shook the stunning redhead's hand. Sassy wasn't sure what to say to the woman or to the man. Something had happened as soon as Bryan had seen these people seated in the hotel lobby. She'd felt it in Bryan's hand gripping hers when he'd completely tensed up and squeezed the hell out of her fingers before the introductions.

Marissa's voice wasn't unfriendly, but it wasn't exactly dripping with enthusiasm for the situation either.

And Sassy could tell the woman was world-class pissed at Bryan. She had a feeling it had to do with her being Trey's sister.

What was going on? Could Sassy trust these two people or not?

"I appreciate everything your organization is trying to do for the Yarboroughs and for my brother. I don't know what we'd do if we didn't have Bryan on our side." Sassy smiled like a good Southern girl and thickened her accent while patting Bryan's shoulder as she would her brother's.

He glanced down at her and gave a slight shake of his head. Was that a warning sign or resignation?

"What are you doing here in Africa?" Bryan asked again.

Marissa studied Sassy openly with her bright green gaze before answering, and it took every bit of Sassy's hard-earned poise not to squirm under the scrutiny. She was the poor country cousin next to the beautiful red-head's elegant ensemble. Sassy's outfit had been pulled together from what Bryan had bought in a glorified grocery store and what she'd been able to salvage from her own clothing by rinsing everything out in the sink last night. Not exactly the height of couture, even here in Africa.

Sassy's clothes fit and didn't smell, but that was about all she could say for her "eclectic" look. Her thick curly hair, normally forced into submission with a blow-dryer and flat iron, was corkscrewing around her face like Medusa's serpents. She'd broken three nails at the quick, and with no makeup, her self-confidence had taken a direct hit.

Normally, she could have dealt with one or two of the issues with aplomb, but all of it together made her feel "less than." Less than put together, less than having her act together. She'd worked her entire life *not* to feel *less than*. Ever since that horrific summer Bryan had left and her life had fallen apart.

"Surely you didn't come all this way just to help us out?" Sassy stood a bit taller, giving the other couple a skeptic's gaze.

She'd never responded well to feeling at a disadvantage. Bryan put a hand on her arm, giving her elbow a slight squeeze as they sat beside each other on the opposite sofa facing Marissa and Gavin.

Another warning?

Most likely. Right now, Sassy didn't give a damn.

Marissa raised an eyebrow at the contact but didn't respond to her veiled comment. Instead, she addressed her remarks to Bryan. "We're trying to find out what's happening with Ernesto Vega and Tomas Rivera. From what we understand, they're behind these trumped-up charges on Gavin."

Bryan hadn't mentioned anything to Sassy about trumped-up charges, but that didn't surprise her. Bryan hadn't said much of anything about his work, today or last night after their mistimed whatever-the-hell-that-had-been and the massive in-room dinner they'd shared.

They'd turned on the television to avoid talking once the dinner had been delivered, and she'd fallen asleep soon after. She assumed Bryan had slept on either the floor or the tiny sofa. When she'd woken up this morning, he'd been in the shower. Their conversation today had been somewhat superficial until they'd discussed Trey's trial date being moved. They had not discussed the legal problems of Bryan's employer.

"Didn't Nick tell you?" Bryan's question pulled her back to the conversation. The heat of his thigh next to hers radiated through her thin cotton dress.

"Tell me what?" asked Marissa.

"Ernesto Vega's dead," said Bryan. "He was killed early yesterday morning near some Algerian oasis. Nick followed the truck of women that Sassy and Jennifer were with to Constantine and got Jenny out of the warehouse before the truck headed for the coast. Sassy escaped when they had a flat tire near the Casbah. I'm still trying to figure out how they knew to pick her up outside the café in Niamey in the first place. Who told them she was part of this?"

"Do you think it was Juan Santos?" asked Sassy. "He knew I was here. He practically told me to come."

She looked at Gavin and made a concerted effort not to outright stare. Movie star handsome, he was in his early to mid-forties—if the salt-and-pepper hair and laugh lines around his eyes and mouth were any indication—and seemed very fit underneath his sport shirt and jeans, pretty much along the same lines as Bryan but leaner.

Bryan might be taller but not by much. The biggest difference she could see was that Gavin had a distinct sadness to his expression, a coolness that was untouchable. Sassy liked Gavin better than Marissa, even if he was intimidating. She knew how to handle men much better than women.

When he spoke, his voice was even and deep with very little accent. "That seems a lot of trouble to go to just to get another woman when they kidnap and spirit away so many. It sounds as if you knew something or were poking round in something they didn't like. Any idea what that could be?"

The lobby was deserted except for the cleaning crew working across the foyer.

Bryan's voice was quiet. "She's a reporter."

Sassy felt a spurt of irritation sizzle in her veins. He made her profession sound like a bad thing.

"I write freelance for the Associated Press. It helps pay the bills and gives me an excuse to ask nosy questions while I'm looking for information to help my brother's case."

"Hmm." Marissa nodded with a look of approval. Surprised, Sassy acknowledged an unexpected spark of gratitude toward the otherwise chilly redhead.

"I found out today they've moved up his trial date. The judge will be handing down a decision just after New Year's."

"That is soon. Are you sure you didn't step on any toes in your research recently?" Marissa asked.

Sassy shrugged, reluctant to acknowledge that she'd wondered the same thing herself. "Possibly. I don't know. A contact gave me a map of supposed routes for smuggling women. I showed the map to Bryan, and that's when everything went to hell in a handbasket."

Gavin nodded. "Do you really think Elizabeth was here?"

"Two days ago I would have said yes, but now I understand that's only been verified by a man with a reputation for habitual lying."

Bryan nodded. "Juan Santos. Nick confirmed he worked for Ernesto Vega and Tomas Rivera, and any other high bidder. Often as not, he's played both sides against the middle. It's very likely he was lying. *Why* remains to be seen. Presumably he didn't need much of a reason."

"Bottom line sounds like you two need to get out of Africa as soon as possible," said Gavin.

"But . . . what about looking for Elizabeth?" asked Sassy. "If we don't find some kind of evidence, Trey will have nothing at trial. He's looking at life in a Mexican prison."

Gavin looked from Marissa to Bryan and shook his head. Before he said anything else, Sassy knew that Gavin had been appointed to break some bad news. And despite the mesmerizing intensity of his gaze, she wasn't going to like what the man had to say.

"We've got some things going on internally with AEGIS. There's zero support from the U.S. government or from our typical sources. With the Ebola outbreak and quarantines east of here, you need to leave now, while you still can. There's no telling what will happen if that chaos spreads across the borders."

"You could have difficulty getting back in time for Trey's trial if they instigate more travel bans," Marissa continued. "If anything else were to go sideways here, there are no resources. I can't stress that enough. These papers will get you back home, but given the nature of all that's happened in the past week, it's entirely too risky to be here without any kind of backup or AEGIS's usual resources. We're under siege."

Sassy interrupted. "But Elizabeth could be here—"

Bryan joined in, speaking right over her. "You missed Christmas with your mother. She needs you. You know she does. I understand she's cleaned up her act, but this thing with Trey has got to be tearing her apart. Go home to see her, talk to Trey's lawyer while we regroup. I'll turn around and come right back to look for Elizabeth if we find any solid evidence that she's been here."

He leaned in, his eyes cool and serious as he crowded her a bit more on the sofa. "You need to go home. We all do."

She wanted to argue despite the prick of her conscience. But sitting here facing these professional "fixers" with her makeshift clothes, no papers, no phone, and not even a penny in her pocket—it was pretty much impossible. Even if her mother didn't need the moral support, Sassy needed a break from the gut-wrenching week she'd just spent chasing leads all over Africa, leads that had only proven how nasty people could treat each other.

If she was honest with herself, home sounded pretty damn awesome right now with a refrigerator full of food, clean clothes, and her old-fashioned claw-footed tub.

But how could she consider that while her brother was in prison? She blushed at the shame of her weakness. "I'll go home. But don't you think for a minute I'm going to sit on my hands. I'm turning in the article I've been asked to write on sex trafficking between Mexico and Africa. My editor left me a couple of voice messages about that earlier as well. He wants a story and he wants it now."

"You'd didn't tell me you were planning to do that," said Bryan.

"Well, I thought the call from Trey's attorney was a little more pressing to share. But in light of everything else, I've got to see if perhaps that will shake anything loose."

"You understand what you're saying? Whoever is behind all this could come after you." Bryan's voice dropped lower and he straightened on the sofa cushion, towering over her with his chest at her eye level. She supposed that posture would have intimidated someone who hadn't known him as long as she had.

She resisted the urge to poke at his torso and stood up instead so that she was head and shoulders above him. "I've got to do something. It's Trey."

"I'm not sure the story is a wise idea," said Marissa, keeping her voice low.

Sassy turned pleading eyes to the woman. "It's not your brother. And no one's leaving me with much choice here."

Bryan put his hand on Sassy's shoulder. "What she means is that the article could do more harm than good."

Sassy shrugged off his hand. "More harm than letting Trey rot in that prison?" She heard her tone change and hated the waspishness of it. Hot tears of despair gathered at the corner of her eyes, and she dashed them away angrily to glare at him as she ignored the others. "I'm not leaving my brother in that hellhole."

Like you left us in Mississippi.

Marissa and Gavin remained silent as Sassy stared Bryan down and her frustration boiled out all over him. She hadn't realized how much unresolved anger she still held onto over his leaving all those years ago. She no longer cared what Marissa and Gavin thought of her. All she could hear was the tick-tock of the rapidly approaching court date. Getting Trey out of jail was paramount.

"We're not leaving him, Sassy. *You're* not leaving him. We'll find the evidence, and we'll get him out. But we've got to be smart about it," said Bryan.

"When? We've got less than nine days." There was no hiding the misery in her voice.

The lobby was unusually quiet. Even the cleaning crew was gone now. Gavin and Marissa looked at her, as did Bryan, but no one answered. There was nothing to say.

Chapter 6

December 26
New York

FIFTEEN HOURS LATER Sassy shivered in her tropical clothing as Bryan paid the driver and they exited their taxi on West Fifty-Seventh Street. It had taken forever to get out of the airport, since they'd had to check Bryan's duffel to transport his handguns. In customs he'd seen multiple officials and walked through the complicated paperwork involved in travelling internationally with weapons. While he had all the proper permits and licenses, the process had been slow.

Before leaving JFK, they'd attempted to make a flight reservation for the next day, but given the holiday crush, they'd had to settle for standby. Standing on the street in Midtown Manhattan, Sassy was dead on her feet.

"There's an ATM down here I need to use. We'll find a hotel after that." Bryan adjusted the duffel bag on one shoulder and his small backpack on the other and started walking at a brisk pace.

Sassy looked longingly at the T.J. Maxx and the

CVS across the street from each other. The day-after-Christmas sales meant practically everything retail was still open. Bryan was focused on finding them a room, but she had to have something warmer to wear or risk pneumonia. She also wanted makeup and her own tooth-brush in the worst way.

She could ask him for some cash but hesitated to be more beholden to him than she already was. How crazy was that? She already owed him more than she could ever repay with his helping look for Elizabeth and getting her out of Africa.

"I need to borrow some cash," she said.

He frowned. "I don't understand. We're going to the bank in the morning. What do you need tonight?"

She sighed. Men truly were clueless sometimes. "It's thirty degrees out, and I'm wearing sandals and a sun-dress." She wasn't going to mention that she'd been wear-ing the same panties for more than a week with just a hand wash in the sink to clean them last night, and that the dress was one she normally wouldn't wear as a Hal-loween costume.

"You see that drugstore down the street and the cloth-ing store across from it? I need a hundred dollars and thirty minutes."

To his credit, Bryan didn't hesitate. Instead, he looked down at the Teva sandals on his own feet and pulled out his wallet. "My God, you must be freezing. I'm sorry I didn't think about that. Here's one seventy-five. That's all the U.S. currency I've got now. I'll go to the ATM on my own and find us a room. There's a hotel around the corner

I've used before. How about I meet you at the checkout counter of T.J. Maxx in forty-five minutes. I need to pick up a couple of things, too."

"Perfect." She took the cash and made a speedy power shopping trip through the drugstore, finding the toiletries she wanted, plus a hairbrush and some very basic makeup that would make her feel human again. She also grabbed a package of Dentyne for Bryan as a peace offering. After checking out at CVS, she headed to the clothing store.

The sales were in full swing and the prices had been slashed on everything. She quickly found a pair of jeans, two basic T-shirts, and a layering sweater, along with an overcoat, some boots, and a fun, oversized handbag on super sale that would carry all her new makeup and toiletries.

She glanced at her watch and saw she had just enough time to go to the lingerie department. She found everything she needed, including a sleep shirt that she couldn't resist, even if Christmas was over. She met Bryan at the checkout with two minutes to spare.

He looked at her CVS bag and the pile of clothing in her arms. "You work fast."

She smiled and handed him the pack of gum she'd just bought. "I always work fast when I'm spending someone else's money. But I will have some of your cash left over."

He shook his head, pocketed the gum, and handed his credit card to the clerk.

"Thanks for the gum. Keep the cash. We'll settle up later, after you get everything figured out with your bank."

She'd never be able to repay him for *everything* he'd done. It wasn't possible. So she wouldn't think about that right now. Like Scarlett, she'd think about that tomorrow.

"Thanks," she murmured.

"I got a double room at the place around the corner I told you about. Since we already shared a room in Constantine, I didn't think that would be a problem."

"Nope, no problem." Her relief was palpable. Despite her usual nerves of steel, she was shaky after everything that had happened in Africa and in the Casbah. She didn't want to be anywhere without Bryan nearby. That alone should have scared her more than anything, but being in New York had the feel of a dream.

The hotel was a short walk away. Once they were checked in, she went straight to the bathroom, where she showered, shaved her legs, washed her hair, and slathered lotion all over herself. She used her toothbrush and dried her hair before slipping into her new nightshirt and panties.

All cleaned up, the butterflies fluttering in her belly were totally different from the shakiness she'd experienced earlier. She was about to be in a bedroom with Bryan with no drama to cloud her overwhelming attraction toward him.

She wasn't in shock or desperate to get out of a hostile foreign country. She was home, she was safe, and she was suddenly extremely, painfully aware of just how much she wanted to feel his arms around her again. But that was a terrible idea, and she knew exactly how to stop it.

She walked out of the steam-filled bathroom to find him sitting at the desk, just like he had been when she'd come out of the hotel bathroom in Africa. That hadn't gone particularly well, but she shoved those disconcerting thoughts aside.

She could do this. She'd bluffed her way through awkward situations with men before, just never this kind of situation. And absolutely never with a man she was so attracted to. Her balancing act tended to fall apart around Bryan. She had to keep a grip on her emotions to shut this down. No matter what happened, she had to stay in control.

He was plugging in his cell phone. When he looked up, his focus zeroed in on her chest. His sigh was one of resignation. "Is that how you see yourself?"

"How I see what?"

"Your shirt." His voice was low and strained.

She knew what was written on the shirt. She'd bought it as part of her "Bryan re-balancing" plan, and because it had been on sale for $2.99. Suddenly this didn't feel like such a good idea, but more like the straw that was going to break the camel's back, or in this case Bryan's resistance.

She could see it in the set of his jaw and in the way his eyes burned a hole through her. She was drowning in nervousness, and her thought with the nightshirt seemed foolish now, with its holly leaves, flirty length, and cursive message: *I'm on Santa's Naughty List. After five minutes with me, you'll be on it, too.*

STARING AT SASSY in her red cotton sleepshirt, Bryan's temperature rose. A pricking sensation of sweat tingled at his hairline as he stood up, towering over her. The thin material outlined her breasts perfectly, leaving very little to his imagination. As if he needed any help at this point.

He'd been imagining what it would be like to have her naked and underneath him since she'd been draped across his lap in the hotel in Constantine. Even though that wasn't going to happen again, he'd thought he could handle one more platonic night together.

Wrong, wrong, wrong.

She took a step back, finally recognizing that he was not in a mood to be joked with.

Yep, that's right. You can't taunt me for days on end and expect I won't react.

She stared at him from a few feet away, daring him with a cool disdain—just as she'd been doing for the past six months. "It's only a joke," she whispered.

He shook his head and balled his fists to keep from pulling her to him. "No, it's not. Not tonight. Why do you do that?"

"Why do I do what?" But she eased back another step as she said it.

He pointed to the shirt and forced himself not to move toward her; otherwise, he was going to do something he'd regret.

"Do I bother you?" She smiled slyly.

He studied her face, knowing she could see exactly what he was feeling. Exactly what she did to him. "Yes, you do."

"Why do I bother you?" she asked.

"You know the answer to that." His voice was tight, and he was clenching his jaw so hard he had to be grinding the enamel off his molars.

"Oh, but I like to hear you say it."

"Sassy, you already know I want you. This just makes the situation harder." He gave up and walked toward her.

She raised an eyebrow and glanced down the length of him. "Harder?"

He shook his head. "Don't do this."

He heard her swallow. "Do what? Isn't that the problem? We're not *doing* anything." Her voice didn't hold the teasing scorn he would have expected with those particular words.

He was standing so close he could feel her body heat. He could smell her, too. The lotion she'd bought at the drugstore combined with the scent that was uniquely hers to make him crazy. He was losing the battle here. He wanted to kiss her more than he wanted his next breath, but it was just so damn wrong, for a whole host of reasons.

He pinned her with his stare. "You know what I'm talking about."

"No, I'm not sure I do . . ." She shook her head even as something in her eyes changed and warmed. She wet her lips with her tongue.

Clearly she knew exactly what he was talking about. He gave up fighting and pulled her against him before he had a chance to think or she had a chance to say anything else outrageous.

Leaning down to press his lips against hers, he wasn't surprised to discover that she tasted even better than he remembered. She felt better, too, all soft curves and smooth skin. He ran his hands up and down her arms before sliding his palms down her back, across her ass and lower. The shock of feeling those warm curves had him pulling back for a millisecond before diving in again. Kissing Sassy was madness, and right now he wanted to do more than just kiss her, because after a moment's hesitation, she was kissing him back.

Her tongue was in his mouth, and her hands were on his shoulders, his waist, and then his hips. Slowly the two of them inched across the room toward the wall. He looked down, reaching for the hem of her nightshirt, and spied the bandage on the side of her neck from the attack in Constantine.

His hand stilled on her leg. It was like having a bucket of ice water dumped on his head, and a sudden semblance of sanity returned. As much as he wanted her, this was a fucking bad idea. He was not doing this. Not with Trey's little sister. Not here, not now.

He wasn't that big an ass. At least he sure as hell hoped not. He took a deep, steadying breath, and instead of lifting the nightshirt, he smoothed it out over her hip and put one hand at her waist as he eased away from her.

The expression in her eyes was slightly dazed, but then it filled with the same look he'd seen in Constantine two days ago. Fear flashed in her widened gaze for an instant, then vanished so fast that if he hadn't been staring into her face, he would have missed it. She pushed against his chest, and he immediately pulled back, dropping his hands to his sides.

Had something happened to her on that trek across the Sahara that he didn't know about? Or had he done something himself just now that scared her? His imagination raced down various unsavory paths.

"What's wrong?" he asked.

She wouldn't look up at him. "Nothing," she muttered. "Shouldn't I be asking you that?" She lifted her chin defiantly, but when she took another step backward into the wall, her panicked eyes met his.

He stepped away to give her space. Something big was going on here.

"Don't worry, Sassy, we're not doing this. And despite what just happened, I'm not going to force myself on you. I'd be a real dick—"

Dammit. He should just give up trying not to curse around her. "What I mean is that I'd be a real jerk if I slept with you and then turned around and left you in Mississippi with everything that's happening. I won't do that."

She was looking down again, so he couldn't tell what she was thinking. It was probably too much to hope that she was smiling. Over the past six months it had seemed to amuse her that she was able to make him cuss when other women couldn't.

He kept talking in an attempt to put her at ease, but he had the distinct feeling he was babbling. "I want you, I think you know that. And yeah, I may need to go take a cold shower, but that's my problem, not yours."

She looked up at him then, but her eyes were shuttered, giving nothing away. "Thank you," she mumbled and turned.

Well, shit. She wasn't going to tell him anything.

He was standing there, hard as nails, staring at her back, and there was nothing to do but go into the bathroom and turn the cold water on. After checking that the door to the hotel room was locked, he left her to do just that.

He shut the door to the bathroom softly, even though he wanted to slam it. What happened to her on that truck? He didn't want to think about her having been assaulted. But something was different.

Her off-the-charts sexuality had always left a distinct impression of über confidence and competence. Yes, some of that was a defense mechanism, but against what? Tonight, and in that hotel room in Constantine, she'd acted anything but experienced. She'd looked scared.

He flipped on the shower and stripped off his clothes, placing his loaded Glock on the bathroom counter. What had happened to her? And when? Was it the kidnapping in Niamey or something earlier? His gut churned thinking about the possibilities.

He unbuttoned and stepped out of his jeans to climb under the water's soothing spray, happy to be in a hotel room with real water pressure. He poured shampoo in the palm of his hand. Looking down, he shook his head and took care to adjust the temperature to a less than comfortable cool.

He needed a new approach to deal with her until he

got her home. He didn't want to wind up traumatizing her further. If she'd been raped on that truck, he needed to know. It made him crazy to think of someone hurting her, but he was just going to have to deal. And he was going to have to talk with her about what had happened, despite how uncomfortable the discussion might be for both of them, particularly as it now seemed they were going to be together for at least another twenty-four hours.

He was rinsing the shampoo from his hair and practicing ways he might start the conversation when he heard what sounded like a scream cut short. He jumped from the shower. Not bothering with a towel, he grabbed his gun from the bathroom counter before charging into the bedroom.

A huge man wearing a New York Knicks sweatshirt had an arm around Sassy's neck, cutting off her oxygen. He wasn't trying to take her anywhere, he was just trying to kill her right there in the hotel room. But she was struggling mightily. So much so that Bryan couldn't shoot for fear of hitting her. When he saw her nose bleeding, Bryan pushed down the black rage exploding inside his chest.

Knick's Fan glanced up as Bryan burst through the door, paying no attention to his undressed state but focusing instead on the .9mm in his hand. The intruder pulled Sassy more directly in front of him to prevent Bryan from taking a shot. At the same time, the man tightened his hold on her windpipe.

But Sassy had learned to fight and wrestle as a young girl, and now she was using all kinds of dirty tricks she'd learned from both Bryan and Trey. She lifted her knee and rammed her foot backward and up, popping Knick's Fan in the kneecap, causing the man to go down.

Bryan was on him in an instant. Despite his wanting to kill the guy outright for hurting Sassy, using a gun here was not the ideal solution. Besides, Bryan needed to know why Knick's Fan was after them, and how he'd known where to find them.

Bryan and the man wrestled on the ground, both getting in some good licks. Bryan's nose was bloody and Knick's Fan had several cracked teeth when Sassy picked up the lamp on the bedside table and tried to conk her attacker in the head. Knick's Fan twisted just as she brought the lamp down, and Bryan ended up getting hit instead.

His hold on Knick's Fan loosened as his vision dimmed. Knick's Fan got a lethal grip on Bryan's throat, pressing into the soft flesh beside his Adam's apple with one hand. Bryan twisted and rolled, then turned and managed to get his hands on either side of Knick's Fan's head.

He had to keep this guy alive so he could find out what the hell this was all about. But now Knick's Fan had a wicked-looking knife in his grasp. He'd pulled it when Bryan was dazed from Sassy's unintended lamp shot.

Knick's Fan drew the knife back to jab at Bryan's belly, and there was no choice. Bryan jerked his hands to the side and heard the sickening snap of the man's neck. Knick's Fan went limp beneath him.

Chapter 7

BRYAN LOOKED UP to see Sassy staring at him with a look of revulsion on her face. He wasn't sure if it was because he was naked with blood smeared all over his face and body, or because he'd just killed a man in front of her. He hoped it was the latter. As the moment wore on, her expression changed from horror to that of distinct embarrassment. It would have been comical if the situation hadn't been so dire.

Without saying anything, she pulled the bedspread from the mattress and gave it to him. "Hand me your gun. I'll call nine-one-one while you get dressed."

Bryan shook his head and bent down to cover the guy with the bedspread, though she would probably prefer he covered himself. He stood and tugged the top sheet from the bed, then wrapped it around his waist.

"I'm keeping the Glock," he muttered. Covering the

body was no panacea for having snapped the guy's neck in front of Sassy, but it was the best he could do for now.

"Are you okay?" He bent to look at her as she nodded.

Her nose was still bleeding like hell, just like his was. She might not end up with a black eye, but the red marks on her neck alongside the cut from two nights ago in the Casbah would become a large bruise. Fury and nausea roared through his veins, and the visceral reaction over what had almost happened to her took him by surprise. A week ago, he'd thought he was numb to those emotions.

Sassy had stopped nodding her head, but she was struggling not to cry. At the same time, she was staring at the blood smeared on his chest, arms, and belly, all while backing away from him. The back of the mattress stopped her. She sat down on the fitted sheet, holding a Kleenex to her nose and vacillating between focusing on the blanket-covered body on the floor and Bryan.

"I'm not very good with blood," she whispered.

Finally she settled on staring at the closed drapes. But it was clear she wasn't okay. Between the blood all over him and Knick's Fan under the bedspread, Sassy the "coper" was on the verge of wigging out.

Not that he was surprised. If anything was going to put her over the edge, it made sense that this would have done it. She'd had a helluva week. But he wasn't going to be able to help her if the sight of him half naked and covered in blood shut her down.

"I'm going to get cleaned up and be right back." He hustled into the bathroom but left the door open while he climbed back into the still running shower for twenty seconds to rinse the blood off his face and chest.

His nose stopped streaming as soon as he tilted his head back. He hurried out of the shower but didn't dress, simply wrapping a towel around his waist before coming back to the bedroom.

What the hell? No one knew they were here. Not even the guys at AEGIS. How had they been located, and by whom?

Clearly talking to Knick's Fan wasn't going to be possible, but until he knew what was going on with the AEGIS charges, having the police investigating him for murder wasn't an option, either. He could end up in jail, leaving no one to take care of Sassy.

He dialed his cell phone with one hand and searched the guy's pockets with the other. Leland answered on the first ring.

"It's Hollywood. We landed in New York earlier tonight and couldn't get a flight out of town till tomorrow. We just had some company. Any idea what's going on?"

Speechless until now, Sassy had been watching him search Knick's Fan's body with wide-eyed astonishment. "What are you doing?" she squeaked. "Aren't you calling the police? Aren't you going to get dressed?"

Leland's voice was filled with humor. "Sounds like your 'company' interrupted something."

Bryan snorted a sad laugh. *If only.* "Hang on a minute."

He didn't muffle the receiver. "Sassy, take it easy. This guy is . . . not going to bother you again. And I've got to find out some things before we get the police involved. Go into the bathroom and get dressed."

"Me, get dressed? What about you?" But she didn't stay to argue her point. Instead, she stomped to the bathroom and slammed the door. Seconds later the door opened. But only her arm was visible as she tossed his dirty jeans and shirt onto the floor and snapped the door closed without a word. Her message was clear.

Get some clothes on.

Bryan was glad to see the feisty side of her back, as opposed to the stark fear he'd witnessed moments ago. If she'd been assaulted on that truck from Niamey, surely she'd be more shaken up now about this hotel room attack?

He filed that thought away and focused on the conversation with Leland as he pulled some sweatpants from his duffel bag and slipped them on. "Okay, I'm back."

"What's happening?" Leland's Southern drawl made it sound as if they had all evening to chat, but Bryan knew better.

"A guy broke into the room. No idea where he came from. He's dead."

"Any ID?" asked Leland. "Tats, anything."

Bryan bent over to check the guy's arms and chest. The chest was clear, but when he pulled up Knick's Fan's shirtsleeve, Bryan almost dropped the phone.

"Shit," he hissed under his breath.

"What?" Leland's radio announcer tone sharpened.

"There's a scorpion tat wrapped in barbed wire on his forearm, just like the one on the shooter who came after Jennifer Grayson in Niamey. The same kind worn by lieutenants in the Vega cartel."

"But Ernesto Vega is dead," said Leland.

"I know that," said Bryan.

"So where did this guy come from?"

"Hang on a second." Bryan snapped a photo of the tattoo and the man's face with his phone and forwarded both to Leland. "I've no idea. But this has to be mixed up with that cluster."

"Clearly," muttered Leland.

"I can't figure out how anyone found us here. Did they follow us from the airport? Are my credit cards being tracked? What?"

The original plan of flying out to Memphis and then renting a car and driving Sassy to her mother's home in Mississippi was not looking like a great idea. And how could he trust Sassy to stay out of trouble once he did get her to a safe place? It's not like she was going to quit working to find answers for Trey. The more he thought about it, the more Bryan realized he couldn't leave her on her own. He might not be getting away from her nearly as soon as he thought.

Jesus. Trying to keep his hands off of her might just kill him if the guys coming after them didn't do it first.

"Have you heard anything from Gavin?" asked Bryan.

"No word since he put you and Sassy on the plane. That's just as well, 'cause there's no good news on the investigation. My sources are telling me that Gavin's about to be 'upgraded' to a terroristic threat because of his ties to the embassies overseas."

"What?" Bryan couldn't wrap his head around the idea. It was too over the top.

"I know. It's all bullshit. But someone, somewhere, is pulling some heavy-duty strings. Everyone associated with AEGIS is going to ground. I have heard from Nick. He and Jennifer are back in the U.S., but I'm not sure where. He was very closemouthed about their plans."

Bryan sighed. "That's not a surprise."

"Given the situation, I told Nick I didn't *want* to know where they were," said Leland.

"Ask him to call me the next time you two talk? He had to toss his phone in Africa. I doubt he's gotten the same number if he's trying to disappear."

"Will do," said Leland.

The last time Bryan had spoken to Nick, he'd been cautiously optimistic about Gavin's innocence. Bryan and Leland were assuming their boss was being set up, but you didn't endanger the people you loved on assumptions. You made damn sure.

After speaking with Gavin in the hotel in Constantine, Bryan was now damn sure the man had been set up. But he couldn't ask anyone else to risk their loved ones based on his own gut feeling. Bryan was loyal, but he wasn't crazy. Afghanistan had taught him that unhappy lesson.

Leland had to consider his own new family—Anna Mercado and her teenaged son, Zach, who was still recovering from a heart transplant. Bryan knew they were tucked away somewhere safe, but he had no desire to know where Leland's safe spot was. He just wanted to get

Sassy to a safe place of her very own and out of all this uncertainty and chaos.

"For tonight, I just need to get us out of this hotel, or at least somewhere with no paper trail. Plus, I've got this dead body."

"Calling the cops will not help you avoid the paper trail. Given your association with Gavin, most likely it would get you arrested," said Leland.

Bryan glanced uneasily at the bathroom door. "You think everything about AEGIS is already in the system? I didn't have any problems at the airport when I was coming back into the country."

"You didn't have a dead body with you then, either. My understanding is the new charges on Gavin haven't been filed yet. But once they are and you're connected, the cops will turn your life inside out if they come to your hotel room to investigate this intruder. At best, you won't be leaving New York anytime soon."

A wave of exhaustion hit Bryan. "That's what I was afraid of. Got any suggestions for what to do with a body?" He was only half joking and was a little stunned when Leland told him exactly what to do.

"That will buy you some time," Leland finished a few minutes later.

"How do you know how to . . ." Bryan wasn't sure how to ask the question without sounding insulting.

Leland's laugh floated over the phone. "I wasn't a hit man in a former life. I just worked for the DEA too damn long. The cartel was filled with sadistic SOBs who were quite creative in body disposal."

Bryan didn't ask any more questions he didn't want answers to. He'd seen enough of the same evil in the Middle East that Leland was referring to.

"How many nights are you paid up in the room?"

"Just one," said Bryan.

"Call the front desk and extend it for three . . . no, make it four more nights. Crank the air conditioning down as far as it will go when you leave. The body will probably be discovered before then, but the AC will keep the decomposition under wraps at least three days. Tell 'em you're on your honeymoon, whatever. Stress you don't want to be interrupted. No housekeeping, no nothing. Hang the Do Not Disturb sign before you leave."

"Right. Got it." As callous as it sounded, Bryan knew Leland was right. This would buy them some much-needed time.

"We'll deal with the police after you two are safe. Risa should be able to help. For now, if we don't figure out this thing with Gavin, we could all be in jail together on more serious charges than murder."

That was a frightening but accurate thought. If Gavin was brought up on charges of terrorism, they were all in very deep trouble. "I'll check us in somewhere that doesn't require ID for registration."

Most likely it would be a rooms-by-the-hour kind of dive. Sassy would not like that. But she'd survive. She'd more than proven that she was a trooper.

"Our main problem is how to get out of town without a paper trail. Renting a car is a nonstarter, and I don't like the idea of a bus."

There was a pause, and Bryan could hear computer keys clicking in the background before Leland finally spoke. "What if you took a commuter train? I'm looking up schedules right now. If you hurry, you might be able to skip the hotel tonight and catch the 12:15 AM to Philadelphia."

Bryan heard the shower kick on as Leland kept talking. "If you use cash, you won't have to put any names on tickets. And even if they check your ID once you're on board, it won't be a computerized check. You could slip far enough down the commuter line to get out of the city that way. You might even be able to upgrade to a sleeper once you get further south. They aren't always very consistent about how they check IDs when you upgrade on the train itself."

"Sounds like a plan," said Bryan. A train wasn't completely invisible, but it was infinitely more so than renting a car or getting on an airplane. "We need to be as anonymous as possible."

"How are you set for cash?"

"I've got some, but it won't last long."

They arranged for Leland to transfer funds online from AEGIS immediately so Bryan could access it from an ATM in New York before they took their train south and disappeared.

"You're going to need a new cell phone," said Leland.

"Yeah I know, dammit. It's going to be tight getting everything done."

He looked at the bathroom door again. From the shopping bag on the floor, he pulled new jeans and the long-sleeve T-shirt he'd just bought. The shower was still running. Getting on a train would be easier than checking into another hotel with Sassy once he convinced her that they were better off not calling the police about their "company." But first he had to deal with the body.

SILENTLY FUMING, SASSY stood before the bathroom mirror. The logical part of her brain said that anger was a healthier reaction than horror, but right now she didn't give a damn. She hardly recognized herself. The red marks around her neck made it clear that the man attacking her hadn't cared if he'd taken her dead or alive.

What had happened to her life? Six months ago she was a freelance writer for local papers; now she was investigating human traffickers and being snatched off the streets of Africa, in addition to nearly being strangled in strange hotel rooms in New York. Everything had started going downhill with Elizabeth's disappearance and Trey's arrest.

She closed her eyes. Was Elizabeth still alive, or was this quest to find her all some crazy pipe dream? Visions of Trey in that filthy Mexican prison danced in her head.

No. Elizabeth had to be alive. There was zero profit in dwelling on any other possibility. For now, the immediate issue was the dead body in their hotel room.

The dead body and Bryan.

Talk about someone who'd changed. Gone was the teenager she'd had such a passion for as a young girl.

This Bryan was completely unflappable and fought to the death with his bare hands.

She replayed his battle with the intruder in the hotel room moments ago. While she might not fully recognize the boy she'd grown up with anymore, she was honest enough with herself to acknowledge her gratitude that this man was willing to do whatever it took to keep them safe.

She gazed into the mirror and snorted at the irony. She didn't recognize much of herself right now, either. Her bottom lip was split and her face was smeared with blood. Her "naughty" nightshirt was ripped from her shoulder to the middle of her arm. Washing her face wasn't going to be good enough.

She turned the water to steaming hot and climbed into the shower for the second time in thirty minutes. Tilting her head back into the spray, she tried to relax her neck. She shampooed her hair again and was just starting to feel the tranquilizing effect of the hot water when she heard the bathroom door open.

Sassy froze, every sense on point.

Chapter 8

"IT'S ME." BRYAN'S voice was pitched low, but Sassy could hear him perfectly from the other side of the shower curtain.

What was he doing in here?

"I need to talk to you." There was an edge to his tone, and she felt a spike of irritation overriding the heart-stopping fear she'd just experienced when the door had opened.

"Can't it wait until I'm out?" She fought the urge to cover herself even though he couldn't see a thing from where he was.

"If it could have waited, I'd have waited." His voice sounded closer.

She grabbed the curtain and shielded her body while sticking her face out. Thankfully, he at least wore jeans now. A naked Bryan Fisher blew every circuit in her brain. His face was clean, but this close, she could see traces of blood on his neck and chest.

She swallowed the bile in her throat. That pretty much zinged the attraction she'd been feeling toward him. Blood freaked her out in a huge way.

"Okay, what is it?" she asked.

"We're leaving."

"When? What about the police?"

"We're not calling the police." Bryan propped himself against the bathroom counter.

"Why not? What about that dead man in our room?" She heard her own voice rise an octave.

Bryan's eyes were cool and emotionless, so different from the man who'd been kissing her less than an hour ago.

"Don't worry about where the guy is. I don't know how he found us, but I do know that he was involved with some bad people, and more of them will come looking for us when he doesn't report back in. So we're getting out of here without a paper trail. The police—"

"Leave paper trails," she finished for him. With the water still streaming down her back, she was surprised at how calm she felt. But she'd seen her world crumble before—her mom's alcoholism, high school, last summer when Trey was arrested. This was just the next layer. Still, she felt cold, despite the hot shower and the steam.

"That's right," he nodded with approval. "We're going to Penn Station."

"Tonight?"

"There's a train leaving for Philadelphia at 12:15. We can start making our way south. But we've got to stay under the radar from now on, so it's travel by train or by bus."

She stared at him a moment. The reality of the situation was finally sinking in. "Are we fugitives of some sort?"

"Not yet, but that could change soon if we don't get out of here."

"What about the body?" The chill she'd felt earlier was turning to ice.

"I think the less you know the better. Right now, I need to rinse off, and we'll be on our way. Hurry up, or I'll assume you want to share that shower."

Was that a threat or a promise?

Every smart-ass retort she'd normally have to his taunt flew right out of her head. At the same time she couldn't help but wonder what it would be like to stand in the tiny enclosure with him.

"Give me two minutes." She fought to keep her voice from squeaking as she dropped the shower curtain. God, she was so off her game here.

She heard him chuckle.

"You have one."

December 27
Late evening

ALMOST TWENTY-FOUR HOURS later, with Sassy dead asleep beside him, Bryan watched the night sky flash by from the window of the Silver Meteor.

"You're terribly lucky," said the conductor as he took Bryan's cash for the upgrade to a sleeper car. "We had a no-show in Richmond. I'll go make sure it's ready before you wake your friend."

Bryan nodded his thanks and leaned his head back to wait. Earlier they'd caught a 12:15 AM commuter train at Penn Station with moments to spare. He had tossed his phone outside the hotel and bought a burner at the station so they couldn't be tracked.

Once in Philadelphia, they'd transferred to another train, hopscotching across different commuter lines all the way down to Virginia. The typical seven-hour trip from New York had taken them over three times as long. Multiple layovers and trains later, here they were.

Sassy was only speaking to him when necessary, but that was fine. There wasn't much that they could have discussed about the situation in public anyway. Still, sitting beside her in silence was driving him nuts. Smelling her, hearing the noises she made as she napped off and on throughout their trek south, was a new form of torture for him.

Her head had tilted and slid to finally end up against his arm. There were dark shadows under her eyes. Bryan knew how she felt. He was so tired, he'd lost count of how many hours he'd been awake over the past three days. But he hadn't been able to sleep.

He could barely think, and he damn sure couldn't let his guard down as long as they were sitting in a crowded passenger car. He had texted Leland when they'd managed to board in Richmond with no ID check. Thankfully, there would be no more hopping on and off for them.

The conductor came back with the tickets and directions to their car. Bryan gently woke Sassy. She was groggy but cooperative when she heard that they had a place to lie down.

Once the door to their compartment was closed and locked, she seemed to perk up considerably as Bryan took the first deep breath he'd had in hours. He shoved his duffel in the corner, sank into the reclining seat by the window, and laid his head back—so relieved he could cry.

The porter had already lowered the beds, but Bryan wasn't going to lie down on that bottom bunk until Sassy was firmly settled on the sleeping shelf above. If he had to sit beside her any longer, he was going to explode. He'd been hard since she'd fallen asleep on his shoulder between Baltimore and Richmond, and the smell of her skin and the feel of her body against his side had put his mind in places that were dangerous for his sanity. Right now, he desperately needed some distance and some rest.

But Sassy had a second wind and was now more than ready to talk. "I need you to explain to me exactly why we didn't call the police in New York, and why we're acting like fugitives. Where are we going?"

Bryan opened one eye. He didn't want to do this. If he could sleep for just thirty minutes . . . Hell, a ten-minute combat nap would put him miles ahead of where he was at this point.

"I can't talk now, Sassy. I'm wiped."

"When are we going to talk?" She crouched down beside his recliner.

"How about when I wake up?" He didn't try to hide the hope in his voice.

The mulish set of her jaw was proof that she wasn't going to wait. He recognized that look from years ago. *Damn.*

He had nothing left in the tank. Zero resources to stop himself from showing her what he wanted to do so badly. Maybe if he let her see all that, she'd leave him alone—at least long enough for him to regroup. In his exhausted state, it seemed like a reasonable plan.

He opened both eyes and stared at her, allowing everything he was feeling and wanting to show in his gaze. He was tired of trying to hide it from her and from himself. He wanted her underneath him in that pitiful excuse for a bed. And he didn't have the discipline or the inclination to stifle his desire anymore.

All the longing and lust he'd been trying to bury for the past six months was at the surface for him, spilling over for her to see. And there was no doubt she saw exactly what was on his mind. She swallowed audibly at his scorching gaze.

"We're fugitives. Don't you get it? Someone is after you. I think it has to do with that story you were working on in Africa about the human trafficking and the cartel connection in Mexico. I can't prove it yet, but that's what I believe is going on."

Now she had a dozen other questions in her eyes. But when she opened her mouth to ask them, he couldn't . . .

He just couldn't do this anymore. He was at the tail end of a rapidly fraying rope.

So he said the one thing he knew would shut her up. The truth. "Sassy, either let me sleep or let me fuck you. I'm open to either option right now, but talking is not on the list."

He cringed inwardly at what he'd just said out loud, but that seemed to have done it. Her mouth dropped open in shocked but blessed silence. The conversation was over, just as he'd known it would be. He was finally going to get some rest, but a niggling voice in the back of his mind told him he shouldn't have gone there. Even if the words were true.

She was still staring at him from her crouched spot when he leaned his head back and closed his eyes again. He took a deep breath, preparing to sleep, when he felt her hand on his knee.

"I'd prefer the latter," she whispered. "If you were serious about the offer . . ."

WHAT WAS SHE *doing? God, what was she saying?* He'd said that to shock her. Eagle Scout Bryan wanted to have sex with her. That wasn't exactly how he'd put it, but it was clear he wanted her.

And she wanted him. Plus, she was tired of pretending she didn't. Tired of guarding her feelings, of being so scared, and now, wondering if they would live through the next few hours. She wanted some kind of control in her life, however fleeting.

But would Bryan still feel the same way when he understood the level of her deception? Most likely not. And that alone had her pulling the old Sassy persona more firmly around her shoulders.

She stood up straight, arched an eyebrow, and shrugged. "You seem so tired, though. Perhaps it would be better to wait till you're rested up and are ready for me?" She was pulling that tiger's tail and damning the consequences.

She smiled her lazy taunt. But he was up and out of the recliner so fast, she didn't have time to step back. Besides, the only place to go was the bed. The converted mattress cushion pressed against the backs of her calves.

Bryan put his hands on her hips and pulled her toward him. He hadn't been joking earlier about wanting her. The undeniable evidence prodded her belly through his jeans. He leaned down and put his face in hers. "Don't say that if you're not serious. I want you, and I'll have you naked and in that bed before you know what happened. But I want you willing, not scared spitless."

Ouch. She deserved that, particularly after the twin freak-outs she'd had in the hotel rooms in Constantine and New York. She stared up at him and gave the barest perceptible nod.

She wanted him, too, and he seemed to sense that this time something was different.

"You're sure?" he asked. Pressed against him, she felt his voice resonate inside her chest.

"Yes," she whispered.

"I don't want to scare you." He touched her cheek as

he studied her face. He was looking for something, but she wasn't sure what. "The only promise I can make is that I won't hurt you."

"I know you won't." And in that moment she believed him.

He kissed her like he'd kissed her earlier, before she'd gotten skittish. His tongue tangled with hers, and a warm tingle worked its way through her body as she kissed him back. He seemed to take her response as a green light, pulling at the sweater she was wearing and quickly slipping it off over her head.

Before she could think clearly, his hands were at her waistline, and he was unbuttoning her new jeans. He slipped them down her legs, but they got caught on her boots. She smiled and started to blush. Then he looked up at her, not staring at her chest as she would have expected him to, but staring directly into her eyes with an intensity that she normally would have found unnerving.

His hands were incredibly gentle as he bent down. "I'll get 'em off," he murmured, kissing the top of her knees as he untied the boots and slid them off her feet.

More of those lovely tingles raced up and down her legs, starting a sudden ache at her center. Finally, she stood before him in her socks, her pale pink panties, and the matching bra she'd bought the night before.

He was on his knees in front of her. After putting the boots to the side, he pulled her down to sit on the lower mattress. His hands were still on her hips. He slid them down the outside of her legs then back up across the tops of her thighs, moving his thumbs closer to the lace edge of her underwear.

All the while he was kissing her belly, her hips, her thighs and making her woozy with the wanting and not knowing where he was going to touch her next. He unhooked her front-closure bra with one hand, then his lips were on her nipple, and it was such an exquisite sensation. She was trying to catch her breath, but that was impossible. She'd never felt anything like this before. A train whistle blew in the distance, reminding her where they were, but the rocking of the train only added to the surreal sensations overwhelming her.

He moved his thumbs higher and higher inside her thighs, occasionally brushing against the silky nylon of her panties and sending sparks skittering through her lower body. She wanted something, but she couldn't name it.

He shifted from one breast to the other, and her unattended nipple pebbled. He put one hand on her shoulder and pushed her slowly to the mattress, following her down. His lips transferred from her breast again to her belly and lower.

Checking to make sure she was okay with this, he glanced up once more before he started to pull her underwear down her legs. She nodded and stared back at him, holding his gaze, because she was so much more than okay. His fingers were on her, touching her in that most intimate place. Then his mouth was there, and instead of being scared or embarrassed, she was floating, focused only on what his fingers and his tongue were doing to her.

As much as she wanted to just drift along, she felt herself building up to something else that was bright and shiny but foreign at the same time. He pressed his mouth more firmly against her, and she was flying through space, shattering into a million pieces.

Floating back moments later, she realized she was lying cattycorner across the bed and naked while he was on his knees in front of her, still fully clothed. Surely they were going to . . .

She had to talk to him. Had to let him know before they—

And just like that, her lovely, floating, blissed-out feeling disappeared. She exhaled. He'd never forgive her if she didn't tell him beforehand.

"You're thinking too much." She felt his words vibrate against the inside of her thigh as he kissed her there before easing up beside her on the bed. "Stop that."

She smiled, not at all surprised that he seemed to read her mind. He sat up on the edge of the lower bunk next to her and took his own boots and socks off, then his shirt, jeans, and . . .

She closed her eyes.

He was going to be naked soon, and she had to say something first. He slid up beside her on the mattress and pulled her back to his front, with his back toward the wall. She felt the insistence of his erection against her bottom.

She started to turn in his arms, but he held onto her with an arm clamped around her waist. "Slow down. I just want to enjoy holding you a while. I've thought about this for a very long time."

Really? That came as a complete surprise. It was on the tip of her tongue to ask *how long,* but when he trailed his fingertips back and forth across her rib cage, she quit thinking. Instead, she sighed in relaxed contentment. "I didn't know it could be like that."

Why had she been nervous about this for so long? She could tell him now. It'd be okay.

He kissed the side of her neck and whispered in her ear, "Well, I promise we're just getting started."

She tensed, and he absolutely noticed but misunderstood the reason.

He gathered her more snugly against his chest. "Don't worry, we can take this as slow as you want."

"You'd do that?" The mixture of relief and disappointment she felt was . . . confusing.

"God, Sassy. What sort of men have you—"

The sound of screeching brakes interrupted whatever else he'd been about to say. Sassy felt the momentum shoving her backward into his chest.

"What's happening?" she gasped.

"I don't know." He tugged his arm from under her body to see his watch. "We're not scheduled to stop for several more hours." The stark change from relaxed lover to alert super soldier was dramatic. "Get dressed. Now."

Bryan hauled himself forward out of bed and started

shoving clothes toward her while Sassy was still playing catch-up. Her panties were inside out, but she slid them on at his urging without fixing them.

"C'mon, Sassy."

The horrific screeching continued, intensifying as she pulled her jeans, sweater, socks, and boots on. She was lacing up as a rumbling shuddering started.

"Fuck," Bryan mumbled.

"What is it?" She finished with the boots and looked up from her crouched position as the screeching abruptly stopped.

"Hang on!" He grabbed for her.

The rail car shifted, and she felt like she was in a carnival house ride as the compartment swayed wildly from side to side. The car tilted, and the bed she was sitting on flew up in the air. She hit her head on the bunk above, and the world went black.

Chapter 9

BRYAN THREW HIMSELF toward Sassy's body as the car uncoupled from the train. Everything was happening in slow motion. He watched in horror as she flew through the air and cracked her head on the bottom of the top sleeping shelf. The contents of their compartment flipped while the car rolled.

The bathroom door swung open, banging into his back, but he focused on getting to Sassy. He managed to grab her, and he wasn't letting go, even when battered by bits of the disintegrating compartment that came loose while the sleeper car tumbled from the tracks. Pieces of broken mirror and plastic, seat cushions, something that looked like pink insulation, and blankets swirled around them in a maelstrom as the car continued to roll. The lights went out in the midst of the chaos. Metal screeched in an ear-splitting cacophony of sound.

He thought he heard someone shouting. Like a nightmare, things took forever to stop moving. When they finally rolled to a halt, the compartment—or what was left of it—was pitch black. Bryan heard more screeching metal, as if part of the rail car was settling now that it had stopped tumbling. Distinct screams and calls for help accompanied the eerie aftermath.

He was on his belly and turned his head, squinting into the darkness. Only now it wasn't quite so dark. The moon shone through clouds and their compartment window with an odd sort of white glow. They'd landed right side up, but that was where any similarity to "right" ended.

The door to the bathroom was lying across Bryan's back while also balanced partially on the bed. Sassy was under his chest. From his vantage point, he couldn't determine the extent of her injuries. But he could feel dampness on her forehead as he ran his fingers over her face. She was out cold.

His back hurt like a son of a bitch, and his left shoulder stung, as if from some sort of cut. Everything else felt in working order. He took a moment to figure the best escape from the wreckage before rising in an odd sort of cobra push-up to move the door and other debris off both of them.

He rolled off Sassy toward what had been the bed, resting on his knees beside her. The moonlight was now a vivid silver. The window, though not broken up completely in the crash, had a spider's web of cracks running all across it that seemed to amplify the light.

He sat back on his knees and looked Sassy over. There

was a cut just above her temple, at the hairline. It didn't look deep, but it was bleeding like mad as most head injuries were prone to do.

Before the crash, his backpack had been hooked over an arm of the reclining chair by the window. When he turned to look for it, he noted the strain in his lower back. The chair wasn't there anymore. There was simply a metal spike poking up from the floor of the car.

Miraculously, his pack was there, too, underneath a broken armrest and other debris. He grabbed for it and pulled the padded strap onto his shoulder, despite the discomfort. The duffel bag was nowhere to be seen, but that didn't matter. Once he got Sassy away from the wreckage, he would see to her head and any other injuries. He tried to stand but found it challenging in what had now become a very confined space.

"Sassy?" He touched her face. She still wasn't moving. "Sassy, baby, wake up." He heard the thread of panic in his voice.

Bryan Fisher, who never got rattled, was flipping out. Nick and Leland would give him hell if they could see him. And he'd happily take all their shit and more if he had one of those guys here with him to help.

He could smell smoke . . . and gasoline. There had been an automotive railcar several cars back. He'd seen more than a dozen vehicles loaded after their stop in Washington, D.C. Since they'd derailed, there was no telling where those vehicles were now. He had to get Sassy out.

Still hunched over her, he looked around for the quickest exit. Their compartment was a ticking time bomb of a death trap. He pushed more debris away and stood. Balancing on one foot, he cleared the remaining rubble off her body. A metal pole with the circumference of a wide broom handle was across her lower legs. He had no clue where that had come from, but he picked it up and moved through the wreckage to the intact window.

Smoke was now curling around his feet, lending an even greater urgency to the task. Where was it coming from? Holding the metal pole like a baseball bat, he slammed it against the glass.

He glanced back at Sassy.

Still no movement.

His throat was dry with fear. *She's okay. She has to be okay.*

He whacked the window again, and it gave way. Shards of glass made a musical-like tinkling sound that was at odds with the piteous screams and moans around them.

More smoke filled the room, but the fresh air did as well. He heard the sizzle and hiss of flames but couldn't see the actual fire yet. He hurried back to Sassy, wincing as he bent over her. With his back hurt, he wasn't sure he could safely carry her. The last thing she needed was for him to drop her.

The smell of gasoline was stronger. From behind them, an orange light suddenly flickered across the wreckage in the broken hallway of the car. This thing could explode any moment. His gaze fell on the door now lying across the bed.

That could work.

He took the thin metal door and balanced it on the ledge of the window, then shoved Sassy's body on top of the door like a bizarre teeter-totter. He looked out the window to double-check. With the car listing to the side, it was only about a four-foot drop to the ground.

Smoke poured into their compartment. Despite the open window, he was choking. Sassy'd be okay . . . as long as she didn't hit her head.

Fuck.

He couldn't think about that now. Holding onto the door with one hand, he took one of the cushions that had flown around the compartment earlier and placed it under the door.

Balancing Sassy precariously with one hand holding the door, he slipped his backpack off the other shoulder and tossed it out the window away from the train. Still holding onto the door, he slipped over the side of the ledge, only letting go of the door when he dropped to the ground. The jolt jarred his entire body, from the soles of his feet to the top of his head.

Shit. He might be hurt worse than he'd thought.

The orange glow of the flames was quite visible now, licking along the ceiling of their trashed compartment. For a moment the door and Sassy remained perfectly balanced on the train's window ledge, then it began to tip toward the ground. He stepped in front of the door, catching Sassy before she could slide onto the rocky terrain.

He went to his knees and knelt a moment with her sprawled across his lap. He glanced over at his backpack a few feet away and weighed the pros and cons of leaving it. Their passports were in it, along with his weapons. Not an option. He'd just have to move his ass.

God, why was he so incapacitated? He was used to running miles at a time for PT and lifting weights. What was wrong with him? He looked back up at the window, now completely engulfed in flames.

This wasn't over. They needed to get away from the train. Sassy was still out cold. He gently laid her on the ground and went for the backpack, settling it on both shoulders. Taking a deep breath, he lifted her back into his arms.

Sassy was ridiculously light, a good thing in this situation. The ground around the train track was covered with rocks, but he couldn't take his time to pick a way through the rough terrain. He was thankful again for the full moon and thin cloud cover.

Fires burned from the wreckage all around them and passengers moved about, some more slowly than others. At least six cars had derailed. With Sassy in his arms, he walked at a right angle to the track, putting as much distance between himself and the flames as possible. He had no idea how volatile the other cars might be. She moaned when he set her down in a field about fifty yards from the devastation.

It was like every derailment photograph he'd ever seen with the immediacy of being there in person. The sights, the sounds, and the smells were all too real. The back of the train appeared to be untouched, while the front looked like he imagined a model train would if an angry toddler stomped on the engine then beat the front cars with a baseball bat.

From where they stood, some pieces of the wreck were unrecognizable as part of a train. Bryan swallowed hard. He couldn't do anything for those folks.

"Sassy? Can you hear me?" He picked up her hand and started rubbing it between his fingers.

It was damn cold out here, and their coats were somewhere back in that morass of twisted metal. Bryan marveled over how the tail of the train was completely stable, with cars still on the tracks. He was considering the possibility of going back for a blanket or something from one of those stable cars when a rumbling explosion detonated toward the back of the wreckage.

Shrieking metal was drowned out by a thunderous roar as what could only be an automotive railcar was caught up in the conflagration, resulting in a small mushroom cloud. Even from fifty yards away, the concussion knocked him on his ass, jarring his back once again.

Where the hell had that come from?

He sat up slowly, staring at the carnage. That part of the train hadn't even been involved in the accident. Now it was completely obliterated, just like . . .

Jesus. It looked just like bombing attacks he'd seen in Afghanistan. Flames stretched toward the sky from the ruins, and what could only be bodies lay beside the tracks.

What was going on? He had no idea where they were. He wasn't even sure what time it was. He'd been cross-eyed when they'd boarded at Richmond. The only upside was that Sassy was awake, blinking and looking at him in total bewilderment.

"Where are we?" she asked.

"You remember the train?"

"Train?" She wrinkled her brow. "I remember . . ." She stopped talking. Even in the shadows he recognized her discomfort as she recalled exactly what they'd been doing before the train wreck.

"What happened?" Her voice was flat.

"The train derailed. Must have hit something at the crossing. Ten minutes later, the back end of the whole thing exploded."

And just like that, he knew this had been about them. It sounded paranoid, but no one survived doing the things he'd done in the Middle East if they didn't consider the outrageous options. And what he was thinking was fantastically outrageous.

Still, you weren't paranoid if they truly were out to get you. This had to be related to the events in Africa. Otherwise, who could be this unlucky—to board a train that derailed, then spontaneously blew to kingdom come?

Wild, improbable thoughts swirled in his head as he looked down at Sassy. She was still trying to shake loose the cobwebs and figure out what the hell was happening, too. Her sweater was torn, her face was bleeding, and it was cold as hell.

When he glanced down at his phone, he could see his breath on the night air. He should call Leland, but he wasn't going to do it. Something wasn't right.

While he didn't think Leland was dirty, he did suspect some part of their communications had been compromised. Bryan had texted him right after they'd boarded in Richmond. Leland was the only one who knew he and Sassy were on this particular train. Barring outright betrayal, corrupted communication was the only explanation for this cluster. So what Bryan was thinking was beyond all reason. He couldn't tell anyone yet, or they just might put him in a straightjacket.

But first things first.

He had to get them out of here before he could do anything about his suspicions. He studied the darkened field. People were rushing in all directions, away from the wreckage, while a few were gathering behind the train about forty yards beyond where he and Sassy were.

Bryan's instinct was to go to ground, but Sassy needed help. He glanced at his watch. It was 1:00 AM.

Sirens sounded in the distance. They must be near a town. He just wasn't sure which one. Sassy's head worried him. He needed to get her looked after before he did anything else.

"Let's see if we can join those other folks," he said. "Think you can walk?"

"Of course I can." She tried to sit up and snorted a grim laugh. "If you help me up, that is."

They started toward the knot of tattered travellers, passing the more extreme devastation along the way. Bryan put his arm around her waist and held on across the uneven ground. Acrid-smelling smoke was thick in the air. They approached two bodies, a man and a woman. It looked as if they'd dragged themselves to this point and just stopped.

"I have to check them, Sassy."

He bent down and put his fingers on the woman's neck, then the man's. Neither had a pulse. He shook his head and sighed. God, this all felt so horribly familiar.

Without speaking he straightened, put his hand back around Sassy's waist, and kept walking up and down over the furrows in the field. The remains of whatever crop had grown there this fall stuck up from the cold surface of the dirt like an old man's stubbly beard.

A little farther ahead, a dozen passengers huddled together. Four others were either sitting or lying on the ground beside the group and being tended. Several of the survivors were staring off into space. One was cradling an ominously silent toddler. The sirens grew louder; lights splashed color across the field from a distance.

"Where are we?" Bryan asked as they approached the group.

An older man answered. "We're outside Kingstree, South Carolina, near as I can tell."

Kingstree.

The name tickled the back of his memory, but Bryan couldn't recall how he'd heard of the place.

The man smiled at his blank look. "It's a small town. Population's a little over three thousand. Agriculture community mostly. Tobacco and cotton. We're near the Francis Marion National Forest."

Bear Bennett. That's how he'd heard of it. *Damn. Of*

all places. But Bear was the last person Bryan needed to be worrying about right now.

Bryan nodded to cover his surprise. "You sound like you know the area. How far are we from Charleston?"

"I work for the South Carolina Board of Tourism. I know all the little towns. We're about seventy-five miles up the road from Charleston." The man pulled his coat more tightly around himself. "You and your woman okay?"

Bryan started at the man's question, but beside him, Sassy didn't respond. *His woman?* He'd never thought of her that way before, having shied away from possessive thoughts of any kind where Sassy was concerned. Tonight he found the idea comforting and fitting. Sassy remained silent as the older man waited expectantly.

"She was unconscious for a while. I expect she's got a concussion," said Bryan. "We were lucky."

The man nodded. They watched the burning wreckage. The man's voice shook when he spoke again. "What in God's name happened here? Seemed like we crashed and after that initial chaos it was all over . . . then all hell broke loose."

Bryan nodded but said nothing. The man was saying exactly what Bryan was thinking. The moon peeked out from behind scattered clouds, and together they peered at the morass of twisted metal.

"I don't know," Bryan murmured, still staring at the broken train.

There'd undoubtedly been a secondary explosion. But what had caused it? Was it something in the baggage compartment, or had one of the vehicles on the automotive railcar simply exploded?

Remembering the destructive power of the detonation, he continued to study the twisted metal. From this distance and vantage point, it was hard to be sure of anything definitive. Even so, he had that prickly feeling along the back of his neck. The train almost looked like it could have been hit with a bomb. But he wasn't close enough to confirm it.

Jesus. Nick had mentioned drones before, and it hadn't really registered. Ernesto Vega had sworn to Nick at The Gaylord that the vet clinic and Thomas Rivera's house in Mexico were both destroyed by drones. Was Bryan looking at a similar attack?

But why? Why would anyone come after Sassy or him in that way?

The sirens had grown obnoxiously loud. Bryan could see the red and blue lights flashing as a police car and ambulance both drove along a turnrow toward the group. For a town of three thousand, the emergency response would be stretched thin with this type of disaster.

He glanced down at Sassy's forehead. She was still bleeding and needed to be seen by a doctor. But he needed her out of the system and off the grid. They both needed to be anonymous.

Bryan looked out over the barren tobacco field toward the man and woman they'd passed on their way to the group.

"Any idea who they were?" he asked the old man, pointing to the bodies a few yards away. An idea was forming that might buy them some time.

A week ago, he wouldn't have thought it possible, and in fact he would have been offended at what he was about to do, at the cruelty he would perpetrate against the families. But that couple was dead, and Bryan was all about protecting the living.

The old man shook his head. "No. I don't know them."

A heavy gust of smoke blew through their little circle and dissipated. The old man coughed as he bent down to rifle through a small bag he'd managed to get off the train. If Bryan was going to do this, it had to be now.

He dug around in his own backpack a moment, then left it with Sassy and hustled over to the bodies, bending down on the pretense of checking for the couple's identification. Both were dressed in street clothes instead of pajamas, which made what he was doing a little easier. A fanny pack was around the woman's waist, and the man had a long billfold in his front jacket pocket. Bryan exchanged their IDs for his and Sassy's, lifting the man's wallet and replacing it with his own, plus exchanging the woman's wallet for Sassy's new passport.

The switch wouldn't hold up for long, but hopefully it would last long enough. The emergency vehicles were close. He pocketed the couple's identification and hurried back to the group.

"Who were they?" asked the old man.

"Guy's name was Bryan Fisher and the woman was Sassy Smith."

"Wha—" Sassy looked up in surprise, but an immediate look of understanding settled over her face when she made eye contact with him.

The police car and ambulance both pulled to a stop beside them and blessedly cut the sirens, even though the lights continued to turn and bathe everyone's faces in macabre red and blue shadows that looked like blood.

Help had arrived.

"I'm James," the older man said in the deafening silence.

"I'm Robert," said Bryan. "And this is my wife, Lisa." He nodded at Sassy. "Robert and Lisa Albertson."

Chapter 10

December 28
Morning
Kingstree, South Carolina

SEVERAL HOURS LATER, Sassy sat on a gurney in the hall just outside an ER exam room and tried to close out all the noise—the overhead paging system, loud voices, louder crying, and beeping monitors. As bad as the hallway was, the ER waiting area was worse, having deteriorated into total chaos a couple of hours ago.

She'd just been wheeled back from a CT scan. With her splitting headache and inability to think straight, she knew without being told that she had a concussion. Bryan was nowhere to be seen, but she assumed he was close by. He hadn't let her out of his sight until they'd insisted she had to go into the room with the CT imaging machine alone.

She was still reeling from everything that had happened, but most of all from hearing Bryan identify himself as Robert Albertson, and her as his wife, Lisa.

He hadn't produced any ID when asked. Instead, he'd

insisted it had been lost in the accident. Sassy assumed the Albertsons were the couple lying dead in the field next to the train wreck.

She understood why he'd had to do that, but it frightened her. On top of the man he'd killed in their hotel room, it made her wonder what she was doing with Bryan. Who was he, really?

His teammates called him "Hollywood." But who had Bryan become? What had he become? She hadn't seen him since they were kids together. Did she know him at all anymore?

He looked the same, if a bit more buff than when she'd lived next door to him in the trailer park. He was still addicted to Dentyne gum. She'd have recognized him anywhere, but the carefree boy she'd known twelve years ago was long gone.

There was something in his eyes that had changed. Sad, somber. Older. What had happened to him?

He'd been in Iraq and Afghanistan. She knew that much from her brother. She also knew he'd been in a horrible accident. It was why he'd missed his grandmother's funeral. Trey had told her that much, but no other real details.

Bryan had gone to visit Trey in Memphis when he'd finally gotten back home from the Middle East, and they'd spent some time together. But the details of how and why he was out of the Marines and working for AEGIS now, she didn't know. She'd thought Bryan was a lifer for sure. Trey had as well. But her brother hadn't shared with her, if he even knew, why Bryan had left the military.

Those were the questions she should look for answers

to. But right now Bryan was the only person standing between her and the people who were intent on killing her. That had been made perfectly clear before she'd been taken for the CT scan.

"You have to play along as Lisa Albertson until we get out of the hospital and away from Kingstree. I know it sucks, but it's the only way to keep you safe," he'd said.

He'd held her hand as she'd lain on the gurney while they'd waited in the hallway for her test. It was one of the first times they'd had even a modicum of privacy since escaping from the train. She'd nodded. She wasn't so scrambled that she thought the train wreck was a freak accident.

"I'm almost certain this has to do with what happened in Africa and New York," he'd continued.

She'd felt her mouth open. Not because it didn't make sense, but because she hadn't walked the train wreck back that far yet. The tech had arrived then and taken her away for her test.

She didn't *want* to believe Bryan's suspicions, but as she'd lain on the table in the imaging room with the tremendous machines and the very loud thumping, she'd come to the conclusion that he was right.

She looked around to see if she could spot him in the waiting room melee down the hallway. The nurse who'd gathered her intake info came by, but still no Bryan. The woman brought a rolling partition and set it up around Sassy before cleaning her face and explaining that it would be a while before the doctor would be available to give her stitches.

As they chatted about inconsequential things for a few moments, Sassy found herself drawn to the older woman. Her name was Tilly and she was a dear, full of conversation and concern for the victims of the train wreck. Tilly told Sassy all about her granddaughter who'd recently moved out of the garage apartment next to her home.

Tilly was most concerned for where Sassy and Bryan would go once they were dismissed from the hospital. She reminded Sassy of Bryan's Gran.

"Can you tell me if the CT scan was okay?" asked Sassy.

"I'm not supposed to, but I can tell you that if there was a problem, the doctor would be in here sooner rather than later. As it is, I'm concerned about the time lapse for getting your head sewn up."

Sassy smiled. *Message received.* Her head was fine. "Can't you or the physician's assistant do the stitching?"

"The cut is on your face. Wouldn't you rather the doctor do it?" asked Tilly.

Sassy shrugged. "It's at my hairline. It won't show much. Besides, I'm sure you do just as good work as that doctor I saw in the hallway who's been practicing for what, fifteen minutes?"

The older woman smiled. "Dr. Xander looks very young for his age." Tilly paused a beat as Sassy raised an eyebrow. "I think he's thirty," she added.

Sassy laughed out loud. "Really, I trust you to do it. And I know there are so many others who need the doctor now more than I do. We can even do butterflies on it if you think that would be better."

THE NURSE WAS tilting Sassy's head back as Bryan stepped into the room, but he'd overheard part of the conversation. "You need stitches," he said. "Butterflies won't work for a cut that deep."

The older woman glanced up and did a double take before nodding and looking back at her patient. "He's right. If you're really okay with my doing it, I can take care of this now."

"Of course," said Sassy. "Stitch away."

Sassy lay down on the gurney and introduced Bryan to her nurse as Tilly readied everything. Bryan caught himself staring, vaguely surprised that Sassy was so blasé about scars. He'd assumed that because of her usual carefully coiffed presentation, she'd howl about not having a plastic surgeon to stitch up her injury.

He'd misjudged her. Was he making other false assumptions about her as well?

His thoughts raced as the two women chatted away. He was grateful Sassy had the distraction of Tilly, because the picture he'd just gathered outside their "partitioned room" was bleak. The police officers taking all the initial information for the accident victims had been full of information.

A grand total of two hotels graced Kingstree, plus one of the local churches was offering a shelter for the accident victims. Not that he figured any of those options would be particularly safe for him or Sassy. They would be the first places someone would come looking for them.

He and Sassy needed to get out of Kingstree, or at least to a safe place where they could regroup and figure out what to do next. While he didn't want to lie any more than he had to, if he wanted the world to believe that he and Sassy were dead, there could be no more contacting AEGIS until he'd figured out their "leak situation."

The immediate issue was getting out of the hospital unobserved by reporters. The cops had filled him in on that, too. The news media had heard about the accident almost as soon as it happened. Reporters from affiliates in Charleston, Greenville, and a couple of national correspondents were descending on the small town like a plague of locusts, salivating for details of the wreck.

How was he to spirit Sassy out of here without the two of them being caught on film? The switch with the IDs at the wreckage site would be all for naught if his face or Sassy's ended up on CNN, even as a background shot for an interview.

His only option for anonymously leaving town was to call someone with no connection to him or to AEGIS. There hadn't been that many choices. Hell, there was really only one.

He'd called Bear Bennett while Sassy was having the CT scan. He hadn't wanted to. The two men hadn't spoken since the day Bryan left Landstuhl Regional Medical Center in Germany and flew back to the U.S. to begin his civilian life.

But Bear had said to call if Bryan ever needed anything. He had even sent Bryan a change-of-address email last year. Bryan had kept up with him, despite their not talking in real time. In an ironic twist of fate, Bear's current work address was less than seventy miles away in the

Francis Marion National Forest. What were the chances?

Today Bryan had dialed the phone and left a message, unsure if the former Special Forces operator would get the voice mail or not. There was no way to know if the man was even on call, particularly during this odd holiday week. He had family, lots of it, as Bryan recalled.

For now, the local motel would have to do. He'd already phoned and made a reservation in Robert Albertson's name, claiming he'd lost his wallet in the accident and was having money wired. The hotel clerk had been quite understanding, since several other guests had had the same issue. Bryan just had to figure out how to get to the hotel, even though he wasn't wild about the whole idea.

"Tilly, how far is the Welcome Inn?" he asked as she finished up Sassy's stitches.

A look of disgust came over the nurse's face. "It's a couple of blocks away, but you don't want to stay there. I was just telling your wife what a dearth of hotels there is here in Kingstree."

"We don't have much choice. The Welcome Inn is the only place in town with a vacancy." And not having a car was an issue. They needed something that was within walking distance.

Tilly finished up the stitches, stepped back from Sassy, and stared at them both a moment before she removed the purple nitrile gloves. "Yes, you do. I have a garage apartment. I was just telling your wife that my granddaughter moved out recently and went back to college. The apartment is simple, but it's clean. You could stay there tonight."

"But we couldn't impose—" started Sassy.

"Spend the night," Tilly interrupted her. "At least stay there today until you figure out how to finish your trip home. I wouldn't wish The Well on my worst enemy. It's a roach motel and a home for bedbugs."

"But—"

"You can pay me. How about half of what The Well charges?"

Sassy looked at Bryan and raised an eyebrow. He didn't want to accept and could tell that Sassy didn't either, but they were completely out of options.

He nodded his agreement.

"Thank you. That's very kind," said Sassy.

Tilly kept talking. "My husband can take you to the house. I'll give him a call. He's here waiting for me right now, 'cause this is the time my shift usually ends, but with the accident and all, it was just extended."

"Are you sure you don't want us to wait?" asked Sassy.

"Oh, I'm sure you don't want to. I'm likely to be here several more hours until they can get more hands on board. Normally we'd keep you for observation on your head injury. But I get the feeling you're not going to go for that, are you, dear?"

Bryan willed Sassy to agree. This was the last place they needed to be. He turned his gaze on her, and she couldn't have mistaken the message in his eyes.

She shook her head and shifted on the gurney. "You're right. We're not up for that."

"So, it's settled," said Tilly. "You go on with my Otis. You can shower and get cleaned up at the apartment."

Sassy had tears in her eyes. "I don't know what to say," she murmured. "Thank you, again."

"No thanks necessary, dear. You just feel better."

"Now, let me look at your man."

Bryan started to protest, but that would be foolish at this point. He needed to be in top shape to get them out of this. Tilly had him sit beside Sassy on the gurney to check his eyes and look at his shoulder so she could determine if he needed stitches, too.

"Got two needles?" he asked with a smile.

Now it was the older woman's turn to sigh.

"Your back has some substantial bruising, and both of you have slight concussions. I don't know which will hurt worse tomorrow—your head, your back, or your shoulder. Take a good hot shower once Otis gets you to the apartment. You might try icing your shoulder some, too. I'll ask the doctor for some anti-inflammatory medication for you."

Bryan nodded and followed Tilly out from behind the privacy screen to finish up the paperwork while Sassy dressed. Afterward the nurse showed them a back door from the hospital so they could avoid the reporters who'd gathered in the ER waiting area.

It was almost 9:00 AM when they walked out of the back hospital exit. Tilly's husband was in the parking lot in a simple silver sedan, just as the nurse had described. "You Tilly's friends?" the older man asked.

Bryan nodded. "Yes, sir."

"Hop on in. She told me to take you to the house."

Without another word, they were off. Ten minutes

later, Otis pulled the sedan into a quiet neighborhood lined with moss-covered trees and sidewalks that looked like something out of Mayberry. He turned into a drive with a detached two-story garage, then parked inside beside something large under a car cloth, leaving his keys in the ignition.

Feeling an unusual need to fill the silence, Bryan nodded toward the tarp. "What do you have there?"

"A '64 Buick Riviera. I just finished restoring her."

"May I?" Bryan put his hand on the material.

Otis nodded, and Bryan lifted the edge of the cloth to reveal a stunning black two-door showpiece. "That's amazing. Is that the dual-quad carb setup?"

Otis beamed like a proud parent. "Found her in a scrapyard. It's taken me four years to finish the restoration. But she drives like a dream. Tilly keeps asking what am I going to do with her. I'd like to sell our sedan and just drive this one."

"Who wouldn't?" agreed Bryan. "You should."

Otis grinned. "Maybe I will." And without further fanfare he directed them to the steps on the side of the garage apartment.

"The key is in the flowerpot by the door. Make yourselves at home. I think there are frozen dinners and perhaps some soup in the pantry from when my granddaughter was here. Help yourselves. Tilly said your wife might need some clothes. There's a closet up there with a white plastic bag full of things Tilly's planning to take to Goodwill. She can pick out whatever she needs. I think Tilly even threw in some of my clothes that don't fit anymore. Grab anything you want." The old man looked Bryan up and down and shook his head. "Not that anything'll fit you."

Bryan glanced at Sassy's blood-spattered sweater. They would both need to change so as not to walk around looking like extras in a zombie apocalypse movie.

"We'll be fine. Thank you, sir," he said.

Otis left them standing at the bottom of the stairs, his sense of welcome obviously complete. They watched him walk into his house, hobbling a bit. Sassy'd been very quiet up till now. Bryan looked down at her, expecting tears or anger.

Instead, she just shook her head and muttered, "Jesus, what a day. And it's not even ten o'clock."

She didn't wait for his reply; instead she started up the steps attached to the garage. He huffed a laugh. Not because the situation was funny, but because she sounded just like the old woman who'd lived next door to his Gran.

Indeed. He walked up the stairs behind her and found the key just where Otis said it would be.

The garage apartment smelled musty, like it hadn't been aired out in a while. But that was to be expected with all the humidity in the area. Still, the place was ruthlessly neat, with a queen bed, full bath, small sitting area, kitchenette, washer/dryer, and a large walk-in closet.

There was no food in the tiny fridge, but in the freezer he found a can of coffee, along with two boxes of Hot Pockets. At this point, Bryan could eat his boot, he was so hungry.

"I still can't believe Tilly offered this to us. She doesn't know us from Adam's house cat," murmured Sassy.

Bryan smiled at the expression. "Me either, but I'm glad she did. Get cleaned up, okay? I'll make us something to eat."

She opened the closet and disappeared inside. "Why don't you go first? I'm going to grab something to change into and throw my clothes in the washing machine. Leave your shirt, I'll wash it, too."

"You sure?"

She stuck her head back around the closet door. "Promise not to use all the hot water?"

He snorted a laugh, slid off his shirt, and stepped into the bathroom. She had no idea how fast he could shower. Six minutes later he was done.

He'd have to wear the same jeans unless there was something of Otis's in the closet that fit. But it was good to have the stink of burning fuel off his skin and out of his hair. For now his jeans would do.

While he'd taken a speed shower, Sassy had hauled out a sack of clothes from the closet and found a long terry robe reminiscent of the one she'd worn in the hotel in Africa. She'd also located an XXL hoodie sweatshirt for him sporting a Dallas Cowboys logo.

"I realize they're not your team but . . . in a pinch?"

He smiled. "This is great. Thanks."

"There's one for me, too." She held up a smaller logoed sweatshirt from the bag before heading into the bathroom, only to squeal in delight as she walked inside. "I've died and gone to heaven. There's a massaging showerhead in here."

"The Four Seasons has nothing on Tilly and Otis. Take your time in the 'spa.'"

"Oh, I intend to. I plan to be one wrinkled prune before I get out of here." She shut the door on Bryan's laughter.

He turned to the frozen ham-and-cheese croissant-like sandwiches and was trying to determine the most appetizing way to reheat them when his phone dinged with an incoming message. It was Bear.

Got your message. Been a long time. What do you need?

Bryan replied: *A ride and a safe place to stay.*

Just you?

Me plus one.

Bear's response was immediate. *Trouble with the law?*

Bryan texted back. *Not what it sounds like.*

You know I don't care. Where do you need to be picked up?

Kingstree. Bryan heard the shower kick on. With a response like Pavlov's dog, he immediately had a picture of Sassy undressing in his head. Even more disconcerting, his heart rate kicked up.

Bear texted back. *Can't be there till almost 4:00 PM. You okay till then?*

Bryan looked around the apartment. This was as safe as it got for now. Tilly and Otis were the only ones who knew they were here, and they thought Bryan and Sassy were the Albertsons.

Yes, he typed back.

Send me the address around 2:00 PM.

Bryan sighed in relief. He hadn't wanted to disclose their location until absolutely necessary. It would have been difficult to say no if Bear had asked for it up front.

Will do. Thanks.

There was no reply, but Bryan didn't expect there to be. The last time Bryan had seen him in Germany, Bear had become a man of few words. It seemed that extended to his text communications as well.

The burner for the hot water heater kicked on with a swoosh. He flipped the switch to preheat the oven, searched for a baking sheet for the sandwiches, and thought about Sassy, wondering how she was doing keeping her stitches dry in the shower. Did she need any help in there?

He huffed a laugh at himself. *Not likely.*

But that didn't stop him from imagining the water beading up on her wet body and running down all the slopes and crevices he'd tasted last night. Places he hadn't gotten near enough of.

The baking sheet slipped from his fingers onto the counter with a clatter, and he mentally slammed the door of his imagination shut on those distracting thoughts.

What the hell was he doing? Thinking about sex with Sassy was the surest way to get them both killed. And despite what had happened on the train before the derailment, sleeping with her was still the mother of bad ideas. Even so, he wondered if she was okay in the shower, particularly when it continued to run for the next twenty minutes.

He was pulling the sandwiches out of the oven when

it occurred to him that with her head injury, she might have tripped. Leaving the oven door open, he rushed into the postage-stamp-sized bathroom, calling her name.

She didn't answer. His stomach tightened when he ripped the shower curtain aside to find her asleep on the tub's porcelain floor with her head leaning back against the tile. Her position didn't look very comfortable, but as exhausted as she was, it wouldn't have taken much. Steam floated around her, and the shower spray was hitting the wall two feet above her head.

"Sassy?" He kept his voice low, not wanting to startle her.

She never stirred, but she'd been crying earlier. That much was obvious from the red splotches around her eyes. And if the sight of her wet body in the shower hadn't brought him to his knees, her tear-splotched face did.

God, please. Let him face another man with a gun and a grenade any day. He had no idea what to do with this woman's tears.

"Sassy?" He spoke a little louder this time.

Was this just the shock of everything catching up to her?

Praying she'd just sat down for a moment and dozed off and that this wasn't some residual effect of the concussion, he reached to turn off the still warm water. *Otis must have a monster hot water heater in this place.*

Ignoring the torque in his back, he grabbed the threadbare towel and borrowed robe from the countertop and reached to pull her up and out of the tub.

When he leaned down over her, her blue eyes flew

open. Only then did she react. But not like he would have expected. She went wild.

"No, dammit. No. Don't touch me . . . don't ever touch me. Just stop! Stop!"

"Sassy? Sassy, it's me." He dropped the robe on her shoulder and leaned back in a squat beside the tub.

Her eyes were glassy and unfocused. She jumped to her feet and covered her breasts with one hand protectively across her chest. He sat on his haunches, taking in the sight of a naked, wet Sassy standing over him. Momentarily stunned, he never saw it coming.

When her other fist connected with his jaw, the cracking sound reverberated around the bathroom. Still in a squat, he tipped backward. His shoulder bounced off the countertop and he landed on his ass directly on the wet linoleum. He felt the jolt all the way up his back again.

Jesus. He'd forgotten she definitely didn't hit like a girl. *Damn.*

The slap of his butt hitting the wet floor seemed to pull her from wherever she'd been. Her eyes widened and her mouth opened in a wide O.

"Bryan. Ohmigod. I'm so sorry. I . . . sat down to shave my legs and . . . I must have dozed off."

The shock on her face no doubt mirrored his own as he rubbed his jaw. "Just glad you weren't holding the razor," he mumbled.

She started to reach for him, then stopped. He saw the moment she remembered she was stark naked.

And instead of reaching for him, she pulled her arms into the oversized robe that he'd tried to drape around her earlier. Exiting the tub, she was struggling to get herself covered and put her foot directly into a puddle of water. Off balance and still trying to drag the robe on, she fell and landed in a heap on top of him.

When she bounced into his bare chest, he went flat, and one of her knees bumped his belly. The other would have had him singing soprano if he hadn't caught her knee with one hand and her naked hip with the other. As it was, she covered him like a blanket in the ridiculously crowded space.

Umph. Bryan felt the impact of her body against him. It should have hurt, and part of it probably did, but at the same time his body was also registering just how good it felt to have all that soft skin against his again.

He lay there for a minute, trying to catch his breath and figure out what the fuck had just happened. But his hands were still splayed across her. She immediately started scrambling, which brought its own set of issues. His body reacted as it normally would with a wet, naked woman lying on top of him. He clamped an arm around her waist as his body tightened further.

"Stop that." His tone was harsher than he'd intended, but he was desperate.

She quit scrambling, which didn't really help the situation at all. The silent drip, drip of the faucet was the only sound as he fought the natural response of his body, a losing battle. Sassy, for the first time he could recall in his entire acquaintance with her, kept her mouth shut.

He felt her body start to shake.

Jesus, she was crying again. And that made him want

to howl. Her tears were his kryptonite. He was forming the words of an apology when he heard her gasp for air and a distinct giggle.

She wasn't crying. The woman was laughing? Not exactly the response a man longed for when he had a raging erection. But under the circumstances, it was better than her tears.

He moved a hand to her face, which was presently buried in his chest, and lifted her chin. The mirth in her eyes was still tinged with tears, but both dimples were out in full force. She was definitely laughing.

Right now, he'd take it.

"Sassy? What the hell are you doing?" He'd completely thrown in the towel on the language issue. At this point, he couldn't control either that or his response to her.

She giggled again and tried to catch her breath but ended up belly-laughing instead. He felt the vibration all the way to his toes.

"God, I am such a mess and this is such a mess. I . . ." She stopped when she saw the expression on his face. She stared into his eyes, and he felt something between them shift. All the sexual sparring, all the verbal clashes of the past six months, seemed to slip away.

"Everyone's a mess, Sassy. Some folks just hide it better than others. That's all."

Her dimples disappeared. "What happened to you, Bryan?"

"More than you want to know." He shook his head slightly and felt the moisture beneath his scalp.

"What makes you think that?" She tried to sit up.

"Hey," he grabbed for her knee again so she didn't cripple him, gently placing it beside his hip versus in his crotch. And this time he did let himself look at her body. He let her see the longing in his eyes, then let her see him shut it down.

The expression on her face changed as she pulled the robe around herself and stood up. "I haven't been fair to you. Will you tell me about what happened in Afghanistan?"

He watched her standing over him. His back was soaked. She was soaked.

"Please. I know something bad happened. You were going to be a Marine for life. Then suddenly you weren't."

"Will you tell me what happened to you?" he asked.

A guarded look came into her eyes.

He nodded. "Yeah, well. I kinda feel the same way."

He didn't want to talk about his past. It hurt too much, and he'd closed the door on what had happened over there. He didn't wake up in a cold sweat anymore from dreams that felt so real, he could taste the grit in his mouth and hear screams in his head. At least not as often as he used to. He retrieved the towel from the floor as he sat up, then stood beside her in the impossibly cramped space and turned to leave.

"Wait," said Sassy. "I'll talk, but let me get dressed first."

He hung the towel over the shower curtain rod. *Good. Clothes would be a very good start.* Maybe between her being dressed and talking about the past, he could keep his hands to himself. But he wasn't going to count on it.

"I'll check on the food."

Chapter 11

FIFTEEN MINUTES LATER, Sassy emerged from the bathroom. She'd had to fight to keep herself from stalling in the bathroom, but she'd been grateful when she'd found a hair dryer. She was still in the damp oversized robe, but with dry hair, she didn't feel quite so vulnerable.

Having lost her handbag and meager toiletries in the train crash, she'd had to make do with what was in the medicine cabinet. She'd rebandaged her stitches and even found some cosmetics that Tilly's granddaughter must have left behind, including blush and a tube of lipstick, which Sassy had disinfected with alcohol before using. She desperately needed armor for the coming conversation, and makeup was the closest she'd ever come to a shield and sword. She couldn't stand the thought of looking like the young girl who'd been so naïve twelve years ago.

Bryan had set the table with paper plates. There was

coffee and sugar and some powdered creamer he must have found after she'd gone to shower. He'd also located a can of corn and heated it to go along with their eclectic lunch.

She sat down at the scarred oak dining table as he put two of the croissant sandwiches on each plate, served some of the corn, and handed it over. "This isn't much, but hopefully it'll stave off starvation."

Sassy nodded. "I'm so hungry, I could eat anything."

He grinned. "That's what I'm counting on."

They sat across from each other, eating in silence for a few moments. As odd as it was, Sassy felt almost guilty for wishing they could stay like this in suspended animation—where there was no ticking clock on Trey's court date, where no one was after them, where there were no strange men in her hotel room, no train wreck, no dead passengers, and where she didn't have to tell Bryan anything about that summer he left Springwater.

"What happened to you, Sassy? What happened after I left home?"

She took a sip of the strong coffee that she'd over-sweetened and swallowed. "I grew up."

He smiled again. "I can see that. You grew up good. You're beautiful."

The words hung there, and she didn't know what to say. As a young girl she'd been infatuated with Bryan. That he would say such a thing now should have thrilled her. But the words only served as a reminder of everything he didn't know about her.

"Something is wrong besides the situation with Trey."

He nodded toward the bathroom. "What just went down in there? Did someone hurt you on that truck in Africa? Please tell me."

"No, it's not that. Nothing bad happened there." What she really meant was that nothing bad had happened to *her*. Other women on the truck hadn't been so lucky.

Sassy looked down. Bryan was gripping his fork so tightly that his knuckles were turning white. God, she didn't want to do this. Didn't want to share this. It was ugly, and so long ago. She'd been stupid, and part of her felt that she should have been over it by now.

But she wasn't. That she'd never allowed herself to be vulnerable to a man proved she wasn't. The incident in the bathroom just now confirmed it. She hadn't freaked out like that since college. It had to be from everything else that had happened this week.

A culmination of circumstances had kept her firmly stuck for so long. But Bryan was turning himself inside out thinking the worst, and she wanted him to know the truth, or as much of it as she could tell.

She took a deep breath. "I wasn't raped."

He exhaled, but the intensity of his gaze didn't let up. "But something happened," he insisted.

"A long time ago. Yes, something happened."

"What?" His voice was strained, even in that one word.

"I had a 'scare.'"

"What do you mean 'a scare'?" he asked.

"Exactly what it sounds like. A group of boys—"

"A group?" he interrupted.

"Will you let me finish?" she snapped.

He nodded tightly and sat back.

"The summer after you left, right before school started, a group of boys from Trey's class asked me to a party at the levee."

She ignored Bryan's groan. Parties at the levee weren't exactly white-tie affairs. "I was going into tenth grade, and I was fairly inexperienced, but Bobby Hughes asked me. You remember Bobby, right?"

Bryan nodded.

She knew he remembered, and that's what made this story so hard to tell. Bryan was two years older than Bobby and Trey, but the boys had all hung out a lot, playing video games at the Hugheses' house and partying together with all the local kids. While Sassy had liked Bobby well enough in ninth grade, by the middle of her sophomore year, she'd understood why the rich kid had "lowered himself" to hang with Bryan and Trey. Bryan was the cool older boy and Trey was the high school football star.

"When Bobby came to pick me up for the party, there were a couple of other guys in the car I didn't know very well. They'd been drinking, but I didn't think anything of it, 'cause Bobby was sober and driving. I felt safe. He was Trey's friend. That was my mistake."

Bryan's eyes bored into hers, and he continued to grip his fork in such a way that it would never be the same when this conversation was over. She shredded the napkin in her own lap as she kept talking. If she stopped, she'd never get through this. She'd been so damn naïve, then compounded the issue by being a coward.

"There was no party at the levee that night, at least not the kind that I'd been expecting." She closed her eyes.

She could still feel the sharp stones biting into her back as Bobby held her down on the ground and the other two boys pulled at her shorts, trying to unbutton them and drag them down her legs. She shook her head to clear the images and took a sip of water before continuing.

She swallowed hard. "Growing up . . . you and Trey taught me a lot about defending myself. But there were three of them. Two were football players."

Bryan was staring at her. The look in his eyes was pure agony. She wasn't giving him all the details, but she knew his imagination was more than filling in the blanks.

"Sassy, please tell me what happened. I'm dying here. I want to go back home and kill Bobby Hughes with my bare hands . . ."

She stared back at him and took another breath. "They didn't rape me, but they got my shorts and T-shirt off. I gave Bobby a black eye in the process. And yeah, I think he would have assaulted me himself if one of the farmers hadn't driven through, checking on some kind of equipment in the fields between the levee and the river. The boys had parked right by the man's tractor, assuming everything was shut down for the night. Old man Foster found me and got me home."

"What happened when you reported it and pressed charges?"

"What makes you think I reported anything?" She'd meant for the comment to sound sarcastic, but her breath caught, and it sounded more like a sob.

"I was from the wrong side of the tracks with a mother who was the town drunk and rumored to sleep with any man who'd bring her a fifth of whiskey. I'd willingly gotten in the car with three older boys. I'd just turned fifteen, but I was old enough to know how that would play."

Bryan shook his head in disbelief as she kept talking. "I didn't report anything. I showed up when school started the next week and acted like nothing had happened."

"Did you ever tell Trey?" Bryan asked, bringing her back to the present.

She raised an eyebrow. "Right. Tell my brother his friend tried to rape me, so he could shoot him or at best beat up the richest boy in town and wind up in jail?" This time her voice dripped with biting sarcasm, and she didn't try to hide it.

"'Course maybe if Trey'd been in a U.S. prison, he might not have wound up in a Mexican jail." She sighed. "God, that's just depressing as hell."

"So you never pressed charges or reported this to anyone?"

She frowned at him in confusion. He was repeating himself, and she wasn't sure why. "No, I never told anyone. You are the first." She sneered at the joke that only she got. "But I learned not to be so damn trusting. It was the most valuable part of my education." And destroyed her own reputation in the process.

The three boys had left her alone all that first week until after school on Friday. Then they'd surrounded her in the very crowded parking lot when they'd known Trey had been on the practice field. There they'd started to insult and harass her, calling her the most horrific names.

They'd drawn quite the crowd. But she'd stood on the tarry asphalt and taken the biggest chance of her life. When Bobby had tried to pull at her clothes again, she'd forced herself to laugh and ask loudly enough for their audience to hear if he thought he could get it up this time as opposed to last week, when he'd just run away.

Every student in the parking lot heard her taunt, and she would have found the look on Bobby's face comical if she hadn't been so scared her gamble would backfire. But it didn't. When they saw she wasn't intimidated, Bobby and his buddies backed down so fast, it made her head spin—especially when she started talking about their lack of "equipment." She'd been stunned at the effect her words had had, and she'd been adopting the same type of self-defense mechanism ever since.

After the levee incident, Sassy became known as the trash-talking daughter of the town whore at Springwater High School.

When Trey heard about the altercation in the parking lot, he completely misunderstood the reason behind it and assumed she really had fooled around with Bobby and his friends. It hurt like hell that her brother jumped to that conclusion, but she never set him straight. After one very uncomfortable confrontation where Sassy told him in no uncertain terms to mind his own damn business, Trey stayed out of it. Only then did she breathe a sigh of relief that her brother and his future out of Springwater were safe.

Throughout the next three years in school, Sassy adopted an over-the-top sexual persona to combat the whispered rumors and gossip. She learned when not to pull the tiger's tail with predator-like bullies, and she developed a radar for who could and couldn't be shut down with some well-timed, cock-shriveling sarcasm.

To say the experience had made her skittish around men was putting it mildly. She didn't let men get close, period. The easiest way to keep them at arm's length was to shut them down with her ego-obliterating disdain when they got too close. That had come with its own downside over the years, but she kept that to herself.

Boys and men alike assumed she was easy and a tease because she talked like she was, but most stayed away from her because she was a ballbuster when it came to the things she'd say in front of anyone. She didn't date in college, and her prickly personality kept colleagues at bay after graduation, too. Her verbal skills served her particularly well in the male-dominated newsroom.

She'd honed her self-defense weapon to a fine point. But there was no doubt that Bryan had her playing with fire where that was concerned, and there was that one little detail she hadn't shared.

In the past six months, she'd shocked herself with some of the outrageous things she'd said to him, and with Bryan she didn't always follow up her big talk with scoffing remarks. He threw her so off-kilter that instead of turning on the usual sexual scorn, she played over-the-top Sassy closer and closer to the edge and its logical end.

She didn't have to be experienced to know that was a

dangerous game. Even as she worried about protecting herself from her own insanity, she knew Bryan wouldn't purposely hurt her. But he could still break her heart without meaning to.

BRYAN STARED AT Sassy over their meal of Hot Pockets and canned corn, processing everything she'd just told him. Some stuff that had been happening between the two of them made sense now, but there were still a few things that didn't.

How Trey hadn't figured out what was up with Bobby Hughes, he'd never know. But Bryan hadn't been there to stop it from happening. So he sure as hell couldn't blame anyone but himself.

When Bryan left Springwater after graduation, he left both Trey and their friendship in the dust, along with Sassy. He'd been so scared he was going to cross some line with her, Bryan hadn't recognized the potential difficulties he was leaving Sassy to wade through without him.

When he'd come back home from Afghanistan in such a mental funk, Trey hadn't said anything about his abrupt departure years before. No blame, no questions. He'd just stepped up and been Bryan's friend again.

As much resistance as he'd had to the idea before, now there was a whole new list of reasons Bryan couldn't be the guy who slept with Trey's little sister. That had some awful implications, especially since Bryan wasn't open to anything permanent.

Was he?

He wasn't so sure anymore and was swallowing a sip of coffee when Sassy said, "Okay, Hollywood, I showed you mine. Now you show me yours."

Her voice was light and teasing. The image was so vivid and unexpected after the story she'd just told, he choked on the coffee and practically inhaled the liquid straight up his nose.

Sassy raised an eyebrow. "So why do they call you Hollywood? You never told me."

He shook his head, still sputtering and coughing.

"It can't be that bad."

He swallowed hard, trying to clear the coffee from his lungs and nasal cavities. If he hadn't caught the expression in her eyes as he was having his coughing fit, the lilt in her voice might have had him thinking she was over the incident she'd just shared from her past. As it was, he was just grateful he'd seen her words for the diversion attempt they were. They'd certainly had the desired effect.

As such, he decided to let it go. She deserved a diversion after this.

She was staring at him now with her usual frank curiosity. "Now, you tell me. What happened to you in Afghanistan? I know something did. You didn't come back for your grandmother's funeral, but two months later you were home for good."

He closed his eyes. He didn't want to talk about this, but he supposed it was only fair. He'd much rather dwell on the *I showed you mine, now you show me yours* part of the conversation.

Not that he'd seen nearly as much of "hers" as he wanted. Not by a long shot. He'd love to see more of her . . . everything. But given what he'd just learned, he wondered if he ever would. One of her brother's supposed best friends had practically raped her. It seemed wrong for Bryan, another of Trey's friends, to be thinking of screwing her brains out.

Bryan knew this was a different situation. He was different. They were different. She was a grown woman, for one thing.

And if the price for making amends to her for past wrongs was laying his soul bare, he could do it. But that didn't mean he had to like it. It hurt too damn much. He didn't want her feeling sorry for him or trying to fix him afterward, either.

"Hey, 'Hollywood.' It's no fair, not sharing after I spilled. Either tell me about your travels to the Middle East or tell me about your nickname."

Jesus. Was he really going to have to do this? He'd only talked to the counselor once at the VA, and that was because they'd insisted.

She was looking at him with an expectant gaze. He took a deep breath.

Tap, tap, tap. The knocking on the door was soft but persistent. He felt a ridiculous sense of relief as he released the breath he'd been holding.

It was Otis, standing on the stairs holding a casserole dish in his hands.

"Tilly had no idea if there was anything in the fridge and figured you two might be hungry. This is our leftover poppy-seed casserole from last night. It's all heated up and ready to eat."

Sassy came to stand beside Bryan and took the dish from the older man's grasp. Bryan asked him inside, longing to postpone the inevitable conversation to come with Sassy.

"No, thank you," the older man said. "You two get some rest now, you hear? Tilly said you'll be wanting to figure out transportation when you wake up. I can take you to the rental car place if you like."

"Yes, sir," said Sassy and Bryan simultaneously. Those deep-seated Southern manners of always agreeing with their elders automatically kicked in, along with a mutual anxiousness to *not* go to a rental agency.

Bryan thanked Otis again and shut the door. "Want some of this?" He glanced at Sassy's half-eaten sandwich.

"Yeah. I don't know when we'll get the chance later."

He served up the casserole and gave himself a mighty heaping as well.

Sassy was right. This was a reprieve. They'd better take it while they could.

"Now where were we?" she asked.

Chapter 12

WHERE THE HELL were they?

The traitor sat in his office and twirled the letter opener as he drank his scotch. Fisher and the woman had been on the train, then after the wreck and explosion they'd vanished. Reports were unclear if they'd died in the crash and explosive aftermath or not. His men at the site reported that their IDs had been found, but no one had actually seen the bodies. And the traitor wouldn't trust anything that wasn't "eyes on" verification.

Fisher had proven himself cagey enough earlier in New York. According to all the intel he was receiving, the former Marine had become appropriately paranoid since arriving back from Africa. The AEGIS connection notwithstanding, IDs could be planted. And Bryan Fisher didn't strike him as a stupid man. So the traitor now had men on the scene checking it out.

How the hell had they lost the woman to begin with? Sassy Smith and Jennifer Grayson were the only two left who could put this together. He needed them eliminated, yesterday. But first he had to find them.

Fortunately, he had the resources; time just wasn't one of them. Everything was coming to a head and in danger of unraveling. God, how could this have happened?

After ten years. Had it really been that long?

He'd flown under the radar until that ridiculous bust last year with the DEA and the snafu with Leland Hollis and the accountant Ellis Colton. Still, there had to be a way to stop it from falling apart.

He'd tried a couple of times. First with the accountant's bust, next the explosions at the Rivera compound in Mexico, then at the vet clinic in Antón Lizardo. He'd finally gone to the "nuclear option" with ordering the deaths of Ernesto Vega and Juan Santos. It was a shame Santos was dead, but that had been inevitable. The man knew too much and talked too much. Vega's death wasn't such a tragedy, but it had been a foregone conclusion, nonetheless.

The traitor still couldn't believe how quickly everything had gone to hell in Dallas, Mexico, and even Africa, of all places. The men at AEGIS and their women were like cats with nine lives. But he was the Grim Reaper. No one could survive him.

His men in Kingstree would find Fisher and the woman. And if they weren't already dead, they would be soon.

Kingstree, South Carolina

SASSY SAT AT the table, looking at Bryan expectantly.

"So where were we? Why did you come back from Afghanistan and boot the Marines? I thought that was your chosen career path. Your Gran sure thought so."

There was nothing quite like getting right down to it. And he hadn't missed the censure in her voice. There was so much she didn't know.

She narrowed her eyes as he stared at her. "Cat got your tongue? Personally, I would have gone for a completely different part of your anatomy."

He swallowed. God, she was doing it again. The woman really would say anything. She was barely five feet tall, yet she consistently shocked the hell out of him. He studied her across the table a moment, letting himself linger on her slicked-back hair and oversized robe. She should have looked like a little girl; instead, she looked like an extraordinarily fuckable woman.

But he wasn't going there, not after what she'd just told him about Bobby Hughes and his buddies. Bryan wasn't going to be another one of Trey's friends taking advantage. At this point, he'd already done enough to mess with her head to last a lifetime. Sassy's brother was one of the only friends Bryan had left after Afghanistan.

Afghanistan. He really didn't want to go there, either, particularly with Sassy. He continued to stare, and as he did, she blinked and glanced away. He got the impression his gaze was making her uncomfortable.

Nah. It couldn't be. She was too bold. Was *everything*

about the bad-girl act just a charade on her part? That hardly seemed possible, but it was an interesting idea.

She looked up again, and her eyes snapped with impatience. "So?" she asked.

He steeled himself and took a deep breath.

"I was in Force Recon, a Special Operations group from the Marines that integrated into MARSOC."

Her forehead wrinkled in confusion.

"MARSOC stands for United States Marine Corps Forces Special Operations Command. There are lots of acronyms involved, but it's probably easiest to think of this as Marine Corps Special Operations."

She nodded her understanding.

"My team was good." They'd been better than good. His team had been amazing. "We did exactly what the name implies, reconnaissance and intelligence. At the end of our third tour together, we were coming back from a mission that involved investigating heroin smuggling routes used by one of the more fickle Afghan tribal chieftains."

Bryan's team had figured out how smugglers were getting the drugs out of the country and had been able to shut down access to a major shipping lane in the Helmand Province. They hadn't shut down anything permanently, but what they'd done had slowed shipments significantly for several months. Hopefully, it had slowed the flow of money to Al-Qaeda and Taliban militants as well.

"We were waiting on transport back to base—talking and making plans for what we were going to do with our time off back home. We'd had a couple of CIA consultants and one DEA guy with us on the mission. At our extraction point, me and one of the other guys were asked to ride in the Jeep behind the main truck to make room for everyone."

Sassy watched him, her gaze never leaving his face. Instead of that making him feel self-conscious, he found himself wanting to tell her the story. He'd kept it bottled up for so long.

If he closed his eyes, he could still see the scene before him—hear the voices, feel the air, draw in the scent of the crisp morning. Afghanistan had smelled different, a difference he couldn't ever quite describe in words. The road was dusty, and the gray-colored grit covered his boots as he walked back to the Jeep with Bear Bennett. Everyone was shipping home the next day for some much-needed R&R. The men were laughing and talking, giving each other good-natured shit as they spoke of plans to see their families and friends.

He and Bear climbed into the Jeep, joking about who would ride shotgun while they snapped on their seat belts. The larger truck ahead of them began moving forward. They were following behind, passing a village boy leading a donkey loaded down with God knew what, and the boy gave them this look.

Suddenly Bryan knew that it was all about to go from sugar to shit. But there was no time to react. Even as the thought registered, the explosion was happening. All in the blink of an eye, while the aftermath felt like a slow-motion nightmare.

One second he was looking at the boy with the donkey, thinking something seemed off. The next, everything disappeared in a cloud of black smoke. The concussion wave turned the Jeep end over end. Bryan came to in a ditch, broken up and still strapped in his seat.

Sassy watched him with unblinking intensity. He hadn't realized he'd said all that aloud, but he was hyperaware now.

"Everyone on the transport was dead—my teammates, the DEA and the CIA guys, our Jeep driver. Bear was in the back of the Jeep with a broken ankle and a blown-out knee. But he was conscious, and he pulled me out of the front seat before the fire spread to our vehicle. I couldn't walk. Could barely crawl. I would have died if he hadn't been there." He looked down at his half-eaten casserole.

He still couldn't wrap his head around why he'd survived. The men on that truck had had wives, kids, parents, girlfriends. Bryan had none of that. Not even a dog. His only relative, Gran, had died of congestive heart failure a few weeks before he'd gotten home after the bombing. He still wasn't over the pain of not being there for her.

So why the fuck had he lived while everyone else but Bear had died?

He didn't share that cheery thought with Sassy. That wasn't anything he was ready to share with anyone.

"I ended up with a broken leg and collarbone, a severe concussion, a ruptured spleen, and some fractured ribs. They tacked several weeks on to my upcoming leave."

Later they'd used the time to investigate Bryan because someone up the chain of command had been convinced his team had been set up.

No shit, Sherlock.

Initially, the powers-that-be were convinced that it was Bryan, Bear, or both who'd betrayed the team, the reasoning being that if they were still alive, they must have been at fault. Convinced to the point where they wouldn't let either man go home, even when Bryan's grandmother died.

They didn't arrest him or Bear; they just didn't release them from the hospital. They were under a sort of house arrest. And they kept them in Germany, despite their being well enough to travel. The unofficial charges had caused Bryan to question everything he thought he knew about the military and what he was doing with his life.

Once both men's names were cleared, his commanders were "oh so sorry." They still had no idea where the information leak had come from that had led to the roadside attack. They'd probably never know. But even with the apology from his superiors, it was too late to change Bryan's feelings about his future with MARSOC.

His trust in the military and that life was completely broken. "I was at the eight-year mark and due to re-up. Instead I got out."

He didn't add that he hadn't been able to stomach the thought of going on. Betrayal did that to him. Once he felt trust was broken, recovery was impossible.

Sassy continued to silently watch him. The homemade casserole had cooled, but he had a feeling she no longer had an appetite. He sure as hell didn't.

What was she thinking? Was it too much to hope that she'd remain silent? He could handle anything but her sympathy.

His burner phone chirped; the soft, mellow tones of the ringer filled the apartment. He didn't recognize the number, but he took the chance to avoid hearing how Sassy would respond to his revelations and answered the call. "Hello?"

"Bryan, it's Nick. I got your number from Leland. Are you in a place where you can talk?"

"Yes." He glanced at Sassy across the table from him. He covered the phone. "It's Nick Donovan."

"Are they okay?" The concern in her eyes was genuine, just as it had been for him.

He stared at her a moment, not registering what she'd asked. *Definitely fuckable.*

He mentally kicked himself, but there wasn't any forgetting that idea. "Are you and Jennifer alright?" he asked.

"We're back home. I've got some information for you, but I don't want to share it over the phone. Probably best to meet in person."

Hearing that Nick was concerned about the integrity of their communications did Bryan's heart good. He no longer felt guilty about not wanting to call Leland after the train derailment. It was an odd sense of relief to know that he wasn't the only one paranoid as hell at this point.

"Where do you want to do it?" Bryan asked.

"Do you remember the boss's cabin?"

Bryan knew it. The place was just outside Broken Bow, Oklahoma. Hell and gone from where he was now.

"We could meet there," said Nick. "You told me I needed a vacation when we were in Skikda."

Bryan snorted a sad laugh. "Yes, I did. But that cabin is over a thousand miles from here."

"Where are you?" asked Nick.

Bryan glanced around the room, cognizant of what he didn't want to say. There was a beat of silence.

"Right. Forget I asked that," said Nick.

"It could take a couple days for us to get there. I don't have transportation at the moment."

"Think you could be there by New Year's Eve?" asked Nick.

Bryan studied Sassy sitting across from him, noted the darkening circles under her eyes. She hadn't slept for more than a couple of hours at a time. Hell, neither one of them had since the hotel room in Africa.

Was that three or four days ago? He stared at the stitches on her forehead. *Someone wanted her dead.*

"Yeah. We can get there by then, maybe before. Let me figure out a car. Count on two and a half days. I'll call you when we're on the road." Bryan closed the phone.

He had no idea how he was going to do it but having Bear come for them might not work after all. They needed transportation now, not four hours from now. He couldn't rent anything with his ID and stay hidden for any length of time. Whatever was going on, the people after them had very long arms.

He glanced at Sassy again. Those circles under her eyes were deep purple. She had to rest, even if he didn't. When they got on the road, they could split up the driving. But she wasn't going to want to sleep until then. He'd bet money on it. She was stubborn that way.

Straightforward would be the best way to talk her into this. But as he recalled, *biddable* had never been a word anyone used to describe Sassy's personality.

He smiled at the thought and took a breath. "You need to rest."

"What did Nick want?" She spoke at the same time he did.

"He wants us to meet him."

"Where?" She stood with her plate and walked it to the sink.

"Oklahoma."

She stopped in the process of scraping her plate into the disposal. "But that's—"

"A really long way from here, yes."

"That could take days. Trey doesn't have days."

Bryan held up his hand. "One problem at a time. First we have to figure out how we are getting out of here, whether we're going to Oklahoma, Mexico, or back to Africa."

She stopped on the verge of what appeared to be a full-fledged rant and nodded. "Okay. So how are we getting a car if you can't use your ID? You think Otis would let us rent that antique under the cover in his garage?"

Bryan laughed and pushed back from the table. "I think Otis would be more likely to give us his house. He loves that car."

She raised an eyebrow. "Well, I suppose it depends on just how persuasive you can be."

He stood and cleared his own dishes. "Oh, I can be persuasive, alright."

She smirked and started filling the sink with water, standing closer to him than usual. "I just bet you can be when you're in the right frame of mind."

Glancing down and trying to ignore the sexual tug, he could smell the floral shampoo she'd used. He also tried, unsuccessfully, not to stare down the front her robe. He failed at both and only managed to give her a look that was partway between scorching and pleading.

Despite the robe's being oversized, Sassy's generous assets were difficult to miss. She was curvy in a way that had him grinding his teeth to keep from saying anything that would lead them further into "bad idea land." Why couldn't he get himself under control around her?

The hell of it was, he strongly suspected that she knew exactly what she did to him. He had to get out of here for a little while, or, despite his best intentions, he'd have her on that table with the threadbare terry cloth open any second.

"I'm going to go talk with Otis," he said.

"I'll get my clothes figured out from what I found in the closet."

Thank God. Out loud he muttered, "Good." Clothes would be an excellent start. Maybe then he wouldn't want to strip her naked, kiss her stupid, or both.

SASSY BUMPED BRYAN away from the sink with her hip. "I'll take care of these." She took a steadying breath as he stared down at her with an inscrutable look.

He said nothing and walked out the door, closing it

with a decided snap. She could almost feel the perspiration popping out on her upper lip. Lord, she had to get out of this robe and put some real clothes on. Dressed this way, she was too vulnerable. Too everything.

The hot water was taking a long time to warm up, so she left the stopper out of the sink and let the water run over the dirty dishes and pan. She'd just turned to move toward Tilly's Goodwill bag when she heard voices outside on the landing. One voice was Bryan's; the other was someone's she didn't recognize.

Before she could move more than a step from the sink, the door burst open, and two men muscled into the apartment on either side of Bryan. Both held guns. Bryan stood silently between them, his face completely blank.

"What's going on?"

The men were dressed in suits and looked official, yet menacing at the same time. When they saw Sassy, something changed in the air. She got a distinct vibe that made her extremely nervous.

There'd be no pulling of the tiger's tail here. These men weren't on any kind of official business; they were up to no good. And if they got their hands on her, she was sunk. Bryan wouldn't fight them if he thought they were going to hurt her. And even if he did try, with their guns pointed at him, he wouldn't get far.

She reached into the sink behind her and grasped the handle of the saucepan that was finally filling with scalding hot water. She swallowed a gasp as it splashed over her hand. "Bryan? Who are these guys?"

The men didn't speak. One of them started toward her

across the small apartment. When he got even with the table, she pulled the pan from the sink behind her and flung the water at his head.

The man howled as the unusually hot water splashed into his eyes. Bryan was on the other man immediately, and they wrestled to the ground. Sassy pounded her downed guy with the saucepan. It probably wouldn't have worked if he hadn't been so incapacitated by the hot water.

She heard scuffling and grunts behind her. A shot rang out. She froze in mid-swing with the saucepan and turned. It was Bryan with the gun. The first man was on the ground and he was dead, if the blood streaming from his head was any indication. Bryan had a bead on the second man even as Sassy was processing it all.

"Don't move, or I'll put a bullet through your brain, too, just like your buddy there," said Bryan.

Sassy did a double take at the tone in his voice. He sounded so different. Not at all like the Bryan she knew. She studied him a moment. His lip was bleeding and his shirt was torn, but the look in his gray eyes had gone from brooding and sexy to turbulent and deadly.

"Sassy, I need you to get something to tie this guy up with. Find something in the closet or the pantry, okay?"

She nodded and opened several drawers but could only come up with a roll of silver duct tape.

"That'll do." Bryan handed her the gun. "If he fights me, you shoot him." No one spoke as he began strapping the guy to an armchair with the tape. It seemed crazy and surreal, like something she'd see in a Quentin Tarantino movie. In a few moments he was finished.

"Why isn't Otis checking this out? Wouldn't he have heard the gunshots?" she asked. Otis didn't strike her as a guy to stand on the sidelines if he heard gunfire on his property.

After the man was secured, Bryan took the gun from Sassy. "Go get dressed. We're getting out of here," he said.

She didn't move. "Won't Otis have heard the gunshot?" she asked again.

"Otis is dead. They killed him."

Sassy's stomach roiled as she cast a horrified gaze at the man strapped to the chair. Somehow she was able to continue speaking in a level tone. "Don't we need to call the police or someone in law enforcement?"

God, when had she become so inured to all this?

The man in the chair cocked an eyebrow, and she felt the first spurt of anger course through her veins.

"Go get dressed, Sassy," Bryan repeated.

The spurt of anger became a raging sea. "No, dammit. What in the world is going on here? Why aren't we calling the police this time?"

She was glaring at Bryan when the man strapped to the chair spoke up. "Well, that might take some explaining, since I'm with the DEA, along with my dead partner over there."

Chapter 13

December 28
Noon
Mexico

THE AIR WAS hot, but the breeze made the temperature almost bearable as Tomas Rivera sat beneath an umbrella outside the coffee shop surrounded by bodyguards. He sipped the iced coffee and wondered for the hundredth time what the hell he was doing here and why he'd agreed to meet Marcus Ramon.

Right now, his remaining "silent partner" was out of control, and Tomas had more to do than deal with a nephew he had never met before. Going to the U.S. to deal with betrayal by a man he'd trusted for over ten years was out of the question. But Tomas had to do something.

Then he'd gotten this phone call and felt compelled to drop everything. Was he becoming sentimental?

He'd certainly come to a deeper realization of just how alone he was in the world with Carlita gone. He was also beginning to see his own mortality with the events of the past month. That, and it had been such a very long time since he'd spoken to any of his own blood relations.

When Tomas left the Mexican Special Forces at nineteen and switched sides to join the cartels, he cut all ties. His family gladly took the money he sent the first five years. But eventually his reputation—or his family's piousness—grew to the point that they asked him to stop sending any more cash. But he kept himself apprised of their lives, even if they didn't want to know anything about him.

When his youngest sister's son sent the cryptic message to him yesterday, he knew exactly who Marcus Ramon was. He'd known the day his favorite sister, Maria, had married a man from Texas and moved to the U.S. It was apparently a true love match, though the man wasn't Marcus's father.

That man had died in a car accident when Maria was still living in Mexico as an unwed pregnant teenager. He'd left her with an infant son to raise, but she'd met and married Marcus's stepfather, who'd adopted the boy and given the child his last name. Marcus Rivera was now Marcus Ramon.

Although Tomas still kept close tabs on Maria, this call had been unexpected. And right now, he had other business to attend to. He desperately needed to be working his contacts to figure out exactly what his onetime partner was in the process of doing. Tomas had no doubt he was about to be screwed, but just how badly depended on how much information he could gather and how quickly he could gather it. He'd rather be in the U.S. to take care of things personally, but that was impossible.

So here Tomas sat. He recognized the young man approaching his table immediately. Marcus Ramon was tall, with dark hair, sharp cheekbones, and eyes that looked so much like his own that Tomas did a double take. While it wasn't unusual for a nephew to bear such a strong family resemblance, Tomas, who had no children of his own, found himself shocked by the disconcerting sensation of gazing into the familiar face without the benefit of a mirror.

The young man sat across the table without preamble or offering his hand. "Hello, I'm Marcus Ramon, your sister Maria's son." The look in his eye wasn't unfriendly, but it wasn't open, either.

Tomas recognized that look, as he'd worn it plenty of times himself. "I know who you are. Why did you want to see me?"

Marcus didn't appear the least bit intimidated. That surprised Tomas and pleased him in a rather perverse way.

"My mother asked me to come. She'd heard about your wife's passing and wanted to send her condolences."

Tomas tipped his head. "That is kind of her. Maria was always a sweet girl. Is she still happily married to her farmer in Texas?"

Now Marcus did look uncomfortable. He wasn't interested in discussing his parents' marriage.

"Let's cut to the chase. I didn't even know of our 'relationship' until a week ago. I've come with a request from my mother. She'd like to see you."

"It's been twenty-five years, and she's never had much to say to me before now. Why the sudden interest? Does she want some kind of mention in my will?" Tomas heard the bitterness in his own tone but didn't bother to hide it.

He saw a barely perceptible wince in his nephew's eyes. "No, this has nothing to do with *your* will."

Rivera could tell by the way Marcus bit off the words that he'd have liked to add *you son of a bitch* to the end of that sentence.

"She's got lung cancer, Stage four. Just diagnosed. She . . . waited a while before she went to the doctor. They haven't given her much time. She's already under hospice care and would very much like to see you before she dies."

Rivera felt his chest tighten and was surprised at the emotion. Even now, nothing could have persuaded him to risk going to the U.S., except this.

Dying . . . Christ. First Carlita, now Maria. God absolutely had it in for him. He didn't allow the devastation to show as he sat staring down his nephew. He *would* go to the U.S., but only after certain precautions were in place.

"Perhaps we can work something out, but I need you to do something for me first."

"Why would I—" The young man stopped.

Although it was obvious he wanted to tell his uncle to go straight to hell, love for his mother kept him rooted to the rickety café chair.

Marcus swallowed and gave an imperceptible nod. "I'm all ears. What can I do for you?"

Kingstree, South Carolina

"WHAT? YOU'RE DEA?" Bryan heard Sassy's strangled whisper even as he cursed under his breath. The only other sound in the room was the radiator kicking on.

Dumbfounded, Bryan turned to stare at the fed, who was trussed up like a Thanksgiving turkey. Still reeling, he flipped on the radio by the stove, turned the volume up extra loud on a Hispanic station, and bent down to search the guy for wires, even though any wires would most likely have been dislodged during their brawl a few moments before. After making sure the guy was clean, Bryan led Sassy into the bathroom to have a little privacy.

By the time he'd partially shut the door, she was livid. "What is happening? I've not asked too many questions, but now I want to know it all, and I want to know now. Or I'm calling the police and turning myself in. So . . . talk."

She was right to ask. He knew that. The problem was, he didn't have answers for her yet. Nothing about the situation made sense.

The man in the hotel, the train crash, now this. God, how did he even begin to explain it? He couldn't. He barely had a handle on his own suspicions. And if he was right about half of what he suspected, he didn't have a lot of time to explain anything.

"Please, Sassy. Can you just get dressed so we can go someplace safe? I'm not sure how much time we've got."

"Time before what?" She narrowed her eyes. "Time before someone else shows up that you have to kill?"

He ignored the jab for now, even though it hurt. Did she really think he was some common killer?

"These guys must have some kind of backup, and when they don't report in . . ." He let the words hang, hoping she would agree to have her questions answered later. The obstinate expression on her face told him that was probably not happening.

He recognized the determined set of her jaw from years ago when Trey would try to boss her around in classic big brother style. Bryan glanced out at the man still tied up in the seat and knew that despite the salsa music's volume, the DEA agent was straining to hear every word.

Sassy shook her head. "No way. I want answers, and I want them now before I go anywhere else with you."

"I don't have any answers. I've told you . . . everything."

She stared up at him in the tiny bathroom with lightning flashing in her storm-blue eyes, so close he could smell the scent of the floral shampoo she'd used. He was crowding her, but that didn't seem to bother her, even after everything she'd told him about Bobby Hughes.

He gazed down at her, and wrong as it was, he knew that the same longing was apparent in his eyes that had been there earlier when they'd been tangled on the floor of the bathroom. She searched his face with an intensity that had him feeling that same sexual pull as before, but this time it was different, awkward for an entirely different reason.

Despite their "audience" in the other room, this felt more honest than most of his interactions with her, including what had happened between the two of them on the train, because she was no longer putting up such huge walls.

His gaze dropped to her mouth. He was a perverse dog to even think it, but his body was operating under a completely different mandate.

She shook her head imperceptibly. "No," she whispered. "Please don't."

And that was all it took to shut down the lizard part of his brain, or at least to stop his acting on it. Whatever had been going on and whatever he'd been thinking of doing were over. He refocused on her eyes and drew her farther into the bathroom, positioning himself so that he could still keep an eye on the man in the chair but keep her behind the bathroom door and out of the agent's line of sight.

"Sassy, I'm sorry, but I don't have answers for you."

"What is the DEA doing here?"

He shook his head. "No idea. But there's a warrant out for Gavin now with some very serious charges. Someone is intent on dismantling AEGIS or, at the very least, defaming the company to the point where no one will believe anything we say. I think the DEA guy out there is dirty or being run by someone who is."

"Who would he be working for?"

Bryan shook his head. "I'm assuming it has to do with what we've been looking into with the sex trafficking and perhaps even Elizabeth's disappearance. It's the only thing that makes much sense. But I can't piece all the parts together."

She nodded, her eyes no longer stormy but serious. "Where is Gavin now?"

"As far as I know, he's still in Africa with Marissa. I'm not sure that he'll be able to come back anytime soon. Unless he can enter the country covertly, he'll be arrested as soon as he lands in the U.S."

"So what do we do?" she asked.

"You get dressed, and we'll get out of here. I'll see about a car." There was no way they could wait on Bear with a dead man in the yard, but he wasn't going into all that.

"Can't we just take theirs?" she asked, motioning toward the door with her head.

Bryan nodded. "We could, but if it's an agency car, it may be LoJacked. I'll figure something out." He took a final look at that robe that was playing such hell with his libido and his resolve to keep his hands to himself. "I never thought I'd say this, but please, Sassy. Get some clothes on."

He turned away before she could see his face, then added, "If we stay here much longer, we'll be in serious trouble on several levels."

He could feel her stare on his back.

"Alright. I'll get some clothes and change," she said.

He heaved a silent sigh of relief. *Thank God.*

He'd figure out what was happening with her later, but as for the DEA agent, Bryan needed to know who the guy was working for now. Not knowing who and what they were up against was going to get him and Sassy killed, sooner rather than later.

It wasn't Leland, he was sure of that. But someone Leland was in contact with?

Perhaps. And wasn't that just scary as hell?

Bryan wanted answers as much as Sassy did, but he didn't have the time or the stomach to do what would be needed to gather any useful information from the man strapped in that chair. For now, he just needed to get Sassy out of here.

"THERE'S NO LoJACK, I swear," the DEA agent murmured. "You don't have to do this."

With a gun in his hand, Bryan leaned over the man and pressed the barrel into the guy's leg. "Who sent you after us?" His voice had an arctic chill.

"Don't make me do this," pleaded the agent. "He'll kill me."

Bryan shook his head. "Who sent you after us?" He repeated the question with a complete lack of emotion.

Sassy heard the words and recognized Bryan's voice, but her skin crawled as she watched him hold the muzzle of his weapon to the DEA agent's knee and never flinch. She'd just walked out of the bathroom in her Goodwill yoga pants, camisole, and sweatshirt.

"Why are you after us?" Bryan asked.

The agent was shaking his head. Bryan hadn't seen her yet. She was horrified and mesmerized at the same time.

"I don't want to do this, but you're not leaving me any choice. I need answers. You and I both know a government paycheck isn't enough to take a bullet to the kneecap. So tell me who sent you and why, or I'm pulling the trigger. And it won't matter how much they pay you, you'll be walking with a limp for the rest of your life. If you don't bleed out before they find you."

Sassy must have made an involuntary sound of some sort, because both men turned to her. Bryan's gaze lasered into hers. The tension was palpable; her heart thudded in the silence.

His eyes weren't cold, they were expressionless, as if he'd completely disconnected from his emotions. But as he stared at her they changed, filling with a new emotion she didn't recognize right away. He turned back to the man tied in the chair before she could identify what she'd just seen.

"Get your things together, Sassy. We're leaving now." Bryan's eyes refocused on the man, and he didn't look up again. For that she was grateful.

"Okay." She scooped her meager belongings into the top of Bryan's pack and slid their still-wet clothes from the washer into a plastic bag. Anxious to get out of the apartment, she picked up the backpack and headed for the door.

"Meet me in the garage," said Bryan.

"What are y—" She stopped herself from finishing the question.

Did she really want to know what he was about to do?

The two men from the DEA had killed Otis. They had tried to kill her and Bryan. She swallowed hard.

No, she didn't want to know. Instead, she opened the door and moved down the stairs. The sun was high in the sky, and it was a beautiful day. But the air was so cool, her breath made small puffs of white clouds as she exhaled walking down the stairway.

A four-door pickup was parked directly behind the gray sedan. Despite knowing he had to be there, she was stunned to see Otis's body sprawled on the lawn, as dead as the brown, winter-beaten grass.

She loathed the thought of Tilly seeing him like that. How could those men have done such a thing? In the garage, she pulled the drop cloth from the antique Riviera and started toward the body.

She was trying to avoid looking at Otis, yet she was morbidly drawn to looking at the same time, like passing a car accident on the freeway.

"Sassy—" Bryan was beside her and physically turning her body away from Otis's before she could place the cloth over him. "We can't do that," he said.

She knew he was right, but she couldn't stomach the thought of leaving the man lying there dead in his yard for his wife to find.

Even so, Bryan was right. They couldn't and shouldn't do anything to compromise the scene, not with the murderers right upstairs. If and when this all got hashed out in a courtroom, leaving Otis where he lay—untouched— was probably the only way to prove Bryan's and her innocence.

"We're taking Otis's Riviera." Bryan steered her back into the garage. "I'd rather not because it's so distinctive. But I don't know if there's any kind of GPS on the DEA guys' vehicle, and they're blocking Otis's sedan. Since

Tilly's not here yet, it might buy us some time before the vehicle is reported stolen."

"Is that guy up there alive or dead?

"What do you think?" Bryan pierced her with that expressionless gaze that was so unlike the man she thought she knew.

"That's the problem. I don't know what to think. About you. About any of this. What was going on up there? I need some answers, Bryan."

He nodded with that unnerving gaze. "I understand. I want answers, too. Let's get out of here first."

With no more explanation than that, he took his backpack from her, helped her into Otis's pride and joy, and tossed the pack into the backseat before climbing into the driver's seat himself.

"Wait, can't we leave a note for Tilly or something?" she asked.

Bryan raised an eyebrow and gave her an incredulous look. "Do you honestly think that will make any difference? We didn't ding the woman's car in a parking lot. Her husband is lying dead on their lawn. There's no way a note will smooth that over."

The words stung even though they were true. The situation sucked, but he was right. It would take more than a hastily written apology to help Tilly.

Not surprising, the keys were under the visor in the Buick. Otis must have thought the car was safe under a cover in his garage. As they backed out of the driveway, she forced herself to look away from his body and shut away the horror of what Tilly would find when she arrived home after an overly long shift at work. Moments later they were out of the neighborhood and on the interstate.

Bryan's deep voice broke the silence. "I need you to send a text for me."

"What?"

His eyes never left the road as he dug his phone out of his pocket and handed it to her. "The last text stream . . . reply to it."

"I don't understand. Who do you want me to text?"

"Bear Bennett, my friend from Afghanistan that I told you about. He was going to come pick us up at Otis and Tilly's house later today. I need him to meet us somewhere else. Since I don't want to drive and text, do you think you could help me out?"

She would have laughed, but instead she was unexpectedly furious. "Let me get this straight. You killed a man in our hotel room in New York, our train was purposely sabotaged, and two men just tried to kill us back there at Otis and Tilly's, yet you won't text and drive because it isn't safe?" She heard the rising hysteria in her tone but couldn't stop herself.

Bryan turned stormy gray eyes on her for a moment before refocusing on the road. "That's right. I can't control much of the shit show that's been happening since we landed in New York, but that's one thing I can control. So would you please help me out here?"

She took a deep sip of air. He was right, and her being a bitch wasn't going to help their situation. "What do you want me to text?"

Bryan's eyes never left the road. "Change of plans. Need to meet sooner and closer to you. Name the place."

The clack, clack, clack of the tires hitting the seams in the asphalt was the only sound as Sassy typed the message. Within two minutes a text dinged back.

The Hot Pot is off US–52 at State Road about ten minutes outside Charleston. I can be there at 3:30.

Sassy read the message from Bear and watched as Bryan visibly relaxed. Now seemed as good a time as any to ask questions. She was beyond frustrated at not having answers.

"Who were those men? Why were they after us? Please, Bryan. Help me understand."

He sighed and checked his rear-view mirror, otherwise keeping his eyes on the road. "All I know is that they worked for the DEA."

"Yes, I know that part." She kept her voice calm. If she lost it now, she'd never get answers. "But why would the DEA be coming after us? Do you think this has anything to do with Trey? Why would they have killed Otis?" She couldn't keep the accusation out of her tone as she spoke.

He locked his gaze on her a moment. "I don't know. Don't you understand? I have no fucking idea. People are dying because I don't know what the hell is going on and I haven't been able to do anything to stop it so far."

His eyes, which had been so empty and emotionless earlier, filled with misery. She understood, but she couldn't back down even as the moment stretched out and he glanced away to focus back on the road.

She exhaled slowly, fighting her own uncertainty and

fear to speak in a reasonable tone. "I'm not asking for all the answers, but don't hold out on me. Every minute we spend on this"—she threw a hand in the air to encompass the road before them—"is time we aren't working on helping Trey. The judge's ruling is coming fast. We have nothing, and Trey's time is running out."

She shook her head and felt the tears burning at the backs of her eyelids. "This will make me sound like an unfeeling bitch, but Otis is dead. I can't change that. All I can think about is Trey spending the rest of his life in prison. He'd rather be dead than face that."

Bryan's jaw tensed, but he didn't answer. How could he?

Chapter 14

December 28
Midafternoon

An hour and a half later, The Hot Pot was bustling. It smelled of stale coffee, fried food, and diesel fuel as Sassy and Bryan grabbed a table in the back of the diner and settled in to wait on his friend. They ordered coffee from the overworked but friendly waitress.

Bryan hadn't spoken to Sassy much in the car, and the tension radiated off him in waves. Sitting across from each other in the restaurant had a completely different vibe than they'd had on the drive. While he'd been quiet then, he hadn't been so edgy.

Here he was on high alert. His back was to the wall, and he looked around the entire restaurant as they sat, his eyes never lingering long on anything or anyone. Sassy knew he had at least one of his guns; she'd seen him put it in a hidden waistband holster as they'd gotten out of the car. He'd said that he didn't know what was going on, but he clearly wasn't taking any chances.

They'd just finished their second cup of coffee when

his phone dinged with an incoming text. "Bear's in the parking lot. Let's go. We don't want to meet in here."

Sassy nodded.

Bryan dropped some cash on the table for the coffee, grabbed his pack, and steered Sassy to the exit. The blast of cool air was a shock. He nodded toward a dark green pickup on the far side of the lot away from all the other trucks and cameras.

"Over there," he murmured.

He glanced around as they walked to the vehicle. The driver never got out or waved any greeting as Bryan led her to the passenger side and opened the door for her. Warmth emanated from the cab of the truck, along with the scent of cinnamon coffee.

The man sitting in the driver's seat turned to her with a curious smile, and she could see exactly where he'd gotten his nickname. Bear Bennett looked like an advertisement for the Smokey the Bear park ranger campaign. He was built like Bryan, most likely as tall, too. But where Bryan was blonde, Bear had longish dark hair and a full beard, with blue eyes almost the color of her own.

He was all muscle dressed in jeans, work boots, and a dark green fleece pullover with the logo of the U.S. Forest Service on his chest. "Hello, Hollywood!" he thundered.

Sassy should have been a little taken aback, but she was so tired and so grateful to see a friendly face that she figured to hell with it and climbed inside the truck.

Bryan crawled up beside her so that she was sandwiched between the two imposing men. Tension continued to pour off of Bryan, and she could feel him vibrating with it beside her as his hip and knee bumped hers.

Bryan exchanged one long glance with the man in the driver's seat but didn't say hello. He simply nodded.

"Anything?" Bryan asked.

"Nothing. But I parked where no cameras could see us." Bear shifted the truck into drive.

"Good." Bryan moved closer to the door so he wasn't squishing Sassy. "The car we drove is on the other side of the building. Let's get out of here."

"You got it." Bear pulled onto the highway. "I'm Bear." He stuck his left hand across his body and took Sassy's in an awkward shake. His hands were huge, but his grasp on her fingers was light. Sassy felt like a Lilliputian between the two men.

"Hello, Bear. Thank you for picking us up." As she pulled her hand from his, his smile deepened, and Sassy did a double take. The dazzle in the man's grin was palpable and surprisingly disarming at the same time, because it appeared that he was completely unaware of its effect.

"No problem. I'd do anything for Hollywood. I owe him."

Bryan still wasn't talking, but he was shaking his head. "You've got that mixed up. You don't owe me anything," he muttered, checking the rear-view mirrors and looking all around them, just like he had in the restaurant.

"Yeah, well, we're just going to have to agree to disagree about that, my friend. Now tell me what you need," said Bear.

"A safe house until I can figure out what's up."

"You okay with coming to my place? I'm right on the edge of the Francis Marion. We drive through the national forest to get there."

Bryan shifted on the seat again. "We're most likely bringing a boatload of trouble that I can't explain. I don't like getting you involved."

Bear shot him an inscrutable look before shaking his head. "Don't worry about me. I can take care of myself."

Indeed. Sassy stole a glance at the man beside her again. Bear Bennett looked like the kind of man who could very much take care of himself with or without traditional weapons, his lethal smile notwithstanding.

Bear continued down the highway, keeping up a constant stream of dialogue about the national forest. On her right she felt Bryan relax, if only marginally, as Bear rambled on in what amounted to a park ranger patter about the area. The man's voice was radio announcer smooth and easy on the ear, not at all the gruff tone she would have expected from one who looked so wild and imposing.

She started to drift.

"I gotta warn you," said Bear. "I live in the boonies. It's fairly rustic."

Sassy's eyes popped open to see the twinkle in his eye now. "How rustic we talking?" she asked.

"Oh, I have indoor plumbing, electricity, and internet that works half the time. But that's about it."

"Sounds perfect. You had me at indoor plumbing." She closed her eyes again in exhaustion as the road blurred in front of her.

Bear chuckled, and the rumble of his deep laughter

echoed inside her chest. She felt truly safe for the first time since Bryan had locked the door to the sleeping compartment on the train.

"You like your job, don't you?" Bryan asked. "You seem much more at ease."

"Well, medication can be a wonderful thing, but I've tapered off most of that stuff. I actually do yoga and shit to control the symptoms now."

Sassy wondered what kind of symptoms he was referring to, but she kept her eyes closed, not wanting to interrupt.

"The job's been ideal. Not many people, outdoors mostly. I do a lot of horseback riding to inspect the trails. That's been helpful. I don't know how you live in the city, Hollywood."

She felt the muscles in Bryan's leg loosen up as the two men talked, their voices quickly lulling her into that blissful twilight state between waking and sleeping.

"Oh, it's not so bad. But I am happy for you, Bear. You seem really good."

She hadn't considered what a change it had been for Bryan to move from the backwoods of Mississippi to the big city of Dallas. Not that he'd lived in Springwater recently. But she still wondered if he missed it—the creek, the outdoors, the smaller town, the slower pace.

She took another deep breath and everything fell away.

BRYAN FELT SASSY completely relax against him and knew she was down for the count. He wasn't sure of the last time she'd slept, excepting her short nap in the shower. On the train, perhaps?

His body tightened at the memory. God, he was so screwed. He was crazy about her. All those feelings he'd tried to quash down over the years were back, and they were tying him in knots.

He couldn't do this. He didn't stick. He wasn't looking for long-term. Knowing that, he had no business even entertaining the idea. Hell, just thinking about it—

"So is this the girl?" asked Bear quietly.

Bryan was grateful for the interruption, but he didn't want to admit anything, least of all to Bear. "What girl?"

"The girl from back home that you never talked about."

Bryan snorted a bleak laugh. Right, the girl he'd never talked about until he'd thought he was dying, and it was too late.

Bear had heard it all as he'd pulled Bryan's butt out of that burning Jeep and kept him awake until just before the evac arrived. When Bryan had woken up in the hospital, he'd been horrified to find he'd shared his deepest secret, and then survived. But Bear had proven to be a solid confidant.

"Yeah, this is the one," Bryan admitted with a sigh.

"She's . . . she's tiny. Aren't you worried you'll . . . whenever . . ." Bear's voice drifted off.

Bryan snorted. "Jesus, Bear." The man's mouth often got way out in front of his brain. That, in addition to his sometimes debilitating PTSD, was why Bear lived in the middle of nowhere, even though he was a technological genius.

Bear could be making a killing, living in Silicon Valley and working for some start-up telecom company, but Bryan suspected there was no way he could handle the people end of that kind of job right now. So he was a park ranger, where the stress associated with his battle fatigue and the opportunity for horrible social gaffes didn't present themselves often enough to irreparably damage his career.

"We're just friends," insisted Bryan.

This time Bear snorted. "I don't think so. You're a lot of things, but *friends* ain't one of them."

Bryan knew Bear was right, but he didn't want to think about it, especially now. "That's not an issue at this point. Her brother's in jail for a murder he didn't commit, and we're trying to find anything we can to help him before the case comes to trial."

"Who did he allegedly kill?"

"Ever hear of Elizabeth Yarborough?"

Bear nodded and sat up straighter. "'Course. Along with everyone else living in the free world with a television. I thought that guy was spending life in a Mexican prison."

"That guy is Sassy's brother, and the judge is handing down his verdict in six days."

"So what are you doing here if your guy is in jail in Mexico?" asked Bear.

Bryan took it as a compliment that Bear accepted his word that Trey was innocent, when the rest of the country was convinced his friend was guilty as sin. He shifted in his seat as Sassy's limp body rested more firmly against his. "Sassy's a freelance reporter and has been doing some investigating into Elizabeth's disappearance possibly being related to sex trafficking. According to her sources, there was a high-level cartel meeting happening at the same resort where Trey and Elizabeth were staying the weekend she disappeared."

"Do you think the woman overheard or saw something she wasn't supposed to?" Bear asked.

"It seems logical, although why they'd frame Trey instead of outright killing him doesn't make a lot of sense."

"Unless they wanted people to stop looking for a woman who was alive," said Bear.

Bryan stared at him as several ideas clicked into place. He wasn't sure why he hadn't considered it before. Perhaps he just hadn't been looking at the situation with the right touch of mania.

"Authorities never found any evidence of the girl's body or any connection to the cartel, but it's hard to know if those authorities were really looking, with all the corruption involved down there," said Bryan.

"So if the evidence is so squishy, what makes you think it has to do with the cartels and trafficking at all? Do you have anything else?"

Bryan suspected that Bear's fight not to give himself over completely to paranoia was what was keeping him sane. It also made him an excellent backboard for bouncing ideas off of, because the man insisted on proof for others' conspiracy theories.

Mindful of and thankful for that, Bryan explained. "We don't have concrete evidence that this has anything to do with Elizabeth's disappearance, but we've got odd coincidences with where the couple was staying and that cartel summit. Undeniably, there was something going on at the resort the same weekend Elizabeth disappeared. That's been independently confirmed by DEA sources as well as Sassy's. She and my partner, Nick, both found connections between those same cartels at the summit and human trafficking in Mexico and Africa. Another source of Sassy's insisted Elizabeth was shipped to Africa via Venezuela. At this point it's all I have to go on."

Bear leaned forward and flashed a grin at Bryan as he drove. "Just so you know, you're making me feel better by the minute about my issues."

Bryan shook his head but smiled, too, relieved his friend could joke about his own situation now. After the roadside bombing, Bear had initially been a wreck.

"So, what else do you have?" Bear asked again. "You're sticking your neck waaay out here, and I think it would take more than just a coincidence to make you do that."

This wasn't just Bear's neurosis speaking. This was his common sense.

"Trey was my best friend growing up in Mississippi, and shit started happening as soon as Sassy began poking around. She was kidnapped off the street in Niamey, and someone's been dogging her ever since." He explained about the men in the hotel in New York, the train crash, and the men at Otis and Tilly's. "I even think that crazy as it sounds, there was something going on with the train crash. How paranoid is that?"

Bear shrugged. "Given everything else, not so very

much at all. Like they say, you're not truly paranoid when someone really is out to get you."

Bryan snorted. Yep. That's exactly what he'd thought after the train wreck. Sassy shifted in her sleep, and he put his arm around the back of the seat to cradle her head.

"I think Sassy found something, or someone's nervous that she's about to. I need a place where we can put all the pieces together from her investigation with what AEGIS has already." He explained about the complication with Gavin and Nick and the government investigation into his employer.

"Do you think one of those guys is dirty?"

"No. But I do believe Leland is compromised in some way. I don't know how, but there's no getting around the fact that every time I've talked to him, something major has happened. There's no other way anyone could be tracking us."

"Hmmm, maybe . . ."

Bryan glanced at him across Sassy's head. "What are you thinking?" he asked.

"There are all kinds of ways to track people these days, particularly in a city like New York. The technology is amazing and scary as hell at the same time. You've heard of nano drones, right?" Bear stared ahead as they drove through the deeply forested area.

As the sun sank lower behind the trees, Bryan watched the shadows deepen all around. "Of course. The military uses them, and now civilians are using them, too."

Bear nodded. "Well, it's more than just wedding photography and paparazzi using drones to get unique pictures. Those suckers are tiny now. Real sci-fi stuff. You can be tracked by something so small you wouldn't necessarily even see it."

Bryan shook his head. "I don't know if I can go there, man. Why? And who would be after us with that kind of technology? After her? It doesn't make sense."

He had to remind himself that Bear lived by himself because he had issues with paranoia, courtesy of his time in Afghanistan. Bryan wasn't sure that he was ready to dive off that cliff with him just yet. But while Bear might be paranoid, the guy wasn't stupid. Bear could read people, and he had to know exactly what Bryan was thinking.

As if he was reading Bryan's mind, Bear changed the subject. "You need to be able to talk to your team without any chance of being traced. Correct?"

"Right. But not in person. We were going to meet up, but that's out of the question now. It's too risky." *We each have too much at stake.* Leland with Anna and Zach, and Nick with Jennifer. "I don't think any of us distrust each other, it's just we know there is something going on that makes no sense."

"Sounds like you need an online chat of some kind that's data rather than text or voice. That way it can't be traced."

Bryan nodded. "Untraceable, yes. Most of what you just said was Greek, but a video chat with Leland and Nick together would be ideal."

Bear slowed at a deep curve. "Well, you're in luck, 'cause I'm sorta an expert at that kind of shit."

Bryan smiled. Whatever other issues Bear might have, the man was a master with telecommunications.

"I can set up some data protocols and no one will be able to track where you are. You could even do a video conference call through a data app if you wanted to." Bear explained the technicalities as they pushed deeper into the woods. The sunset painted the sky an exotic mix of purple, red, and gold, but there was no snow, despite the bitter cold.

Bear turned from the main road onto a gravel one, continuing on a rutted mud track that curved and twisted quite a ways into the forest, finally petering out in front of a surprisingly modern-looking two-story log cabin. The structure was all square angles and glass, with planter boxes filled with hardy winter evergreens and a deck overlooking a sheer drop. Even in the twilight Bryan could tell that the view of the valley would be spectacular during daylight hours.

Solar panels adorned the cabin's rooftop. On the wood deck, a black wrought-iron table and two massive chairs with upholstered cushions were arranged near a fire pit. Black iron lamps set on posts lit up the darkening night around the seating area. Bryan was momentarily awestruck. The cabin could have been in a magazine for upscale outdoor living. He'd underestimated Bear's domestic capabilities.

Sassy stirred between them.

"Did you do this yourself?" Bryan asked.

Bear nodded. "Mostly. I hired someone to dig the water well and install the solar panels. But I did the other construction. I like my privacy, but I didn't want to live in a shack."

Sassy was rubbing her eyes and taking in the cabin as well. "This is remarkable. I can't wait to see the inside."

Bear smiled shyly as he turned off the ignition and unfastened his seat belt. "Thanks. It's still a work in progress. I finished up most of it in October before the real cold set in, and I've got more work to do in the spring. But it's been warm, and the electricity and water supply have been good so far this winter."

They all got out of the truck and walked toward the cabin. A dog was barking as they climbed the front porch steps.

Bryan stared at Bear in shocked surprise. "You have a dog?" This man had done a 180 since Bryan had known him.

Bear nodded and unlocked the door. "Come meet Lily."

"Lily?" Bryan laughed and followed Sassy inside. Lily turned out to be a four-month-old English bulldog who was growing into her dinner-plate-sized feet and had a serious snorting issue.

Despite her name, she was not going to be a delicate flower. But she was friendly and thrilled to have company. As soon as Bear had opened the door, she'd stopped barking and started dancing on her hind legs behind a baby gate in the kitchen area. Bear lifted the gate, and she obediently went straight outside.

"Okay. I'm officially impressed. You've got her housebroken? I thought you barely were yourself," said Bryan.

Bear shook his head. "I'm not sure who's training who here. It was a lot harder than they said it would be, but yeah, finally. Both of us."

Bryan took a moment to look around. While the cabin had a second floor, the "footprint" was tiny. Bear had gone with the "less is more" decorating method, and in the very modern log house, it worked. A massive sofa and fireplace dominated the main room. The small kitchen area to the side had a breakfast bar and high-backed bar stools made of split logs with cushioned seats.

"Bedroom's up there." Bear pointed to the spiral staircase leading up to a loft. "I'll take the sofa while you're here."

Bryan nodded his thanks. He wasn't going to argue about who was sleeping where. He was so wiped, he wasn't even worried about how he'd deal with lying beside Sassy and not touching her. The thought of being able to close his eyes without being on alert was a siren call.

Bear would take care of them tonight. Bryan felt himself starting to unwind and anticipated the oblivion of his head hitting the pillow.

Lily came trotting back in the front door, and Bryan was headed for the stairs to the bedroom when he felt the buzzing vibration at his hip. There was an incoming text on his cell. Sassy was beside him at the bottom of the staircase and moving to pet the dog. She stopped in midstride to glance at the screen when he pulled it from his pocket.

The text was from Nick, but there was also a photo. At first the message didn't make sense. So Bryan tapped the screen to enlarge the picture, and he heard Sassy's sharp gasp.

The photo was of him and Sassy side by side in two separate shots: one picture was from his driver's license and the other from Sassy's press ID. He still wasn't clear on what he was looking at until he saw the CNN caption emblazoned across the bottom. It was a snapshot of a CNN news bulletin on a television screen:

Fugitives sought for killing spree in Kingstree, S.C.

Under the picture was a one-line text from Nick:

WTF, Hollywood?

Chapter 15

OH SWEET JESUS.

Sassy felt sick as the realization of what she was looking at hit. "They think we killed Otis, too?" She squeaked out the question as Lily sniffed around her shins and feet.

Bryan didn't answer. Instead, he turned to Bear. "Did you say you have internet access?"

"Sporadic, but yeah, I have it. I use a personal hot spot when—"

"Can you get me a streaming news channel?" Bryan interrupted, the tension obvious in his voice.

"Got a preference?" The big man was seemingly unbothered by Bryan's terse tone.

"Try CNN."

Bear nodded and headed to a sophisticated-looking computer setup in the corner on a desk that Sassy hadn't noticed until now.

Her chest felt heavy. She'd been holding her breath.

"They think we killed Otis," she murmured again aloud. "Poor Tilly. That man in the apartment you were talking to . . ."

"Was alive when I left and works for the DEA. He spun the story exactly the way he wanted it," said Bryan. "I didn't expect any less."

"But the evidence. The gun that was used."

"Won't come out until after we've been apprehended . . ."

Or killed in the process. The unspoken words hung in the air. He didn't have to add them, it was understood.

Her brain felt numb, but that didn't last long once Bryan found the news channel. CNN had a live report from the train wreck site that segued into how Sassy and Bryan had killed and robbed a man in a New York hotel, then shot a DEA agent in Kingstree as he was trying to question them about their recent travels to Africa.

The report implicated their connection, as well as AEGIS's, to a drug and human trafficking ring. The newscaster alleged that Bryan and Sassy had killed not only the DEA agent and Otis, but Tilly as well. "The fugitives" were thought to still be in the area.

"No." Sassy couldn't breathe anymore and sat down hard on the bar stool. "They murdered Tilly. Why?"

Bryan's jaw hardened as he watched.

"Killing spree, drug dealers, sex traffickers." The reporter's voice droned on for another horrifying two minutes with just enough truth twisted into the lies to make Sassy and Bryan look guilty as sin.

"But why kill Tilly?" Sassy whispered. "She knew nothing, not even our real names."

"They're tying up loose ends." Bryan's voice was glacial, and he never looked away from the computer screen. "They didn't know how much we told her, or if she talked to Otis before he was killed."

Sassy's stomach roiled. She was going to be sick now. "Bear, where's the bathroom?"

Her tone and the question had him ushering her upstairs to the spartan but modern bath off the bedroom. She hit her knees, lifting the toilet lid just as her stomach revolted. She kept her eyes closed as gentle hands held her hair back from her face and she emptied the meager contents of her stomach. Afterward, as she leaned her head on the cool porcelain and flushed the toilet, she heard water running in the sink behind her.

Too miserable to be embarrassed that her host had seen her throw up, she was just grateful she'd made it to the bathroom in time. When she saw it was Bryan who had bent down beside her to lift her hair and put a cool rag on her neck, she burst into tears.

Surprisingly, it didn't matter that he'd seen her at her most humiliating moment. Sassy wasn't a pretty crier; she never had been. And tonight was no exception. She clutched at his shirt, curled into his chest, and blubbered like a baby.

It was simply too much. She grieved for Otis and Tilly, even the man in the hotel, and the other at the Kingstree apartment, despite their wanting to hurt her. She didn't understand the details yet, but she knew the train wreck had something to do with this nightmare as well. The thought of all those innocent lives lost, and the guilty ones also, overwhelmed her.

Bryan rubbed her back as she cried. Once she thought she felt him kiss the top of her head, but she was beyond caring. Gradually she quieted but found that once her emotional storm had passed, she couldn't bring herself to look up at him.

"My God, Bryan. What are we going to do? By the time we straighten this out, it'll be too late to help Trey. He's going to spend the rest of his life in that jail."

Leaning against the glass shower door behind them, Bryan held her as she curled deeper into his arms. He smelled like Dentyne again. The familiar cinnamon scent was comforting.

"We're going to figure this out, Sassy. It's going to be okay."

"How?" she mumbled into his chest, painfully aware that in addition to all the other indignities, her breath could drop an elephant about now.

"I don't know yet. I need to talk to Nick and see what we can do. This is part of the same people discrediting AEGIS, and I've got to get all the pieces on the table before I can fit them together. I could use your help." He continued rubbing her back in tiny circles.

"But how will we do that and keep our location secret? There's no way we can drive across the country now to meet your friends with our pictures plastered all over the news."

"Bear is handling the communications end of things. That's his specialty. He can help us contact Nick online without being traced. It may take a while to set everything up, but he'll do it." This time she was sure when he kissed the top of her head.

She looked at him then and considered the quiet confidence she saw reflected in his eyes. "Let me get cleaned up a bit. I've got to borrow some of Bear's toothpaste or mouthwash or something."

Bryan pulled her up with him as he stood. A beveled glass medicine cabinet hung over the sink, which was a repurposed galvanized bucket set inside a tiled countertop. He located a bottle of mouthwash and handed it over. She smiled at him in the mirror before taking a swig and gargling.

He left her alone to wash her face.

What are we going to do?

Despite Bryan's assurances everything would be okay, she was very concerned it wouldn't be. How in the world would they clear their names? Turning themselves in was out of the question. She knew how the system worked. By the time they were given the opportunity to present their evidence to those who'd listen, they'd be halfway to federal prison, and entirely too late to help Trey.

She had to find a way to circumvent the process. She'd do anything to save her brother. The only card she had was her job with the AP and her relationship with her editor. Would Howard Spear listen, or at least consider publishing a story that was from an alleged spree killer?

Howard was fairly pragmatic about that kind of thing. Spun the right way, the story could sell like proverbial hotcakes. But she had to have a good angle.

She sighed and stared around the bathroom. She did have a story of sorts. She'd lost her physical notes during the kidnapping in Africa, but she'd stored some things in her online cloud account. If she could access those digital notes, she could write about the trafficking and her experience in Niamey, along with what had happened to her there when she'd started asking questions.

And Howard would publish it. She knew he would. He'd left her those messages earlier this week clamoring for the story. But she needed more, a deeper angle.

Elizabeth couldn't be definitively connected to Sassy's information, at least not with anything that would hold up under scrutiny. The tiny bit of information Sassy did have so far was compelling, but it wasn't proof. She needed to know *who* was behind it all.

That would be a story no editor could turn down, and the kind of evidence that would save her brother as well as get her and Bryan out of this mess.

THE TRAITOR SAT in his office, fuming. One agent that worked exclusively for him and one cartel contractor dead, plus a trainload of people. Christ, this situation was completely out of control and had been for over a month now. How the hell had one woman overhearing a conversation caused so much shit?

If he could, he'd kill Ernesto Vega all over again, for being such a fucking idiot and insisting on taking Elizabeth Yarborough to the brothel instead of killing her outright, as they'd agreed.

It should have all been a slam dunk. The whole world thought the boyfriend had killed the girl. But if that reporter wrote a story detailing what Santos had told her about Venezuela, everything was screwed, and the house of cards he'd so carefully constructed over the years would tumble down within hours.

Why Juan Santos had told anyone outside the organization about the girl, he had no idea. Money, power—whatever the reason, the snitch had paid the ultimate price for double-crossing his employer. Ten years of successfully covering himself and working both sides quite profitably had been blown to hell when Santos had spoken to Sassy Smith. It was still hard to fathom.

He'd had the initial threat of Reese Donovan successfully eliminated years ago . . . by Santos, of all people. Then disaster had struck with that Colton raid earlier this year. The biggest damn coincidence was that Max Mercado's wife had ended up in a hotel room next to Leland Hollis. God, one freaking chance in a million.

After that things had tumbled completely out of control with the Riveras and the Vegas. But even that had eventually worked to his advantage. Everyone had been too busy accusing each other to recognize that their silent partner was the real rat in all of it.

He had to find the reporter, or he was screwed again. And this time there'd be no coming back from it.

STILL FEELING SHAKY, Sassy crept out of the bathroom and down the stairs. She needed to get a grip. She'd been taking care of herself for quite some time now and hated feeling so vulnerable, so helpless. Deep down, she knew Bryan wouldn't take advantage of that, but her adult track record with men stepping up to the plate to help out when she needed it wasn't good.

She stopped midway down the staircase. Bear and Bryan were huddled over the computer, deep in a conversation filled with techno jargon she could barely follow. Bear was typing as Bryan dictated. "Ambushed. DEA killed old man and wife. Use the following apps for communication to avoid detection."

Lily pranced over as Sassy's foot hit the bottom step. Bear looked up from the computer screen and grinned.

"We're using email to contact Hollywood's friend, Nick, so our location can't be traced. No one can find us if we do this, at least not for a while. But it'll take time to download the apps. Those burner phones can be slow. The microprocessors are underpowered, and they don't have enough memory."

Sassy felt her eyes glazing over. Tech speak was not her thing, even when she was at her best. Bear recognized the signs and turned back to Bryan. "I'll need to set up something else if you want to have a real-time conversation."

Bryan nodded. He still hadn't looked up at Sassy or acknowledged her presence. She came closer, the puppy following, and sat down on the sofa to pet Lily as the men continued focusing on the screen.

After a couple of minutes, an apparent reply came through from Nick. Bear read it aloud. "'Are you in a safe place?'" Bear glanced up at Bryan. "What do you want me to say?"

"Tell him yes, but that we need to talk in real time. Remind him to use those apps."

Bryan straightened and turned away from the captain's desk. The unusual piece of furniture with the scrolled edges and antique-style legs seemed out of place here in the rustic surroundings.

"'Not in a place I can talk now,'" read Bear.

"Call when ready," dictated Bryan. His gray eyes met hers and filled with a heat she wasn't expecting; her breath caught.

She swallowed hard, and her hand stilled on Lily's head. "How long will it take them to get everything together?" she asked.

"Depends on how fast they can download the applications and where they are. Could be a couple of hours," answered Bear over his shoulder. "Hey, Lily really likes you."

Typing at a breathtaking speed, he turned back to Bryan. "I'll set things up to bounce the signal around a few places because I don't know what your man Nick is using on his end. I've set the perimeter alarms here, and I've got cameras, too."

Bear pointed to a separate monitor beside the larger screen he was working at and reached for a set of headphones. *Perimeter alarms? Cameras?* Why would a park ranger living in the middle of nowhere have such an elaborate alarm system?

It was on the tip of her tongue to ask when she recalled his words to Bryan in the truck.... *Medication can be a wonderful thing, but I've tapered off most of that stuff. I actually do yoga and shit to control the symptoms now.*

PTSD? Had to be after what Bryan had told her about the roadside bombing.

"Why don't you two get some rest? I'm gonna listen to some music and set everything up for the call. If you want to get cleaned up or . . . something. I can keep watch and work at the same time. The alarm is programmed into my stereo system." Bear put the headphones on and glanced back at Sassy.

He nodded as his fingers flew over the keyboard. Sassy watched, still a bit stunned at the speed at which he typed. What he implied wasn't registering until Bryan reached for her hand and led her toward the staircase.

"Grab whatever you need from the closet," Bear shouted, not realizing how loud his music was. The screaming guitars of Pearl Jam leaked from the headphones across the room. "Top left dresser drawer has clean T-shirts and other stuff."

Sassy blushed. The top dresser drawer had other stuff? What did Bear think they were going to do upstairs in an open loft with him just below them?

Bryan said nothing, raising one hand from the banister to signal his understanding as he climbed the spiral stairs and pulled Sassy along behind him. "I put our wet clothes in Bear's dryer."

"Great." That was a relief. She didn't like the whole commando thing she had going on right now.

He threaded his fingers with hers on the way up the staircase. She held on tightly, not realizing until they hit the top step that she was blowing her intentions of establishing equilibrium.

She hadn't paid attention to the room earlier on her mad dash to make it to the toilet, and she'd been too out of it afterward to notice. Bear's bedroom wasn't at all what she would have expected, but the man was full of surprises and conundrums.

The walls were an unsanded wood stained a deep mossy green. The massive king-size bed was made of black iron and covered with a taupe-colored duvet that had a weave like burlap, but the fabric felt infinitely softer when she reached out to touch it. A huge picture window looked out over what must be an incredible view in the daylight hours. The textures, colors, and everything about the room were all so unexpectedly beautiful, yet completely masculine at the same time. Bear clearly had hidden depths.

She turned to Bryan, wanting to tell him what she'd decided about writing the story. But one look at his face, and she knew he wasn't in any shape to hear it. The deep shadows, along with the lines bracketing his eyes, were evidence of his exhaustion, but there was something else in his expression she couldn't identify. The heat she'd glimpsed downstairs seemed to have disappeared.

"Hey," she murmured. "You should rest for a bit like Bear suggested. Maybe try to take a nap?"

He shook his head. "I'll sleep for hours once I go down."

"Well, why not go for it? Bear's up and will be for a while, from what it looks like. Being tired puts you at risk of making mistakes. Even I know that."

He stared at her a moment, processing it all. She could tell he wanted to argue but couldn't justify a reason. He was about to agree, so there was no sense in poking at him anymore. Coaxing would work so much more effectively anyway.

She didn't try to stifle her own yawn. "I'm tired, as well. Why don't we both lie down? You look entirely too tuckered out to cause me any trouble." She was keeping her voice low, even though she knew Bear couldn't hear them over his heavy metal music.

Bryan cocked an eyebrow at that. But she took his expression for a halfhearted attempt to call her last statement into question. He was fading fast.

"Well thanks, kick a guy while he's down," he mumbled.

Before she could stop herself, Sassy gave him a slow once-over that was meant to cajole. Instead, it backfired and had her blood warming and his eyes opening back up again with more than a little interest.

Attempting to get the upper hand and that elusive equilibrium back, she spoke before she thought it through. "You're not down, not by a long shot, as far as I can tell." She rolled her eyes and laughed.

God, what was she trying to do? She wasn't sure herself anymore. She didn't want to push him away, but she'd been playing this game so long, she didn't know how to pull him closer, either.

She swallowed hard. "Besides, we're just friends, right? I think you'll be safe from me."

Chapter 16

FRIENDS? THOUGHT BRYAN, remembering Bear's comment from the drive earlier. *Not hardly. You sure as hell won't be safe from me.*

His head was spinning. He fought not to let everything he was feeling show in his face, then decided to hell with it. Exhausted as he was, they needed to tackle this thing between them once and for all. He was damn tired of fighting it and walking on eggshells when it came to showing her how he felt.

He thought about their time on the train and silently laughed at himself. It wasn't as if he'd done that great a job of hiding his feelings. He stared at her, letting her see everything—the wanting, the pain, and the anger at her choosing now of all times to tease.

Logically, he knew the banter was her way of distancing him, but he hated that kind of shit. And even though he was dead on his feet, he wanted her so damn bad he couldn't see straight. The expression on her face changed when she realized, too late, what she was dealing with.

"Sassy, I'm not your *friend*. I'm your brother's *friend*. And despite having grown up with you from the time I came to live at Gran's in Springwater, I've pretty much wanted to screw your brains out since you turned fourteen. Surely you've figured that out by now."

He moved closer to her, crowding her into the wall beside the bed. Even with the story she'd told earlier, he knew he didn't scare her. She'd made it perfectly clear that she was comfortable with him physically. That was the problem.

Her story had only confirmed for him that he shouldn't be with her. Hell, he'd practically been responsible for her attack in high school. She'd assumed because of him that all of Trey's friends were to be trusted.

More than anything, he needed to make sure Sassy understood that there was nothing *friendly* about wanting to fuck your best friend's little sister and this steamy double entendre thing she did made him crazy. She didn't seem to understand what a very bad idea her way of dealing with him and their sexual tension was, or whatever the hell *Cosmo* magazine term one wanted to call it. Her verbal sparring diffused nothing for him. If anything, it only made him want her more.

God, he was twisted.

He took a deep breath and tried to chill. But her smell, that scent that had been driving him crazy as long as he could remember, hit him between the eyes and much, much lower.

"Jesus, I left to keep from doing this. To keep from doing you. So don't go talking about *friendship* now, then look at me like you can't wait to go to bed with me. If it weren't for Trey, I'd have you on your back so fast, it'd make you dizzy. I've wanted to be inside you for so long, I can hardly remember a time when I didn't. That hasn't changed. In spite of everything, I still want you all the damn time."

Her eyes widened as he sucked in another deep gulp of air and kept talking. "So don't tease me with sideways glances and then think you're going to cajole me into napping like a five-year-old. I'm not a boy, Sassy, even though I've dreamed about you since I was a teenager. Unless you plan on letting me fulfill that particular fantasy, I think you'd better head back downstairs with Bear. 'Cause if you get in that bed with me right now, we're doing a helluva lot more than napping."

Her eyes had changed during his little speech. But his "big talk" was having no effect, and she'd only moved closer as he spoke.

"So do you want me or not?" she asked, reaching out to touch him. No hint of the earlier taunt was in her voice now.

He kept his hands to his sides and stayed silent. A wave of exhaustion and resignation washed over him, even as his lower body responded with a very enthusiastic and evident *yes*.

"You're scared of this because of what I told you about that summer, aren't you?" She put her arms around his waist and pressed her curvy body against him.

Damn straight. I feel responsible. He was gritting his teeth to fight responding to her touch. But at this point that was futile and, most likely, slightly insane. Fighting his attraction to Sassy was over.

He deliberately unclenched his jaw. "You thought you could trust Trey's other friends like you could trust me."

She looked up, and this time there was nothing but sincerity in her eyes as she rested her chin in the center of his chest. "No, that's not it. I was furious. And I didn't trust you at all. Not after you left Springwater. Not until you came back last summer to help Trey."

The words stung. But in a way, it was an odd relief to know she hadn't gone with Bobby Hughes and the others because of some misplaced confidence in him.

"You shouldn't trust me now, either," he murmured.

"But I do. You're different."

She pulled him closer, and he felt every inch of her as she took her own shaky breath. His defenses melted like butter on a hot griddle. He'd lost all perspective with her. Of their own volition, his arms went around her, and he was done.

Her voice was muffled against his chest, but he heard each word. "What happened with those boys had nothing to do with their relationship with Trey. If anything, they were weaker afterward because of their friendship with him."

Exactly, he thought. *I'm no different. I'm completely vulnerable to you. To whatever you want to do to me.* But that kind of exposure, that kind of loss, hurt too much. He couldn't risk losing another part of himself like that again. He'd given it up voluntarily once when he'd left

Springwater. Left Gran and the only family he knew, including his best friend. He'd done that for Sassy.

He'd opened up and risked letting himself care again in Afghanistan with men who'd become like family, and he'd lost his team, his job, everything. Afterward he'd shut that part of himself down and made a promise. No more risk taking in relationships for him.

To open himself to Sassy now scared the hell out of him. He'd been protecting himself and his heart for so long, it was second nature.

"I want you, but I'm not interested in a long-term relationship with anyone, so I'd be an ass to start something with you. I won't be 'that guy.' Not with you. Not with my best friend's sister. It's wrong." But he was still holding her as he spoke.

"I want you, too, Bryan. Hasn't that ever occurred to you? This wanting is a two-way street. I get it that you feel awkward about my being Trey's sister. But does that make me undesirable or not good enough for you?"

Sassy was changing all the rules and turning his argument on its ear. She sidestepped away from him. *Thank God.* It was the only time in this conversation that she'd backed off. But what she was saying was all wrong and upside down, yet she was finally retreating.

His brain scrambled to catch up to what was happening, because his body had pretty much been running the show since he'd taken her hand and started up the staircase. They were finally getting to the heart of the matter, but Sassy was steadily backing away from him toward those same stairs, and she was mad as hell.

"Screw that. I've spent my whole life fighting the feeling of not being good enough. Growing up in a trailer house in the middle of a cotton field, I was the girl from the wrong side of the tracks who was looked down on by everyone in town because of what my mother was. It was the reason I worked my butt off to get out of Springwater. To get away from all that. Trey did, too. He just worked on the football field to do it. I sure as hell don't want that attitude from you."

She stood at the top of the staircase with her arms firmly crossed across her chest. Bryan sucked in a final gulp of air. For the first time in what felt like hours, he didn't smell her when he inhaled. She had it all wrong, but she was leaving him alone, and that was what he wanted, wasn't it?

"Sassy, that's not what I've been saying."

"Then what? It sounds an awful lot like you want me, but you think that's a bad thing because I'm defective in some way. And you're fighting it all the time. Well, let me take temptation the hell out of your way. I want someone who wants me and can't wait to be with me. Someone who is excited to be with me, not dreading the fact that he's crazy about me. So get over yourself, Bryan Fisher."

She glanced down at the very evident bulge in his jeans and eyed him with grim distaste. "Take care of whatever needs taking care of and spare me the pity fuck from my brother's best friend."

Sassy turned to leave, not stomping as he would have expected, but softly, as if she was concerned the steps might break if she stepped on them too hard.

Her walking away was what he'd wanted, right?

No. Not by a long shot. God, he was an idiot.

It was hard to catch his breath now, but he pushed the words out, because she had to know.

"Pity would be the very last thing on my mind."

SASSY HESITATED ON the staircase, her heart breaking and her blood boiling. That Bryan had made her feel this way about herself was such a kick in the teeth. She'd fought her entire life against feeling "less than" and was furious with herself that she'd allowed a man, even this one, to make her feel that way again. Especially about sex.

"Pity would be the very last thing on my mind." Bryan's voice sounded rough and strained. Against her better judgment, she turned back to him. He was still beside the bed, and he looked . . . miserable.

Good. He deserved that after how he'd made her feel.

But his face was awash in regret. "I can't let you think that. Even though it's giving me exactly what I want. I can't let you walk away believing that."

"And pray tell, what *do* you want?" She sighed.

He walked toward her and took her hand, gently tugging her up the steps. "I want you, Sassy. I've wanted you for as long as I can remember. That's why I left."

"But why do you think you still can't have me?"

He took her hands in both of his. "Because I'm the one who's broken. Everyone I cared about in Afghanistan died. There's a loyalty issue here that's very difficult for me to get past. I don't have many close friends. Your brother is one of the few I have left. I wasn't so sure how he'd take it."

His grip tightened on her fingers. "And I didn't know how you felt about me these past few months. Every time we've been together since last summer it's been . . ."

He looked down at her and shook his head as he let go of her hand. " . . . impossible. I can't let myself be vulnerable again in that way. Everyone I have ever cared about has died on me except for you and Trey."

She swallowed hard. With all her big talk, she'd almost convinced him that she didn't care. Her own defense mechanisms had gotten in the way. She moved into him, covering his heart with her hand. "I was protecting myself, too, you know. Not wanting to be vulnerable. I've been doing that for a long time and for a lot of reasons. I'm not going anywhere, I promise you. And Trey . . ."

She thought of her big brother and wondered for a moment what he would think. If, given his current situation, this would be something he would ever even know. " . . . Trey will be okay with this. He loves you like a brother, Bryan. He'll want to see you happy."

The hint of her flirty smile was back. "I, on the other hand, have slightly different feelings for you."

He shook his head, reached for her hand again, and gave it a slight squeeze. "Sassy, you're killing me."

She grinned at him and tipped her head up. His eyes, always so serious, were filled with the heat she'd only caught glimpses of these past months. He pulled her closer and, suddenly shy, she looked down, pressing her face against his chest. He was so ridiculously tall compared to her, warm and solid beneath her cheek. She felt his heart beat steadily against her temple.

"Tell me now if this isn't what you want." The words rumbled through his chest, reverberating inside her.

She didn't say anything. She wanted this. She wanted this badly.

He tipped her chin up. There was a question in his eyes, but he must have seen what he was looking for, because he leaned into her, brushing his lips against hers.

He was so gentle, she could have easily pushed him away or moved back if she felt uncomfortable. But she was ready. She leaned forward and into the kiss, opening her lips slightly, and licking into his mouth. He made a sound— almost like he was in pain—and then his hands were at her hips, and he was picking her up and pulling her lower body into his.

She wrapped her legs around his waist as he turned and walked to the bed. When he leaned forward to lay her down on the mattress, she loosened her ankles. He stood above her, staring into her eyes with a look of such intensity that she couldn't look away. He only broke eye contact when he pulled his sweatshirt over his head.

She came back to herself for a moment. They were about to have sex, and he didn't know yet. Didn't understand that she'd never done this before. Would he be horrified or turned off or—

His hands settled on his belt buckle, and her thoughts scattered. He raised an eyebrow as if to ask *You're sure?*

She nodded. Yes, she was sure. She wanted him. She wanted this with a fervency that once would have frightened her because of the vulnerability she was about to expose. But she'd had more than enough time to think about it.

As the heat pooled deep in her belly, she found that she wasn't thinking much at all anymore. She just wanted Bryan. She watched, mesmerized, as he slid his jeans and boxer briefs down to the floor.

But she should tell him, shouldn't she? After everything they'd just talked through. Before he got so far down the road, so to speak, that he couldn't turn back.

It wasn't fair to not let him know, even though the thought of him stopping was more than she could stand. This was as vulnerable as things got, and she'd meant to explain the why of it all on the train. But the accident had stopped her, and now . . . here they were.

Shouldn't she tell him that she was a virgin?

Chapter 17

BRYAN STOOD AT the edge of the bed, staring down at Sassy. She was everything he'd ever wanted. She was also his best friend's sister, and he was about to have sex with her.

You're thinking too much.

That's exactly what he'd told Sassy on the train. Her gaze met his, and she smiled tentatively. He put a knee on the mattress and knelt down to slip off her leggings. She sat up partway and peeled off her own sweatshirt, along with the camisole. Then she was lying before him . . . gloriously naked.

He stood back a moment and stared, struck dumb by the lush curves of her body.

She smiled again, but there was something off about her expression. "You're making me nervous, you know. Not saying anything."

"I just want to look at you, savor this. You're so damn beautiful."

She snorted a laugh. "I can't beli—" She stopped, and her expression sobered. "Thank you for saying that. I think you're beautiful, too." She reached for his hand and pulled him down to the bed.

He worried about crushing her and was careful to lie beside her rather than on top of her. She rolled into his side and ran her fingers tentatively over his chest, before her hand headed south. He hissed in a deep breath as she wrapped her fingers around him.

"I never thought—" She stopped.

"You never thought what?"

"I never thought we'd be like this . . . together. I've wanted it. I just never thought it would happen for me."

Something about that statement struck him as odd. But he was too tangled up in lust and exhaustion to puzzle it out.

"I didn't think it would happen, either," he said. That was unquestionably true. As much as he'd wanted Sassy over the years, he'd never thought he'd end up in bed with her.

She was starting to say something else, until he brushed a fingertip across her nipple. She exhaled when he leaned over to kiss her breast and work his lips farther south, past her belly. She was breathing hard as he kissed the inside of her thighs, then he was between her legs with her hands in his hair.

He loved going down on her. The sounds she made, the taste of her. Moments later, her entire body stiffened in his arms and she arched her back, coming in a lightning-fast rush. She whispered his name once as he kissed his way back up her stomach to lie beside her. When he gathered her close, she curled into him, sighing once more.

He grinned. A speechless Sassy was a rare thing.

Rolling onto his back, he pulled her across the top of his chest, nuzzling her neck at the same time. She was limp as he stretched her across his body. He ran his fingers down her back, cupping her ass in his palms. After a moment she sat up, pressed her hips into him, and leaned her head back.

Her hands ended up beside his head, her knees on either side of his stomach. He was directly against the slick heat of her. He wanted to be inside her so much right now that his own hands shook as he lifted his fingers to touch her face.

She opened her eyes and moved against him. "I need to tell you somethi—"

His eyes pleaded with her as he put a finger to her lips. "Tell me later?" He might come before he got inside her if she didn't stop that.

She smiled and leaned down to kiss him, her nipples brushing against his chest, sending a tidal wave of heat straight to his cock. As she slid across him, he reached behind her to guide himself inside her.

She gasped and took their kiss deeper, leaning forward on her knees to press herself down centimeter by centimeter. He closed his eyes. It felt incredible even as she paused a moment and took a deep breath. *Damn.* She was so very tight. He wasn't halfway inside her, and it felt like—

His eyes flew open to see her brow furrowed in a tiny grimace.

God, no.

Suddenly the odd words earlier made perfect sense. *I never thought we'd be like this . . . I never thought it would happen for me.* Now he knew exactly what she'd meant.

But . . . she couldn't possibly be. Not after all her brazen talk of the past six months. Maybe it had just been a long time since she'd had sex? God knew it had been for him.

He held himself back even though his hips naturally wanted to roll forward and press deeper. He studied her face. Her eyes were scrunched closed as she took another audible breath and pressed herself all the way down the length of him, burying him inside her. She opened her eyes to meet his gaze and froze, the expression there telling him everything he suspected.

She'd never done *this* before.

Sassy was a virgin. Or had been until about thirty seconds ago.

"Why didn't you tell me?" he whispered.

She swallowed hard, pressed her lips together, and gave her head a tiny shake, tightening those muscles around him that were already so impossibly snug.

And despite what he knew was happening here, he fought his body's natural response, because this had suddenly become all about making her first time special rather than losing himself inside her.

He was Sassy's first time. If he thought about that too much, he'd lose it.

"Are you okay?" He loosened his grip on her hips and started to pull away.

He needed to get out of her, now. He wasn't even wearing a condom. They'd gotten to this point like it was his first time as well as hers. And there was no excuse for that, except his own stupidity and the fact that he wanted her like he wanted his next breath.

Of course, the damage was already done. This was reckless as hell on both their parts. He knew he was clean, and, given the circumstances, she most likely was, too. But there could be other long-term consequences.

"Wait. Please. I'm okay." She pressed down further against him. "I just need a second to . . ."

She pulled herself up, and the exquisite sensation had him taking a deep breath himself. He knew they needed to stop, to talk. But he had to be as gentle as possible.

"Sassy, I'm not wearing a—"

She nodded, and that action was more than his body could stand. Of their own volition, his hips rolled forward, pressing deeper into her, once, twice.

"I can't believe you are giving me this . . . gift, but I can't—" He searched her face as he pushed into her a third and final time. Gripping her hips, he pulled back and lifted her up and away from him as he came, in what felt like a free fall from the edge of a cliff.

SASSY LAY BESIDE Bryan and stared at the ceiling. She was a little scared to look at him. He was on his back, but he hadn't turned to face her yet. She didn't have a clue what to say.

I didn't want to tell you I was a virgin because I didn't think we'd have sex if I did?

That would be stating the obvious. No way he'd have done anything if he'd known. Lying beside her, he was still so very quiet. She had to say something. She just wasn't sure where to start.

Then the moment was gone as he stood and walked into the bathroom without a word or a backward glance.

Her heart stuttered. Without question, she'd gone into this with false pretenses. Was he mad? Sad? Irritated? She had no idea.

She took an audible breath. "I'm sorry I didn't tell you about . . . before," she whispered to herself.

She heard water running. A few moments later, he was back to sit beside her with a warm washcloth. Without speaking, he gently wiped it between her legs.

Somehow the act felt more intimate than what they'd just done. As he finished, she could feel his eyes on her face, but she couldn't meet his gaze. Instead, she felt a lump in her throat.

What could she say to this man?

"Thank you," she finally managed.

Bryan shifted his weight on the mattress. "Why didn't you tell me? I could have made this better for you if I'd known."

She wanted to laugh, but she felt the maddening trickle of tears burning at the edges of her eyes.

"Don't worry. It was fine for me." She heard her own derisive, bitchy tone but couldn't stop herself.

If he continued to be this nice, she'd fall so hard and so fast she'd never recover. She needed to make him mad, to hurt him. It was her old standby and the only way she could think of to protect herself.

"Don't do this, Sassy. Please." She could see him shake his head out of the corner of her eye, but his tone was filled with resignation, not anger. "I'm really sorry. I didn't mean to hurt you."

As much as she wanted to protect herself, she couldn't let him think that. "You didn't hurt me," she murmured, turning to look at him. "I just . . . it needed to be done."

"Okay, now you're making it sound like losing your virginity was the equivalent of having a root canal. The sound you hear is my ego shattering." He gave her a grim smile. "Why now?"

"You mean why not in high school or college?" She finally rolled onto her side to look him squarely in the face.

He nodded.

She laughed, but there was no humor in the sound. "My mother was the town drunk and, occasionally, the town whore. I wanted out of Springwater so badly that there was no way in hell I was sleeping with anyone in high school. And yes, what happened with Bobby Hughes and company had something to do with it."

Bryan winced, but she kept talking.

"After that I got pretty particular about who I trusted. And I never found the right guy who'd . . ." Her voice trailed off.

Be patient enough to deal with me and my baggage.

Over the years, she'd assumed there would be ghosts

from the past when she finally had sex. But up till this moment, there'd been no memories of that awful night intruding. It had just been Bryan, and despite what he thought, the experience with him had been amazing.

But how she'd ended up still being a virgin at twenty-six years of age was not something she wanted to discuss with anyone, much less the man who'd relieved her of the "burden."

"It needed to be done," she repeated irritably, embarrassed at having to explain.

At the same time she knew this wasn't about Bryan. It was about her and how she'd put up walls to protect herself since she was a teenager. Now it would be about tearing those walls down. She just wasn't ready to begin the demolition project tonight. How she dealt with Bryan had to fundamentally change. But exposing herself to him like that was riskier than anything else she'd ever done. If he rejected her now, she'd never recover.

Bryan's forehead wrinkled in confusion. "But this was a big deal for you. It was a big deal for me, too. To be your first. That's an amazing experience to give me. To give to anyone. I just wish I'd known. I would have . . ." He sighed in what she was beginning to recognize as frustration with himself.

"Worn a condom?" she asked, piling on instead of backing off. It was so much easier to go back to automatic pilot and old patterns than to risk any more of herself.

"Well, yeah." His cheeks turned pink, but he didn't look away from her. "Among other things. Don't worry. I'm clean and tested. I know you don't have any issues with that, but there's the more immediate aspect of all this. Where are you in your cycle?"

Hell to the no. While she didn't ever want him to think that what they'd just done had hurt her physically, they were not having *this* conversation.

"If I got you pregnant just now, I'll do whatever you want," he said.

Oh good lord.

She hadn't thought the mortification could be any worse. She'd been dead wrong. He was making her feel like shit without meaning to. And it was so not his fault.

He thought he was just being responsible, but she couldn't stand it anymore. He had to stop talking like this. Her options were to lighten the mood, or shut this conversation down cold. Otherwise, who knew what he'd say or do . . . and how much further she'd fall.

"Don't worry. I won't make you marry me." She glanced up at him to see how that hit him.

He never even blinked. "I would, you know. Marrying you wouldn't exactly be a hardship."

She stared at him, completely flabbergasted. What did that mean? He'd said he wasn't looking for anything long-term.

The lump in her throat was back. He was watching with such earnest concern, she couldn't come up with any kind of snappy response other than "Don't sweat it. I'll deal with it."

"But you'd tell me, right? If you were pregnant?"

Probably not. But she couldn't look away from him. She'd been expecting his expression to be one of horror or laughter when she made the marriage comment. Instead, she was stunned by the sincerity in his gaze.

"Of course," she mumbled and stared back at him, at a complete loss over what to say.

She looked around the room, spying a robe hanging on the back of a closet door. Getting up and leaving seemed the best way to escape what had become a most uncomfortable conversation.

"Do you think Bear would mind if I borrowed that?" She nodded toward the garment.

Bryan searched her face once more, the look in his eyes so tender she might start to weep again despite all her efforts to maintain her topsy-turvy equilibrium. He seemed to be trying to decide whether or not to say something more himself. She desperately hoped he wouldn't.

"Hey, Hollywood, you guys awake up there?" shouted Bear from downstairs. "Your friend is ready to talk."

Thank you, Jesus. She was saved, for the time being. Sassy cocked an eyebrow and gave Bryan a rueful smile. "So are you ever going to tell me why they call you Hollywood?"

Bryan exhaled, and the moment and whatever he'd been about to say were gone. But the look in his eyes was heartbreakingly soft.

"That's a long story we don't have time for today. Maybe another time?" He pulled the edge of the spread over her hips, smiled softly, and she was lost.

Who was this man?

"Yo, Hollywood!"

"Be right there," called Bryan. Sassy pulled the bedspread to her chest as his gaze locked with hers. Now she could feel a blush heating her face.

"I'm sure Bear will be fine with your borrowing the robe." He rolled to a sitting position, tucked more of the covers over Sassy, and started pulling his clothes back on. Against her will, her heart melted a little more.

Standing, he zipped his jeans but never took his eyes from hers. "You are beautiful, you know." Before she understood what he intended, he was leaning down and kissing her, softly but thoroughly. She was so shocked, she didn't respond, even as he walked away barefoot down the steps.

Chapter 18

WHAT THE HELL was he doing?

Bryan shook his head as he walked downstairs. He had just done exactly what he'd promised himself he wouldn't. He'd made the colossal mistake of letting his guard down to the point where he had allowed himself to make love to Sassy. But try as he might, he couldn't be sorry.

His only regret was that this was going to hurt people. Sassy most likely and, of course, Trey, if he ever found out. Bryan didn't include himself, because he already knew he was toast. He had accepted that fact when he'd kissed Sassy the first time in the hotel in Constantine. There was no way he was making it out of this insanity with his heart intact.

By the time he hit the bottom step with those unhappy thoughts, Bear was vibrating with impatience.

"Your friend Nick is ready to chat. We can do this

with a voice call or even by video conference, since you are both using data only. There's no way it can be traced tonight. What's your preference?"

Bryan's head was still reeling from the past hour as he sat beside Bear at the desk.

"Video." There was something reassuring about seeing another man's face and reactions when this much was at stake.

Bear tapped a few keys, and a window popped open on the computer screen. Nick Donovan was in the center of the monitor with Jennifer Grayson seated next to him. Beside them were Leland Hollis and Anna Mercado. Leland's leg was propped on a coffee table in a walking boot. A crackling fire was visible behind the two couples.

Bryan recoiled internally. He hadn't been expecting Leland, and the expression on Nick's face was grim. But Nick was ex-CIA; he'd always looked grim until earlier this month, when Jennifer had appeared on the scene.

"Who the hell are you?" Apparently Nick could only see Bear on the screen.

Bear smiled into the monitor's camera. "I'm just tech support. Here's Hollywood." The big man stood and gave Bryan his seat. "I'll put you on the headphones so you can have some privacy. I'm going to fix something to eat."

Privacy? Bryan shook his head. *What for?* Nick had invited the entire flippin' world. "That's not necessary. We need all the help we can get to figure out what's going on."

He caught a glimpse of Sassy coming down the stairs in Bear's huge robe. He might have to eat those words. He didn't want her here, looking like that. Was it as obvious to everyone else that they'd just had sex?

The velour garment came to her ankles. Seeing her in another man's clothing bothered him. If she was going to wear any man's clothes, they should be his.

What the fuck was happening to him? He shook his head to clear that bit of insanity and focused on Nick and Leland, reassuring himself with Bear's earlier declaration that no matter what, this call couldn't be traced.

He was surprised when Jennifer started the conversation. "You guys in a safe place?" she asked.

Bryan nodded. "You?"

Nick put his arm around Jennifer as he spoke. "Safe as we can be for now. We're at Gavin's lake house."

Bryan wasn't sure how they'd managed to gather there with the cloud of suspicion Gavin was under, but it made sense. Once the cabin had been searched for evidence and ruled out by investigators, the house would no longer be on anyone's radar.

Sassy stood just out of sight of the computer monitor's camera. "Is it okay if I join you?" Her scent wrapped around him once again and messed with his head. He so did not need this right now. But she seemed oblivious to her effect on him.

Bryan nodded without looking up at her. *Why the hell not?* They were practically having a slumber party here. This was not what he'd envisioned when he'd planned to talk with Nick.

Jennifer smiled as Sassy came into view on the camera. "I'm so glad you're okay. I was worried for you."

Sassy nodded, surprisingly quiet, and took the seat beside the desk Bryan had just vacated. He glanced at her, but she didn't meet his gaze.

Was she regretting what had happened upstairs between them? He wasn't sure, but right now that was the least of their problems and definitely not something he should be focusing on.

Could he do that?

"What is going on with you, Hollywood?" Leland's deep, Southern-fried voice sounded so clearly through the computer's speakers, he might have been across the room rather than across the country.

Was it that obvious?

Bryan was shocked by the question before he understood what Leland was really asking. And wasn't that the question? What *was* going on with him?

Bryan was still recovering from the shock of seeing Leland there on screen with Nick and Jennifer at the cabin. Nick was the most suspicious-natured person on the AEGIS team. But if Leland was clear in Nick's eyes, the man must be clean.

Even so, it bugged the hell out of Bryan that every time he'd talked to Leland about where he and Sassy were, someone had found them. The obvious answer to that was to avoid discussing their location. But there was no way to go forward until he dealt with the issue head-on.

"Someone is tailing us," said Bryan. "They have been since we got back to the U.S. First there was a break-in at our hotel room in New York, then the train crash. Leland, it happened every time I talked with you. I think someone has a trace of some kind on your phone. You need to do a sweep."

Leland tilted his head as he peered back into the screen but said nothing.

"What are you saying exactly?" Nick leaned forward with an intensity that would have intimidated most people, but Bryan was used to it.

"I'm not accusing Leland of anything. However, I am pointing out the obvious. Someone knows Leland is the contact person in AEGIS we all call when we need something. Whoever this is has a bug or a trace of some kind on him. Our conversation is going to be over before it starts if you won't accept that and do something about it."

Leland nodded, looking unhappy but resigned. "Of course I'll do something about it. I just can't figure out how anyone could've gotten to me or my phone. I haven't been anywhere or with anyone that had access since this start—" He stopped. "Holy shit," he muttered under his breath.

"What?" asked Bryan and Nick together.

Anna's eyes widened in alarm as Leland stood.

"I don't want to believe this. Give me a minute." Leland hobbled away from view of the camera with one crutch.

"Do you need your other crutch? It's in the bedroom with Zach," said Anna. There was a garbled reply, most likely positive, since she stood as well.

Nick glanced over his shoulder at something not visible onscreen. "Okay, he's checking it out, in another room I might add. What do you have?"

"The train wreck. This sounds crazy, but after everything was over, it looked like some of the drone attacks I saw in Afghanistan."

"Tell me about the crash.". Nick took a sip from a coffee mug on the low table before him.

"After the initial derailment, the back of the train was intact and undamaged. Several minutes later, there was a massive explosion."

"But couldn't that have just been a secondary detonation from a leak inside the crash?" asked Nick.

"When I saw the train right after the wreck . . . when we got out of our sleeper car, the back cars were on the track and the least 'disturbed' part of the entire wreckage site. They hadn't been touched. It doesn't make sense that something in the back of the train exploded after the initial impact up front."

Bryan heard the fire popping over the computer microphone as everyone absorbed the information. Jennifer leaned her head against Nick's shoulder, twisting a ring around her finger. Anna settled into the sofa cushions.

"Then the attack on Tilly and Otis, the nurse and her husband who helped us in South Carolina. I can't figure out why that happened, but I have to believe it all goes back to things that went down in Africa. I don't know if it's wrapped up with the human trafficking or the cartels themselves. But someone is driving all of this. I just can't pull the pieces together. That's why I wanted to talk. I thought if we laid everything out from the very beginning, it might make more sense."

Nick nodded. "When do you think this all started? When Jennifer was taken?"

"No," Sassy spoke up for the first time. "If everything is connected, it started long before that. It started last summer, when Elizabeth was taken. She and my brother were at the resort in Mexico where Tomas Rivera and Ernesto Vega were meeting at the same time. Elizabeth disappeared and Trey was found passed out in the boat they'd rented, covered in blood. He was arrested almost immediately for Elizabeth's alleged murder."

Anna nodded. "At the end of November my son was taken by the Riveras, and Leland went to Mexico to get him."

Nick took a sip of his coffee. "When Anna and her son were safe and it was over, Carlita Vega, Rivera's wife, was dead in what Rivera says was a drone attack on his compound that no one has yet claimed responsibility for. Carlita's brother, Cesar Vega, died the next day, trying to kill me."

Jennifer reached for his hand as Nick kept talking. "While I was recovering from the gun battle at Rivera's compound, Jenny was taken from my brother's home by Ernesto Vega in retribution for his own brother's and sister's deaths. Vega put Jenny in a cartel-run brothel in Mexico and joined forces with Tomas Rivera to get even with me and AEGIS because he thought we were the people responsible for killing their loved ones."

"How did Jennifer get away from the brothel?" asked Sassy.

Bryan turned in his chair to answer her. "Nick and I went to get her out. We had help from an informant. But there was a deliberately set fire. Everyone at the brothel was killed in an ambush, except Jennifer. It didn't make sense then, and it doesn't now. That place was run by Rivera, but Vega was supposedly cooperating with him at the time." Bryan turned back to the screen. "Do you think Vega was playing both sides?"

Nick took another sip of coffee as he contemplated an answer. "In Algeria, just before we left Africa, Rivera told me he'd learned that someone else was responsible for the attack on his compound where his wife died and the vet clinic where his brother-in-law Cesar was killed. He claimed that someone he trusted had betrayed him. By then Ernesto Vega was already dead. So it couldn't have been Vega that Rivera was referring to. If what Rivera said about a betrayal is true, it makes sense that the same person could have been responsible for the attack on the brothel and the attack on the Niamey dig site as well."

Bryan hadn't been there when the Niamey dig site attack occurred, but he'd seen the aftermath. The camp had been burned to the ground. Several Tuareg guards had died, along with a professor from Abdou Moumouni University, but no foreigners. So there wasn't much news coverage for what had been labeled a "tribal uprising" in an area of Africa that hadn't seen "tribal uprisings" in decades.

Nick was still explaining his part of the story to Sassy. "When Jennifer got home from the brothel kidnapping in Mexico, Rivera came after her and bombed her house. He came after her in Niamey last week, too. There was an actual contract on her life. Rivera thought killing Jenny would be the best way to get revenge on me for what he saw as my part in killing his wife, Carlita. Until a few days ago, he was convinced that I had something to do with bombing his compound where Carlita died. In Skikda, he claimed that he knew who the person was who had 'betrayed his trust.'"

Bryan nodded. "So someone else has been playing both sides against the middle, maybe trying to pit the two cartel leaders against each other. The question now is who?"

"And why did Jennifer end up on that truck with me?" asked Sassy. "Was it all about revenge, or was someone else after her? Rivera had her in Mexico at the brothel—why didn't he just kill her there if that's what he was all about? At the time he still thought Nick was responsible for his wife and brother-in-law's deaths." Sassy leaned toward the computer screen. "Sorry, Jennifer, I have to ask."

Jennifer nodded her understanding at the bald statement. Sassy kept talking.

"If Tomas Rivera wasn't responsible for the attack on the Paleo-Niger Project, who was? And why did they take you and Nick from the site and put you on those trucks, instead of just killing you there at the dig site? Every other time Rivera's men got near you, they tried to kill you."

Jennifer stared a moment, not speaking, along with Nick. That hadn't occurred to either of them. Finally Nick spoke up. "You're right. Taking us from the dig site wasn't about revenge. Rivera made it clear that his attempts to hurt Jennifer were all about hurting me. Killing her would have been the most painful thing for me."

Sassy nodded. "But taking Jennifer from the dig site was different. Who did that and why? Did she see something in Mexico she wasn't supposed to?"

"I considered that after the house bombing," said Nick, "but we never came up with an answer."

Bryan listened as Sassy put pieces of the puzzle together that his team had been too close to see. Her reporter's mind was making some connections he hadn't considered before.

"I've been over and over the time there in Mexico," said Jennifer. "It's fuzzy. I was drugged until just a few hours before Nick arrived. I only talked to one of the girls. Mia." She shook her head and turned the ring on her middle finger once more.

"Could you have overheard something from her that would explain or reveal who this other person w—" Sassy quit talking.

Bryan glanced over to see what had interrupted her train of thought. She was riveted to the screen and leaning even closer.

"Jennifer, could you hold your hand up to the camera, please?" Her voice shook when she asked the question.

Bryan turned to her as Jennifer's hand filled the screen, along with a very distinctive ring—an older silver design with a large crystal stone in the center and several smaller crystals around it.

"Oh my God," Sassy whispered. "That's Elizabeth's engagement ring."

KAY THOMAS

Chapter 19

"How do you know that's Elizabeth's ring?" Bryan asked.

"I was with Trey when he bought it," said Sassy, her eyes never leaving the monitor. "It's a one-of-a-kind estate piece. Where did you get it?"

Bryan watched as Jennifer pulled her hand back from the computer screen and her eyes filled with equal parts surprise and sadness. "A young girl at the brothel gave it to me. Her name was Mia. She died in the ambush. She said I was kind to her 'like the other *guera*' there had been. I assumed it was costume jewelry. I had no idea."

Bryan's gut clenched remembering the little girl and how scared she'd been when he'd met her. He'd given her his shirt so she'd have on more clothes than the sleazy lingerie the madam had dressed her in, and he'd almost gotten her out of that place. Hell, he'd thought she was out and safe, until he'd met Jennifer and Nick behind the house and learned the child was dead. One more person who'd died on his watch.

The parallel to Sassy's experience after he left Mississippi that long-ago summer was too painful to think about for long. At least he hadn't gotten Sassy killed . . . yet. He mentally pushed those unproductive thoughts away. He couldn't brood over that right now, or he'd completely lose focus.

Jennifer gazed at the ring on her hand before looking up again. "Rivera noticed this ring, too, when Nick and I were in the café in Skikda. What would your brother's engagement ring have been doing with a child in a Mexican brothel?" She reached to take it off as she looked at Nick. "I can have it sent to you."

Sassy nodded. "Yes, thank you. But not for the reason you think." She was way ahead of both of them. "Don't you see? That's the proof Elizabeth was alive after Trey was arrested. She was there at that brothel, and she was alive. Trey gave her that ring the night she disappeared. He told me about it when I saw him at the prison." Sassy squeezed her eyes shut, trying to remember exactly what Trey had said.

"He proposed to Elizabeth the night they rented the boat, but she wanted to think about it. She was still upset about their argument over the Peace Corps. He convinced her to put the ring on anyway, especially since they were out on the water. That was part of the reason the Mexican authorities were so sure he'd killed her. They were convinced he'd flown into a rage because she'd turned down his marriage proposal after their argument earlier."

Bryan was shaking his head. "Sassy, just because her ring was there doesn't necessarily mean that Elizabeth was at the brothel. An argument could be made that whoever killed her would have taken valuable and identifying jewelry off her body before dumping it. It could be that one of the murderers involved went to the brothel later and perhaps paid for services with the ring."

"But the girl who gave it to Jennifer said she'd been kind to her 'like the other *guera*.' *Guera* can be a reference to a fair-skinned Latino, but it can also mean a blonde woman. Elizabeth is blonde."

"Sassy, that's a stretch." Bryan worried she was twisting the facts to fit the story.

"No, that's reasonable doubt. Combined with my source who claimed they saw her board a boat in Venezuela."

"A source that's notoriously unreliable," argued Bryan.

Sassy ignored him. "She's alive, or she was after Trey was arrested. This is exactly the kind of evidence we need for the judge."

Bryan heard the determination in her voice. There would be no changing her mind. He recognized that set of her chin.

"But how can we prove it? I understand this is the right evidence for reasonable doubt. But no judge is going to take our word for it, particularly now that AEGIS, and you and I in particular, are under such suspicion," he said.

"I'm afraid he's right," said Nick. "None of us are considered reliable witnesses at this point."

"Don't worry about that. I can get traction for this if I write a story putting it all together like we've done here."

"I hate to point out the obvious, but you're wanted for murder right now," said Nick.

"And what editor wouldn't want that kind of an exclusive? They'll title it something outrageous like 'Why I Did It' or some such nonsense. I can get this story out. I know I can. But I want to make sure I have more detail. Can we go over it again?"

Bryan sighed inwardly but listened carefully as everyone talked through the details once more. He didn't want to rain on Sassy's good news, but he didn't think this was going to work. Leland hobbled back into view on his crutches as Nick was recounting the sniper attack at the Grand Hotel du Niger. His expression was more intense than Bryan could ever recall and rivaled Nick's at this point.

"What is it?" Nick asked.

"We've got to get out of here, now. There was a bug in my phone." Leland's voice, normally smooth and calm, sounded ragged and weary.

Nick stood, pulling Jennifer with him. "What kind of bug are you talking about? Where's the phone?"

Leland reached for Anna's hand as he spoke. "It's the efficient kind. And the phone is now at the bottom of the lake. I tossed it from the pier in a plastic bag with a brick. I couldn't get any further away on these sticks. I don't know if the person on the other end listening realizes what's going on yet, but we need to leave. They could have been tracking us before this video chat started."

"Who could have bugged your phone?" asked Bryan, understanding—possibly better than they did—the eminent danger. Without a word, Nick disappeared from the screen, taking Jennifer with him.

Leland turned to the computer as he tucked Anna to his side. "Several people have had access besides you and Nick."

"Who?" Bryan pushed and heard the dread in his own tone.

"Gavin, Marissa, Anna, and Zach."

Police sirens suddenly echoed in the background, and on screen everyone froze for a moment.

"Oh my God," murmured Anna, looking away from the computer. There must have been a window just out of sight of the camera. "Six police cars are in the driveway!"

Leland shook his head, the expression on his face so sad. Running with Anna was not an option for them with Zach there, too. The boy's health was still fragile after his heart transplant in November. Leland kept talking as if the inevitable wasn't coming. "The only person in this scenario that makes any sense to have bugged me is my old boss at the DEA, Ford Johnson."

"The man in charge of the AEGIS investigation?" asked Bryan.

Leland nodded as his eyes hardened. "The man I couldn't reach the day of the Colton bust." All hell was about to break loose, but Leland was incredibly calm.

Nick came back into view with Jennifer, and Bryan knew. They were all going to surrender. There was no other way, with their women there and the boy with them. Giving Bryan all the information they could before they were taken was the best option.

"The Colton bust?" asked Sassy.

"This must have started back then," said Leland, talking faster. "Staring at that phone outside, some things clicked into place for me. Juan Santos was the informant for that Colton bust that went so horribly wrong. The location was wrong, the supposed perp was wrong. I told my immediate boss at the DEA not to believe Santos, but he wouldn't listen. When I tried to reach Ford Johnson to talk with him about the situation, he wasn't available."

"Juan Santos," echoed Sassy. "Santos was my informant on the trafficking routes in Africa and the Venezuela connection."

Leland nodded unhappily. "Doubtless he was working both sides. Santos has always gone to the highest bidder. It follows that Ford Johnson was working with the cartels. It all makes sense in a way. With his position within the DEA, Johnson had insider access to know when each and every bust was going down. He could easily have played both sides."

In the background, Bryan heard the doorbell ring and someone shouting, "Police! Open up."

"There's more we could piece together, but we're out of time," said Leland. "Be very careful. Ford Johnson's connected in a huge way."

"Get in touch with Gavin if you can." Nick was typing on his phone as he talked, never looking up. "I'm texting him now, but he'll need the details from you. Don't forget what else I told you about at the café in Skikda. About my father. There's a link there."

"I remember," said Bryan, reeling to take it all in.

Could this really have had something to do with Reese Donovan's murder ten years before? *Suspecting* a DEA officer of being dirty wasn't the same thing as *proving* it. They were a hell of a long way from proof.

"You really think it reaches back that far?" Bryan asked.

"I don't know, but if Vega was to be believed, someone else was calling the shots when Reese died. It would make sense if that someone calling the shots was playing both sides."

The pounding on the door became louder. Bryan nodded. "We'll get you guys out of jail as soon as we can."

Nick looked up then and shrugged. "Oh, I think we're about to be there for the duration. Just get word to Gavin and Risa."

"Of course," said Bryan, hating the inevitability of what was to come. "I'm . . . I'm sorry. This is some vacation I set you up for."

Nick shook his head and smiled. "Not your fault, man."

"Bear! Bear!" called Sassy at the same time. "Can you make this thing record?"

Bear jogged over from the kitchen and leaned over Bryan to hit a couple of keys before straightening. "It's recording now."

Out of sight of the screen, they heard the sound of splintering wood as the door burst open. Nick and Leland didn't move.

"What do you need, Officers?" asked Nick. "We're happy to cooperate."

Bodies filled the screen as multiple officials poured into the room and started barking orders. Bryan counted eight different officers and an alphabet soup of agencies, if the navy-colored windbreakers were any indication—DEA, FBI, even ICE. Several people were shouting, but Nick and Leland remained calm. Bryan could see Nick being handcuffed and heard Anna's protest as Leland's crutches were taken away.

"He needs those," Anna cried. "He recently had surgery and can't put all his weight on that side yet."

"Well, he's shit out of luck today," said one of the ICE officers, pushing Leland away from her.

There was a scramble as Leland stumbled against the sofa and fell forward. Without his hands to catch him, he headed down like a felled tree, straight toward the coffee table.

Anna screamed at the officer. "Help him, plea—" The sound was cut short as the computer was knocked from its perch and Bear's monitor went black.

Jesus. Bryan clenched his hands and gritted his teeth as feelings of helplessness and rage swirled inside him.

Sassy sat watching the screen with tears running down her face. "What's going to happen to them?"

Bryan shook his head. God only knew what would happen to his friends. They'd been arrested because they'd been trying to help him. He and Sassy were wanted for murder, and the man they suspected of framing the entire AEGIS team was in charge of the investigation.

December 28
Africa

GAVIN SAT IN the hotel room, staring at the text message from Nick. This was the cherry on the cake of his shitty day. He and Risa had found Elizabeth Yarborough . . . or rather, what was left of her.

She'd come damn close to making it out of Africa alive. At least he assumed that was the case, if the location of the mass cremation gravesite was any indication. Witnesses from an aide organization in Sierra Leone reported that a young white woman matching Elizabeth's description had been in their village before she had succumbed to Ebola.

But no one could confirm seeing her body after she'd died. That wasn't unexpected. She'd most likely been cremated, along with fifty other villagers who'd died the same week. Forensics testing wasn't going to be possible.

Hell, at this point travel wasn't even possible, but Gavin was working on it. He wanted to speak with the aide workers face-to-face.

The entire continent of Africa was in a justifiable white-hot panic over the Ebola outbreak. There was no way to get the proof Sassy Smith needed to save her brother. But even without Yarborough's body, the circumstantial evidence was compelling. There just weren't that many young white women missing in Africa who would have been wearing a Peace Corps T-shirt along with University of Texas gym shorts.

He needed to let Sassy and Bryan know what he'd

found out, despite the fact that the current evidence was only hearsay and assuredly not proof enough to bring the Yarboroughs closure or to help Trey Smith with anything other than further heartbreak in his court case.

Then there was the message from Nick: *Need help from Risa. About to be arrested at your cabin with Leland, Anna, Zach, and Jenny. Bryan wanted for murder.*

Jesus. When had it all gone to hell?

Before Kat had died or after? The last time Gavin could remember sleeping through the night had been what, three months ago? No, maybe six. He couldn't recall. It was sometime during Kat's last remission, before the long slide into the horror show of her last two months.

God, he was tired, and he had been for so damn long. What was he doing here? How did he think he could possibly help?

He had no fucking idea. He just knew that he had to do something. If he stopped moving, the grief overwhelmed him. So Gavin made sure he never stopped moving.

And despite his efforts, his life and his livelihood were simultaneously circling the bowl. He was struggling with major depression. There was a warrant out for his arrest in the U.S., and he was on the verge of sleeping with the woman who'd been his lover before he married.

So here he was, at one of those major fork-in-the-road points of life. Was he going to make the hard choice or take the easy way out?

He knew what he should do. And he hated it. He strode to the adjoining room to show the text to Risa.

"Hey. What's up?" She was wrapped in a barely there

robe, and her hair hung in dark wet ringlets all around her face and shoulders.

"They've got trouble back home."

"What kind of trouble?" She scraped the hair away from her face and bent over at the waist. They weren't shy around each other, and she treated Gavin more like a brother than a former lover at this point. Their whole setup here felt wrong and simultaneously so right that it scared the crap out of him.

"Nick and Leland are being arrested at my lake house as we speak. Bryan and Sassy are wanted for questioning in the murder of a DEA agent in South Carolina. It's time for you to go home."

Risa stopped in the process of wrapping her hair in the hotel's threadbare towel. "You sure? I thought you were going to try to get to Sierra Leone to investigate the information you just got about the Yarborough girl."

"I'll do it on my own. If you don't leave Algeria now, you may have trouble getting home, depending on what happens with the quarantines."

"What about you?" Risa asked with her husky voice.

He looked at her, really studying her, and felt the slow burn he always did when he looked at Marissa Hudson for more than a few moments. Like staring at the sun, gazing at Risa for too long had always singed him a bit.

Lovers long before Marissa had introduced him to Kat, they'd peeled the paint off the ceilings of quite a few bedrooms together. But once Gavin had met the woman who would become his wife, that was over. He'd taken one look at Kat Deveraux and he'd been a goner, head over heels.

That should have made his current relationship with Marissa awkward and weird as hell. But since Risa had made it more than clear she never wanted to marry him, they had been okay. Comfortable to the point that they'd all remained very good friends, with him and Marissa even opening their security consultant business together.

Because even though Marissa had never wanted a permanent sexual relationship with Gavin, business-wise they were a perfect match, and the physical didn't enter into running AEGIS. *Thank God.*

Yet slipping back to that old pattern and comfort would be entirely too easy right now, and completely unfair. Because Gavin was hurting like he'd never hurt in his life. And the thought of taking solace in their physical relationship, no matter how brief, was incredibly seductive. But he wasn't that big an ass. At least he hoped he wasn't. Until now, anyway.

He cleared his throat. "They need you back home. To get their butts out of jail if nothing else."

She flipped her head up and twisted the towel, tucking the edges under in a move that puzzled and fascinated him at the same time. He never could quite figure out how women managed to do that thing with the towel.

"What makes you think my butt won't end up in jail as well?" she asked.

"You're too quick and your connections are too good. Whoever's behind this would have to have an awful lot of clout to put Senator Hudson's daughter in the pokey." He grinned to soften the message that he wanted her to leave.

She gave an indelicate snort. "I wouldn't count on that. What are you going to do?"

"I'm going to Sierra Leone and try to confirm the information on Yarborough."

"You really think that's possible . . . or even necessary? She's dead, Gavin."

He stood. "Maybe."

She stared at him without speaking, and God help him, he felt like squirming.

He swallowed. "Okay, probably. She's *probably* dead. I don't have much else to do right now, since going back to the U.S. is off the table."

She studied him a moment longer but never moved close enough for him to feel she was being the least bit inappropriate or suggestive.

"Are you okay?" she asked.

He gave a half smile. "Define *okay*."

"Hmm . . . That's what I thought."

He shook his head. "Risa, this is hard as hell. I miss Kat every minute of every day. My only remedy is staying busy. Getting arrested would be disastrous for me because I wouldn't be able to move around and do something to keep my mind off how bad I fucking hurt. I'd be stuck, unable to think about anything but the pain. I can't handle that yet. I'm not sure I'll ever be able to handle that. So yeah, I'm going to try and find out what happened to Yarborough. Was she really trafficked here from Mexico? And if so, how did she end up in a mass grave of Ebola victims?"

Risa was listening, and not disagreeing. "Where will you start?"

"I've still got contacts here from my DEA days. I'll get into Sierra Leone somehow. For now, I need you to go home. They need you."

And that was true. The AEGIS team needed her to work her magic and get them out of jail. He knew she wasn't happy about leaving him, but it was time.

They didn't need to be together. They didn't belong together. An intimate relationship at this point in both their lives would be disastrous. They had just enough history together to screw each other up but good.

So she had to leave. Now. Before he did something they'd both regret, something that would make it impossible for them to work together anymore.

She tilted her head and studied him a moment longer. "I've known you a long time, Gavin. I never figured you for a coward."

He shouldn't have been surprised that she'd figured out what he was thinking. But she had. Stunned and a little embarrassed, he didn't know how to respond. Then the opportunity was lost when she turned and headed for the bathroom in that slow saunter that had him wondering why in God's name he was sending her away.

She paused in the doorway and glanced back over her shoulder with a sad smile. "Don't worry, your virtue would have been safe with me."

His laugh was wistful, rueful. "Perhaps. But yours wouldn't have been with me."

He didn't wait for her reply as he headed back to his own room to make arrangements for her flight home. He simply shut the adjoining door with a firm snap.

Chapter 20

December 28
Evening
Bear's cabin

SASSY SAT IN stunned silence, unable to believe what had just unfolded on the screen in front of her. What was happening to Nick, Jennifer, Leland, Anna, and Zach right now? Would they be all right? Were they safe?

What were she and Bryan going to do? She knew what she could do. A story. And not just any story but one that an editor would take and run with.

"Bear, are you sure you got this recorded?" she asked. "How far back did it start?"

He was looking straight at her when she asked, so she caught the hesitation in his eyes. She suspected that under the beard there was a flush in his cheeks.

"I recorded the whole thing," he said.

"But . . . What?" He'd only come over at the end of their video conference and hit record.

Bear put his hands in his pocket and shrugged. The blush was undeniably there. She could see it on his cheekbones and forehead. Despite his size, the man looked like a little boy who'd gotten his hand caught in the cookie jar.

"You never know when you'll need something. This conversation seemed really important, so I recorded it. If Bryan hadn't needed it, I would have erased it afterward."

Bear leaned over the computer screen and hit a couple of buttons, and the last few moments of the chat replayed: Leland and her discussing Juan Santos and the mention of Ford Johnson, Nick telling them to call Gavin to get help figuring this out, the sound of the authorities beating on the door.

After that the audio was garbled because there were so many people talking at once, but it was clear what was happening. As Leland fell, she could see the look of horror on Anna's face. The screen froze there.

Sassy fought to detach herself from the nightmare of this happening to people she knew. She had to see it strictly as a news story. It took a few moments to unhook her emotions, but years of practice got her there.

Yes, Howard, her editor, would love the story.

And if Trey's case could be linked to this?

"Bryan, I'm so sorry. I—" She turned to face him and stopped. His gaze was on the screen, but his mind was far away. His eyes had turned a chilling ice gray.

"Bryan," she repeated.

He blinked and refocused on her face, but his expression was glacial. She kept talking, because at that moment she had no desire to be privy to the dangerous thoughts swirling behind his emotionless gaze. This was the Bryan she no longer knew. The boy who'd grown into the lethal man she didn't understand.

"I can work with this. I can write something that will help your friends at AEGIS and Trey. Particularly with the video. The idea of dirty cops and dirty feds. It's tantalizing to the media and to the public. That mixed in with what was . . . with what *is* just a hot mess in general . . ."

She leaned toward him. "It sounds crazy, but we can make this work to our advantage. We might even be able to get some viral traction with the right story and that video."

Bryan's expression changed as she spoke, and she didn't have to be a mind reader to know that he hated the idea. His feelings were now obvious from the look on his face. Still, he said nothing. Instead, he closed his eyes and took a deep breath.

She kept talking. If he balked, they were out of ideas. "I understand you may not care for the story premise, but I can't think of any other way to do this."

He opened his eyes and the internal struggle was gone, no sign of any hesitation visible. He hid it so well, she might have imagined what she'd seen moments before.

His tone was cool and unaffected. "I hate it, but you're right. We need publicity and a lot of it if we're going to sway public opinion. We can't let Johnson do this in the dark, and that's exactly what he'll do unless we have some way of letting people know what's happened."

She nodded, relieved at his change of heart, and looked for paper on the desk to take notes. "Nick said something during the conversation about his father's death. Tell me what that was about."

"He told me about it in Algeria. His father, Reese Donovan, died ten years ago in a car accident along with Nick's mother. Afterward it came out that Reese had been embezzling from his clients. In Africa, Nick learned that his parents' car accident wasn't an accident. They were murdered by Juan Santos on orders from a cartel member. Apparently Reese was working with the federal government trying to gather evidence against the same cartel that he was laundering money for. When the cartel found out what he was doing, they had Reese killed. Santos told Nick that someone outside the cartel ordered the hit."

"Do you think this is related?" she asked.

"I don't know if it's even true. We are talking about Santos, the habitual liar. If there is a dirty DEA agent in our mess, it could *possibly* be the same dirty agent that was operating ten years ago. But not necessarily. Still, with either the Riveras or the Vegas involved, the chances of it being the *same* dirty DEA agent go up exponentially."

Sassy felt the spike of adrenaline that came from working a story that was suddenly coming together. Despite the circumstances, a tingle of anticipation was there. She'd caught the main thread of the idea. It was going to require some digging, but she could unravel this. She knew it.

God, this kind of story would be huge. Beyond huge. Drugs, human trafficking, dirty DEA agents ordering hits on American citizens? This story would be massive, with the explosive effects rippling out through multiple branches of law enforcement.

And it had just the kind of tie-in they needed to help

Trey. Years ago, she'd given up feeling guilty about the excitement she felt in this kind of situation. She craved finding answers. It must be a lot like what a detective felt on a murder case when he pulled all the pieces together. While part of her was sick over the circumstances, another part of her was so damn jazzed to have figured it out.

She just had to make sure she got everything on paper with the right tone and inflection so it didn't come off like conspiracy theory tabloid sensationalism.

"Bear, can I access the cloud from here without being picked up by everyone looking for us? I have some notes I took in Africa that I stored there."

He bit his lower lip before he answered. "I'm not sure. Let me look at your application. We can probably figure out some way to access your account anonymously, but it may take a while."

"Okay." She needed to let this all percolate a little more before she started writing, but she was so keyed up and excited about the possibilities.

Bear glanced at Bryan, then back to Sassy. "Why don't you get some rest?" he suggested. "Hollywood and I will take turns with a watch. I'll be up a while figuring the encryption out for your account." He sauntered back over to the kitchen to finish eating.

She glanced at Bryan and could tell from just looking at him that he was still far away, thinking hard.

"Thanks." She looked around the desk once more but couldn't find anything to write with or on. "Bear, can I get some paper before I go upstairs? I need to make some notes before I try to sleep."

"Of course." He reached into a drawer and pulled out a yellow tablet and a pen.

The drawer screeched a bit as it closed, and Bryan's eyebrows snapped together. He was back from wherever he'd been.

"You're going to work now?" he asked.

"Just a little. I want to make sure I have everything straight in my head while it's still fresh from the conversation."

A bit distant, Bryan nodded, and she turned to walk upstairs. What was going on with him? She had no idea. And if she focused on it, something she could do nothing about, she'd make herself insane. Things were already crazy enough.

She got up to the bedroom, slipped off her shoes, and crawled into the middle of the bed with the yellow notepad in her lap. She was still so revved up that at first she wasn't sure she'd be able to write.

She scooted back to lean her head against the headboard. A ceiling fan mounted on a long bronze pole stirred the air overhead, keeping the temperature evenly distributed. She stared back down at the paper, took a deep breath, and started. After a few sentences, the ideas began to flow, with the narrative practically writing itself.

The stories Leland, Anna, Nick, and Jennifer had told individually were compelling. Together they created a startling bombshell. The big picture had only emerged after everyone had sat down together, albeit online, to share those individual pieces of the puzzle.

She'd been working for the better part of an hour when

the air seemed to change. She looked up to see Bryan at the top step, watching her. His intense gray gaze was different from earlier, when they were downstairs. More like the old man's eyes that she'd become accustomed to over the past six months. Still, there was something else in his expression that she couldn't identify, and that mystery bothered her.

"Hi," she murmured, suddenly shy.

He nodded.

"I didn't hear you," she added.

"I figured."

"How long have you been standing there?" Her unease at not being able to identify his mood grew.

"A couple of minutes. You were really . . . involved. I need to talk to you about this story." He walked toward the bed, and it was her turn to nod.

This was something she was comfortable talking about. And maybe, just maybe, they weren't going to revisit what had happened up here earlier. Particularly if she could get him involved with another topic.

"Yeah, I get lost in this. I usually set alarms for myself if I'm working at home, or I lose track of time completely." She glanced down at her notes. "I've got the beginnings of a good story here. My editor will take it. I know he will. I just need to clarify some things, but after that . . ." Her words trailed off. She was babbling, while Bryan continued to study her with that inscrutable expression as he stood next to the bed, his eyes never leaving hers.

"Sassy, I need you to promise me you will not go off on your own as we do this." His voice was insistent, urgent, not unlike the way it had been a couple of hours ago when he'd made love to her. That realization had a shudder working its way down her spine.

"I'm not sure I understand. What do you mean?" She stalled for time, hoping to distract him.

Her usual methods no longer worked. But that look on his face was warming her in places she didn't want to be warmed, unless she was up for a repeat of earlier. Not that she didn't want to go to bed with him again, she absolutely did. But it was a terrible idea.

If she didn't stop herself now and figure out how to guard her feelings, she'd become too attached. As if she wasn't already. So she had to be careful, or she'd get her heart stomped on all over again. And Bryan would never know he'd done it.

"You know what I mean. You're used to doing everything yourself. To taking care of yourself in some pretty rough places. I know that. But I need you to promise that you'll work with me here as we figure this out. I want to be able to trust you."

Her brows furrowed as her temper spiked. His words were the perfect remedy for the warm feelings she'd been harboring. "I'm not going to leave my brother twisting in the wind just to keep you informed."

Bryan sighed. "This is not just about your brother. It's about my friends, too. They're up to their necks in this, and while they're not in a Mexican prison, they are in a very dangerous position. I believe the man responsible for all of this is in charge of the investigation. There is no telling what he could do to them before we get it all unwound."

"I don't think—"

Bryan interrupted, and the irritation was obvious in his tone. "That's right. You don't always think, and you don't know all the details involved. What you don't know could get you and others into deep trouble."

Now she was mad. "Well, tell me what I don't know."

"You don't understand. None of us knows what we don't know. There are layers to this thing we're just uncovering. I've told you all I can, but there are issues at play here that go far beyond what I understand at this point. So don't go off half-cocked. I know you. I know your temperament."

Even as she wanted to be angry at his assessment of her "temperament," she couldn't be. He was right; and with that knowledge, her chin dropped. She could no longer stare belligerently into his eyes.

She did tend to be a "me against the world" kind of girl. But she didn't like to think that she'd purposely put others in danger. It hurt that he would think that. And it brought up a whole different kind of emotional storm.

To her surprise, she felt tears pricking at the edges of her eyelids. *No.* No damn way was she going to cry. Not in front of him. Not now. Not after everything that had happened. She'd rather die. She picked at the bedspread, refusing to look up even when he spoke to her again.

"We need to talk, you know. About earlier."

Yes, she did know, and she didn't want to talk about it. Didn't want to discuss what losing her virginity with him meant. Didn't want to examine why what had seemed such a good idea two hours ago was pretty much the worst idea she'd ever had. Most of all she didn't want to think about why she still felt the need to protect herself, even after everything she'd laid bare earlier. Exposing her real self was too frightening, too risky. Even with Bryan.

But he was standing right there in front of her, and she knew she had to face him sooner or later. She took a silent breath and glanced up before cutting her eyes back to her notebook. Tears fell in earnest off the end of her nose, splattering onto the ink-filled pages.

She couldn't believe this. She swiped at her eyes and felt the bed give way as Bryan sat on the mattress edge beside her. Then he was pulling her into his arms.

"Don't cry," he whispered. "It's okay. It's going to be alright." He gathered her against his chest and wrapped his arms around her. His heartbeat was steady and strong below her cheek, and he smelled like wood smoke from the fireplace downstairs. Wood smoke and man.

She felt so secure and safe at this moment. Like nothing could harm her. The irony was that the man holding her could break her heart into tiny little pieces without half trying. She snuck a peek at him again, this time attempting a smile.

But it was no use. She couldn't do it. She only succeeded in crying harder. His pity was worse than any indifference he might have shown.

When Bryan had left all those years ago, she'd cried till she hadn't been able to see straight. Then she'd dried her tears and decided never again to let a guy make her feel that way. It only made sense that Bryan would be the man to make her weep like a child all over again.

"You're killing me here. What is it, baby? I promise I'll take care of you. I'll marry you if you're pregnant."

Whoa. That statement brought her up short. Her tears stopped as if she'd turned off a water faucet.

Hadn't they covered this already? And how had they gotten from her sleeping with him without telling him it was her first time to his saying he would marry her?

That's not what she was crying about. It was everything else: Trey and Elizabeth, Bryan's friends, Otis and Tilly, and her life feeling so out of control. A marriage proposal was definitely not what she was after and positively the absolute last thing on her mind. God, what were they doing even talking about this when the rest of the world was going crazy?

"That's not what this is about." She heard the world-weariness in her voice. "It's just. I—"

She looked up at him to try and explain, but the words died on her lips. The expression on his face was so intense. So . . . hot. He looked like he would inhale her if she'd let him.

She was taken aback to the point that she forgot what she was about to say. She forgot about being tired and upset, too, as she stared with her head tilted back in what must have appeared a blatant invitation.

Bryan smiled ruefully and shook his head. "Dammit, Sassy. I forget everything when I'm with you except how much I wa—" He didn't get to finish the sentence, because instead of pulling away and protecting herself, she leaned up and into him, covering his mouth with her own and licking at the seam between his lips.

He groaned as she wrapped herself around him, kissing him with all of her own pent-up frustration and longing. Everything else was too much—too confusing, too overwhelming, too messy, too god-awful—to deal with right now.

This was the one man she wanted. She kissed him because it hurt too much to think of doing anything else. It would eviscerate them both to unwind all the misunderstandings and miscues of the past two hours, much less the past six months. The one thing she knew for certain was that Bryan could make that pain and confusion go away, at least for a little while.

At first she wasn't sure he was going to respond, then he opened his lips to hers and consumed her. None of the hesitation from earlier today was there. He undressed her as though unwrapping an anticipated present, all the while kissing her with a reckless intensity that had her melting inside. She was naked and beneath him in moments, then she was helping him undress.

He stopped only to pull a condom from his pants pocket before he was balanced over her. The shyness she'd felt before was gone. She just wanted him and the blessed oblivion he could bring her. She didn't want to think right now. She couldn't think, or she might start crying again.

Not for what she'd lost earlier tonight, but for the comfort she and Bryan had both missed out on these past months by alienating each other so much. If she allowed herself to focus on that for too long, she'd weep for it all—Bryan's dead comrades, his AEGIS friends, for Trey, and for the tragedies she'd discovered in Africa when researching the story on Elizabeth.

Instead, she leaned into Bryan's kisses and focused on feeling, on all the new sensations she was experiencing. His chest pressed hard against hers, and his body pushed her into the mattress. But he was careful not to crush her as he moved his lips down her neck and focused on her breasts. Cool air from the overhead fan raised goose flesh on her arms, but she was far from cold by the time he'd kissed his way across her body past her navel, then lower.

Why had he stopped fighting their attraction now? She couldn't figure it out.

He stopped kissing her at the edge of her hip bone. She glanced down to see him resting his chin lightly on her belly and looking her in the eye.

"You're thinking too much again. Stop that. Just … feel." He pressed his lips to her tummy, moving lower before pausing to gaze up at her again. "Come on. I dare ya."

She laughed. He was right. She was doing exactly what she'd just promised herself she wouldn't do—she was thinking too much. And she'd never been able to resist one of Bryan's dares.

She huffed a laugh and smiled. "Game on."

Chapter 21

December 29
Early morning

BRYAN WOKE IN the dim light of early morning with Sassy wrapped around him like a vine. For just a moment he let himself revel in the memory of the hours before—of how it had felt to hold her and to make love to her. Before he could have second thoughts about getting out of bed, he untangled himself, being careful not to wake her. He knew that if he didn't leave now, he never would. If he stayed with her here, he'd only endanger her further in the manhunt that was sure to expand today.

Their only salvation lay in finding who was responsible for the attacks on AEGIS and the disaster that had occurred in Kingstree. While he was almost positive that Leland's old mentor, Ford Johnson, was behind it all, Bryan was a long way from proving that or being able to do anything to stop the man. Plus, there was the cartel issue, in addition to Trey's upcoming trial.

Sassy was convinced her news story would make a difference, but Bryan wasn't so sure. People with as much power as Ford Johnson generally had a way of making the media work for them, not against them. How much truth would Sassy really be allowed to share in her news exposé? He suspected her editor would revise the story to some sanitized version.

Putting a stop to all this once and for all was going to be complicated, but it was possible. Bryan just needed to be able to work by himself. If he had to split his attention between worrying about Sassy and worrying about putting all the pieces together, he wouldn't be able to do a competent job of either.

It was time to go.

He showered and dressed quietly before creeping downstairs. The fire was only embers now, but Bear was up and at the computer, with Lily snoozing at his feet. The scent of freshly brewing coffee filled the downstairs. Bryan poured himself a cup, snagged what appeared to be a homemade muffin, and moved to sit beside the desk.

Bear's fingers were tapping at the keyboard like a concert pianist's.

"You got a text." Bear handed over the burner phone Bryan had bought at Penn Station a little over two days ago. It felt more like a month. "It's okay to access the message, but don't answer it from the phone. We'll communicate from my computer instead."

The text was from Marissa: *Layover in Paris. Call me on the scrambled number.*

"We can do that," said Bear with no apology. Apparently he'd already read the message.

And what had Bryan expected? This had become about Bear's safety, too. That was why Bryan had left his phone downstairs last night. "Okay, let's do it."

Bear took the cell back and typed for another moment. "Alright. I've got things set up where you can call her from the computer over a data line, not voice. It'll be untraceable, or at least much harder to trace." Bear stood and swapped places with Bryan.

"Thanks." Bryan took a swallow of the strong coffee and settled into the leather office chair.

"I'll give you some privacy." Bear moved toward the kitchen.

Bryan raised an eyebrow. "When did that become an issue?"

"I'm trying to at least give the appearance of being hospitable," Bear mumbled as he pulled milk out of the refrigerator.

Bryan shot a glance over his shoulder at his host. "I know. I'm not trying to be an ass. It's just . . ."

"It comes naturally?" asked Bear, shaking his head.

Bryan turned back to the computer screen and bit into the muffin. "Right," he muttered. " 'Fraid so."

Bear stopped in the process of refilling his own coffee mug. "You're not used to people knowing your business. I get it. This is an extraordinary circumstance, though, so you're going to have to deal."

"A bit of the pot calling the kettle black, isn't it?"

Bear shrugged and stirred the milk into his coffee. "Yeah, but I can recognize the tendency in others a hell of a lot easier than I can in myself."

Bryan snorted his reply.

"Make the call. I'll go outside so you can have real privacy." Bear headed for the patio door.

Bryan slid on the computer headphones with the built-in microphone and made the call like Bear had shown him last night. Marissa's number only rang once from his end before she answered.

"Hollywood?" Her husky Texas twang was there, even when she just said his name.

"Yeah, it's me."

"I'm about to board a plane into Hartsfield. I've got a meeting in Atlanta tonight to get the scoop on Tomas Rivera and a possible dirty DEA connection."

Bryan was stunned. He always was by the depths of Risa's sources. "How did you get the intel?"

And so fast?

"I have a friend in the Justice Department."

Of course she did. Risa had "friends" everywhere.

"I don't use him often, but his information is always good, and the contact is invaluable."

Bryan didn't doubt that. "What do you want me to do?" he asked.

"Meet me in downtown Atlanta at the Glenn Hotel on Marietta. Alone. I want you to hear what this source has to say. You can question him yourself. You'll know things to ask that I won't. Can you get there by nine PM?"

Bryan took a sip of coffee as he thought through the options and his answer. Atlanta was over six hours from Bear's home. It would take longer to get there if he had to take back roads. Leaving Sassy here would be best; he knew that. They were wanted by police everywhere in the Southeast.

Travelling together was dangerous. He'd seen the evidence of that last night with Nick and Leland. You were completely out of options when the woman you loved was with you and the police came knocking.

The woman you loved?

Did he love Sassy? This sure as hell wasn't the time to be contemplating that question. And it wasn't like he didn't already know the answer.

That, more than anything, had him answering Marissa in the affirmative. "Yes, I can be there. Not sure exactly what time I'll get to town. I need to arrange transportation first. But I'll be there for your meeting. Where exactly at the Glenn will you be?"

"The SkyLounge on the rooftop."

"Got it. Text me when you land at Hartsfield." Without Bear's intervention, Bryan wouldn't be able to call Risa back without being traced, but he wasn't going to go into all that with her now. Besides, once he was away from here without Sassy, his concerns over being traced wouldn't be as significant.

"Sounds good," she said.

He heard the announcement for Risa's flight over the phone as he ended the call. The sun was rising, and he headed out to the deck, where Bear was stacking wood by the sliding glass door. The air was cool and crisp. "God, it's beautiful here. I see why you'd never want to leave."

Bear stopped working to sip coffee from a thermal

mug and stare out over the golden-tinged valley. "I love it." His breath puffed gray smoke around his mouth as he spoke. "What do you need?"

"How did you know I'd need—" Bryan stopped and appreciated anew his friend's intelligence, even with the social gaffes.

Bear took another slug of coffee and turned from the spectacular view. "You weren't going to talk to someone in Paris and not need something."

"I need transportation. I have to be in Atlanta this evening."

"Are you particular about four wheels, or can it be two? I already offered my truck to a family friend today to move. There'll be questions if I undo that. But I've got a motorcycle in the storage shed. It'll take you every bit of seven hours to get to Atlanta, but it's doable. Unless . . . Wait a second. You're not taking Sassy, are you?"

"A bike is fine." Bryan didn't want to talk about this with Bear or anyone else.

"What about Sassy?" asked Bear. Bryan could feel his friend staring at him. "Have you told her that she's not going? Why aren't you taking her?"

Uncomfortable, Bryan shifted under Bear's steady gaze. He couldn't take Sassy for a number of reasons, limited transportation options being just one. But that was the perfect excuse, a way out.

Bear started shaking his head even before Bryan could supply his manufactured reason. "I understand not wanting to take her because it's dangerous, but when are you going to tell her that you're leaving without her?"

Bryan kept his eyes on the incredible vista before him. He didn't want to answer that or fess up to what he was about to do.

Bear's tone changed from concern to chagrin. "Well shit, Hollywood. You're going to leave me with a furious woman in the middle of nowhere, aren't you? That's not a nice thing to do."

Bryan's laugh was rueful. No, it wasn't a *nice* thing to do at all, to either of them. He finally met his friend's gaze, prepared to fall on his sword. "I know. But if she wakes up, there'll be no getting away from here on my own. She'll wear us both down."

Bear raised an eyebrow. "You're scared of a woman who doesn't weigh a hundred pounds soaking wet?"

"Hell, yes. And you would be, too, if you knew what was good for you."

Bear snorted. "She's got your number, doesn't she?" He shook his head and shut the woodbox before sliding off his work gloves. "Come on, let's get you ready to ride. You're going to need more substantial clothing than what you're wearing. I've got something that should fit." They walked down the stairs, heading for the shed on the other side of the cabin.

Thirty minutes later, Bryan stood in the kitchen, outfitted in a black leather jacket and pants with multiple layers, insulated gloves, and a helmet. He was ready.

"Take more food," suggested Bear. "You won't want to stop along the way. At least not for meals."

Bryan nodded, and Bear handed over a half dozen protein bars and four bottles of water for the bike saddlebags. "If you plan to be gone before she wakes up, you need to leave now," he warned.

"Yeah, I know."

Now that it was time, Bryan was hesitating. He knew he was making a mistake to go without telling Sassy goodbye. But it was the classic damned if he did, damned if he didn't scenario.

"Tell her . . ." Bryan's voice drifted off. He didn't know what to tell her. That was the problem.

"What can I say that won't have her mad as hell at the both of us?" asked Bear.

Bryan sighed. "Are you a coward?"

Bear laughed, seeming to take no offense at the question. "Nope. But I'm no fool. I'm no hero, either, especially when it comes to dealing with angry women."

But Bryan knew that Bear would guard Sassy with his life. No matter what the man said about not being a hero.

"Just tell her I'll be back. Tomorrow evening at the latest."

"Got it," said Bear.

Bryan climbed onto the vivid black bike and settled into the leather seat. The Harley had a definite retro look with all the chrome and tank flame graphics. But everything about it was state of the art, from its Twin Cam engine to its next-generation security system. It occurred to him that Bear was loaning him his most treasured possession.

"I know this is above and beyond. I don't know how to thank—"

"What is this?" interrupted Bear. "Get out of here before that woman wakes up."

Bryan smiled. In deference to the cold weather, he swiped the starter button before holding it down ten seconds later. The engine roared to life, breaking the silence of the early morning air.

"Thank you," Bryan mouthed over the rumble of the exhaust.

"Go," demanded Bear, refusing his gratitude.

Bryan revved the engine once more and drove out of the clearing beside the house. For better or worse, he was on his way to Atlanta.

SASSY WOKE TO the sound of an engine revving. It wasn't a car; it had to be a motorcycle. She reached out and touched only covers where Bryan had been lying earlier.

He wasn't there. The sheets weren't even warm. Her feet hit the floor, and she rushed for the window as that engine sound rumbled farther away in the distance.

She knew, without going downstairs, that it was Bryan.

He'd left her. Again.

After everything.

After all his talk of feeling guilty over what had happened after he'd left Springwater, she was on her own once more to make things happen and to get Trey out of jail. She'd been right to worry about trusting Bryan completely.

In his defense, he'd warned her last night.

You shouldn't trust me. . .

Sassy flopped back on the bed, trying to wrap her head around what had just happened. The faint scent of wood smoke and Bryan clung to his pillow. The front door opened and closed. That would be Bear.

She lay in shock on top of the duvet. No reason to rush downstairs. *What was the point?*

She showered before going to talk with Bear, hoping the extra time would help her pull it together. He had to be dreading the conversation. As much as she'd like to, she wasn't going to sharpen her teeth on that gentle giant of a man. He'd gone above and beyond what Bryan had asked.

Was it just yesterday afternoon that they'd met him at the diner outside Charleston?

In the shower she washed her hair and thought through the options. The only thing she could do now was write the story and get it to her editor. So that's what she'd do. She dressed and went down to find Bear at his computer, along with a cheery fire burning. He looked up as she hit the bottom step, and his expression changed from concentration to wariness.

"Morning, Bear. Bryan's gone, isn't he?"

Bear nodded and pushed back from the desk to face her. "You heard the motorcycle? Bryan said to tell you he'd be back tomorrow night."

She shrugged but said nothing. Tomorrow night would mark yet another day gone. The clock was ticking so loudly for Trey right now, she could hear nothing else.

"Sassy, he couldn't take you. Not with your pictures

plastered all over TV and you both wanted for murder. Half the country's law enforcement agencies are looking for the two of you."

She nodded. "I know. There's always a logical and reasonable explanation."

But the bottom line was she was here alone while Bryan was gone. Perhaps he was "saving them." He didn't think her news story was going to help anything. He'd made that perfectly clear.

So, she'd prove him wrong.

Like she'd done to every other naysayer in her life. Howard would want this story. Sassy was certain of it. And it could be the start of breaking down the walls to Trey's release. She could do it on her own.

A voice in her head warned that she wasn't supposed to go off all "half-cocked," as Bryan had said, but she ignored it. If she did nothing, Trey would spend the rest of his life in a Mexican jail. Besides, she wasn't going off "half-cocked." In fact, she wasn't going anywhere.

Bear was studying her with the wary expression of a sailor watching violent clouds gather on the horizon. Reminding herself that blowing up at her host would do nothing to help the situation, Sassy tamped down her frustration and tempered her smile.

"Can you bring up my research again that I was looking at last night?" She bent over to pat Lily and got an enthusiastic puppy kiss for her effort.

Bear nodded. "Sure, just give me a couple of minutes." He looked decidedly relieved at the passing of Storm Sassy and began typing on his keyboard.

Sassy washed up before grabbing some coffee and a muffin the size of her hand from the kitchen. The warmth of the cup was a small comfort. She was cold all over, but it hadn't registered before now. Feeling abandoned had that effect on her. After a couple of moments, Bear stood, turned the computer over to her, and walked upstairs.

Using her yellow legal pad, Sassy worked from her online notes and interviews, including the conversation with everyone last night. Pulling the story pieces together from Leland's experience with Ford Johnson and the Colton bust, she looked up some old news stories and pulled quotes from Johnson himself at the civil trial that had taken place when Ellis Colton had sued the government for his wife's injuries and his baby's wrongful death.

Sassy laid out what she'd learned from Nick and Jennifer as well. She layered in what she'd discovered about the cartel involvement and the human trafficking situation that spread from Mexico to Africa, details she'd picked up while looking into Elizabeth's disappearance. There were passages that could use more filling in, but that could be done later. The story was intricate, and would lend itself to being a multi-piece series.

It was late afternoon when she finally stood up from the computer and stretched. She was done, or at least as close to done as she needed to be before talking to Howard to see how interested he really was and when he might be able to run a story like this. She typed out a quick message with just enough of an outline to whet

Howard's appetite: murder, drugs, government conspiracy, sex trafficking.

Given her communication limitations, she went in search of Bear. She found him outside, just off the patio with its stunning overlook. He was splitting wood and humming a James Taylor song as he worked. She knew the moment he heard her approach, because he abruptly quit doing both.

"Can you help me send an email without its being traced?" she asked.

"Absolutely. Whatcha got?"

They headed back into the cabin, where she showed him the message for Howard. He talked her through the steps of sending it so it wouldn't be traceable. After thirty seconds, the telltale swoosh of an outgoing email tone sounded.

She looked up with a smile. "Excellent. Now how about some lunch? I make a mean omelet, and I'm starved."

"Lunch? Woman, lunchtime was hours ago. I was about to throw a couple of steaks on the grill. How about some wine to go with them?"

Sassy didn't hesitate. "Sounds great."

Bear nodded, and she heard the distinctive pop of a cork being pulled as she went up to grab her shoes and put on another layer, since the sky was growing darker by the minute. The Cowboys sweatshirt made her think of Tilly and Otis. She remembered her clean clothes in Bear's dryer and realized she could wear something else that didn't make her feel so depressed.

She wondered briefly what Bryan was up to, but she forced herself to leave that sad topic alone as well. "Nothing but heartache all around," she murmured to herself and headed back downstairs.

Bear was back at the computer when she came down. "Hey there, you have a reply already. Sorry, the window was open, and it popped up while I was sitting here."

She wasn't all that surprised at the speedy response. Howard was a workaholic. "What does it say?"

"'Call me ASAP,'" read Bear.

She sighed and reached for the glass of wine he had poured for her. "Of course it does."

"You *can* call him, you know. We'll just use the data port instead of the phone. Want to do it now before we start cooking?"

"Yeah, let's. Can I check my other email first? I didn't do that earlier. I just sent the one to Howard."

"As long as you only download plain text and don't click on any attachments," explained Bear.

She nodded and came back to swap places. He headed for the kitchen to give her privacy. Sassy was grateful she was sitting down when she read her messages. One required immediate attention. She glanced up, debating whether or not to share the contents with Bear. He was making some kind of exotic-looking salad, while Lily wandered over and flopped down in her dog bed near the desk.

Her reporter's instinct kicked in. *Nope. Not happening.* Sassy wasn't sharing until she had more information. She took a deep breath and dashed off a reply, carefully following the earlier instructions for sending an untraceable email.

Now she was ready to talk to her editor.

Bear directed her from across the room. She slipped on the headphones and dialed the phone the way he instructed. Moments later, she could hear it ringing on Howard's end. He answered on the first ring.

"It's me, Howard."

"Sassy? Where the fucking hell are you?" Her editor's language was colorful even when things were going his way. When he was stressed, it became even more so.

"You know I can't tell you that. Can you use the story?" she asked.

"Depends. When can I see the copy? How reliable are your sources? I warn you, you're going to need thorough corroboration, because the DEA and the FBI will be all up my ass as soon as this goes live."

"You want my sources?" She heard her own voice squeak on the question.

"If you weren't wanted for murder yourself, it wouldn't be an issue. But I have to know that this is legitimate information. Do you have anyone who's not wanted by the FBI or the DEA who can corroborate?"

Sassy sighed. "I'm going to have to think about it."

Howard's muttered epithet was one of his more anatomically creative. "You do that. I want the story as soon as you're finished. And I'll need at least one witness who is not an alleged criminal."

"What about Ellis Colton?"

"The guy whose wife and kid died in that botched drug raid?"

"Right. I'm not sure I can get an interview with him at this point, given the circumstances. Perhaps he would talk to you?" she suggested.

By now she imagined Howard was leaning back in his office chair, staring at the ceiling and chewing on the tip end of his red Bic pen.

"I remember the Colton mess. It was quite the juicy story when that DEA officer, Leland whoosits, testified against his own team. Colton was explicit about not wanting to talk with the media after that. But for the right reasons, he might be willing to break his silence. Like maybe to apprehend the man responsible?"

Sassy gulped a silent breath of air. Howard was buying in. This was good. "How long do you suppose this will take? We don't have a lot of time here for my brother."

"We've got to get it right, Sassy. You can't go off half-cocked."

She struggled not to grind her teeth on hearing that term again. Why was everyone calling her on being impulsive?

Howard's voice brought her back to the conversation at hand. "And we're ignoring the elephant in the living room. The warrant out for your arrest."

"Bryan and I didn't kill that couple."

"I assumed so. But it looks bad."

Sassy leaned back in her own chair. "Use that to make

the story current. Relevant." She had to give Howard an angle to get this story out there in time to help Trey.

"I suppose that could possibly work. I'll see what I can do and be in touch. If you find a legitimate corroborating source, let me know."

And that was as much of a promise as she was going to get from him.

"Alright. Thanks, Howard. I appreciate it. I'll keep working it for you."

"You do that. Without a credible source, this will only be seen as a tabloid piece."

"Right." She hung up and turned to Bear, thankful that she'd been on the headphones and had had a semi-private conversation.

She would have to get the more compelling evidence herself. Howard wasn't going to do it for her, at least not within a time frame that was going to suit her. But she'd keep that to herself. At least she had options. Suddenly the email from earlier took on an even greater importance, and she was glad she hadn't said anything about it to Bear.

She slipped the headphones off to talk to him. "Hmmm. Not sure this is all the way over the goal line, but it's as far as I can take it this evening." That wasn't exactly a bald-faced lie. "So where are those steaks you promised?"

"Right this way, ma'am."

She checked her email one last time. Not surprisingly, a new reply had arrived while she'd been speaking to Howard. The content had her hesitating only a beat before she answered Bear. "I'm right behind you."

She closed the window to her email account and followed him out to the patio, taking smaller sips of the cabernet than she would have normally. Her evening was just getting started.

Chapter 22

December 29
Late evening

FOUR HOURS LATER, Sassy was alone in Bear's truck, bumping along the dark road out of the Francis Marion National Forest. A friend of his had stopped by after dinner to return the vehicle. She'd waited until Bear had gone up to shower before she'd snuck out.

Bear hadn't even wanted to leave her alone downstairs, but she'd insisted and finally prevailed in convincing him to take a shower and a nap before taking the evening watch. She claimed that since she'd had such a good night's rest the night before, she'd be staying up a while to work anyway.

He'd reluctantly agreed, showing her how the alarms and surveillance cameras worked before he went upstairs. She'd sent another email, and as soon as she'd heard the shower kick on, she'd disarmed the system and snuck out of the house to—basically—steal his truck.

Yes, a horrible way to repay his kindness. But she'd do that and worse if it meant saving Trey. Besides, she planned to return the vehicle. But tonight, she needed it for a little while.

The email message she'd received before dinner was too tantalizing to resist.

I need to talk with you. Alone. You name the time and place. Near Charleston, perhaps? I can be there within the hour. It concerns your brother's welfare and his possible early release from Mexican incarceration.

She'd known the sender was serious, addressed as it had been from Tomas Rivera. He was assuming, just as law enforcement was, that she and Bryan had holed up in the area after the train wreck.

She'd emailed Rivera back, telling him to meet her at The Hot Pot, the same diner where Bear had picked her and Bryan up the day before. She'd almost said something to Bear over dinner, but he would never have agreed to this.

With the truck's GPS, she assumed she could find the diner easier than anything else in the area. But she wasn't sure how long it would take her to get there, so she'd given herself plenty of time and set the meeting for 2:30 AM. If she'd been willing to wait until tomorrow night, she supposed Bryan could have come with her to the meeting. But she'd dismissed that idea out of hand.

Rivera had said to come alone. And Trey's current timetable didn't allow for her to wait on anything. Besides, she wasn't all that convinced Bryan was coming back. No matter what Bear said.

She wondered what Bear would think when he realized she was gone. Hopefully he'd come out of his shower and go straight to bed for a while to rest, but she doubted it. Realistically, she had a twenty-minute head start.

But Bear didn't know where she was going, so she comforted herself with that. She got lost twice but pulled into The Hot Pot with thirty minutes to spare.

She remembered to park the truck out of sight of the surveillance cameras that they had avoided yesterday, then made her way to the door of the diner. She could see truckers and waitresses through the foggy windows and thought she could use a cup of coffee herself.

She was stepping onto the sidewalk when she heard the door open on a Lincoln Town Car beside her. The windows were so heavily tinted, she couldn't see inside.

"Miss Smith?"

She turned.

A young man stood beside the back passenger door. At first it didn't register who this could be. The man was too young to be Rivera.

"Mr. Rivera would like to see you, now. Get in, please."

She stopped. Her foot felt leaden on the sidewalk. The door to the diner was right there. She could reach out to open it and be safely inside. "I told him I would meet him in the restaurant."

"That's not how he wants to do this, ma'am. Please come with me."

His polite demeanor surprised her. Under the circumstances, she should be grateful the man said please and wasn't manhandling her into the car. She'd known all along how crazy stupid and incredibly dangerous it was for her to be here alone; that fact was amplified for her now. But this was the price she would pay to help Trey. She'd go with this man to meet whoever she had to in order to save her brother.

She ducked and slid into the backseat through the open door. The sound of it slamming behind her further rattled her unsteady nerves. The scent of expensive cologne and extravagant tobacco clung to the air.

Sassy wasn't alone in the backseat.

December 30
Midnight
Atlanta

BRYAN SAT WITH his back to the glass-paneled wall highlighting a dramatic skyline view in the dark bar filled with last call patrons, smoke, and the throb of club music. They were starting the meeting late because Risa's flight had been significantly delayed. She'd been picked up at the airport by her contact rather than Bryan because there wasn't enough room on his bike and the concern over his being identified. So Risa and Bryan had had no time to talk privately beforehand.

Despite the SkyLounge's lush surroundings and plush cushioned sofas, or perhaps because of them, Bryan was struggling to relax. With the dim lighting, someone would practically need night-vision goggles to recognize him, but he still felt exposed. And he wasn't exactly dressed for clubbing.

Earlier, in the bathroom downstairs, he'd managed to

peel off some of the thermal layers and run his fingers through his hair so he didn't look so out of place in his black leather jacket and pants. After driving Bear's bike like a wild man to get here, he'd had more than three cups of coffee while he'd waited for Marissa and company to arrive. The waiter offered Bryan another refill when he dropped off drinks for Risa and her contact, but Bryan shook his head. He was wired enough already.

Risa's guy wasn't exactly an ass, but he was an intense fellow. Bryan had the distinct feeling they were not going to get along. The man's name was David Nightshade, and from his initial conversation Bryan assumed the guy had been working in the Justice Department for a long time. It was obvious that David and Risa had a past, but neither had enlightened Bryan as to what that past entailed.

As the waiter walked away, Nightshade leaned into Bryan's personal space and gave what Bryan guessed was his threatening stare. Bryan ignored it. He'd disarmed that kind of mind-game shit years ago. And while he was willing to put up with Nightshade's intimidation tactics and more to get help, it didn't stop him from fantasizing about punching the guy in the nose.

Nightshade frowned at Bryan's lack of response before he started talking. "What I'm about to tell you is classified, and I'll have your ass in jail if you breathe a word of it to the press or to anyone else."

Bryan nodded and fought to push aside his frustration at the melodramatic tone. He supposed Nightshade could be menacing looking in the right setting. But there wasn't much that scared him anymore, particularly when his friends' lives were on the line. At the moment, Bryan just felt an extreme sense of irritated impatience brought on by too much caffeine and worry over what was happening with Nick and Leland, their women, and the boy.

"For God's sake, David. Will you zip it and put the tape measure away? Bryan's not going to call CNN. He knows you're putting your job on the line by talking with us. Speak." Risa's tone was glacial. She'd never been one to waste time with posturing.

Well, we're not calling CNN yet, thought Bryan. *But there are no guarantees.* He wondered how Sassy's "story" was coming. He'd been dismissive of her idea last night, and that had been a mistake. He'd been thinking of her all day.

He should have woken her and said goodbye this morning, another huge error on his part. He wanted to talk with her, but calling to apologize wasn't an option, given the tracing issue. He'd have to wait until he got back to Bear's and give his apology in person. And that was enough thinking on that, or he'd forget the whole reason he was here.

Bryan focused on Risa instead, silently cheering her handling of Nightshade. The man was quiet for the first time since they'd arrived, simply staring at her. And even if Bryan didn't like the guy, he couldn't blame the man for that.

Risa had the timeless beauty and carefully coiffed look of a woman who could be anywhere between thirty and forty-five. Her history with Gavin had him assuming she was at least thirty-five, but beyond that, her age was a mystery.

What was not a mystery was how scathing she could be when angered. Bryan had been on the receiving end of Risa's wrath before. It wasn't fun. To have her sharpen her claws on your pride hurt.

Nightshade didn't seem too bothered. "You know I wouldn't do this for anyone but you, Risa."

"I do, and I so appreciate it." Her words should have sounded trite or dismissive, but Risa's tone was completely sincere.

Nightshade smiled at her before turning back to Bryan. "Ford Johnson is most likely your man. Currently he is under investigation by the internal affairs arm of the DEA."

Bryan exhaled, relieved to have the suspicions confirmed by someone else besides AEGIS. "What's Ford Johnson being investigated for?"

"Multiple offenses ranging back over the past decade. Most recent was unauthorized approvals for the use of an experimental drone system in Mexico. Johnson helped himself to several test drone programs, both large and small. The one that bit him in the ass was the swarm quadrotor system. Those drones are smaller than a kid's mini remote-controlled helicopter and have very targeted firepower. When used in multiples, a swarm of the nano quadrotors can take out a specific person in a vehicle of a convoy or even in a specific room of a building. It gives a new definition to the term *surgical strike*."

Risa was drinking her wine and watching the room

as Nightshade talked. She'd obviously heard some of this before.

"The DEA's Office of Professional Responsibility discovered discrepancies in the approval system on a routine report audit a couple of weeks ago. They're still unwinding everything, but I understand the inspector general of the Justice Department is involved now. They're planning to file charges." Nightshade leaned back and lit a cigarette.

"Are they sure Johnson used those drones?" Bryan sat up straighter in the booth. "Ernesto Vega swore that the clinic where Cesar Vega died and the home where Tomas Rivera's wife died were both hit by drones. Could Ford Johnson have been behind that?" But Bryan already knew the answer.

"It sure as hell wasn't sanctioned by the U.S. government," said Nightshade. "The drones in our program are experimental, to be used strictly for observation."

"Even those quadrotors?" asked Bryan.

"Their use is classified. But I assure you that program was not tasked with anything having to do with Ernesto Vega or Tomas Rivera." Nightshade already sounded like he was testifying before a subcommittee.

"Does Johnson know that he's about to be busted?" asked Marissa.

Nightshade shrugged and tapped the ash off his cigarette. "He shouldn't, but if his network is as good as I think it is, he might. I have no way of knowing for certain. The guy has a sixth sense about some of this stuff."

Bryan was itching to ask how certain Nightshade was of the intel, but that wasn't why Marissa had invited him to this meeting. If she trusted the man's information, Bryan was going to have to trust it, too. That bombshell about the drone investigation was proof enough that Ford Johnson was their guy. And if an inspector general was involved, this wasn't some harebrained theory.

"What do you know about Johnson's past? How long he's been with the DEA?" asked Bryan.

Nightshade sipped his overpriced IPA and shifted in his seat. "Johnson was there when I got to the Justice Department ten years ago. He's done a little of everything stateside and more recently overseas in Afghanistan."

"Afghanistan?" The sense of foreboding was so overwhelming that Bryan almost missed what Nightshade said next.

"Johnson's been running an investigation into cartel involvement with the chieftains living in the central and southeastern provinces for several years now. When I started, he was one of those fair-haired boys from the DEA heading up a joint task force in California. I remember because lots of heads rolled in both agencies when their case against a suspected cartel kingpin fell apart after the main informant died unexpectedly in a car crash. It was some attorney."

Bryan was reeling from the possible Afghanistan connection, but as he looked into his cooling cup of coffee, several things fell into place.

He decided to start with the one that would initially keep his blood pressure lower. "Was the dead attorney's name Reese Donovan?"

Nightshade cocked an eyebrow and crushed out his

cigarette. "Yeah. Turned out the lawyer had been laundering money for the cartel and embezzling from his clients at the same time. DEA bet on the wrong horse in that investigation."

Marissa looked stricken. "How did you know about that, Bryan?"

"When Leland, Nick, and I talked online last night, we put some pieces together. That was the one that we couldn't make fit. It makes sense now." He turned to Nightshade. "Reese Donovan was murdered. Juan Santos confessed to Nick Donovan in Africa last week that he did it on 'orders' from someone else."

"You're sure?" asked Nightshade.

"Positive."

Nightshade nodded. "I'll let my office know. We've suspected for a while that Gavin and AEGIS were being set up, but there's no way to stop the investigation without tipping off Johnson. We've got him under observation. They should have him in custody soon."

Bryan clutched his hands around the cup to keep from reaching across the table.

"Your office has known we were being set up and did nothing?" Marissa's voice took on a dangerous tone as she asked the question, and Bryan could sense the storm coming. Any sane man would. But apparently Nightshade did not have the proper radar. Bryan was in no mood to throw the idiot a lifeline.

"If what you are saying is true, Ford Johnson has been dirty for over ten years, and no one ever caught him." Marissa's scathing tone could have flayed skin.

Nightshade looked slightly embarrassed, as if he might not want to hear any of this. But the record needed to be set straight.

Bryan clenched his jaw in frustration to keep from howling. "Reese Donovan wasn't embezzling or laundering money. Did it not occur to anyone that he could have been set up by Johnson, his handler?" Challenged to keep the disgust from his tone, Bryan let the accusation sink in for a moment.

Was Johnson behind his own team's betrayal in the Helmand Province two years ago? Bryan wasn't sure he could think about that right now without leaving blood on the walls of the trendy bar.

"Johnson's slippery as an eel. Unless you have him in custody already, I don't see how it's going to happen any time soon," said Risa.

Nightshade puffed up in indignation, but there wasn't any way to argue the obvious. He'd already confirmed the Justice Department's inept handling of the matter. The meeting was over.

Marissa was quietly furious, and it was unclear how long she'd keep those feelings under wraps. She asked Bryan to follow them to the Best Western, where she had a reservation. That way he wouldn't be trying to rent a hotel room with his face all over the television.

After checking in, she handed Bryan her keycard in the hotel parking lot and left with Nightshade. Bryan had no idea what was going on there. But by that time he was so exhausted and angry at the disaster that was the Justice Department's ongoing investigation that he didn't care. Maybe Marissa would shoot Nightshade and save him the trouble.

He took a shower to wash off the road grime and fell into bed, only to feel the quiet hum of caffeine overload buzzing in his veins. If he thought of what Nightshade had revealed about Johnson and Afghanistan, he wouldn't be able to function.

It was just too much. He had to shut that shit off for now. He could always pull it out and agonize over the situation later, 'cause this was gonna be a damn long night.

Chapter 23

December 30
Early morning

WHEN THE PHONE rang, Bryan had slept just long enough to be groggy and disoriented. One glance at the hotel clock and he knew it wasn't good news. No one ever called with good news at 2:00 AM.

It was Bear. Bryan didn't even have to hear his frantic explanation before an aching sense of unease settled and brought him fully awake.

"Sassy's gone. I came downstairs after taking a shower and . . . a nap. The alarm was turned off, and my truck was missing. There was no sign of forced entry."

Bryan knew without being told that she hadn't left under duress. He didn't know what had happened, but he didn't believe anyone had stolen her away from Bear's. No, Sassy was out doing exactly what he'd asked her not to—trying to do something for Trey on her own.

Dammit.

"Was she on the computer before she left?" Bryan asked.

"Yeah. She was working on her story and . . . shit. She checked her email." Bear's voice was full of self-reproach. "I never should have gone upstairs to rest. I should have known something was up."

Bryan shook his head. *Hell, Sassy. You said you wouldn't do this.*

"Don't blame yourself, Bear. This is what she does. Is there any way to see what she was up to on her email?"

"Yeah. Give me a minute."

While Bryan was waiting for Bear to hack into Sassy's email, he started texting Marissa. There wasn't much his boss could do. She'd pulled in all her big favors for the meeting with Nightshade.

The man had made it clear that he would do nothing to endanger the corruption case against Johnson. Helping Sassy would surely fall into that category. But Risa would want to be kept in the loop, plus she had that uncanny ability to pull rabbits out of hats.

Bryan finished the text as Bear came back on the line. "Sassy's gone to meet Rivera."

"What?" Of all the crazy scenarios, Bryan had not seen that one coming.

"Rivera emailed her and asked to meet. Said he has valuable information that can help her brother. She emailed him back and agreed to meet at The Hot Pot . . . about thirty minutes from now."

Shit. He was six hours away at best.

"And I'm fresh out of transportation," said Bear.

Sassy had done exactly what she'd promised she wouldn't. Bryan shook his head as disbelief morphed from disappointment to anger then dread. Was she that impulsive? *God, the woman needs a keeper.*

She'd promised not to go off on her own. He understood how Rivera's holding out a helping hand to Trey would have caused her to reconsider. But he couldn't believe she was naïve enough to believe the man would keep his word.

Desperation made one gullible.

Gullible wasn't a word he'd normally associate with Sassy. Did she honestly believe that Rivera would help Trey? Or was this about getting a scoop for her story? The idea burned as his hand tightened on the cell phone.

He could see Sassy meeting Rivera to get Trey help, but the way she'd done it made him livid. He didn't want to think about her going behind his back and stealing Bear's truck. That she trusted him so little after everything they'd been through together hurt like hell.

You shouldn't trust me now, either.

Damn. That wasn't what he'd meant last night. But he could certainly see how today, after he'd left without saying goodbye, she might have taken those words way out of context.

Christ. He wasn't going to think about that, or he'd make himself nuts. He needed to focus on how to find her.

Why would Rivera have come into the United States? The man was on the DEA's most wanted list. He'd never risk capture on U.S. soil. What would motivate the drug dealer to do such a thing? The answer dawned with stunning clarity and dismay.

Revenge.

It was the only motive that would make a man take that kind of crazy personal risk. Rivera knew Johnson was the one who'd sold him down the river and killed his family: his wife, Carlita Vega, and his brothers-in-law, Cesar and Ernesto Vega. He'd told Nick in Skikda that he'd been betrayed by someone he trusted.

Rivera had figured it all out before anyone at AEGIS or the Justice Department had. And Rivera had made it clear that he wasn't after AEGIS. They were "off his radar" if what he had said to Nick in Algeria was true.

So why did Rivera want Sassy now? What could she possibly bring to the table?

She wasn't involved in any direct way except for her relationship with Trey. Bryan had left her at Bear's believing that she'd be out of harm's way and could work on her story. The story that wasn't such a Hail Mary idea after all, particularly after his meeting with Nightshade and Marissa.

The answer was right in front of him, but he couldn't put his finger on it. He sat and stared at the generic hotel room: the desk, the sofa, the complimentary newspaper on the dresser.

Of course. He smiled grimly as the idea dawned.

Sassy's news story. That was what Rivera was after. And why the man had wanted to meet Sassy.

They were so screwed.

December 30
Early morning
Washington, D.C.

FORD JOHNSON SAT in his plush office, staring at the message on the computer screen. Tomas Rivera was here in the U.S., and he wanted to meet. But Ford had no illusions about the situation. Rivera wasn't making a social call.

Discovery had been inevitable, and Ford was running out of options unless he took some drastic action. He knew that, even if he couldn't believe the day was finally here. Since he and Rivera were the last men standing, it only made sense that Tomas had figured things out. Whether Rivera recognized just how long he had been played wasn't really important.

Ford had a contingency plan that he'd been working on for a long time. He pulled up a new window on his computer screen, clicked on a map, and made note of the target before typing in the authorization codes for the launch.

He knew all about the Justice Department investigation, but that was being taken care of. When he bagged the DEA's and FBI's most wanted cartel leader here on U.S. soil, the investigation of Ford Johnson would simply go away. All would be forgiven.

Still, investigative news reports were not so easy to cover up. But Ford could escape unscathed *if* the AEGIS team played this out as expected. Heroes were so predictable. Loyalty was their downfall, particularly when one knew how to exploit it.

December 30
Early morning
The Hot Pot

SASSY TOOK A shallow breath through her mouth in an attempt to calm her racing heart. The scent of rich leather seats, expensive cologne, and velvety tobacco combined to make her slightly nauseated.

"Miss Smith. Thank you for joining me." The voice was smooth and slightly accented.

The driver's door slammed, and the car backed out of the parking place. She glanced out her window as they pulled onto the highway.

A spurt of anger had her snapping out a reply with her usual snark. "It's not like I had much choice in the matter."

She was grateful her voice was strong. She inhaled slowly and bit her lower lip to stop it from trembling. She'd been insane to come alone and meet Rivera without leaving word. Right now she was just grateful the backseat was dark enough that her captor host couldn't see the panic in her eyes.

"Ah, I disagree. You came to the diner alone, as I asked. You didn't have to do that." There was a grudging note of respect in his tone.

"You said this was about my brother. I'd do anything to help him."

"Ah, yes, Trey Smith. Your brother has had quite the hard road through no fault of his own. He was just in the wrong place at the wrong time."

"I'd say that he and Elizabeth Yarborough were both in the wrong place at the wrong time." Sassy couldn't believe she was being so waspish, but she hated this game they were playing. As if this encounter were all so civilized.

"Agreed." Even though the car was dimly lit, she could see the man shake his head in the shadows.

"Do you know where she is?" Sassy demanded.

"No, I do not. That fiasco was all Ernesto Vega's doing. He was supposed to dispose of her in Mexico, but he couldn't stand the thought of it. The last I heard the girl was in West Africa, but I'm afraid the knowledge of her exact whereabouts died with Vega." Rivera made it sound as if they were talking about a lost umbrella rather than a living, breathing person.

"Do you think she is still alive?" Sassy struggled to keep the anger in her voice to a minimum. It would do her no good to antagonize this man.

"I seriously doubt it, given the current state of West Africa. Vega had her in a brothel there for a time, and from what I understood when we spoke of her last, she was quite ill."

"Ill? What was wrong with her?"

Rivera shrugged. "Take your pick: malaria, an STD, Ebola? I believe there may have just been too much unpleasantness for her to deal with."

Unpleasantness?

That was the understatement of the decade. Even if Elizabeth had survived an African brothel, with its rampant STDs, HIV, and abuse, surviving the rampages of Ebola would have been impossible.

The thought of it all would normally have had Sassy in tears, but tonight she didn't have the luxury of allowing herself to feel. She had to put the thought of Elizabeth's horrible fate away. She'd grieve another time.

For now, Sassy had to focus on why she was here. There was no reason to play coy or beat around the bush, so she kept silent on all the unasked questions about Elizabeth and jumped straight to the heart of the matter. "How can you help my brother?"

In the shadows, Rivera nodded at her question. "I have special 'relationships' with some of the judiciary in my country. The judges have a great deal of latitude in the Mexican legal system. I can have your brother's charges dismissed with a phone call."

Her jaw dropped. She didn't doubt what Rivera said. The Mexican court system was infamous for its corruption. Judges investigated cases themselves and were subject to bribes and intimidation by the cartels. Incorruptible judges were as rare as snowflakes in July. Cases against drug dealers were dismissed all the time.

She turned to face Rivera on the soft leather seat. "It's not that I don't appreciate the offer, but why would you do that?" she asked.

Rivera chuckled. "I appreciate your candor, Miss Smith. You have a directness that's most refreshing."

Sassy pulled her old armor around her and sat up straighter. "I'm delighted that I amuse you. What do I have to do to get you to make that phone call?"

"Not much." Rivera didn't even bother to act as if this wasn't a quid pro quo situation. "I just need you to kill the story you are currently working on for your editor."

"I'm currently working on several stories. Which one are we talking about?" Her tone was light and flirty even as her stomach knotted. *How did he know?*

She needed to make sure which story was at issue here, although she was certain she knew the one they were discussing. Even so, she didn't want to tip her hand. This was familiar ground, and a game she was used to playing. The stakes were just much higher this time around.

Rivera sighed. "There's no reason to be coy. The story about sex trafficking in Mexico and Africa. The one that speaks of the relationship between myself, Ernesto Vega, and Ford Johnson."

"What makes you think I'm working on such a story?"

Rivera shook his head. "Please, do you mind if I call you Sassy?"

"Of course not. You can call me whatever you like," she murmured.

"Well, Sassy, let's dispense with the charade. I don't like explaining myself. But I'm going to make an exception because . . . you amuse me. I have many business associates and contacts around the world, many of whom would rather not be 'known.' Opening that door so publicly—for instance, with a news story—into the private workings of my associates . . ." He let the words hang for a moment. "Let's just say it would be bad for everyone."

The time for game playing was long past, and Sassy knew she had to lay everything on the table here or risk

Trey's freedom. She swallowed hard. "But Ford Johnson betrayed you. Why wouldn't you want him exposed in the most public forum possible?"

Rivera's laugh was chilling. "Oh, don't worry. I have plans for Ford Johnson."

Sassy's mind raced. Quashing the story went against everything she believed in as a journalist. But for Trey, she'd do this, and more. Bryan and his team would be abandoned, though, with zero support against false allegations in the press. She hated that.

But for now, she didn't see a way out of it. It was Bryan's team in a U.S. jail for a few weeks until this was all unwound or Trey in a Mexican prison permanently. She closed her eyes and made the only choice she could.

"I can stop the story." *If I desert Bryan and the others.* "How soon can you speak to the judge about Trey?"

"I'll take care of it immediately." She saw his smile flash in the glow of the dashboard. Perhaps it was because he was doing something for Trey, but she wasn't nearly as put off by the smile as she had been earlier.

She took a deep breath for the first time since she'd sat in the car. Rivera handed her a phone. "It's clean. No one can trace it. Call your editor," he instructed.

Sassy didn't hesitate and dialed Howard's number to leave a message: "Hey Howard, it's Sassy. I'm not coming up with any more sources on that story. I'm going to table it for now, but I'll keep digging. I'm sorry. I'll call you if I find anything."

She hung up and handed the phone back. Rivera stared with a raised eyebrow.

"If I announced I was dropping the story completely, he'd suspect something was wrong," she explained.

Rivera nodded as he dialed, then began speaking in rapid-fire Spanish. Sassy recognized Trey's name and understood just enough of the language to grasp that Rivera was doing what he'd said he would. He was telling the judge to let Trey go.

Could it be that easy? She could scarcely believe it. After all these months, the man responsible for her brother's incarceration was negotiating his release.

Euphoria overrode her anger in a dizzying rush. She was glad she was sitting down, or she might have fallen over. Rivera was talking about the judge's family.

Jesus, was he threatening them? She didn't have it in her to be disgusted. This was about getting Trey out of a snake pit, where his life was threatened on a daily basis.

She glanced out the window. The moon illuminated a deep ditch running along the right-hand side of the road and a several-hundred-foot drop on the left. She'd been so sleepy yesterday, she hadn't noticed the ravine on the drive with Bryan and Bear.

Bryan . . . God, what was she going to tell him about all this? She'd gotten Trey out of jail, but would Bryan ever trust her again?

Rivera ended the call. "It's done," he announced.

"Thank you." The relief had her feeling as if she was swaying from side to side.

It took a moment to register that this wasn't only relief but real motion on the road. The car had been swaying from side to side and now began to swerve violently from one shoulder to the other in broad, evasive maneuvers.

Rivera leaned forward to shout at the driver. "What the hell is going on?!"

Sassy fought to hold herself still long enough to peer through the front windshield. Something was floating in front of the car. She blinked hard.

What was that? *Tiny helicopters?*

It didn't make sense. How was that even possible?

She was wearing a seat belt, but the action of the car's swerving didn't stop her head from hitting the window as they continued to careen from one side of the road to the other—running off one narrow shoulder, swerving sharply back up onto the highway, then sliding off on the other shoulder.

The driver cursed vividly in Spanish. Once more they slid to the left side of the road and off onto the shoulder. Rivera shouted; Sassy cried out. This time they didn't make it back up onto the asphalt. Instead, they were airborne in a stomach-clenching, weightless free fall before hitting hard.

Air bags deployed, but the car didn't stop rolling. Tumbling end over end, the Town Car fell down the embankment at a terrific rate of speed. After the third flip, all Sassy could hear was a roaring in her ears and the screech of tearing metal.

She felt a final, tremendous jolt, searing pain, then nothing.

Chapter 24

December 30
Morning

IT WAS 7:30 AM and a thick fog clung to the interstate, obscuring the road and the sky as Bryan sped back to Bear's house. Surely the sun would burn through it soon. Cold as hell, Bryan was as exhausted as he could ever remember being. But his fear over what was going on with Sassy kept him wide awake while he chewed through a pack of Dentyne he'd found in his backpack, the gum Sassy had bought for him in New York.

He was two hours out from Kingstree and had to stop for gas and coffee. He pulled the motorcycle helmet off but replaced it with a baseball hat pulled down low over his forehead. He had multiple missed calls from Bear and dialed back as he filled the tank on the bike.

Bear answered on the first ring.

"It's me, what do you have?" asked Bryan.

His friend didn't answer.

"Bear, you've called me eight times. What the hell?"

"Not great news, Hollywood. There's been an accident." Bear's typically laid-back tone was fraught with tension, and his voice broke on the word *accident.*

"What is it?" A cold ball of horror settled in Bryan's stomach as he stared unseeing at the gray sky. He didn't want to hear this. Somehow he just knew that whatever Bear was about to tell him was going to change everything.

"A car accident, about ten miles out from your favorite diner. Rivera's dead."

"How do you know this?" Bryan squeezed his eyes shut, dreading the details but pushing forward anyway.

"I have a police scanner. The accident happened on a big embankment, the car went off into a ravine. From what I could tell, there was some kind of freak explosion."

The breath swooshed out of Bryan's body, but he held onto the handle of the gas nozzle with numb fingers. He had to force those roiling emotions away for now. This was a time for facts only.

A freak explosion was entirely too coincidental when they were talking about the drone technology Johnson had access to. It took more courage than he thought he had to ask the next question. "Was Sassy in the car?"

Again, Bear hesitated, his silence telling Bryan everything he needed to know.

"I'm so sorry, man. The scanners reported that the driver and passenger were burned beyond recognition. They didn't say who was who. I haven't heard anything else since they cleared the road. They must have switched to another frequency."

Burned beyond recognition.

Bryan swallowed hard and struggled to focus on Bear's words, instead of the stupefying pain exploding in his chest. But the pounding in his head was overriding everything, building to an unholy crescendo.

And Bear was still talking with that flat voice. "I called the diner. My truck is in the parking lot. I'll . . . I'll try to find out more." It was obvious that he thought Sassy was dead.

Bryan wasn't wrapping his head around the concept yet, even as the burn of hot tears stung his eyelids. The frigid December wind gusted through the gas station. He'd felt this kind of overwhelming pain once before. Two years ago, when he'd lost his team in Afghanistan, he'd been swallowed up in an abyss of hopelessness. He'd never thought to experience that kind of misery again. He'd closed himself off from relationships to guarantee it.

So why did this hurt so much?

Without realizing how exposed he'd been, he'd clawed his way out of that hole these past months, inch by miserable inch—ever since he'd started working with Sassy last summer.

Why was this hitting so hard?

The answer was simple and fucking heartbreaking at the same time. He was still in love with her, after all this time. But he'd waited too damn late to figure it out. Too late to tell her anything except how he wasn't looking for anything permanent.

Was she really gone?

He couldn't believe that. Not yet. A paralyzing chill

swept through his body, and he sagged against the gas pump. He was going to be sick.

"I'm going to have to call you back, Bear. Find out what you can and let me know." He ended the call without waiting for a reply and shoved the gasoline nozzle back in the pump.

He headed for the bathroom at a sprint. It was an older station, with restrooms outside the building. The heavy door opened with a teeth-setting *screech,* and he pushed through to lock himself in. He'd barely made it to the dingy toilet before his stomach revolted.

Afterward, he leaned back against the cinder-block wall, hot tears rolling down his cheeks. If Sassy was dead, he was done.

Over.

Everything he thought he'd been digging himself out of these past two years was through. He'd been fooling himself all along. He hadn't been able to protect her. Just like when he'd left her in Mississippi all those years ago. He'd been lying to her and to himself by thinking he could keep her safe.

He wasn't sure how long he sat there with his head against the wall, crying like a baby. His legs were stiff by the time he got up. He flushed the ancient commode, went to the sink to rinse his mouth out, and splashed some water on his face. The hand dryer sounded like an airplane taking off. When the dryer shut down, the silence was deafening. The wind whistled outside as he gazed into the dingy mirror.

His eyes were bloodshot from tears and lack of sleep,

plus his nose was Rudolph red. He looked as if he'd been kicked in the head. He stared at his reflection, desperate to pull himself together despite the bleakness in his expression.

"Snap the fuck out of it!" He spoke the words aloud, but his voice sounded rusty. Even if Sassy was dead, it didn't change what had to happen next.

Who the hell was he kidding?

Sassy's death changed everything. He'd waited too late to tell her how he felt, and now it was much too late for anything. He was alone, without even the memory of telling her the truth to warm him. The world was a cold place and about to get colder still.

The hum of the ancient fluorescent light fixture grew louder as he continued to study his reflection in the dirty glass. The tears dried, and his cool gray eyes cleared to the soulless stare he'd honed in Afghanistan. The man responsible for this, Ford Johnson, would pay.

No matter what it took. No matter what it cost. If Bryan had to die himself to make it happen, Ford Johnson would pay.

A LONG SERIES of black skid marks tattooed the lonely stretch of highway where Rivera's car had careened over the embankment and down into the ravine. Bryan slowed as he passed the flame-blackened slope. Bear had texted him the exact GPS coordinates at the gas station, along with the admonition not to lose hope, since they didn't know for certain what had happened . . . if Sassy was alive or dead.

But Bryan was miles beyond lost hope.

Everything in the media about the accident had been locked down and shut up tight as a drum. The police scanners, even the ones Bear could access, were strangely silent.

Bryan had ridden for another hour and a half to get here, trying not to think about what he would find once he arrived. To keep himself from howling at the insanity of it all, he allowed himself to focus only on finding answers. Even revenge would have to take a backseat to that for now.

Marissa remained in Atlanta, working to cut the AEGIS guys loose from custody, along with Anna, Zach, and Jennifer. The red tape occasionally required more time to hack through. The crazy thing was that even with the evidence the Justice Department had against Johnson, an indictment wasn't a slam dunk. In the current political climate, the U.S. government wasn't too concerned about the illegal use of drones in Mexico against drug dealers.

The narrow highway along the ravine was unremarkable except for those stark black marks and the remains of flares where the emergency vehicles had set up earlier to investigate the wreckage. Following the skid tracks, Bryan could see that Rivera had fought hard to stay on the road for several hundred yards before ultimately losing the battle.

He stopped the motorcycle a few feet beyond the last burned-out flare canister and gazed over the bleak hillside, forcing himself to look toward the bottom of the ravine. Tree limbs rattled in a steady north wind that had picked up throughout the day. The temperature was dropping. Most likely there was a front coming through, but he was beyond caring.

If there were tears in his eyes, they were only from the frigid air gusting across the road. Beyond feeling, he was numb. He had been since he'd walked out of that restroom at the gas station. He wasn't sure he'd ever be warm again, and right now he didn't give a damn.

His phone vibrated in his pocket with an incoming text message. He ignored it, assuming it was Bear. Again. He'd been texting Bryan more information after finding another way to access the police scanners.

Investigators were puzzled by the wreckage. Something about the burn marks was off. Two people were confirmed dead at the scene, but no names had been released.

Bryan didn't need names. He knew Sassy was gone. Despite the punch to the gut at seeing that blackened slope, he was morbidly relieved to view the accident site for himself—to confirm what he had felt in his bones when Bear had first told him the news.

He walked back to the spot in the road where the skid marks abruptly stopped, then he carefully picked his way along the burned path that Rivera's vehicle had taken. There was a massive boulder at the bottom of the ravine, blackened across one side and split on a corner.

He swallowed hard. He wasn't sure what he'd been expecting to see. He wasn't an accident investigator himself, but one thing was clear from the scorched earth leading from the road at the top of the embankment to the bottom of the steep slope: The vehicle was on fire before it left the road and flipped several times on the way down.

He stared at the soot on the boulder and chewed at his lower lip. A multitude of things could have caused the car to catch fire before it left the road, but only one made sense. The same thing that had taken out the train he and Sassy had been on three nights ago.

The phone buzzed once more. This time it was a call. Bear was going to keep at it until Bryan picked up. He reached for the phone, but the screen showed a D.C. area code.

"Who is this?" Bryan demanded.

"That's not a very pleasant greeting." The voice had a sharp Boston accent. "Besides, I think you've figured that out by now. But just in case, my name is Ford Johnson."

Bryan swallowed the fury clogging his throat. "What do you want?"

"To make a trade."

"What do you have that I could possibly want?" asked Bryan.

You've already taken everything.

"What an interesting question." Johnson laughed, and Bryan wanted to reach through the phone and kill him. "Check your sources, Mr. Fisher. I'm sure you know by now that there's been a tragic accident. But what you may not know is that there was also a survivor . . . Do I have your attention?"

Bryan gripped the phone but said nothing.

"I have someone that I believe you want very much," said Johnson.

Bryan exhaled. "She's alive?"

"For the time being. Yes, Sassy Smith is alive."

Bryan felt his knees start to give way and put his hand on the boulder to catch himself. *Sweet Jesus.* She was alive. But Johnson had her. So how long she would stay alive was entirely dependent on what happened next.

He squeezed his eyes shut and swallowed the lump in his throat, willing his mind to clear as he slipped into combat mode. "Is she okay?"

"A little banged up. But she's alright. She's tough for such a little thing."

Damn straight. Bryan knew that firsthand. Sassy was tough, and he'd bet she was feisty as the devil in this particular situation.

"I want her back without any more bumps or bruises. What do you want in exchange?" What Bryan was willing to trade for her safety right now should have frightened him.

Johnson didn't hesitate. "This is a discussion better held face-to-face. Meet me in Atlanta tomorrow at noon. I'll contact you in the morning with the address. I don't need to tell you to come alone."

"Of course." Bryan ended the call. Weak-kneed with relief, he sat down hard on the ground beside the scorched boulder. He'd allow himself this moment.

Sassy was alive. She wasn't dead. She was alive and right now possibly giving someone hell about what they were doing. He couldn't believe it. This time he was happy to feel the hot tears scald his cheeks. He shook his head as the knowledge sank in.

She's alive. No matter what happened, no matter the cost, he planned to keep her that way.

Chapter 25

December 30
Late afternoon

SASSY WAS ENVELOPED in cotton, clawing her way out of a suffocating cocoon. She couldn't breathe, couldn't speak, couldn't move. Despite her rising panic, she kept telling herself it was all a dream as she swam her way back to consciousness—not because she wanted to, but because someone in the room was prattling on and on and wouldn't shut up. She longed to tell them to be quiet and to let her rest. But when she was finally coherent enough to understand what she was hearing, reality came rushing back, along with an excruciating headache.

She'd been in the car with Rivera. There'd been an accident. Then . . . nothing? There was a hazy memory of fire and someone screaming—another dream, perhaps? She took a deep breath, and the scent of singed hair and smoky clothing assaulted her nostrils. Her eyes flew open. That was no dream.

Her heart rate sped up as she took note of her surroundings despite the pounding in her temples. She was alone in a huge bed, facing a balcony window with a stunning view of the sunset over a massive lake. Treetops were at eye level, and mountains shrouded in mist were painted brilliant oranges and purples in the dying light. She wasn't sure if she was in a hotel or a private residence, but she heard what sounded like the engine of a small plane in the distance, although the plane itself was invisible in the twilight.

She turned her head, aware of an overwhelming need for a bathroom. Her vision swam. She closed her eyes until everything stopped spinning and cautiously opened them again.

The room was spectacularly decorated in antiques. A large television was on, tuned to a twenty-four-hour cable news channel. At last she'd located the source of that incessant chatter.

She tried to sit up—big mistake—and her head felt as if it were sliding off her shoulders. She lay back down and closed her eyes once more, willing the agony to subside. Even the light from the sunset hurt. But the need for the toilet won out over the headache and she stood, spying the sumptuously appointed bathroom from the bed. Surprisingly, once she was upright, her head felt markedly better.

Where was she? Why was she here and not in a hospital after that accident? Who had her?

She headed for the bathroom and took care of the most pressing issue first, then washed her hands and face. When she finally braved glancing in the mirror, she was sorry she had. Her hair was matted along the side of her face, and she was working on a pair of serious black eyes. She looked as if she'd been in a bar fight. How long had she been out?

Despite her dirty face, the bandage from her stitches in South Carolina had been changed. She had a huge bump on the back of her head and a new small cut above her eyebrow, but no memory of hitting her head. It had to be from the accident but . . . God, why couldn't she remember anything?

The effort of thinking about that, plus the bathroom lights, were making her headache worse. She made her way back to the bed and was just lying down when she heard the door open. She lay very still with her eyes closed, trying to peek out between her lashes.

A man moved into the room, but she couldn't tell much beyond that. He stopped beside the bed, and she could practically feel the impatience rolling off him in waves.

"It's no good, Ms. Smith. I know you're awake. I heard the water running earlier." The accent was pure Boston, with a definite nasal twang.

Sassy exhaled and opened her eyes. The man staring down at her was of average height and build. With his thinning gray hair and unfashionable glasses, he looked like an accountant. Probably somewhere between forty-five and fifty-five, he was completely innocuous looking until she got a closer glimpse at his clear blue eyes. The lack of emotion there was startling. His lifeless expression made her want to burrow under the covers for warmth.

"Who are you?" Her voice sounded rusty. She had a pretty good idea of who this was already.

The man studied her a moment, his cold stare giving nothing away. "My name is Ford Johnson."

Sassy froze, and Johnson smiled faintly. "I see you've heard of me."

She didn't reply. Instead she listened, maintaining a blank expression. She'd never been much of a poker player, but she had learned a lot over the years about lying to men. She was an expert when it came to hiding her true feelings.

"Sit up. We need to talk."

Sassy slowly pulled herself up in the bed. "Is Rivera dead?" she finally asked.

Johnson smiled more broadly this time, his eyes actually taking on some warmth. "Yes, he is. He and his driver died in the aftermath of the car crash."

"Aftermath?" Sassy remembered snatches of the ride and swerving on the road, but she had no real recollection of the crash itself. Her blinding headache was bound to have something to do with that.

"The fire," said Johnson. While his eyes had warmed, his voice was still quite cold.

She wasn't a fan of Tomas Rivera, but what a horrible way to die. "How did I . . ." She didn't remember anything about a fire beyond those hazy dream images.

"How did you survive?" Johnson finished for her.

She nodded, but the motion had her closing her eyes against the fresh wave of throbbing pain in her temple.

"My men pulled you out of the car."

"Could they not get to Rivera and his driver in time?" she asked.

Johnson shrugged. "I didn't ask them to. I only needed you. I didn't realize you were with Rivera until we'd arranged for the accident. And I knew you could be of much better use to me alive."

Sassy tried not to visibly shudder. This man was a monster. She'd known it intellectually after talking with Nick and Leland, but to hear him speak so casually of people's usefulness and living and dying was stunning, nonetheless.

"I need you to do something for me that only you can do, Ms. Smith."

If her head wasn't already spinning, the casual segue to her doing a favor for him would have made her dizzy. "I don't understand." She stopped herself just in time from shaking her head from side to side.

"I need you to write a news story for me."

Sassy pulled back as a bizarre sense of déjà vu settled over her. How surreal that Johnson would want a story whereas Rivera had asked her to stop one.

"What kind of story?" she asked.

"Oh, something like what I imagine you were already writing for your editor . . . but with a twist."

"How did you know I was working on something for my editor?"

Johnson stared and shook his head. "You don't think I could get access to your online storage account?"

She sighed. *Of course.* With his resources, hacking her account would be child's play.

"The story you've written is quite good, but I need a few things tweaked."

She frowned and felt the zing of her headache when her brow crinkled. *Tweaked*? She truly hated that word when someone was applying it to her writing.

"What kind of things do you need 'tweaked'?" she asked.

Johnson settled a hip on the edge of the bed. "I've discovered that the public will forgive quite a few sins in the pursuit of the war on drugs, but some things will not fly. Sex trafficking is one."

Sassy frowned. "But the main point of my news story is the human trafficking in Africa."

He nodded. "I understand. This is where the adjustment comes in. I want you to present evidence that AEGIS used their resources to cover up their own involvement in human trafficking in order to frame me."

"What?" This time she forgot about her headache. Raising her eyebrows merely intensified the pain once again.

"It's quite easy. Bryan Fisher kidnapped you in New York after you found out what AEGIS was doing. You barely managed to get away from him after the train wreck in South Carolina, but tragically an older couple was killed in the cross fire."

She stared at the man in shock. Ford Johnson was a diabolical liar and possibly a bit mad. But there was just enough truth in the story he wanted her to fabricate to make things believable. Just enough truth for a twenty-four-hour news cycle that wouldn't fact-check the details too closely before putting out this version of the tale.

"You don't honestly think you can keep your job, do you?" she asked.

"Stranger things have happened. At this point, I only need the government to hesitate in firing me. Consider this story a way of buying me time."

He shrugged as the realization dawned on her. *Of course he'd keep his job.*

"The U.S. government won't care that I used drones illegally in Mexico, as long as I neutralized the two biggest cartel kingpins and didn't run any kind of guns."

"But you killed a baby, crippled a mother, killed a young woman, and were complicit in wrongfully incarcerating a U.S. citizen in Mexico."

"I understand Rivera called the judge about your brother. I believe he will be released despite Rivera's untimely departure."

"How—"

"We're tapping that particular judge's phone." Johnson leaned closer. Now his eyes held a maniacal light that frightened her. "I can undo Rivera's call to the judge just as quickly as Rivera made it. Don't fuck with me. Write the story. Fisher will be here later, and you can go home with him. It won't matter to me where you go after the story is released."

He turned off the television and studied her. She stared back in silence. A plane buzzed in the distance.

This felt like some kind of dream—that someone else was asking her to change the story, that everything could shift so fast, that Trey could be set free, that Bryan was coming to take her home. Though she wasn't really buying that last part.

This couldn't possibly be as easy as Johnson made it

sound. For one, she'd need to get that slight change in focus for the story past Howard Spear, plus she'd need that elusive source. But she wasn't going to worry about that now.

"You were behind it all, weren't you? From the very beginning."

Johnson's gaze never wavered from hers. "I believe you already know the answer to that."

Sassy sat up straighter in the bed. "You set up Ellis Colton and his family to make him look like a drug runner, didn't you?"

Johnson tilted his head. "You're very well informed. That was a necessary evil. We had a transportation issue with a shipment and needed a credible distraction. The Coltons were unfortunate collateral damage."

"And Nick Donovan's father, ten years ago?"

Johnson shook his head. "I'm not going into this with you. Write the story as I've asked, or I'll simply kill you, have someone else write it, and put your name on it before sending the file to your editor. Doing it my way means you get to live. Hell, you can leave with Fisher as soon as the story goes public. Although for his sake, I'd suggest someplace out of the country with no extradition."

"You don't worry that I could tell them what you made me do?" she asked.

"Given your present circumstances, that would sound a bit fantastic, wouldn't it? After you write a story about being kidnapped by AEGIS . . . only to write of being kidnapped by me, a respected government official, all while being wanted for murder yourself? You'd have a significant credibility issue and be like the little boy crying wolf."

He was right. The convolution of facts and the way he was twisting it all around was crazy. But he would come out smelling like a rose, because the indisputable fact was that two of America's most wanted cartel leaders were dead on Ford Johnson's watch.

Sassy, on the other hand, would sound like a lunatic conspiracy theorist if one story was released then she claimed something else. It could all be cleared up eventually with a thorough investigation into her cloud storage account. But that would take months, and Johnson would be long gone.

She was stuck. Johnson had access to her and her story. And he could do whatever he wanted with it.

Arguing was pointless. She was going to do this, because she wasn't going to die for the job. The idea might sound noble, but she wasn't a writer willing to die for her craft. She'd rather live with her brother free from a Mexican prison and with Bryan. . . .

She shut down that train of thought. Any kind of relationship with Bryan most likely wasn't going to happen after she wrote this story. It would have been one thing not to write about Johnson, but to craft a story hanging all the blame on AEGIS—he'd never be able to get past that.

Hell, was any of this even possible? Was Johnson going to let her go?

After all this, it would be anyone's guess. Cooperating would buy her time, Trey's freedom, and a chance—however small—to figure out what was going on with Bryan. He had left her yesterday. Perhaps he truly was on his way to get her today.

God, she hoped so. She didn't normally allow herself to hope like that.

"Where am I?" she asked.

"Towns County. Lovely, isn't it?" Johnson stood at the window and gazed toward the water and the rapidly darkening sky. "I'd been planning to retire here. The builder just finished this place. That's Lake Chatuge." He pointed toward the glass. "Those are the Blue Ridge Mountains. There's quite the posh resort in the next cove."

"Is this Georgia?"

He nodded.

"What day is it?" she asked.

He chuckled, but it wasn't a pleasant sound. "You got quite the head shot there, didn't you? It's December thirtieth. Tomorrow is New Year's Eve. 'Auld Lang Syne' and all that."

Sassy fought the feelings of helplessness and nausea that simultaneously swamped her. Suddenly she knew. Johnson was lying.

While he might leave Trey's release alone, and Bryan could very well be looking for her this instant, Johnson would never just let her go. Sassy knew too much. As soon as he got what he wanted, she was dead.

She would only speed that time line up by saying she wouldn't cooperate. She was on her own to get herself out of this. She swallowed hard. She needed a plan. Now.

"Could I have some paper, please?" she asked.

Johnson stood and opened the drawer beside her bed. He handed her a yellow legal pad and pen.

She froze but recovered quickly. Was it just yesterday she'd held a yellow pad in her lap and worked on this story at Bear's computer? "Exactly what do you want me to say about AEGIS in the article?"

Johnson began to dictate. He started with the night of the Ellis Colton bust, blaming Leland Hollis for the mistake that brought a SWAT team down on the innocent civilian's family. He outlined how Leland was part of a group of former DEA and ex-CIA operatives who had used their knowledge to set up a sex trafficking network with Gavin Bartholomew heading up the entire operation.

Johnson could have been a novelist in another life. He twisted the facts and crafted a remarkably credible narrative that was bound to sell papers and launch numerous investigations into AEGIS. In defiance of her pounding headache, Sassy took careful notes. When he had finished talking, she leaned back against the headboard.

If she followed Johnson's directive, she would have to do a complete ax job on Bryan and AEGIS. It could all be straightened out over time, but the reputation of AEGIS and its employees would be forever tarnished.

Could she do that to save Trey?

How could she not? Despite the gut-wrenching choice, she'd do anything to save her brother. She comforted herself with the fact that Bryan would want her to do this for

Trey, too. Nonetheless, she kept her eyes down. "I need some time to write the story as you want it."

Johnson nodded. "You have two hours."

"Two hours?" she squeaked. That wasn't long enough. She needed every last minute he'd allow.

"I saw the rough draft, Ms. Smith. You already have most of it written. Isn't this just changing some facts around?"

Again, arguing was pointless. She had no illusions as she fought the paralyzing panic rising up inside her. As soon as he got what he wanted, or if she was foolish enough to say out loud that she wouldn't cooperate, she was dead.

"I want my freedom. The only way I can secure that is by giving you exactly what you've asked for. I want to make sure you receive my best work."

"I'm sure it will be."

"May I have a computer to work with and my original story notes from the cloud account?" she asked.

"Of course." Johnson opened the door, and a guard walked in with a laptop and a tray table, along with a small plate of food and a bottle of water.

She started to refuse the food, but she needed fuel if she was going to work. Eating would likely help her headache, too.

"There's no internet connection," explained Johnson. "We just downloaded the contents of your cloud account into a file."

"I understand." Sassy opened the computer, hoping she looked appropriately eager to start working.

"Anything else?" asked Johnson. "A shower, perhaps? I can have some clothes brought to you. Donald will be right outside your door."

She nodded. "I'd very much like to get cleaned up." A shower might help her pull it together. "Could I have some aspirin, please?"

"Of course." Johnson spoke to the guard who'd dropped off the food. He was back moments later with a small bottle and a stack of clothes: sweatpants, a long-sleeve T-shirt, and underclothes.

"I'll give you an extra hour to shower and eat, but I need the story before eight, Ms. Smith." He pointed to a large clock on the bedside table. "Don't disappoint me."

He closed the door behind him with a resounding snap.

She focused on the lushly carpeted floor for a moment, then turned to the clock. It was 5:05 PM. This was really happening.

She gazed at the computer and the bottle of pain reliever. There was no way she could write until her headache was under control. And whatever else happened this evening, she was going to make sure her brother's deal wasn't jeopardized. If there was any chance of saving Trey with this story, she'd do it. She unscrewed the top on the bottled water and popped three of the caplets.

Three hours. She checked the sliding glass door to the balcony. It was locked down with some kind of mechanism that required a key. She supposed she could try breaking the glass, but that would have to be a very last resort, since the guard would hear the noise and come running.

She went to the window in the bathroom. The same kind of locking mechanism was there as well. She studied the high-tech shower and glanced down at her wrinkled, smelly clothes.

There didn't appear any way out. But in the time it took to shower, perhaps the aspirin would kick in. Maybe then she could pull her scrambled thoughts together enough to figure a way out of her lovely prison or write the hatchet piece that would destroy AEGIS.

How had it come to this?

Chapter 26

December 30
Evening

How HAD IT come to this?

Bryan gave his parachute one final check and pulled himself out of the airplane's doorway onto the strut of the Beaver float plane.

He ground his teeth as he held on and prayed for the jump to be over.

"You hate this, don't you?" shouted Nick from the door.

Bryan nodded once. *Oh yeah.* He loathed skydiving. Night jumps in particular. Not that he wasn't proficient; he just couldn't get used to the sensation of falling through the inky black sky.

"Still can't believe you're a Marine who hates skydiving," said Nick.

"Screw you," shouted Bryan, happy for the opportunity to let the primal scream out that had been building ever since the plane had taken off. The wind buffeted his body as he stood on the strut, freshly reminding him of why he did not like this.

He was thankful Nick was there. Nightshade had pulled a 180 and the stick out of his ass, cutting Leland and Nick loose, along with Jenny, Anna, and Zach. He'd also supplied them with equipment, including a plane and pilot, less than fifteen hours after meeting Bryan in the Sky-Lounge. Bryan didn't want to know what Risa had done to make that happen. He was just grateful for whatever it was and had decided Nightshade might be an okay guy after all.

Leland was back on crutches full-time after the fiasco at Gavin's lake house. He had stayed behind in Atlanta with Anna, her son, and Jennifer. Leland was running comms from there, making sure Bryan and Nick could access everything Bear had for them that was hackable. Nick wouldn't have felt right leaving Jenny unprotected, even though he had more reason to want Johnson than anyone, given what the man had done to his parents.

The pilot had their plane cruising at around 120 miles per hour. Nick climbed out beside Bryan on the strut. Jumping from a float plane was a challenge but not impossible. Still, it had never been on Bryan's bucket list of things to do before the year ended.

He shouted to be heard over the engines. "Meet me by the resort's dock."

Nick nodded, his teeth and eyes the only areas visible on his cammied face. They were about to parachute into the largest resort on Lake Chatuge. Two hours from every conceivable airport, flying had been the quickest and quietest way in. Johnson's compound was locked down like Fort Knox on its own private island across the lake from the White Pines Resort.

The pilot would land on the other side of the lake and wait for word from Bryan to come pick them up when this was all over. Part one of the never-ending fun that was this evening included Bryan and Nick parachuting into White Pines, "borrowing" transport from the resort's boathouse, and getting to Johnson's island. Bryan heartily wished they could skip to the part where they were finding Sassy and getting the hell out of Dodge.

Discovering where she was being held had been part luck and part science. Bear had done it, and on a hunch, too. Working all night, he'd "set traps" on Sassy's various cloud and email accounts that she'd used while at his house. They'd gotten lucky when Johnson had called Bryan at the accident site. Bear had taken that information and used it to locate Johnson when he hacked Sassy's cloud account an hour later.

Nightshade had done the rest in total secrecy. Nothing was official. Bryan wasn't even sure it was entirely legal, but he hadn't questioned the man's methods. He'd needed help getting Sassy, and he wasn't too proud to admit it. He also wasn't looking over that proverbial gift horse too closely.

Unfortunately, parachuting in was the only way to get to the area undetected. While Bear had been snooping around electronically, he'd found that Johnson's house was more of a compound. Even now Bear was working hard at hacking into the sophisticated security system. Bryan and Nick had to find a way to neutralize that system to get to Sassy.

"You ready?" called Nick.

"As I'll ever be." Bryan sucked in the largest breath he possibly could and took a giant step from the strut. The wind was still blasting away at his body, but as he plummeted through the air at over 110 mph, it was surprisingly quiet. Most people loved this part of the jumping experience. For Bryan, it was miserable.

He gritted his teeth. Lights from the resort glowed like jewels on the velvet blanket of the lake's shore. Moments later he deployed the chute. One hundred feet from the ground he lost the reflection of the ambient light, falling into what felt like a black hole before suddenly touching down on the grassy slope beside the water. He felt the jolting smack all the way up his sore back.

Light from the restaurant didn't quite reach his landing area. No one would have seen him unless they'd been looking up as he landed. He glanced up himself but couldn't see Nick, then he began folding the black chute into a stuff sack before heading to the dock. This would be the place he was most likely to be seen. The outside of the boathouse was lit up like a Christmas tree. A black shadow materialized from the other side.

Nick stepped forward, and one of the lights caught the green, brown, and black streaks covering his face. "You okay?" he asked.

"We're on the ground, and I didn't break anything. That's all that matters." Bryan straightened the pack on his back that held his weapons.

Nick snorted a quiet laugh, and they headed for the boathouse, taking care to keep to the shadows as long as possible. Finally they were able to duck inside and be completely out of sight. A fishing boat with a trolling motor was tied next to a larger ski boat.

Bryan spied a couple of paddles and opted for the fishing boat. "We can get away from the dock and start the motor once we're further out."

"Good plan." Nick nodded, and they went to work.

The stars illuminated the sky and the lake. It was a beautiful night, but on the water the bitter cold seeped through every layer Bryan was wearing. Once they were halfway across, he contacted Leland on the combination high-tech SAT phone and computer Nightshade had sent with Nick. Bryan had never seen anything like it before and assumed this was some kind of top-secret prototype. Bear would likely give up a kidney to get his hands on it.

Bryan was careful to keep his voice low, knowing the sound could easily carry and amplify over the water. Through the magic of the prototype's technology, Leland's voice was vivid and distinct in both Bryan's and Nick's earpieces. "I've been talking to Bear. He's got some news. I'm patching him through."

There was a moment of static, then Bear's voice was clear also, as if he was sitting right beside them in the boat instead of three hundred miles away. "I hacked the builder's computer system and hit the mother lode. Found the blueprints for Johnson's place including the security schematic. I'm forwarding both of those to you now through Leland. Bad news is that besides being state-of-the-art security, everything's bulletproof glass and wired out the wazoo."

"Do you have any good news?" asked Bryan.

"Yep. I do. I hacked the contractor's email while I was on the builder's site. There was some big brouhaha about the client wanting sensors that wouldn't show on all the sliding glass doors and windows. They had to be special ordered. A gazillion of the suckers. This place has a lot of sliding glass doors and windows."

"Is there a point to this?" Nick turned off the motor and picked up the paddles, preparing to row the rest of the way to the island.

"The sensors haven't all been installed yet due to holiday slowdowns in postal delivery, plus they got shorted on the last shipment. Lots of nasty emails back and forth between the contractor and the security sub-guy. Some of the second-story windows are uncovered."

"Unless they've been shipped and installed in the past twenty-four hours, you've got a clear path in," said Leland.

"You're kidding." Bryan suppressed a whoop and strained to see the lights of the compound on the island ahead of them.

"Nope. I'm not kidding. And here's the best part. Johnson doesn't know," said Leland.

"What?" hissed Bryan.

"The sub and the contractor discussed it at length. Decided not to tell the client," explained Bear.

"And they put that in an email? They should know better in the security business." Bryan kept his voice quiet, but inside he was doing handstands.

"Some folks are box-of-rocks stupid. Ain't it grand?" said Bear.

"Thank God for that," said Bryan, still incredulous. "Any idea where Sassy is located in the house?"

"No," said Bear. "But I'm looking at the blueprints and can give you an educated guess about where she's not."

"We're too far out of range to use them yet, but once we land, we've got thermal imaging optics." Nick rowed as he spoke, drawing them ever closer to shore.

"Excellent," said Bear. "There are two sets of bedrooms suites on the second floor of the southeast and northwest corners. Kitchens, living areas, workout room, dining room, office are all on the first floor. She's probably upstairs."

Bryan scanned the fast-approaching island with the regular night-vision goggles provided courtesy of Nightshade. "Once we're closer, we'll start with the bedroom suites."

"You'll have to do a little climbing to get to those second-story windows," said Bear.

"Tell us exactly which windows are uncovered," said Nick.

Bear gave them the details and explained what needed to happen on their end to get in without tripping any internal alarms. "It'd be best if you could use the southeast corner," he finished.

"Got it," said Nick.

Bryan put down the goggles and looked at Nick. "Thanks, guys. We couldn't do this without you."

"No problem, Hollywood. Just get her out safe," said Bear.

"That's what I intend to do."

SASSY ENDED UP tweaking the story to Johnson's specifications *before* cleaning up. Once she was finished writing, she climbed into the high-tech shower to wash away the dirty feeling it had given her to twist the facts and lie about AEGIS. The article of fiction wasn't her best work, but it was finished.

She'd just turned off the blow dryer when she heard what sounded like thumping and a sliding glass door opening in her bedroom. She rewrapped the luxurious towel around herself and opened the bathroom door. Curtains from the balcony billowed in a frigid breeze, and two hulking men in dark clothes and fully camouflaged faces stood just inside the doorway with automatic weapons hanging from their sides.

How had they gotten in? That balcony door had been locked when she'd checked earlier. She fought the scream rising up in her throat, recognizing both Bryan and Nick a split second before she let loose with a banshee yell.

Bryan moved toward her with an expression that was hard to read through the cammo paint, but his eyes were a molten gray. "Oh my God," she murmured in a squeaky sigh. "It's you."

Under Bryan's hot stare, she pulled the towel a little tighter around her chest and barely stopped herself from stepping forward into his arms. Instead, she remained rooted in the doorway, forcing him to come to her.

He'd left her yesterday morning without a word. He couldn't be here out of anything more than an overblown sense of obligation. While she was extraordinarily grateful he was here, she wasn't going to embarrass him or make it more than it was. She couldn't trust him with her heart. He was standing just inches away from her as she struggled to puzzle it all out under his mesmerizing stare. Heavy footsteps sounded in the hallway.

Bryan put a finger to her lips, reminding her of the last time he'd done that under such different circumstances. There was a knock at the bedroom door. Nick melted back onto the patio, but there was nowhere for Bryan to go except against the wall behind that bedroom door. He flattened himself against the paneling, but he would be seen as soon as the door opened if Sassy didn't do something. Fast.

There weren't many options. *Hell.* There was really only one. Her stomach churned at the thought, even as she made up her mind to do it.

Taking a deep breath, she stepped into the middle of the room as the door opened and let the towel drop to the floor.

BRYAN'S HEART CLENCHED even as he took in the splendor that was Sassy Smith in the nude. The guard stopped in the doorway as if he'd been struck dumb. Bryan truly understood why.

Sassy au naturel was a sight to behold.

Given everything she'd told him earlier about what had happened to her in high school and the fact that she'd never slept with anyone until forty-eight hours ago, he had a pretty good idea of what it had taken for her to drop the towel. And she'd done it to protect him. Bryan wanted to pick the bath sheet up and wrap it around her himself. Because while she might talk a big game, underneath that tough exterior was a fiercely modest person.

"What do we have here?" the guard mumbled under his breath even as he leered, never taking his eyes from Sassy's body.

"I need to get my clothes," she murmured in a breathy voice that sounded like something straight out of a porn movie.

The guard said nothing but continued to ogle her lasciviously as Bryan stepped from behind the door and hit the man in the back of the head with the butt of his MP5.

The guard sank to the floor. Bryan closed and locked the door. When he turned back, Nick was already tying the man's hands and feet as Sassy scrambled for her towel. She was trying hard not to moon anyone in the process. Not that Bryan would have minded.

"Don't think I'm not grateful you hit him over the head, but what in hell were you waiting for?" she asked, rewrapping herself in the bath sheet.

Feeling inexplicably happy given their current situation, Bryan shrugged and smiled. "I was caught up in the glory of a naked Sassy Smith."

She frowned and stared at him a moment as if he'd lost his mind. "It's nothing you haven't seen before," she retorted.

There was a long pause. A blush bloomed across her face and neck as she belatedly recognized what she'd alluded to in front of Nick. There was nothing Bryan could say that wouldn't make this exponentially worse. He wisely chose to keep his mouth shut.

Nick had no such inclination as he disarmed the unconscious guard. "I promise I didn't see a thing. But if I had, I'm sure I wouldn't have been able to move or speak, either." He winked at her before shoving the guard's prone body into one of the partially empty closets.

Sassy shook her head, but she was smiling, too, even as her blush deepened. "You're both nuts. But I'm awfully glad you're here, even if you are crazy. How did you find me?" She directed the question to Nick. Apparently, she wasn't speaking to Bryan anymore.

"It's complicated. Let's just say Bear Bennett is incredibly resourceful, and we all should buy lottery tickets when this is over."

She cocked her head. "I don't understand."

"You weren't in the southeast corner, but he hacked the system from three hundred miles away, and that's pretty damn good," explained Nick.

"I still don't—"

"It doesn't matter," interrupted Bryan. "Get dressed so we can get you out of here."

She started to nod, then furrowed her brow instead. "No. If I leave before giving Johnson this story, he will undo a deal that was made to get Trey out of jail."

As she explained the situation, Bryan glanced at Nick. Hearing Sassy tell what Johnson wanted her to do with her story—blaming AEGIS for everything—made it clear that Johnson thought he was above the law. There was only one thing to be done. The one thing he and

Nick were both very good at: tracking and eliminating targets.

Ford Johnson wasn't going to get the chance to undo anything. He was going down, tonight. And while there was no way Nick Donovan would be willing to walk away without going after Johnson, Bryan wasn't taking Sassy along for the ride while he and Nick searched the compound and took care of the man.

Bryan was confident that between the two of them, he and Nick could keep Sassy safe, but this was about not wanting her to see what they were going to do. Because Ford Johnson wasn't going to be arrested or taken into custody. They were way beyond that.

"A pilot is waiting in a float plane on the other side of the lake. Ready to fly over here and scoop us up as soon as I make the call. Let me get him here now to pick you up, while Nick and I look for Johnson."

Even before Bryan finished speaking, Sassy was shaking her head. "No way. You're not leaving me behind."

Bryan hadn't really thought that would work, but he had to try. "Be realistic. You're not at a hundred percent. You've been in a serious car accident." Going for guilt might be the only way to handle her. "If we're worried about keeping you safe, we won't be able to do this."

"So quit worrying about me. I'll be fine." The stubborn set of her chin concerned him. She wasn't budging.

Nick shook his head and spoke up. "We don't have time to argue about this. Sassy, stay here and keep the room clear for us. Hollywood and I'll be coming back this direction. It's the only way out on this side of the house that doesn't set off every alarm in the place. Leave the balcony open for now. We don't know what is hooked up where, and I don't want to set off anything accidentally."

Surprisingly, she was listening as Nick gave orders, and the mutinous expression she'd worn earlier began to fade. "Johnson said he'd be back here by eight o'clock to get the story."

"Then that gives us our timetable. Look at the clock. It's seven fifteen now. If we're not back in twenty minutes, go out the window and down the rope off the balcony. Make your way to the shoreline, but on the opposite side of the island from the dock of this complex. If the pilot hasn't heard from us, he'll be there on the opposite side of the island by eight thirty."

With Nick giving the orders instead of Bryan, she was much more amenable to cooperating. Bryan tried not to be irritated.

Nick handed her the downed guard's handgun and a small flashlight. "Keep an eye on this guy. It'll probably be easier to just conk him in the head again if he comes to. I saw you do it in Africa with one of your shoes, so I know you're more than capable."

She gave him a grim smile and shivered. "Right." Clad in only a towel with the winter breeze gusting through the open balcony door off the water, she had to be freezing.

Bryan offered the only advice he thought she'd take from him. "Get dressed and be ready to go. We'll be moving fast when we get back."

"What are you going to do?" she asked and surprised him by reaching for his arm.

He put his hand over her chilled fingers and took a moment to meet her gaze before giving her palm a squeeze. Still, he kept his answer brusque. He couldn't sugarcoat this. "Come on, Sassy, you're a reporter. Use your imagination."

Chapter 27

December 30
Evening

SASSY'S TEETH WERE chattering by the time Bryan and
Nick left. She locked the bedroom door behind them and
went into the bathroom to slip on the sweatpants and T-
shirt that had been brought to her, along with the sweater
she'd been wearing in the car accident. If she was going
outside, this would be all about layering. She slid on the
dirty socks she'd taken off before her shower and the
boots she'd been wearing earlier. She looked around to
see if she could find any other kind of jacket in the closet.

The guard was still out cold. She was relieved she
didn't have to deal with him, even though she knew she
could if it came to that. She found a long woolen scarf in
the closet, some oversized gloves, a beanie hat, and an
empty cloth messenger bag. Another gust of wind blew
through the open balcony door. As she stuffed the gear
in the messenger bag and slung it across her body, she
wondered how long she might have to wait in the woods
or out on the water for rescue. Feeling nervous, she wasn't

sure what to do with herself. She checked on the unconscious guard again, then glanced at the clock and went back to the bathroom to brush her teeth. Bryan and Nick had been gone thirteen minutes. She had seven minutes left until she would need to make her way out by herself.

Nick had mentioned climbing down from up here. She didn't want to think about having to do that on her own, but she needed to explore the possibility, so she walked out onto the redwood balcony. From the deck area she could see much farther than she had from inside. Johnson's home was extensive.

A pile of coiled rope lay on the boards. Her stomach churned, but she forced herself to look at the braided nylon. One end of the rope was tied to the railing. Beside the rope was a climbing harness that she recognized as rappelling equipment. She'd tried to rappel. Once. For a story she'd been working on. She had a lovely scar on her ankle to show for it, too.

She sincerely hoped she didn't have to use any of that equipment by herself. To take her mind off the possibility of climbing down that rope and revisiting her fear of heights, she looked out over the well-lit property.

There were two outbuildings between the main house and what she assumed must be the shoreline. The outbuildings were connected with an illuminated walkway between them. Elaborate, well-lit paths led from both sides of the main house through the trees down to those same outbuildings, and one larger path curved and wound around from the front door of the main house down to the shoreline.

As she stood taking it all in, a figure exited the out-building closest to her and started up the side walkway. Deeply involved in conversation on what appeared to be some kind of two-way radio, there was no stealth in the man's movements as he headed for the side door of the main house. He had no idea anyone was up here watching.

But standing on the balcony, Sassy was silhouetted by the light in the room behind her. She dropped to her belly on the deck and scootched into the shadows as best she could. The balcony door was wide open. If the man looked up, he would be able to see that. Thankfully he was much too involved in his conversation. He was going to pass right beneath her and go directly inside.

"Yes, sir. I've rigged all the buildings except the boat-house, Mr. Johnson. They'll blow simultaneously. I'm on my way to get the computer and Donald. The men from AEGIS should be here soon. The remote trigger you have is now live. Are you sure there's no way to salvage the house?"

There was another pause. What was going on? How did they know about Bryan and Nick?

"I understand. It's just . . . it's a pity. It's a lovely place."

The man had stopped walking and was now directly underneath her. If he looked up, he would see her staring straight down at him through the boards. She lay perfectly still and strained to hear what he would say next.

"Yes, I understand. I'll make sure of it. It will look like a gas leak. I'll get the computer, take care of the girl, and gather your papers before I meet you on the dock. The remote will work up to a mile away."

Sassy didn't move. The house was set to explode? Did they know Nick and Bryan were already here? Who had set them up? The only thing she knew for certain was that Johnson was at the dock with a live remote trigger.

She had to warn Bryan and Nick, but she was stuck on the balcony until the man moved out from under it. And she wouldn't have much time, because he was on his way upstairs to get the computer from her. She glanced at the coiled rope. God, she was going to have to do this.

Finally he moved inside. She lay still a moment, waiting until she heard the door close beneath her before scrambling to her feet. Racing to the bed, she grabbed the computer and stuffed it into the bag, replacing the gloves and scarf. There was no way she was leaving that story behind.

She stared at the rope like it was a snake. How fast could she get down that thing? And where should she go when she reached the bottom? After Johnson, or after Nick and Bryan?

She tossed the rope over the balcony and took a deep breath. She could do this. After clipping herself into the harness, she attached the carabiner to the rope. God, she was sweating like it was high noon in August, and it was only thirty degrees out.

She swung her leg over the balcony next to the wall, straddling it for a moment, getting used to the weight of the bag and the feel of the harness. She'd done this before. Plus, she'd read extensively on the subject so she could finish that damn story, after she'd hurt her ankle. *How bad could it be?*

She swung her other leg over and looked down, possibly a huge mistake. If she fell, she'd doubtless break . . . something. *Don't think about that.*

She had to do this. The guard would be in the room any second. She squeezed her eyes shut, put one foot at a time on the wall beside the balcony, and took the first step back.

Ten seconds later she hit the mulched flowerbed with a muffled *humph*. Relief flooded her system as she looked up at the rope dangling from the railing. She'd done it, and she'd survived.

There was no way to hide her escape route. The guard would know AEGIS was there as soon as he saw the rope. But he'd still need to get her computer before his boss could blow the house.

Stopping Johnson before he did anything with that trigger was foremost in her mind. She unsnapped from the harness, dusted herself off, and ran.

BRYAN AND NICK were on the first floor and having no luck. The place was empty. Where were the guards?

Bryan had that funny prickly feeling on the back of his neck, like something was about to go tits up in a big way. This place should have had more security. Where was everyone?

They'd searched the entire second story and every room except the kitchen on the first. It wasn't just dumb luck that they weren't encountering any kind of resistance. Something was bad wrong.

Bryan had the overwhelming urge to go back upstairs and check on Sassy. He'd learned enough over the years not to ignore that gut instinct.

"Nick, this doesn't feel right. I'm going back to get Sassy."

"I'll check the kitchen and meet you down by the lake in ten."

Bryan nodded and headed for the second floor, flattening himself against a wall as he heard a door to his right open. *Finally*. It was a guard tucking a radio into his pocket.

The guard walked up the steps Bryan had been planning to use and headed straight for Sassy's room. When the guard closed the door behind him, the final sound of a lock sliding into place had Bryan sprinting after him. All he had was the element of surprise.

Without hesitation, Bryan threw himself against the door, breaking the lock and knocking the guard to the floor. Where was Sassy? He wrestled the man on the ground, and they rolled onto the balcony through the open glass door.

Sassy was nowhere to be seen, and Bryan wondered briefly if she'd given up waiting and had gone over the side of the balcony the same way he and Nick had gotten in. She'd freeze to death if she didn't have any more clothes on than he'd seen her in earlier.

He saw the flash of a knife and felt a sharp stinging pain as the guard got a good swipe in. Bryan was about to get himself killed if he didn't focus. He threw a punch and caught the guy on the side of the head. The man's grip on the knife loosened. The metal handle made a distinctive sound as it skittered across the boards and over the side of the balcony. The guard followed the movement with his eyes, and Bryan hit him again, knocking him out cold.

Bryan stood and studied his shoulder where he'd been cut. He was bleeding, but he was pretty sure the guard hadn't hit anything vital.

He scanned the room. Sassy was plainly not here. He looked out over the top of the balcony and saw a small figure rushing down the path toward the water. It was Sassy, but what was she doing?

She was headed for the dock. *Big surprise*. She was not going through the woods like Nick had asked her to and like Bryan would have expected her to, if she was meeting them on the opposite side of the island. Where the hell was she headed?

The guard's radio squawked. "I've got movement on the path. What's going on up there? I need you to get one more thing from my office before we blow the buildings."

Blow the buildings? Shit! Who did he go after? Nick or Sassy?

Dammit. There was no choice. Sassy wasn't inside. Nick was. Bryan turned from the balcony and ran for the stairs.

He found Nick in the office going through file folders and papers on what had to be Johnson's desk.

"You won't believe what I've found." He held up a handful of manila folders. "Hell, it's all here. These files go back years. The cartels, the trafficking. There's even something with Dad's name on it. But I don't understand why Johnson left it all out like this. Something's seriously fucked."

Bryan longed to stop and see if there was anything about Afghanistan and his team in the Helmand Province, but they were out of time. "Nick, we gotta get out of here. Now! The place is rigged to blow."

"What?" Nick clutched several folders and glanced longingly at the others on the desk for a split second before joining Bryan to head for the exit. "Where's Sassy?" he asked, stuffing the files inside his shirt.

"She's headed for the lake. I saw her upstairs from the balcony of the bedroom." Bryan explained what he'd overhead on the two-way radio as they sprinted for the front door.

SASSY HUSTLED ALONG the path with the messenger bag banging into her hip, wondering if she was making the biggest mistake of her life. She wasn't sure she could have gotten past the guard downstairs to find Nick and Bryan without alerting Johnson that something was up, so this seemed the best plan.

Johnson wouldn't blow his house up with the news story he wanted still inside, would he? Although what she'd do when she got to the lake, she had no idea. Distracting him seemed like the obvious choice.

Once she got past the outbuildings, the main path to the lake was curvy, and some places were better lit than others. She rounded a particularly dark corner, and suddenly there was the boathouse and dock. She skidded to a halt and stepped off the path.

Johnson stood at the end of the pier. She recognized him because the light caught his silver hair and the glint off his glasses. How could she divert his attention without him setting everything off?

He had that remote trigger somewhere that would blow up the house and outbuildings, along with Nick and Bryan. That was exactly how he'd planned to take care of his loose ends after she got his story written—all in one big, not-so-tidy package.

The guard up at the house would be wondering what was going on by now. What should she do? Go back for Nick and Bryan? She crouched beside a tree, frozen in indecision.

Johnson was prepping a boat. She wasn't sure how long he'd wait for Donald and the other guard, but she got the feeling Ford Johnson was not a patient boss. He tossed a bag into the craft and lifted a walkie-talkie to his lips. His voice carried, and she heard the anger in his tone.

"Where are you, dammit? We need to be gone. Now."

The radio remained silent. Johnson stood in the middle of the dock, peering through the shadows toward the house. Sassy shrunk back further into the darkness.

"Shit." He reached into his jacket and pulled a device from his pocket. It was the size of a cell phone. He walked up the path, staring into the night before heading back to the dock.

Oh God, was that the remote control? How horribly

had she miscalculated? She should have found Bryan and Nick before coming this way. Was he going to blow the house with them still inside?

Johnson held the walkie-talkie in one hand and stood in the middle of the pier, holding the other device at an odd angle.

"No," Sassy cried, rushing from her hiding place. Johnson looked up in surprise as she ran toward him. He dropped the walkie-talkie and pulled a gun from his waistband with one hand, still holding onto the cell-phone-like trigger with the other.

Behind her, she heard a huge rumbling. The ground shuddered beneath her feet. Johnson was aiming the handgun as she tackled him. She heard a shot as together they went off the side of the pier into the icy water.

Chapter 28

SEARING PAIN TORE along her hip as water went up her
nose. Sassy struggled to stay afloat while pushing down
on Johnson at the same time.

No! He'd detonated the explosion. Were Bryan and
Nick out of the house or inside when it went off?

Johnson wrenched an arm behind her. His hand was
on her head, pressing downward. The messenger bag
filled with water, pulling her under. The water was deep.
She kicked with the leg that wasn't feeling so numb, but
the pressure in her lungs built as her body began to crave
oxygen.

She needed air, now.

God, she was drowning. She'd calculated everything
wrong, going off on her own.

She kept kicking with the one leg but made no progress. She wasn't going to make it. Her headache from
earlier was back with a vengeance, and her vision began

to waver when she heard what sounded like firecrackers exploding.

The messenger bag continued to pull her deeper even as the pressure on the top of her head lessened. She was able to give a final, halfhearted kick, but it was no good. She was sinking, no longer able to tread water. Her lungs burned and her vision grayed out. She closed her eyes, feeling the weightlessness even as she sank.

Something was pinching her wrist and pulling her up. Her head broke the surface, and she gulped in sweet air.

Dizzy and nauseated, she coughed and sputtered. She heard shouting voices and lots of splashing. A body floated motionless beside her.

Bryan was there, holding her wrist, pulling her into his arms and toward the dock. "It's over," he said. "You're okay. It's over."

She stared at him as if waking from a dream. The lights from the dock were bright on the water. His face cammo was smudged. His eyes were unreadable, and his shoulder . . .

"Your shoulder is bleeding. Are you okay?"

"I'm . . . I'm fine." But he didn't look at her as he answered.

Other hands lifted and pulled her from the water. "What about you? That was some swan dive." Nick was tugging her up onto the dock and draping his jacket over her shoulders, but she heard the concern in his voice. Then Bryan was climbing up beside her, pulling her away from Nick, and back into his arms.

"What the fucking hell were you doing, Sassy?" Bryan's tone was rough and brusque, but there was nowhere to look but up into his face as he pulled her closer. "You could have gotten yourself killed." He kissed the top of her head, and it was then she saw the white-hot panic in his eyes. "What were you thinking, baby?"

She reached up to touch his face. "Hey, I'm okay. Really."

She smiled up at him as he kissed her forehead this time, but then she made the mistake of glancing down. Blood was streaming from her hip, down her leg, and onto the dock. Suddenly she wasn't so okay.

The dizziness was back, and once again her vision became hazy around the edges. She'd never been very good with blood.

For the second time in twenty-four hours, everything went black.

December 31
Evening

BRYAN SAT BESIDE Sassy's bed in the small regional hospital, waiting for Sassy to open her eyes. The first time she'd woken up, he'd been getting stitches in his shoulder downstairs and being debriefed by Nightshade and his alphabet soup cronies. By the time the nurse had located him, Sassy had been out and down for the count.

That was when Bryan told Nightshade that if the feds couldn't talk to him in Sassy's room, they'd have to arrest him. He wasn't leaving her side again until she was awake and telling him to go away herself. Everything else could wait. And while Nightshade had cussed and fumed, eventually, he'd left them alone.

A few hours after that Marissa had suggested that perhaps a shower really shouldn't wait, and Bryan had reluctantly agreed. While he'd been showering, Sassy had woken up a second time. To her credit, Marissa had burst into the men's shower room to get him, surprising one very disgruntled and naked surgeon in the process.

True to Murphy's Law, by the time Bryan had gotten the soap out of his eyes and a towel around his waist to dash up to her room, Sassy had fallen back asleep. The doctors had said not to worry.

But that had been three hours ago, and no amount of coaxing could blast Bryan out of the room now. So here he sat, with stitches in his shoulder that hurt like a bitch, in a leatherette recliner made for a midget. If he leaned his head back against what passed for a headrest, his legs hung over the end at his knees so that he cut the circulation off in his shins and feet. If he pulled his legs up to calf height on the footrest instead, he'd be hanging himself upside down from the other end.

It wasn't as if he could sleep anyway. Whenever he closed his eyes, he saw Sassy diving off the end of that pier, directly into Ford Johnson's gunfire. All to protect him. The nightmare didn't stop until he saw her covered in blood and passing out in his arms.

The doctors assured him that she would be okay. It was more about a concussion combined with anesthesia and exhaustion than the gunshot wound. But he needed to see her awake and talking to believe that she was all right.

After that he would get as far away from Sassy as he possibly could. Not because he didn't want to be with her but because she wasn't safe with him.

After meeting him for coffee in Niamey, she'd been kidnapped. After flying back to New York with him, she'd almost died more times than he could count. The thought of something happening to her because of him was beyond what he could stand.

If it didn't hurt so damn much, his situation would be laughable. He'd thought he didn't stick or want a long-term relationship, but that couldn't be further from the truth.

It was killing him, but he now knew that the kindest thing he could do for Sassy was to leave her the hell alone, no matter how much he cared for her. He'd go to Mexico and see what he could do for her brother. But first, before he left, Bryan had to see for himself that she was really okay.

He didn't even look up from his pity party when the door opened. The nurses were in about every thirty minutes.

"Jesus. And I thought I looked like hell. What have you been doing to yourself, man?"

Bryan jerked his head up at the familiar voice. Trey Smith stood in the doorway, skinny as a scarecrow and leaning on a cane. But he was alive, and he was here.

In shock, Bryan sat for a moment before scrambling to his feet and out of the ridiculous chair to embrace his friend.

"What? How?" He hugged Trey and patted him on the back but made sure not to hit too hard. Trey was so horribly thin.

Trey shook his head. "I'm not sure I even understand what happened. Last night I was asleep in my cell. When the guards came to wake me I thought . . ." His voice cracked, and he shook his head. "Two hours later I was on a private plane. Some guy named Nightshade met me at a regional airport and then drove me here."

Bryan felt the tears prick at his eyes. Nightshade had just become his new favorite person. "You alright?" he asked.

Trey looked at Sassy, and his eyes filled, too. "No . . . but I'm gonna be." He walked over to the bed, but he didn't touch her. "How's our girl? Nightshade said she got shot?"

Bryan offered the recliner, then dragged a straight-back chair from across the room and sat, still marveling that his friend was here and safe. He filled Trey in on Sassy's injury and everything that had happened since last summer. Well, practically everything. He wasn't telling Trey all that he'd done with his sister.

"The doctors assure me that she's going to be okay, but I want to see for myself," he finished.

"That's good. What are you gonna do after?" asked Trey.

"After what?"

"It's obvious you care for her. You gonna make an honest woman of her or just string her along?"

"Umm . . . what?" Bryan stuttered. Wasn't that perfect and not at all obvious?

"Come on, Bryan. You've been crazy about Sassy since before you graduated high school. It sounds like you've spent a shitload of time together these past few months. I might be a little slow about picking up on this kind of thing, but I'm not blind."

"It's hasn't been like that. I mean. It wasn't until—" He stopped as a grin spread over Trey's face. "You knew?" he asked.

"Of course I knew."

Bryan shook his head. "I've been crazy about her for such a long time. Somehow I thought you'd have a problem with it."

"A problem with my best friend being with my little sister? I might not have understood the attraction on your part when we were younger, but I can't think of anyone I'd want for her more. You'd sacrifice anything for her."

"I . . . I love her," Bryan whispered, surprised he'd said the words out loud.

Trey nodded, as if that was understood. "I know you do. So what are you going to do about it?"

Still reeling, Bryan leaned back against the hard backrest and sighed. "Once she wakes up, I was planning to leave."

Trey raised an eyebrow. "Where the hell are you going this time? You're too old to run away and join the circus."

Bryan flashed a sad smile. "As much as I've tried to help her the past few months, she's almost been killed multiple times because of me. I'm no good for her, and I'm damn sure not relationship material."

"Excuse me while I call *bullshit*."

"Were you not listening earlier to all the crap that's happened while she's been with me?"

"I *was* listening," insisted Trey. "Were you?" He reached for his cane and stood. "You're going to have to figure this out for yourself, friend. I'm too tired to argue with you."

Bryan looked up at him a moment before standing, too. Trey moved slowly toward the door.

"Your buddy Nightshade's taking care of things. I think I'm going to be talking to a lot of different folks over the next couple of days, a debriefing of sorts. He said we'd normally go to Washington for this, but he's going to do it in Atlanta. So I can be closer to Sassy." Trey stopped at the door. "One more question. Do you think Elizabeth is alive?"

With the burning query reflected in his eyes, Trey studied Bryan. He deserved the truth, even if it hurt like hell. Bryan hadn't even told Sassy what he really believed. For so long, finding Elizabeth alive had been her only means of getting help for her brother. Because that was no longer a factor, Bryan had to tell the truth about what he really thought.

He took an audible breath and met Trey's gaze. "No, I don't think she survived. The conditions she would have been subjected to in both Mexico and in Africa, if she got that far, were extraordinarily harsh. I don't believe Elizabeth, or anyone, could have survived, given all the other factors at play."

Trey glanced down at the linoleum floor a moment before nodding and taking a deep breath. "Thank you for being honest. As one who lived with it for months, I've got to say—false hope is an awful thing." He looked up with a sad smile. "I'll see you soon."

Bryan opened the door. Marissa and Nightshade were waiting in the hallway.

Bryan nodded at them. "I can't thank you enough for this." He patted Trey on the back and shook his hand again. "I'll talk to you tomorrow?"

"Sounds good." Trey smiled again, but he looked completely exhausted.

Nightshade took one look at Trey and hustled him off to the elevator. Risa stayed a moment and tried to talk Bryan into going back to the hotel to get some real rest, but he refused.

"I'll see you in the morning," he told her. He watched her get on the elevator before closing the hospital room door.

Sighing, he climbed into the medieval torture rack that was disguised as an easy chair. He'd just gotten his feet at a good angle without having his head tipping over backward when he glanced up to see Sassy awake and blinking at him.

Chapter 29

"I JUST HAD the most amazing dream that Trey was here. It was a dream, right?"

"Nope. Not a dream. He's home. He's here. And you're awake." Bryan grinned as he scrambled from the chair and moved toward the bed.

Trey was downstairs and probably halfway across the parking lot by now. No way was Bryan walking out of this room to go get him. She might be asleep again before they made it back.

Sassy's eyes rounded, along with her mouth. "He's free?" Bryan was a foot from the bed when her face crumpled, and she burst into tears.

Oh Jesus. He never knew what to do when she cried.

"He's okay?" she asked, with tears streaming down her cheeks.

Should he go after Trey in the parking lot? Making a

snap decision, he sat on the edge of the bed and gently leaned over to hold her.

"Yes. He's . . . he's going to be okay. I can try to catch him downstairs if you want. He was just really tired. That's why he didn't stay."

Her tears were soaking through the thin scrub shirt he'd been loaned. She shook her head. "No. Don't do that. I—" She hiccupped through the tears. "He must be exhausted." She slipped her arms around his neck and inadvertently pulled on his shoulder with the stitches. He winced.

She let go, tilting her head up to look at him. "You're hurt."

"So are you. You got shot." His throat tightened as he said the words. He kissed her forehead and leaned back to study her face. He should call the nurse. They'd want to know she was awake. "Are you hurting? Do you need any pain medication?" he asked.

She shook her head. "It'll make me too sleepy. And more emotional. I feel like Rip Van Winkle as it is. What time is it?"

"About six thirty PM."

Her eyes widened. "What day is it?"

"New Year's Eve."

Her dimples appeared. "Wow. I've been out a while, haven't I?"

Careful not to jar her hip, he nodded and reached for her again, so very grateful she was awake and talking. He needed to be touching her.

She was okay. Before he'd seen Trey, his plan had been

to leave after confirming this. But how could he bring himself to do that now? He had no idea how to proceed. On the bright side, her tears were subsiding.

"So who'd have thought we'd be spending New Year's Eve together?" She cocked an eyebrow, but the saucy inflection in her voice sounded different. He assumed that was a side effect of the medication in her system.

"Sassy, I—" He leaned closer. Happy to be exactly where he was, even if he didn't know what in hell he was doing. He needed to leave soon, but he wasn't ready yet.

"What are you going to do now?" she interrupted.

He smiled at the question mirroring his own thoughts. "I don't know. I was going to Mexico to try and help Trey, but since that's no longer necessary . . . I guess I'll get back to Dallas and start helping put things back together at AEGIS. There's a lot to sort out after everything with Johnson's allegations."

He saw the vulnerability in her eyes as she deflated in his arms.

"What about me?" she whispered.

"What?" But he knew exactly what she meant.

She inhaled, clearly coming to a decision. "What are you going to do about me? About wanting me?" She gave a nervous laugh as she glanced at the IV pole beside the bed. "What is in that bag? My God, I've never said anything like that to a man in my life." She shook her head, refocusing her gaze on him. "But hell. What about us?"

He let her go and straightened up, barely staying on the mattress. "Sassy, I'm no good for you. I don't open up in relationships anymore. That vulnerability hurts too much. Yes, I want you." He swallowed hard against the admission that scared him spitless. "I love you. But I damn near got you killed. More than once. I can't keep you safe. And I can't give you what you need long-term."

I can't even stop cussing around you.

She took his hand but didn't answer until he was looking her in the eye. "I don't need you to keep me safe. I just need you to love me. To trust me. And I don't want to be rescued. I simply want to be with you. I know I'm not easy. I never have been. But I want to build a life with you. To know you. To be known by you. Isn't that rescue enough, vulnerable enough, for the both of us?"

"But—" He stopped. What was he doing? He wanted this. He wanted *her* so much. He'd been wanting her for so damn long. And he'd never thought it would be possible.

Could he do it? Was exposing his heart again worth the risk?

"Yes." He blew out the breath he'd been holding. *I love this woman.* That wasn't nearly as frightening to think about as it had been just moments ago.

She tilted her head against the pillow and arched an eyebrow. "Yes what, Hollywood?" That sensual lilting tone returned as she dragged out the syllables in his name, but the look in her eyes was a sincere promise.

He felt a smile tug at the corner of his mouth. To know and to be known by this woman would take a lifetime. He couldn't imagine needing anything else. "Yes, that's more than enough."

She nodded. Reaching up to touch his face, she

stopped with her hand in mid-air. "Hey. What kind of nickname is that, anyway?"

He leaned forward to kiss her. "It's a long story and kinda boring. You don't want to hear it now."

Her dimples were back as her fingertips traced his cheek. "Sure I do. We've got lots of time. Come on . . . tell me. I dare ya."

Epilogue

THE WOMAN WOKE slowly, to stare at a canvas tent ceiling. The muscle aches and chills that had racked her body for days had finally subsided. She hadn't vomited the last two times she'd been awake.

That was a very positive development. She knew because she'd heard the health care workers say so. They hadn't realized that she was conscious and could hear them talking about her. She'd learned to keep her eyes closed and her head down when she was unsure of her surroundings.

Opening her eyes, she lay still and listened to the voices around her. The beds on either side of hers were empty. Had those women recovered or died?

Two people dressed in hazmat suits were at the cot two spaces down, dealing with another patient.

How long have I been out of it?

Days? Weeks? She'd lost track of time long before the

devastation of the illness had overtaken her. Yet, remarkably, miraculously, she was alive.

People would think she was insane if she said Ebola was a blessing, but for her it had been a deliverance. When her fever had spiked and she'd been left behind, she'd thanked God. She'd known she was going to die, but even the ravages of Ebola were more merciful than what she'd been facing.

A worker in protective gear came toward her bed.

She couldn't see a face clearly through the mask, but she could hear excitement in the man's voice when he saw that she was awake.

"Doctor! Doctor!" The worker turned back to the others.

She closed her eyes. When she opened them again, an older man dressed in a blue hazmat suit was looking down at her. It was easier to see his face.

You're back," he said. "That's excellent. How do you feel?"

Like Lazarus.

Certainly better than the last time she was awake.

Her throat was so dry, she couldn't speak. So she nodded and tried to smile her answer instead of talking. Her lips were swollen and chapped from lack of moisture. They cracked at the movement. She tasted the faintest hint of copper on her tongue.

The doctor patted her arm and picked up a cup with a straw in it, holding it to her mouth. "We'll get something for your lips. Can you tell me your name?"

She took a deep breath, surprised at the tears stinging

the corners of her eyes. Her throat was cotton dry, even after the sip of lukewarm water. Her mouth stung, but the pain reminded her that she was alive. She'd survived.

For months she'd longed for someone, anyone, to ask for her name. She coughed and cleared her throat, but her voice was still rasping when she finally spoke.

"Elizabeth."

Acknowledgments

FIRST, THANK YOU to my readers for your excitement and enthusiasm about this series. I've loved hearing what you think of my Elite Ops heroes, and I appreciate your taking the time to write. Your messages have always seemed to arrive just when I've needed the encouragement. I'm grateful.

Writing *Easy Target* was an adventure I did not embark on alone. Having a mystery arc that stretched across three books was a challenge requiring a host of folks to keep me on track. Sassy and Hollywood's story wouldn't have been possible without the feedback and help I received from many generous people, several of whom have been working with me from the first manuscript. Many thanks to Ellen Henderson and Joyce Ann McLaughlin, who read and reread this story as we worked out the kinks. Thanks also to friend, author, and graphic artist Kathleen Baldwin, who continues to go above and beyond.

Many thanks to Mike Simonds, Don Ring, Tim McManus, and my brother, Tim Luster—the men who helped with a multitude of technical details about things like body decomposition time lines and international firearms transportation. Any mistakes are mine and mine alone.

As always, thanks to my editor extraordinaire, Erika Tsang, who pushed me to make Sassy and Hollywood's story the best it could be, along with all the folks at HarperCollins who work so hard on my behalf including—the fabulous art department, Chelsey Emmelhainz, Heidi Richter, and Judith Gelman Myers. Thank you to my agent, Helen Breitwieser, for her continued support.

Thank you to the "Bulletproof Babes" for their passion and encouragement for my work. Your enthusiasm is contagious!

Thank you to the Writer Foxes—Lorraine, Addison, Suzanne, Alice, Sandy, Julie, Jo, Tracy, and Jane—for your unwavering supply of wisdom and wine. Cheers!

Finally, thanks to my family. This book took more time to finish than I'd planned, and you gave me the time and the space to write during a decidedly busy season of life. My parents and daughter were particularly understanding about phone calls rolling to voice mail. My husband and son ate lots of meals without me. Thank you, Tom—for making me laugh, keeping me sane, and loving me, even when I'm grouchy (and hungry). You always make it fun to "come home from work."

Can't get enough of Kay
Thomas's Elite Ops team?
Keep reading for an excerpt from Book One,

HARD TARGET

Available now from Avon Impulse

"COULD YOU HAND me my top, please?"

Leland bent down to retrieve Anna's shirt and turned away, staring at the floor in front of him to give her privacy. What the hell was he doing? At least he'd given the room a cursory inspection to rule out cameras or bugs before he'd practically screwed her against the bedroom wall.

What he'd really wanted to tell her, before they'd gotten sidetracked with the birth control issue, was the same thing he'd wanted to tell her last night. She didn't have to do him to get Zach back. Whether or not they had sex had no bearing on whether he'd help find her son.

Not that he didn't want her. He did. So much so that his teeth ached.

He hadn't known her long but what he knew fascinated him. To have dealt with everything she had in the past year and to still be so strong. That inner strength captivated him.

It was important she not think he expected sex in exchange for his help. Sex wasn't some kind of payoff. He needed to clarify that right away.

Besides, neither of them was going to be able to sleep

now. He sighed, zipped his cargo shorts and pulled on his t-shirt and shoulder holster with the Ruger. He shoved the larger Glock into his backpack. This was going to be a long evening.

The night breeze had shifted the shabby curtain to the side, leaving an unobscured view into the room. He turned to face her, wondering if anyone on the street had just gotten an eyeful.

A red laser dot reflected off the wide shoulder strap of her tank top. Recognizing the threat, he dove for her, shouting, "Down. Get down!"

Leland tackled Anna around the waist and pulled her to the floor. A bullet hit the wall with a *sphlift*, right where she'd been standing a half second earlier.

He climbed on top of her, his heart rate skyrocketing, and covered her completely with his body. His boot was awkward. His knee came down between her legs, trapping her in the skirt. More shots slapped the stucco, but they were all hitting above his head.

The gunman must be using a silencer. A loud car engine revved in the street. Voices shouted and bullets flew through the window, no longer silenced.

How many shooters were there?

A flaming bottle whooshed through the window. Breaking on impact, the fire spread rapidly across the dry plywood floor. The pop of more bullets against the wall sounded deceptively benign.

"What's happening?" Anna's lips were at his ear.

Her warm breath would have felt seductive if not for the shots flying overhead and fire licking at his ass. He was crushing her with his body weight but it was the only way to protect her from the onslaught.

"Why are they shooting at us?" Her voice was thin, like she was having trouble breathing.

He raised up on his elbows to take his weight off of her chest but kept his head down next to hers. "They want the money."

"How do they know about the ransom?" she asked.

"Everyone within a hundred miles knows about it." He raised his head cautiously.

They were nose to nose, but he ignored the intimacy of the position. They had to get out of the smoke-filled room. In here, even with just half the money, they were sitting ducks.

He needed his bag. It held all his ammunition and the Glock 17. And they couldn't leave the cash, not now anyway. Having the money might be the only thing to keep them alive when they got out of here.

"Come on." He rolled to the side and tugged Anna's hand to pull her along with him. "But don't raise your head."

Another bullet hit the wall where she had been moments earlier. God, how many men were there? Knowing that could make a difference in getting out of this alive.

Keep reading for an excerpt from Book Two,

PERSONAL TARGET

Available now from Avon Impulse

THE WOMAN AT the vanity turned, and his breath caught in his throat. Nick had known it would be Jenny, and despite what he'd thought about downstairs when he'd seen her on the tablet screen, he hadn't prepared himself for seeing her like this. Seated at the table with candles all around, she was wearing a sheer robe over a gray thong and a bustier kind of thing, or that's what he thought the full-length bra was called.

He spotted the small unicorn tat peeping out from the edge of whatever the lingerie piece was and his brain quit processing details as all the blood in his head rushed south. He'd been primed to come in and tell Jenny exactly how they were getting out of the house and away from these people and now . . . this. His mouth went dry at the sight of her. She looked like every fantasy he'd ever had about her rolled into one.

He continued to stare as recognition flared in her eyes. "Oh my God," she said. "It's . . ."

She clapped her mouth closed, and her eyes widened. That struck him as odd. The relief on her face was obvious, but instead of looking at him, she took an audible breath and studied the walls of the room. When she finally did glance at him again, her eyes had changed.

"So you're who they've sent me for my first time?" Her voice sounded bored, not the tone he remembered. "What do you want me to do?"

What a question. He raised an eyebrow, but she shook her head. In warning?

Nothing here was as he'd anticipated. He continued staring at her, hoping the lust would quit fogging his brain long enough for him to figure out what was going on.

"I've been told to show you a good time." Her voice was cold, downright chilly. Without another word she stood and crossed the floor, slipping into his arms with her breasts pressing into his chest. "It's you." She murmured the words in the barest of whispers.

Nick's mind froze, but his body didn't. On autopilot his hands automatically went to her waist as she kissed his neck, working her way up to his ear. This was not at all what he'd planned.

"I can't believe you're here." She breathed the words into his ear.

Me either, he thought, but kept the news to himself as he pulled her closer. His senses flooded with all that smooth skin pressing against him. His body tightened, and his right hand moved to cup her ass. Her cheek's bare skin was silky soft, like he remembered. God, he'd missed her. She melted into him as his body switched into overdrive.

"What do you want?" She spoke louder. The artic tone was back. He was confused and knew he was just too stupid with wanting her to figure out what the hell was going on. There was no way the woman could mistake the effect she was having.

She moved her lips closer to his ear and nipped his earlobe before she spoke in a hushed tone. "Cameras are everywhere. I'm not sure about microphones."

And just like that, cold reality slapped him in the face. He should have been expecting it, but he'd been so focused on getting her out and making sure she was all right. She might be glad to see him because he was there to save her, but throwing her body at him was an act.

Jesus. He had to get them both out of here without tipping his hand to the cameras and those watching what he was doing. He was crazy not to have considered it once he saw those tablets downstairs, but it had never occurred to him that he would have to play this encounter through as if he was really a client.

He slipped her arms from around his neck and moved to the table to pour himself some wine, willing his hands not to shake. "I want you."

About the Author

KAY THOMAS didn't grow up burning to be a writer. She wasn't even much of a reader until fourth grade. That's when her sister read *The Black Stallion* aloud to her. For hours Kay was enthralled—shipwrecked and riding an untamed horse across desert sand. Then tragedy struck. Her sister lost her voice. But Kay couldn't wait to hear what happened in the story—so she picked up that book, finished reading it herself, and went in search of more adventures at the local library.

Today Kay lives in Dallas with her husband, two children, and a shockingly spoiled Boston terrier. Her award-winning novels have been published internationally. For more information on Kay, please sign up for her newsletter at *www.eepurl.com/TBUI* or visit her website: *www.kaythomas.net*.

Discover great authors, exclusive offers, and more at hc.com.

Give in to your Impulses . . .
Continue reading for excerpts from
our newest Avon Impulse books.
Available now wherever e-books are sold.

HEART'S DESIRE
By T.J. Kline

DESIRE ME NOW
By Tiffany Clare

THE WEDDING GIFT
A Save the Date Novella
By Cara Connelly

WHEN LOVE HAPPENS
Ribbon Ridge Book Three
By Darcy Burke

An Excerpt from

HEART'S DESIRE
by *T.J. Kline*

Jessie Hart has a soft spot for healing the
broken, especially horses and children, but her
business is failing. The one man who can save
Heart Fire Ranch is the last man she wants to see,
the man who broke her heart eight years ago . . .

Jessie heard the crunch of tires on the gravel driveway and stepped onto the porch of the enormous log home. Her parents had raised their family here, in the house her father had built just before her brother was born. The scent of pine surrounded her, warming her insides. Even after her brother and sister had built houses of their own on either end of the property, she'd remained here with her parents, helping them operate the dude ranch and training their horses. She inhaled deeply, wishing again that circumstances hadn't been so cruel as to leave her to figure out how to make the transition from dude ranch to horse rescue alone.

Leaning against the porch railing, she sipped her coffee and enjoyed the quiet of the morning. When a teen girl walked toward the barn to feed the horses, she lifted her hand in a wave. The poor girl was spending more time at the ranch than away from it these days, since her mother had violated parole again, but Jessie loved having her here. Aleta's foster mother, June, had been close friends with Jessie's own mother, and she understood the healing power horses had on kids who needed someone, or something, just to listen. Now that Aleta was living with June again, she was spending a lot of time at the ranch.

Jessie looked down the driveway as Bailey drove her truck closer to the house. She could just make out Nathan through the glare on the windshield. The resentment in her belly grew with each ticking second at the sight of him. Clenching her jaw and squaring her shoulders for the battle ahead, Jessie walked down the stairs to meet Justin's former best friend and the man who'd broken her heart.

The truck pulled to a stop in front of her, and Bailey jumped from the driver's seat wearing a shit-eating grin. Jessie narrowed her eyes, knowing exactly what that meant—she was in for a week of hell from this pain-in-the-ass, penny-pinching bean counter.

She didn't understand why he'd insisted on returning to the ranch. If Justin hadn't begged her to give Nathan a chance to help, she would have been perfectly content never to speak to his lying ass again.

She watched him turn his broad shoulders to her as he removed his luggage from the back seat. When he faced her, Jessie was barely able to contain her gasp of surprise. After he left, she'd avoided any mention of Nathan Kerrington like the plague, going as far as changing the channel when his name was mentioned on the news. She'd been praying that the past eight years had been cruel, that he'd gained a potbelly, or that he'd developed a receding hairline. She pictured him turning into a stereotypical computer geek.

This guy was perfection. Well, if she was into muscular men who looked like Hollywood actors and wore suits that cost several thousand dollars. Every strand of his dark brown hair was combed into place, even at six in the morning, after a flight from New York. There wasn't a wrinkle in his stiffly starched shirt.

His green eyes slid over her dirty jeans and T-shirt before climbing back up to focus on her face. Memories of stolen kisses and lingering caresses filled her mind before she could cast them aside. His slow perusal sent heat curling in her belly, spreading through her veins, making her feel uncomfortable. Was he just trying to be an ass? If so, it was working. She felt on edge immediately, but she wasn't about to let him know it. She crossed her arms over her chest and kicked her hip to the side.

"Nathan Kerrington. You've got some brass ones showing up here."

An Excerpt from

DESIRE ME NOW

by Tiffany Clare

Amelia Grant has just escaped her lecherous
employer with nothing but the clothes on
her back. In the pre-dawn hours of London,
a horse and carriage comes barreling
down on her, and a stranger rushes to
her aid, sweeping her off her feet . . .

"**W**hy did you kiss me?" She wasn't sure she wanted to hear the answer, but a part of her needed to know. And talking was safer right now.

"I have wanted to do that since you first stumbled into my path. Do you feel something growing between us?"

She'd been ignoring that feeling, thinking and hoping it would pass with time. She'd assumed she'd developed hero worship after Mr. Riley had rescued her and then taken care of her when she'd been at an ultimate low.

She couldn't deny the truth now. She did feel something for him; something not easily defined as mere lust but a deep desire to learn more about him and why he made her feel so out of sorts with what she thought was right.

Not that she would ever admit to that.

Who was she to garner the attention of this man? Women probably threw themselves at his feet and begged him to ruin them on a regular basis. That thought left her feeling cold. She eyed the door, longing for escape.

"Do not leave, Amelia." He stepped closer to her, near enough that she could kiss him again if she so desired. She ignored that desire. "Work for me as we planned. Just stay."

There was a kind of desolation in his voice at the thought

of her abandoning him. But that was impossible. And she was reading too much into his request. Logically, she knew she couldn't feel this sort of attachment to someone she had just met. Someone she didn't really know.

"I am afraid of what I will do," she admitted, more for herself than for him.

"Then do not think about it. Go with what your instincts tell you. If there is one thing I have always done, it is to follow my first inclination. I would not be in the position I am today, had I ignored those natural reflexes."

He caressed her cheek again. She nearly nestled into his palm before realizing what she was doing. With a heavy sigh, she pulled away from him before she made any more mistakes. This was not a good way to start her first official day as his secretary.

She couldn't help but ask. "And what do your instincts say about me?"

"I do not need my instincts to tell me where this is going. It is more base than that. I desire you. And there is nothing that can stop me from fulfilling and exploring what I want. You will be mine in the end, Amelia."

Her heart picked up speed at his admission. Her breathing grew more rapid as she assessed him. She desired him too. She, Amelia Marie Somerset, who wanted nothing more than to escape one vile man's sick craving to marry her and claim her, was willing to let the man in front of her ruin her, only because she felt different with him than she had with anyone else.

What would she lose of herself in the process of courting dangerous games with this man? Focusing on the hard angles of his face and the steady expression he wore, one thing was certain.

This man would ruin her.

And more startling was the realization that she would do nothing to stop him.

An Excerpt from

THE WEDDING GIFT
A Save the Date Novella
by Cara Connelly

In the next Save the Date novella, mousey
Jan Marone finally allows herself to live,
laugh, and love . . . with a sexy fireman
during a weekend wedding in Key West!

"I'm sorry, ma'am, there's nothing I can do."

Jan Marone wrung her hands. "But I have a reservation."

"I know, I'm looking at it right here." The pretty blonde at the desk tapped her screen sympathetically. "I'll refund your deposit immediately."

"I don't want my deposit. I want a room. My cousin's getting married tomorrow, and I'm in the wedding."

The girl spread her hands. "The problem is, when one of the upstairs tubs overflowed this morning, the ceiling collapsed on your room. It's out of service for the weekend, and we're booked solid."

"I understand," Jan said, struggling to remain polite. Hearing the same excuse three times didn't make it easier to swallow. "How about a sister hotel?"

"We're independently owned. Paradise Inn is the oldest hotel on the island—"

Jan held up a hand. She knew the spiel. The large, rambling guesthouse was unique, and very Old Key West. Which was exactly why she'd booked it.

"Can you at least help me find a room somewhere else?"

"It's spring break. I'll make some calls, but . . ." A discouraging shrug and a gesture toward the coffeepot.

The girl didn't seem very concerned, but Jan smiled at her anyway. "Thanks, I appreciate you trying."

Parking her suitcase beside the coffee table, she surveyed the lobby wistfully. The windows and doors stood open, the wicker furniture and abundant potted plants blurring the line between indoors and out. The warm, humid breeze drifted through the airy space. Her parched Boston skin soaked it up like a sponge.

To a woman who'd never left New England before, it spelled tropical vacation. And it was slipping through her fingers like sand.

Growing ever gloomier, she wandered out through a side door and into a lush tropical garden—palm trees, hibiscus, a babbling waterfall.

Paradise.

And at its heart, a glittering pool, where six gorgeous feet of lean muscle and tanned skin drifted lazily on a float.

Ignoring everything else, Jan studied the man. Thick black hair, chiseled jaw, half smile curving full lips. And arms, perfect arms, draped over the sides, fingers trailing in the water.

He seemed utterly relaxed, the image of sensual decadence. Put him in an ad for Paradise Inn, and women would flock. Gay men would swarm.

As if sensing her attention, the hunk lifted his head and broke into a smile. "Hey Jan, getcha ass in the water!"

Mick McKenna. Her best and oldest friend.

He rolled off the float and jacked himself out of the pool. Water streamed from gray board shorts as he crossed the flagstones.

Stopping in front of her, he shook his hair like a Labrador.

"Geez! Don't you ever get tired of that?" She brushed droplets off her white cotton blouse.

He laughed his big, happy laugh. "Never have, never will. Get your suit on. The water's a perfect eighty-six degrees."

"I can't. They don't have a room for me."

The grin fell off his face. "What the hell?"

"Water damage." She shrugged like it wasn't tragic. Like she hadn't been anticipating this weekend for months.

"They must have another room." Mick started to go around her, no doubt to raise hell at the desk, McKenna-style.

She stopped him with a hand on his arm. "I tried everything. They're digging up a room for me somewhere else on the island."

He tunneled long fingers through his hair. "Take my room," he said.

An Excerpt from

WHEN LOVE HAPPENS
Ribbon Ridge Book Three
by Darcy Burke

In the third Ribbon Ridge novel from
USA Today bestseller Darcy Burke,
Tori Archer is about to discover that even the
best kept secrets don't stay buried for long . . .

Tori Archer sipped her Nocktoberfest, Dad's signature beer for the annual Ribbon Ridge Oktoberfest, which was currently in full swing. She clung to the corner of the huge tent, defensively watching for her "date" or one of her annoying siblings that had forced her to go on this "date."

It wasn't really a date. He was a professional colleague, and the Archers had invited him to their signature event. For nine years, the family had sponsored the town's Oktoberfest. It featured Archer beer and this year, for the first time, a German feast overseen by her brother Kyle, who was an even more amazing chef than they'd all realized. Today was day three of the festival and she still wasn't tired of the fondue. But really, could one ever tire of cheese?

"Boo!"

Tori jumped, splashing a few drops of beer from her plastic mug onto her fingers. She turned her head and glared at Kyle. "Did you sneak through the flap in the corner behind me?"

"Guilty." He wore an apron tied around his waist and a custom Archer shirt, which read CHEF below the bow and arrow A-shaped logo. "How else was I supposed to talk to you? You've been avoiding everyone for the past hour and a half. Where's Cade?" He scanned the crowd looking for her not-date, the engineer they'd hired to work on The Alex, the hotel and restaurant venue they'd been renovating since last spring. With a special events space already completed, they'd turned their focus to the restaurant and would tackle the hotel next.

Tori took a drink of the dark amber Nocktoberfest and relished the hoppy flavor. "Don't know."

Kyle gave her a sidelong glance. "Didn't you come together?"

"No. Though it wasn't for your lack of trying. I met him here. We chatted. He saw someone he knew. I excused myself to get a beer." *An hour ago.*

Kyle turned toward her and frowned. "I don't get it. Lurking in corners isn't your style. You're typically the life of the party. You work a room better than anyone I know, except maybe Liam."

Tori narrowed her eyes. "I'm better at it than he is." Their brother Liam, a successful real estate magnate in Denver, possessed many of the same qualities she did: ambition, drive, and an absolute hatred of failure. Then again, who *wanted* to fail? But it was more than that for them. Failure was never an option.

Which didn't mean that it didn't occasionally come up and take a piece out of you when you were already down for the count.

Kyle snorted. "Yeah, whatever. You two can duke it out at Christmas or whenever Liam decides to deign us with his presence."

Tori touched his arm. "Hey, don't take his absence personally. He keeps his visits pretty few and far between, even before you moved back home. Which is more than I can say for you when you were in Florida."

Kyle's eyes clouded briefly with regret and he looked away. "Yeah, I know. And hopefully someday you'll stop giving me shit about it."

She laughed. "Too soon? I'm not mad at you for leaving anymore. I get why you had to go, but I'm your sister. I will always flip you shit about stuff like that. It's my job."

He returned his attention to her, his blue-green eyes—nearly identical to her own—narrowing. "Then it's my duty to harass you about Cade. He's totally into you. Why are you dogging him?"

It seemed that since Kyle and their sister Sara had both found their soul mates this year, they expected everyone else to do the same. Granted, their adopted brother Derek had also found his true love, and they'd gotten married in August. What none of them knew, however, was that Tori was already spoken for—at least on paper.